THE LISBON CROSSING

Also by Tom Gabbay

The Berlin Conspiracy

THE
LISBON
CROSSING

TOM GABBAY

wm WILLIAM MORROW *An Imprint of* HarperCollins*Publishers*

This book is a work of fiction. References to real people, events, establishments, organizations, or locales are intended only to provide a sense of authenticity, and are used fictitiously. All other characters, and all incidents and dialogue, are drawn from the author's imagination and are not to be construed as real.

HarperCollins books may be purchased for educational, business, or sales promotional use. For information please write: Special Markets Department, HarperCollins Publishers, 10 East 53rd Street, New York, NY 10022.

FIRST EDITION

Designed by Betty Lew

Library of Congress Cataloging-in-Publication Data

Gabbay, Tom.
     The Lisbon crossing: a novel / Tom Gabbay.—1st ed.
        p.   cm.
     ISBN: 978-0-06-118843-5
     ISBN-10: 0-06-118843-3
     1. World War, 1939–1945—Portugal—Lisbon—Fiction.   2. Lisbon (Portugal)—
     Fiction.   3. Motion-picture actors and actresses—Fiction.   I. Title.

     PS3607.A226L57 2007
     813'.6—dc22
                                                                        2006046955

07 08 09 10 11 DT/RRD 10 9 8 7 6 5 4 3 2 1

For Julia, again,
of course.

Also
Jared, Jake, Max, and Sophie.

The Wehrmacht marched into Paris on June 14, 1940.

As England steeled herself for the inevitable invasion,

I sat by the pool and read the *Hollywood Reporter.*

Just another war to end all wars, I thought.

Nothing to do with me.

Looking back across the stern from my solitary post on the prom-
enade deck, I lit a Lucky, leaned into the clean, white railing, and
watched the last splash of crimson spill across the western horizon.
9.17 P.M., mid-Atlantic time. Back in Hollywood they'd be polishing
off their three-martini lunches and slipping behind dark glasses as
they stepped out into the blinding afternoon heat. I felt a twinge of
regret. Tinseltown wasn't all it was cracked up to be, not by a long
shot, but it had given me a good run for my money, and leaving
hadn't been in my plans. I told myself it was just a tactical retreat, but
deep down I guess I knew the party was over.

It was my own damn fault, of course. Falling in with Mrs. Charlie
Wexler wasn't the smartest move I ever made, but then one look at
her and common sense went straight out the window. She was what
you call "drop-dead gorgeous," and if I'd stuck around L.A. much
longer I would've been the one doing the dropping. Oh, I'd been in
hot water with jealous husbands before, but Charlie Wexler wasn't
your average outraged mister. To begin with, he was a bona fide psy-
chotic. Anywhere else in the world he would've been doing a life
term in the loony bin, but this was Hollywood, so he was head of

production at Metro, making him one of the most powerful lunatics in the business. The kind of powerful that could walk into any restaurant or nightclub in town, empty a .38 into my back, then stop at the bar for a whiskey sour, secure in the knowledge that every so-called witness in the place would suffer from sudden, catastrophic loss of memory. No one in Hollywood was dumb enough to fuck with Charlie Wexler. Except for me, of course.

I flicked the remnant of my Lucky, watched it float out across the cool night air like a lost firefly until it ran out of steam and arched downward, swallowed up by the darkness as it headed for burial at sea. I straightened up and buttoned my dinner jacket against the chill. Lili would still be holding court at the captain's table and wouldn't miss me if I disappeared into a bottle of scotch.

The cabin-class smoking lounge was a strange mix of Surrealist paintings, brightly colored armchairs, Oriental carpets, and odd Gothic touches like the two gargoyles that grinned down from above the cast-iron fireplace. Scattered around the room were small groups of well-heeled travelers, all men, sitting under dense clouds of cigar fumes, arguing the business of politics and war in the whispered tones of a half-dozen languages. I headed for an empty spot at the back where the barman set me up with a bottle of Highland malt and a crystal tumbler. He poured a double dose, neat, and left the bottle on a silver tray. I rolled the glass around in my hands for a minute, savoring the anticipation, then tossed it back. It was a relief, after all that frosty dinner champagne, to feel the smoky liquor melt into the back of my throat and infiltrate my brain. Slumping into the soft leather, I lit another smoke and went to work on getting thoroughly stewed.

I woke up feeling surprisingly fresh in spite of the empty bottle lurking by the side of my bed—the difference between a good single malt and the two-dollar blend I'd gotten too used to soaking up. I stretched out under the cool white linen and surveyed my surroundings. First class. It's the way to travel, all right. I'd been up and down enough times in my twenty-five years to know the difference, but I also knew it was a mistake to get too comfortable in the lap of luxury. You start thinking you deserve the good life and one day you wake up to find yourself staring at the inside of a boxcar. That was my experience anyway.

I felt like staying put for a while and there was no reason not to. It wasn't even eight yet and Lili never appeared before ten-thirty, sometimes not until noon.

Hollywood didn't make them any bigger than Lili Sterne, although her star didn't shine quite as brightly as it had five years earlier. They'd called her "Germany's secret weapon" then; now they whispered "box-office poison." Lili pretended not to care, but as much scorn as she poured on Hollywood, the truth was that she needed it more than it needed her, and she could feel it slipping away. It wasn't fair, of course—Lili was still stunningly beautiful and she was pure magic on the screen—but nobody cared about fairness. Leading ladies just don't turn forty.

I'd met her the previous year on the set of *Ride the Wild Wind,* a misguided attempt by Warners to match her up with Errol Flynn in a western. I didn't see how a Tasmanian Don Juan and a former showgirl from Berlin teaming up to save Dodge City would add up to box-office gold, and the great American public agreed—they stayed away in droves. It didn't help that Lili and Flynn hated each other's guts, to the point where they wouldn't even stand in the same room together. The director ended up having to shoot each star delivering his or her lines to an off-camera extra, then put it all together in the cutting room. The result didn't work out too well, especially for Lili, who was pretty much reduced to a cameo.

In fact, I probably had more screen time on that picture than either one of them. I'd been stunting for Flynn (who couldn't so much as look at a horse without breaking a bone) since *Robin Hood* a couple of years earlier. The money was better than daily work, and when you're doubling a star some of the perks rub off, so I smiled and put up with the fact that he was a miserable bastard. The kind of guy who gets a kick out of pushing people around, especially the ones who can't push back. When Lili saw that I didn't take any shit from him, she decided to induct me into her camp, which was a hell of a lot more fun than his camp. At first she just wanted ammunition against her costar, which I happily supplied, but we hit it off and over the course of the film we got to be friends. The fact that it never got romantic was probably why we stayed that way.

Don't get me wrong. It wasn't like we were soul mates. Lili was a lone wolf who liked to keep people at a safe distance. I might not hear from her for weeks, then I'd get a call out of the blue and the next thing I knew I was escorting her up some red carpet, or backstage at the Coconut Grove getting drunk with Artie Shaw. So I wondered what was on the cards when the phone rang late one Thursday night and I was greeted by the famous husky voice:

"You've been keeping secrets."

"Lili…?" I coughed into the receiver, groping the bedside table for my smokes.

"Did I wake you?"

"Not yet," I croaked.

"Charlie Wexler is looking for you."

I pulled myself up to a sitting position.

"Are you awake now?" she purred.

"Yeah, that pretty much did it," I said, finding an empty pack of Luckys, which I crumpled up and tossed across the room. I was living in a rented wreck up in Bronson Canyon, nothing much to look at it, but it was private and it had a nice view of the city. It suited me fine.

"What's he want with me?" I asked, although I had a pretty good idea.

"You'd better come see me tomorrow," she said. "One o'clock, I'll give you lunch." And she clicked off.

• • •

The next day, Lili's Louisiana-born butler, Wilson, showed me around to the back of the house (if you can call thirty-seven rooms a house), where I found Lili standing at the terrace bar.

"I hope she was the greatest fuck in the history of sex," she said, mixing a gin and tonic with a wry smile. "Because it's going to cost you—plenty."

She raised a finely plucked eyebrow above the lens of her Italian sunglasses, swung her hips around the bar, and sauntered down to the Olympic-size pool, installing herself on one of the army of sun loungers surrounding the water. A five-foot Mexican was carefully skimming the surface for stray leaves that didn't exist.

There was no need to ask how she knew about Wexler. Lili had a network of informants that would make J. Edgar Hoover turn green.

"I'll just have to lay low for a while," I said, stripping off my jacket and helping myself to the bar.

"That's right." She laughed. "You just lay low and Charlie Wexler will forget the whole thing. Maybe you can become great friends! Let bygones be bygones!"

I packed a highball with ice and swamped it with Johnnie Walker.

"She probably was, you know."

"What?"

"The greatest fuck in the history of sex."

"I'm so happy for you," she sneered, squeezing a wedge of lemon onto her tongue. In spite of our platonic relationship, there was always an undertow of something when we got onto the subject of my love life. Not jealousy. Something else.

"Have you seen her?" I sat down and sipped at the cold scotch.

"I really wouldn't know, darling," Lili replied in her bored stiff voice. She stood up and slipped out of her robe, revealing an athletic build—all sharp angles, with thin boylike hips, long slender limbs, and skin so white it was practically transparent—then she strode over to the pool and dove straight in, hardly disturbing the water's surface.

I watched her swim a few laps then met her at the steps with a towel. "Charlie Wexler fucks every starlet that comes through the gate at Metro," I said. "He owes her a couple."

Lili shot me a "gimme a break" look as she wrapped the towel around her head and bundled herself in the robe, letting it slip stylishly off her left shoulder. She retrieved one of the English cigarettes she smoked, banged it up and down on the pack a couple of times.

"Why is it that normally intelligent men become complete imbeciles when their penises are involved?"

"The way we're built, I guess." I lit her up. "I wonder how Wexler found out. We were pretty careful."

She smiled like a cat and snagged me with the pale blue eyes. "I'm sorry to disappoint you, darling, but the little woman told him herself. She confessed in a flood of tears."

"Really?" was all I could come up with. I gave myself a minute to confirm that my guts weren't gonna cave in or anything drastic like that. Maybe I should've felt let down or betrayed, but I was fine. It's not that I didn't care. Mrs. Wexler and I had been as intimate as you can get and I'd even enjoyed her company when we had our clothes on, but I knew what the deal was from the first day. She'd picked me up on the Metro back lot, where she spent a lot of lonely time waiting for her husband to finish screwing the chorus line. I guess she got tired of waiting and decided it was time to send him a message. My ego might've been a bit bruised to find out that I was just her shill, but I decided to take comfort in the fact that she didn't have to stick around for three weeks of unbridled sex. She could've confessed her infidelity after the first night if she wasn't having fun.

Lili sauntered up the marble steps onto the terrace, where lunch was being laid out. "I suppose you thought you had her under the Jack Teller spell."

"Something like that," I said, following her up.

She sat down in the shade of a big umbrella and stared at a seafood salad. Taking a long drag off the Rothman, she showed a trace of a smile as she let the smoke escape between her lips.

"Really, Jack. Of all the horny wives in Hollywood, you had to pick Charlie Wexler's!"

I smiled and shrugged. "What d'you think he'll do?"

"Shoot you!" she said with a little too much enthusiasm. I grunted and we fell into silence.

"Maybe I'll shoot him first," I said, and she fired a look across the table. I'd kept Lili in the semidark about my New York days, but she seemed to know enough not to dismiss the possibility that I might be serious.

"You'd be a hero, darling," she smiled. "But I have a better idea."

"I'm all ears." I realized I was hungry and started in on the crab. The cracking seemed to annoy Lili, so I kept at it.

"You need to disappear for a while . . ."

"Maybe," I mumbled, and she treated me to one of her lingering looks. "What am I supposed to do? Run off with my tail between my legs?"

"At least you'd still have a tail."

"I'm not worried about Charlie Wexler," I lied.

"You should be."

"Yeah, well, I can take care of myself." I fumbled my claw, and it fell onto the floor. Lili watched with a combination of amusement and contempt as I scooped it up and threw it back on my plate.

"Do you own a tux?" It was my turn to give her the look. "It doesn't matter. I'll have one sent over."

"What are you talking about, Lili?" She pushed her plate away and sat forward, folding her arms on the table.

"I'm planning a trip," she said. "And I need an escort."

"An escort?"

"That's right."

"What kind of a trip is it?"

"A cruise."

"To?"

"Does it matter?"

"It'd be nice to know."

"Lisbon."

"Lisbon, Portugal?"

"Is there another one?"

"I think there's one in Ohio. Or is it Indiana?"

"The one I'm going to is in Portugal," she smiled, not so sweetly.

"What's there?"

"I'll tell you about that later—if you decide to come."

"I don't know," I said, not wanting to buckle too quickly. "It seems kind of extreme . . ."

"Would you rather be shot in the back by a deranged studio executive?"

"I hear they're shooting people over there, too."

"Not in Portugal."

"Yeah, well, give 'em time." I speared a prawn.

"Look, Jack," she said, losing patience. "You can stay here and face the music if it makes you feel like more of a man, but I'm leaving tonight, and if you're not willing to help me I need to find someone who is."

"Tonight, huh?"

"The sky sleeper to New York and we sail the day after."

I narrowed my eyes, looked her over for a minute. "When you say you need an escort, Lili, I have this feeling that you're not talking about a dancing partner." She held my look for a moment then reached for another cigarette.

"I need someone who can handle himself . . ." she said, watching me with one eye as she lit up and allowed herself a long drag. ". . . and who doesn't necessarily play by the rules. I believe you have experience in both areas?"

I didn't answer, but I could see from the cagey way she looked at me that she knew she had her escort.

. . .

It turned out that Lili knew more about my New York days than I thought she did. She knew about Johnny Kaye and the Kit Kat Klub and the graft, bribery, and corruption that went with it. She knew about Arthur Wahlberg, too, the two-bit Broadway director that Johnny wasted for fucking his girlfriend and then tried to pin on me. It was my one-way ticket out of the rackets and onto the rails—two years drifting west, broke, and trying to steer clear of the law. As it turned out, there was no need. When I hit L.A. I found out that Johnny had shot the girl, too, then swallowed a bullet himself. The cops decided to drop the whole inconvenient mess, but the idea that I was the guy who killed Wahlberg never quite died.

Lili played all this back to me on the flight east, implying that a guy with my kind of history might be useful in whatever it was she was up to. I didn't say anything one way or another, which she seemed to like, probably assuming it meant I was a cold-blooded killer.

I didn't get her story until two days later, as we were sailing out of New York Harbor. Lili looked every inch the star in dark shades, white tailored suit, and matching silk scarf tied around her chin. The July sky couldn't have been more blue. We watched Manhattan slip into the distance for what seemed like a long time, then Lili turned around and handed me a grainy photograph of a young woman in a small boat, the kind you rent in a city park on a bright summer's day. The girl was seventeen or eighteen, I guessed. More striking than beautiful, at least in the Hollywood sense of the word, she had long, dark hair that swept across high, delicate cheekbones and landed gently on her shoulders. Her gaze met the lens straight on, but her eyes were in shadow, protected from the harsh light by an extended right hand. She had a warm, natural, unguarded smile, but she kept something in reserve, too.

"Who is she?" I asked.

"A friend. From long ago. She's the reason we're going to Lisbon." Lili waited for a reaction but I didn't give her one, so she continued.

"Her name is Eva . . . Eva Lange. I've known her since I was nine years old, when she moved into the apartment below us in the Kreuzberg. Her father had come home to Berlin after Eva's mother, who was English, died suddenly in London. Eva was a quiet, lonely thing . . . younger than me by four years, but there were no other children in the building, so I took her under my wing. We became inseparable. We even made a blood oath once that we would always stay together."

Lili smiled bittersweetly as the memory washed over her.

"But life took over, of course. We grew up. Eva went on to university and I went onto the stage. We saw less and less of each other and then we lost touch altogether. Until May of 1927. As I was packing to go to Hollywood, I received an invitation to a concert. Eva played the cello, quite beautifully. But on that night, she was exceptional. She played like an angel, and I felt as though it was for me alone."

"I brought flowers backstage and took her to the best restaurant in Berlin. We drank too much champagne and laughed a lot, then . . . well, we went our separate ways. Eva promised to visit me in America, but . . ." She shrugged, letting all the reasons hang in the air.

"You never saw her after that?"

"No." Lili turned her face into the breeze. "Now I want to get her out of that insanity over there."

"What makes you think she's in Lisbon?"

"Last September, when the war broke out, I decided to find her. I should've done it years ago, but . . ." She remembered her cigarette, took a cursory drag, and tossed it overboard.

"I made inquiries, phoning old friends and neighbors, but it was impossible. Even when I could get through, nobody was willing to talk. It was strange. They'd all changed. As though they'd become different people." She paused for a moment, then shrugged it off.

"It seemed hopeless, and I was ready to give up. Then, two months ago, a letter arrived. It was postmarked from Zurich, but it was from Eva's father, in Berlin. He'd been looking for his daughter since the war broke out, when she disappeared from Hamburg, where she'd been living. Just vanished, he said. When he heard I was looking for her, too, he thought I must be the answer to his prayers. Surely a big star like me could find his daughter before the Nazis did." She gave me a look. "What hope is there for the Third Reich when a star as big as Lili Sterne is involved?

"Anyway, it made me more determined than ever to find her. If she was running from the Nazis, there must've been a reason. Her father had heard a rumor from some of her friends that she'd gone to Amsterdam, but he hadn't been able to reach her at the address he'd been given. Then, in May, Holland was invaded. Perhaps she'd escaped again, perhaps she'd gone into hiding, or perhaps she'd never been there in the first place. He didn't know. He gave me the address and telephone number in Amsterdam and wished me good luck. There was no return address on the envelope."

"Not much to go on," I said.

"No," Lili agreed. "But being me has its advantages. I spoke to a friend I have in Washington. He arranged for the American ambassador to go around to the address I'd been given."

There was no need to ask who her friend was. Even though she never talked about it—not with me anyway—it was common knowledge that Lili enjoyed a "special relationship" with Roosevelt, regularly dining at the White House and seeing the president when he came west. If I had to guess, I'd say that there was nothing romantic about it, but I could've been wrong. After all, he was married to Eleanor—quite a lady, to be sure, but not exactly oozing with sex appeal.

"The ambassador found out from the neighbors that Eva had indeed been there, but she'd left quickly, shortly after the Nazis had marched in. The neighbors thought that she'd gone to Paris, but they couldn't be sure. At any rate, they had no name or address."

"I'd say it sounds like a dead end if we weren't on our way to Lisbon."

"I was planning to go to Paris myself, but the Nazis got there first," Lili said. "So I hired Eddie Grimes."

Eddie Grimes needed no introduction. He was a run-of-the-mill snoop from San Francisco who'd managed to convince the Hollywood elite that he was a combination of Sherlock Holmes and Dick Tracy. If you had a problem and lots of money to waste, Eddie was your man. There were plenty of better guys around, but nobody half as overpriced, and that meant a lot to Lili's crowd.

"I told him I wanted him to drop everything and go to Europe. I didn't care what it cost." My mind boggled at what he must've been soaking her for.

"I'm not sure Eddie Grimes was the right guy to—"

"He phoned me a week later with news that Eva was in Lisbon."

"Like I said, there's nobody better than Eddie."

"He told me she'd arrived from Paris a few days earlier. She'd been trying to get passage to London, but as far as Eddie could tell, she had no money and wasn't going anywhere. I instructed him to make contact and hand her the letter I'd given him for her."

"What did the letter say?"

"To go with Eddie to New York, where I would meet them."

I waited for more but nothing came. Lili removed a piece of folded paper from her handbag and gave it to me.

"This arrived the next day," she said.

I unfolded the thin sheet, which turned out to be a Western Union telegram. It was dated the same day Lili had phoned me at home and invited me to lunch.

It went like this:

MISS LILI STERNE
228 ROXBURY DRIVE
BEVERLY HILLS CALIFORNIA USA
JUNE 26, 1940, 11:32 AM PST

APOLOGIES TO REPORT MISTER E GRIMES DEAD IN CAR STOP BE-
LIEVE HE WAS IN YOUR EMPLOYMENT STOP PLEASE CONTACT ME,
YOUR SERVANT, CAPITAO J CATELA
GUARDA NATIONALE REPUBLICANA, LISBOA END

The coffee was as thick as black crude, but it delivered a nice kick, so I signaled the waiter for another. I had an hour to kill and it felt good to be soaking up sun on dry land, a soft morning breeze gently rustling the poplar trees overhead. I sat back and breathed it in.

The *Manhattan* had slipped into her berth early, just before dawn, and I was roused a few minutes later by a sharp knock on the door. Dressed to the nines with two dark-skinned porters and a pile of Louis Vuitton in tow, Lili greeted me with a look of disdain, apparently annoyed that I was still in my pajamas twenty minutes after the sun had cracked the horizon. She breezed past me and did a quick turn around the cabin while informing me that a car was waiting on the dock to take me to police headquarters. I'd meet up with Captain Catela then proceed to the Hotel Palacio, a five-star beach resort twenty miles west of the city, where she'd be waiting for my report. It wasn't put in the form of a suggestion, so I didn't bother with a protest.

The Hollywood rumor mill was already grinding out whispers about Eddie Grimes's demise, so it was no surprise that Lili had a last-minute change of heart about meeting up with the Lisbon police.

It seemed unlikely that even Hedda Hopper would have operatives in Lisbon, but you never know, and if the rags linked Lili to Grimes's death, they'd have a field day. Anyway, I was happy enough to be on my own. Shadowing a screen goddess wasn't the easiest way to travel.

The waiter appeared and looked me over carefully while he served up my second cup.

"American?" he ventured.

"That's right." I nodded. He leaned over the table, brushed some imaginary crumbs onto his tray.

"I get you big money for American passport." He shot me a knowing look, stepped back, and waited for a response, tray tucked neatly under his arm.

"What would I use, then?"

"I sell you one," he winked. "I make you nice price. You make a profit."

"I'll keep it in mind," I said, and he waltzed off happily, whistling a tune as he went. Business was too good, I guess, to worry about one reluctant customer.

I sipped the coffee and thought about the best way to handle the authorities. I knew they knew that Eddie was working for Lili, but I had no idea what else they knew. I'd have to play it by ear.

Captain Jose Luiz Ernesto Teixara da Catela sprang to his feet, scurried around his hand-carved seventeenth-century desk, and was halfway to the door before he realized that no movie star would be coming through it. He came to an abrupt halt and stood at attention, his left eyebrow punctuating his face with a question mark.

"Jack Teller," I said, stepping forward with an outstretched hand. "I represent Miss Sterne."

The captain's square-jacketed shoulders sagged perceptibly. "I see," he said, forgoing the handshake and motioning me into one of two armchairs sitting across from the desk he'd just abandoned.

"I understood that Miss Sterne would herself be present this morning," he said in heavily accented, but pretty good English. "I hope she's not unwell."

"Just a little tired after the long voyage," I said, my voice bouncing between the high ceiling and the hard tiles on the floor. It was a large room, empty but for the big desk and a few dark paintings on the wall. No windows, just a set of French doors looking out onto a lush terrace garden.

"Understandable," he nodded as he found his seat. "Perhaps we can arrange for a more convenient—"

"I'll try not to take much of your time," I interrupted.

He sat back, drew a long breath through his nose, pursed his lips, and ran the tip of his finger across an impeccably trimmed pencil mustache. Catela was a man who liked what he saw when he looked in the mirror. In his midfifties, with heavily lidded dark eyes, olive skin, and thinning black hair that was greased straight back, he must've been the most groomed man I'd ever laid eyes on. The kind of guy who shaves twice a day.

"I'm sorry," he said, leaning forward. "I've forgotten your name."

"Teller," I repeated. "Jack Teller."

"Yes, of course . . . May I ask, Senhor Teller, what is your position in the matter?"

"I'm a friend of Miss Sterne."

He nodded and stared at me, stone faced, across the antique surface. The long silence was supposed to make me feel uneasy, but I was happy to sit there all day. "She didn't mention your name in our telephone conversation," he finally said.

"She must've forgotten," I said coolly, aware that the only communication had been an exchange of telegrams to set up the meeting. "If I could just ask you a few questions about Eddie Grimes . . ."

The captain performed a deep sigh and frowned. "As you must be aware, Senhor Teller, I am the deputy chief of the national police force of Portugal." He spoke slowly, letting the gravity of the statement sink in before continuing. "Do you really believe that I would concern myself with the death of an insignificant tourist in a motoring accident? Is that the sort of incident that, under normal circumstances, you would expect a man in my position to take an interest in?"

My initial aversion to the guy was blossoming into full-blown contempt. I had to bite my tongue, though. The best shot I had at finding Lili's friend would be to get hold of Grimes's notebook. Overpriced snoops-for-hire like him were very conscientious about keeping detailed notes. They liked to provide their clients with long, single-spaced reports that made it look like they'd actually earned their ridiculous fee. Assuming he was no exception and there was a notebook, Catela would have it, and it looked like there was only one way he was going to give it to me. I cut to the chase.

"You'd like to meet Miss Sterne," I said.

"Bravo, senhor." He smiled and leaned back in his chair. It was just as well that Lili hadn't come along, I thought. If Catela had her in his grasp, he would've strung us along for all it was worth. At least this way I had something to bargain with.

"I'll tell you what," I said. "Give me what you have on Grimes and I'll see what I can do."

"This is what I love about the American people," he smiled. "Always straight to the point. So let me be equally forthright." He leaned across the desk. "Whatever your business here in Lisbon, I am in a position to be of great service . . . Or I can make things very difficult."

"Sure," I responded flatly. "But then the closest you'd ever get to Lili Sterne would be the front row at the Saturday matinee."

The captain slowly unfolded a grin wide enough that I could see the gold in his back molars. "I believe I could learn to like you, Senhor Teller."

"I wish I could say the same for you." I smiled. "But I've got this problem with authority figures. Nothing personal."

Catela laughed heartily. "You see what I mean about Americans?" He removed a gold cigarette case from his breast pocket and offered it across the desk. I waved it off and reached for my Luckys.

"Eddie Grimes," I said.

"Yes. Eddie Grimes." He sat back, ready to be of service.

"Your cable said he was killed in a car accident."

"That's correct."

"How did you know he was working for Miss Sterne?"

"We found a contract among his possessions. In his hotel room."

"Which hotel was that?"

Catela gave me a look. "I promise you, senhor, I have no reason to mislead you."

"I'd just like to have a look. If you have no objection, of course."

"The Imperial," he said, but not very happily. "Quite a modest accommodation, considering the value of his contract."

"Did you find anything else?"

"What are you looking for?" He lit one of his gold-tips and let the smoke drift up into his nostrils before sucking it in.

"Papers," I said. "A notebook maybe."

"No." The captain shook his head. "There was nothing more than a few articles of clothing and the contract. I'm certain of it."

"How about a passport?"

The captain shook his head.

"Wallet?"

"No papers were recovered. Other than the contract, of course."

"And that was in his hotel room?"

"As I said."

"So how did you identify him?"

"I'm sorry?"

"You wouldn't have known where he was staying until you identified him, and if the only identification you found was in the hotel room . . . see what I mean?"

"The vehicle number plates," he said. "It was a leased car." He sat there with a smug look on his face, waiting to bat the next one away.

"He must've had a passport," I said. "Did you check the hotel safe?"

He gave me a look. "Of course, senhor, the safe was checked. The passport and other papers were most likely on his person at the time of the accident."

"But you said no papers were recovered . . ."

"Since the body was not recovered, we would not have recovered any papers that were on the body."

"The body wasn't recovered?"

"That's correct. Therefore, the passport and wallet—and perhaps even the notebook you hope to find—are most likely to be in the pocket of the corpse, which is currently being thrashed about by the waves at the bottom of o Boca do Inferno." The captain was enjoying this a lot more than I was.

"Boca do . . . ?"

"The Mouth of Hell," he translated. "A rock formation at the base of a one-hundred-foot drop into the sea. Apparently, your detective drove over the cliff sometime during the night."

"That's unlucky."

"Yes. A tragedy, of course."

"I meant for me," I said.

The captain smiled. I asked him if he was going to recover the car.

"You haven't seen o Boca do Inferno, senhor. Time and the sea will save a great deal of effort."

"Can I talk to the witness?"

"Witness?" he said, looking surprised. "No, there was no witness."

"I'm sorry, Captain, but that doesn't make any sense," I said.

"In what way does it not?" he said breezily.

"You said you identified Grimes through the car's plates."

"Correct."

"How did you get the number if the car went into the water? How did you even know it went over the cliff?"

"You don't seem to trust me, Senhor Teller."

"Like I said, I've got this thing about authority."

The captain smiled cagily. "The back portion of the vehicle is visible at low tide. A local fisherman reported it shortly after dawn . . . Why should I keep anything from you?"

It didn't really matter. Even if Grimes had a notebook with him, it wouldn't do me any good after a couple of weeks in the drink. I contemplated my options, which weren't many.

"I guess that leaves me with you," I said.

"Putting me in a very good position," Catela grinned.

"Looks that way," I said. "So how would you feel about joining Miss Sterne and myself for dinner tonight?"

"I would prefer it without you . . ."

"I'll try to fade into the background," I said.

He leaned forward. "How can I help?"

"Eddie Grimes was hired to locate a friend of Miss Sterne's. A woman named Eva Lange." I considered showing him the photo that Lili had given me, but he'd want to keep it, so I didn't.

"Eva Lange . . ." he ruminated. "German?"

"That's right. A refugee."

He chuckled.

"Is that funny?"

Catela gestured in the direction of the outside world. "Lisbon is filled with refugees. Tens of thousands and more arriving each day. They roam the streets, worn and dirty, trying to beg, borrow, or steal passage on anything going to America . . . What is your country's expression? 'Give me your tired, your poor, your . . .' How does it continue?"

"'Huddled masses . . .' Or something like that," I said.

"Yes. These people, they actually believe it." He shrugged. "I suppose they have no choice. There's no place left for them to go. A few with money might be fortunate, but most will sell the last of their possessions to buy a ticket on a ship that doesn't exist. So they steal in order to eat and I am obliged to put them in jail. Others choose a more permanent solution. Do you know that in the past month we have had over one hundred suicides in Lisbon?" He stubbed out his cigarette. "But you must pardon me. These are my problems. Please continue with yours."

"That's about it," I said. "A few hours before Grimes drove off the cliff, he phoned Lili—Miss Sterne—and told her he'd traced the girl to Lisbon. Said she'd been trying to get passage to London."

"London?"

"That's what he said."

"Not the best place to go if you wish to escape the Third Reich. I would certainly be looking west, across the sea."

"Maybe so," I said. "But Grimes thought she was broke anyway, so there's a good chance she's still in Lisbon." In fact, I thought the chances were a lot better that she was long gone, but there was no point in telling him that.

"Think you can locate her?"

"Perhaps," Catela said cautiously. He narrowed his eyes, gave me a penetrating look. "Do you know why this woman left Germany in the first place?"

"Maybe she didn't like the long winters," I said. "What difference does it make?"

"If she is a fugitive, she will be traveling on false papers," he replied.

"I don't know why she left," I said, which was true. I stood up abruptly, taking the captain by surprise. "But I've taken enough of your time."

He rose to his feet. "It may be very difficult to locate one individual . . . As I said, there are tens of thousands . . ."

"Miss Sterne will be very grateful if you can tell us anything. We can discuss it over dinner."

He performed a shallow formal bow. "You're staying at the Palacio."

"Have you been spying on us already?"

"Everyone who is anyone in Lisbon stays at the Palacio. I myself often spend the evening at the casino there."

"And I bet you win."

"No one can win every night," the captain smiled, coming out from behind his desk and leading me to the door. "But in the end, I always seem to come out ahead."

• • •

The route to the Imperial Hotel took us through the market district of the Baixa, a grid of expansive boulevards that was built in the aftermath of the massive earthquake and subsequent tidal wave that flattened Lisbon in 1755. I got an earful on the subject of the country's long history from my good-natured driver, Alberto, a barrel-chested chatterbox with legs too short for his body and the furriest arms I'd ever seen. He spewed forth with unstoppable enthusiasm as we drove through the crowded streets, covering two thousand years in about ten city blocks, from the Phoenicians, through the Greeks, the Carthaginians, Julius Caesar and the Roman Empire, to, finally, the Moors, who were defeated by the Christians in the twelfth century after a four-hundred-year siege. When he took a deep breath and started to launch into Napoléon, I decided to fast-forward.

"Who's next?" I said, and he paused, stole a glance in the rear-view mirror.

"Senhor?"

"The Germans seem to think they should be running Europe," I said. Alberto paused to think his answer through.

"We are fortunate in Portugal to have a strong and wise leader," he said. "Dr. Salazar will keep the latest conqueror from our door."

"I'm sure you're right," I said, thinking they'd probably been saying something pretty similar in Paris not too long ago. Anyway, it put an end to my history lesson.

I felt like stretching my legs, so I told Alberto to pull up. He found a shady spot for the car and, anticipating the bonus of an unexpected morning nap, launched into a long-winded dissertation on the best route to the hotel while he sketched it out on the back of an old newspaper. He looked a little heartbroken when I told him he was coming along. Even if I could find my way based on his dubious instructions, I'd need a translator once I got there.

Alberto kept racing ahead, then stopping to let me catch up

before pulling in front again. I didn't need a midday sprint through the July heat, so I kept my own leisurely pace. He led us off the main drag into Lisbon's oldest district, the Alfama, a hilly maze of narrow lanes where traders in denlike shops and Arabs in open stalls bought and sold everything from fresh fish to the family silver. We could've been in Istanbul or Cairo.

It was the first time I noticed the refugees, who congregated here in the shadowy backstreets, where they could trade the contents of their suitcases for the hope of a future. They weren't what I expected. Sure, they were tired and dirty and looked utterly defeated, but underneath all that you could see fathers and mothers, sons and daughters, aunts and uncles who, until recently, had worked, lived, and died in the towns and villages built by their grandparents and great-grandparents. A few weeks ago, they'd been proud people and now they just wanted to be invisible, averting their eyes as you passed them in the street. Except the children, of course. They didn't know enough to look away.

We found the hotel stuck between a dark funeral parlor and a fragrant cheese shop. It wasn't exactly a dive but it was pretty damn close. You had to wonder why a guy on fifty bucks a day would choose to stay in a place like that, but I suppose he was just trying to make a dime on his expense account. Or maybe Grimes just felt more at home on the seedy side of life.

The lobby was small and dark, the only light emanating from a twenty-watt lamp standing on the small, curved reception desk. A large arrangement of decomposing white orchids—probably leftovers from next door—languished on a side table, overwhelming the room with a sickly sweet fragrance that didn't mix too well with the faint aroma of aging cheese that wafted in from outside. The proprietor shuffled out from a back room and greeted us with a blank expression. Pushing seventy, with close-cropped white hair and a mustache to match, he looked at us through dark, weary eyes as he buckled his pants up. His wrinkled white shirt seemed to be several sizes too large.

"*Boa tardes,*" he mumbled suspiciously, well aware that we weren't there to book a room. Alberto returned the greeting, established that no English was spoken, then explained the reason for my visit. The old guy glanced over at me, shook his head, and muttered something as he headed back to where he came from, probably to complete his siesta.

"He says he has answered all the question from the police," Alberto explained.

I took my wallet out, removed a crisp ten-dollar bill, and placed it on the desk. "Sorry that I don't have escudos," I said. "Ask him how he feels about the Yankee dollar?"

The old man stopped in his tracks and, not waiting for the translation, picked up the note and folded it into his shirt pocket.

"I'd like to see the room," I said. He nodded and removed a key from the wall behind him. I didn't expect to find anything up there— the authorities would've been through everything—but I had to get away from the smell of dead orchids and ripe cheese.

The room wasn't as bad as I'd expected. It was tidy and cheerful enough once the old man pulled the shutters back. The furnishings consisted of a double bed with a large crucifix hanging over it, a wardrobe, and a set of drawers. There was a sink in the corner and the toilet was just across the hall. Not exactly deluxe, but I'd seen a lot worse.

I took a look around, checking under the bed, on top of the wardrobe, and inside a few drawers, more for show than anything else. I told Alberto to ask the old guy how much he charged and how many days Grimes had paid for. I thought it might put him on the defensive, and it did. He claimed that the American had settled up daily, but you could tell he was lying, that he'd been paid in advance for a few of the nights that Eddie had spent underwater. I couldn't have cared less, but I let him know with a look that I was onto him. People who've been caught in a lie tend to suddenly get a lot more talkative.

"Did he have any visitors?" I asked, and a lively dialogue ensued, the two men chattering back and forth like a couple of old ladies at the back fence. I gave them a minute before clearing my throat.

"Ah, senhor . . . *Desculpe*," Alberto apologized. "The gentleman tells me some quite interesting facts about your friend."

"He wasn't my friend but go ahead."

"It seems he had a big interest in the women." Alberto gave me a knowing look. "He takes a different one each night."

"Hookers?"

"Yes, senhor. Like that. Hookers. And not the nice ones. The kind of the street." It was mildly interesting and it explained Grimes's choice of accommodation, but as much as it amused Alberto, it didn't help me any.

"Ask him if he remembers how many bags the American had."

Alberto shrugged, wondering why I would want to change the subject to suitcases, but he put the question. After some additional discussion he said, "Just one. The one the police took away."

"Did he see the American on the night of the accident?"

"*Sim, Sim,*" the old man responded, providing another round of long details in Portuguese. He was being very talkative now, enjoying the gossip, and it occurred to me that Alberto might be useful to have around. I'd get Lili to hire him on for the duration.

"Yes, the American was here on that evening," Alberto relayed. "He has arrived a few minutes after nine o'clock."

"How does he remember the time so well?"

"Because the girl, she was waiting for him. She had been arranged to arrive at nine o'clock."

"How long did she stay after Grimes arrived?"

"Not long," Alberto answered without referring to the old man, having by now elicited the whole story out of him. "Five minutes only." He made his face into a shrug.

"Five minutes?"

"*Sim.*"

"Was she that good or that ugly?" I said, which gave Alberto a good laugh. He translated for the old man, who managed something approaching a smile.

"No, senhor," Alberto explained. "The reason she has left was because the second lady comes."

"Second lady?"

"*Sim.*" Alberto beamed.

"Who was the second lady?"

"This gentleman thinks that maybe she is the wife of the American."

"Why does he think that?"

"Because the first girl—the hooker—she has run away in such a big hurry when the second lady comes. And then, a few moment later, the second lady is run away, too, and not looking very happy. Then the American, he comes after, putting on his clothes while he runs out the door. And, after . . . he don't come back." Alberto pantomimed the action of a car sailing over a cliff and hitting with a splash.

This was getting interesting. I reached for my wallet again, held it in my hand without cracking it. "Ask him if he spoke to the second woman," I said to Alberto.

"Yes," the old man said, eyeing up the billfold and dropping the pretense of a language barrier. "I speak her."

"In what language?"

"She speak Portuguese."

"She was Portuguese?" I asked, surprised.

The old man frowned and shook his head. "She speak a bad Portuguese. She German."

I showed him the photo of Eva Lange. It was small and grainy and fifteen years out of date, but he dutifully studied it, holding it a couple of inches from his face and squinting hard, before returning it.

"He say it could be this lady, but it could be not," Alberto explained. "He say she has a kind of red hair."

I put the photo away and extracted another ten from my wallet. "I want to see the hooker that Grimes saw that night. Can you arrange it?"

The old man closed his eyes, meaning if enough currency appeared when they opened, he could. I removed two more notes, held all three in front of his face.

"The Hotel Palacio," I said. "Midnight."

The old man nodded, so I folded the bills over and stuffed them into his shirt pocket.

It looked like the search for Eva Lange might be over before it started. I wondered how I'd tell Lili that her overpaid private eye had, in all likelihood, driven her childhood friend over a hundred-foot cliff into the sea.

I decided to wait until I had a little more to go on.

"When's low tide?" I asked Alberto as we pulled onto the coast road heading toward Estoril.

"Oh, it comes, I think, about one hour ago," he replied, checking the sun's position in the sky.

"Are we going anywhere near this Boca do Inferno?"

"O Boca? Yes, she is very close the hotel."

"Okay, let's have a look."

Alberto nodded and settled in behind the wheel. Maybe he sensed that I wanted quiet or maybe he was just talked out, but either way I was grateful for the lull. I smoked and stared out the window as the car rattled along the road heading out of the city, hugging the Rio Tejo until it disappeared into the deep blue waters of the Atlantic. We skirted a wide, sandy beach, empty but for a couple of old fishermen hauling the day's catch out of a brightly painted wooden skiff, then the road sloped upward, winding its way to the top of the rocky cliffs that rose vertically out of the Atlantic. It was quite a sight.

We pulled up on the verge of a craggy headland jutting out into the open sea. Alberto yanked the hand brake and jumped out of the car.

"From here we must walk a little," he said. By the time I stepped into the sea air, he'd already clambered down a shallow bank and was heading out onto the cliffs.

"This way, senhor!" He waved and shouted over the roar of the ocean crashing onto the rocks below. "I show you!" I slid down the incline and picked my way over the rocks until I reached the edge of the bluff, where Alberto was waiting for me.

"O Boca do Inferno," he said almost reverentially, pointing further up the peninsula toward an underwater cavern at the base of the formation. "The Mouth of Hell."

"How'd it get its name?" I asked.

"Because, like hell, you can believe you are a safe distance away, but the current is too strong. Once it catch you, you no can get away. It pull you in."

"I know the feeling."

Alberto shrugged. "I think there are many unfortunate souls at the bottom of this place."

I scanned the water for any sign of Grimes's car. I didn't see anything at first, but then the sunlight glinted off some chrome trim near the cliff's edge, and I could make out a taillight and the rear fender of a red car just under the surface of the churning waters. The vehicle had landed headfirst and stayed upright, lodged in the rocks. A hundred-foot drop from the road, it must've been quite a ride. No more than a couple of seconds, but it would've felt a lot longer sitting there watching your life flash before your eyes. It gave me the shivers.

With nothing more to see, we headed back to the car. I noticed a villa overlooking the site from a larger promontory to the east. We must've passed it on our way, but the estate was hidden from the road by a dense cluster of pine trees. A relatively new building, three stories high, with dormer windows on a pitched roof, wooden shutters, and a wraparound porch, it looked like a white stucco version of a Cape Cod. A gated wall surrounded the compound, which included a garden and swimming pool that overlooked the sea, as well as three smaller structures, probably a garage and a couple of guesthouses. There was something forlorn about the place, but I couldn't say why. Maybe it was just the remote position.

Alberto fired up the engine and we pulled away. It was late afternoon and the sun had dropped a few degrees, taking the heat out of the day. Lili would be wondering where the hell I was.

I found her on the tennis court at the back of the hotel, serving up a junior diplomat from the U.S. Mission. His name was Richard Everett Allan Brewster III, which pretty much said it all. After Groton and the Yale debating society, he'd followed Brewster I and Brewster II into the State Department. At twenty-six, he was on top of the world, a real Brylcreem Boy with a mouthful of perfect white teeth and a great jawline, a guy who was going places and knew it. Lili was in the process of taking him apart.

"I was starting to think that you'd run off with somebody else's wife," she said when she spotted me.

"Just seeing the sights," I said, and sat down on a bench facing the court. Lili stared down her opponent then wound up and sent her service wide. She looked at me like it was my fault.

"Didn't mean to break your concentration," I deadpanned. She grunted and turned her attention back to the boy wonder, blowing her second serve by him with ease. I enjoyed watching Lili embarrass him for a while, then it got monotonous. The light was fading and I needed a drink when she finally aced him for game, set, and match.

"I'm sorry you had to witness that," Brewster puffed as he sauntered over to check me out.

"You put up a good fight," I lied.

"Don't get much time for tennis, I'm afraid." He flashed his dental work and offered up his hand. "Richard Brewster, assistant deputy to the ambassador. Call me Dick."

"Jack Teller," I responded.

"Yes, Lili was telling me about you . . ."

"I didn't say anything nice!" she interjected as she pulled a sweater on over her whites and walked across court to join us.

"Shall we have a drink?" Brewster suggested.

"I'd love to, darling," she said, lacing it with irony. "But I have a dinner engagement." She shot me a withering look. "With a police captain."

"Word travels fast," I said, trying a smile.

"He sent two dozen roses to my room."

Worse things could happen, I thought, but Lili didn't seem to think so, so I didn't push it.

"Thank you for the match, Mr. Brewster," she said, propelling her hand forward. "Perhaps I'll give you a chance to redeem yourself before I leave Lisbon."

"I'll work on my game," he answered lamely.

Lili offered him a strained smile, suggested that I not be late for dinner, then made a quick exit along the lush garden path that led back to the hotel. I was in the doghouse, but she'd get over it.

"Is she always like that?" Brewster asked, zipping a light cotton jacket against the cool evening air that was moving in off the sea.

"Like what?"

"A ballbreaker."

"She's a star," I explained.

He gave me a patronizing look and started along the path, expecting me to follow. "Well, whatever she is, she certainly has pull. The secretary himself cabled instructions. We're to provide any and all assistance."

"Glad to see my tax dollars at work," I said, making him wait while I took my time firing up a Lucky. He got his own pack out of a jacket pocket and I lit him up, too.

"Was Catela any help?"

"He said he'd have a look around."

"I wouldn't count on him if I was you."

"I never count on anyone," I said, and he nodded, like he was concurring, but I didn't think he was listening. I started up the path again, letting him trail behind this time.

"What do you know about this girl she's looking for?" he asked. "This Eva Lange?"

"Not a lot."

"Are you sure she's in Lisbon?"

"I'm not sure of anything," I said. "Eddie Grimes thought she was, though."

"Did you know him?"

"Grimes?"

"Right. Grimes."

"Just by reputation."

"Which was?"

"Hollywood's favorite dick."

Brewster nodded again, as if I'd just said something important. "I was supposed to notify the next of kin," he said. "But I couldn't find any."

"Then I guess no one'll miss him."

Brewster stopped at the end of the path, had a look around, and spotted a black coupe parked up the drive at the side of the hotel. The driver spotted him, too, and started the engine.

"Well," he said, signaling the car to swing around and pick him up. "Give me a couple of days. I'll get to the bottom of it."

"Actually," I said slowly, "I'd appreciate it if you didn't."

"Didn't what?"

"Mention it to anyone."

"Jack," he said, sighing. "I know how to be discreet. It's in the job description."

"No, I mean, I'd appreciate it if you didn't do anything about it or discuss it with anyone."

"What the hell are you talking about?" he said, getting edgy.

"I'd rather you just left it alone," I said. Lisbon didn't strike me as the kind of place where a junior diplomat with a nice smile would open doors.

Brewster looked me up and down, then put on a crooked smile that was supposed to let me know that he wasn't too impressed. "Look," he said stonily. "I'm sorry to be blunt, but the secretary of state explicitly directed me—"

"I don't give a monkey's tit what the secretary of state directed you."

"Hold on, Teller. Just who in hell do you think you are?"

"The guy who holds your career in his hands, Dick. That's who I am."

It stopped him cold.

"You wanna explain that?"

"Sure," I said, and paused long enough to make him uncomfortable. "You don't think the secretary of state really gives a damn what happens with Lili Sterne and her childhood friend, do you? Of course he doesn't. So why would he make such a fuss about it?"

"You tell me."

"Don't you read the gossip columns? You really should, you know. A guy in your position needs to know these things."

He was all ears by this point. "Know what things?"

"You really don't know?" I chuckled, just to rub it in a little more.

"Look, Teller, I'm—"

"Come on, Dick, think about it. Why would the secretary of state care about Lili Sterne?"

Nothing.

"Who does he answer to?"

It started to dawn on him.

"The—"

"That's right. The guy whose picture hangs in your office."

"I'll be damned . . ." He was impressed. "Are they—?"

I shrugged. "Your guess is as good as mine."

"Well, all the more reason—"

"All the more reason to do nothing," I said.

"What the hell are you talking about?" he said, frowning. I was gonna have to spell it out for him.

"The only thing you care about is getting a good report card, right?"

"Well, I wouldn't put it . . ."

"Maybe you wouldn't put it like that, but that's the way it is," I said. "So while I appreciate your offer, the kind of help I need right now is for you to forget the whole thing. If I need something from you—and there's a good chance that I will at some point—I'll let you know. And if you're happy with that arrangement, I promise that you'll get an A-plus on that report card. You happy with that?"

Brewster narrowed his eyes and pursed his lips. I waited while he figured out where his interests lay, and it wasn't long before he was smiling again. He produced an engraved business card from his bill-fold, turned it over, and scribbled something on the back. "My home number," he said, handing it over. "Anytime."

"Thanks," I said.

The car pulled up and Brewster flashed his teeth one last time. "You know," he said as he slipped into the backseat, "she looks a lot older in person."

I decided to let him have the last word.

There was just enough time before dinner for a wash and a shave before donning my dinner jacket and heading downstairs. I considered stopping at the bar for a quick one, but I skipped it and went straight to the dining room. I needed a few minutes alone with Catela before Lili arrived.

Chances were pretty good that Eva Lange was dead. The old man at the Imperial might not have been the most reliable witness on the planet, but I had little doubt that she was the one who'd been to see Grimes on the night he drove off a cliff. The rest wasn't hard to guess. Grimes had probably been in touch with her, maybe arranged a meeting at his hotel using Lili's letter as bait. When Eva showed up at an awkward moment, accidentally walking in on whatever perversions he was up to with his two-dollar hooker, she did a runner and Grimes went after her. He got her into his car, maybe against her will, and one way or another they took a nosedive into the Mouth of Hell.

It was the most plausible scenario, all right, but I couldn't be sure unless I got Eddie's car pulled off the rocks. Catela had dismissed that idea, but he seemed like the kind of guy you could do business with. I'd go with the tried and true—hard cash—and see where that got me. I was pretty sure Lili would shell out without asking questions, but if she did ask, I'd just say that I thought there might be something in the car that would tell us what Grimes knew about Eva. There was no reason to talk about my suspicions, not yet.

The dining room at the Palacio was every bit as formidable as the rest of the place—white marble floor, towering crystal chandelier, thirty-foot arched windows and straitjacketed waiters who didn't talk much but who knew how to bow and scrape. I was led to a table in the back where I found Catela in the company of a uniformed German officer. My first Nazi.

Catela smiled when he saw me, the German didn't. In fact, he looked a bit queasy, like he'd been drinking sour milk.

"Ah, Senhor Teller," the captain welcomed me. "Please sit down. Allow me to present Major Ritter."

"Hello," I said, noticing the distinctive SS insignia on his lapel. Ritter offered a slight nod in response, making it clear that he didn't welcome the intrusion.

"Major Ritter has arrived recently in Lisbon, as well," Catela explained.

"On holiday?" I said, digging out my smokes.

Ritter allowed for a half smile. "Take one of mine," he said, offering a polished silver cigarette case. "French."

"Thanks," I said. "But I don't like the smell."

"As you wish." Ritter shrugged and offered one to Catela, who accepted, providing the major a light in return.

"Major Ritter has been in Paris," Catela said as Ritter smirked.

"Hanging swastikas?" I asked, but Ritter already knew the speech he wanted to make.

"I was fortunate enough to accompany the Führer on his tour of the city," he said, puffing his chest out. Major Ritter wasn't a particularly imposing man. He was probably in his late forties, of average height and average build, with unremarkable features on an unremarkable face. The uniform was his only distinguishing characteristic.

"Quite an honor," I said, and he nodded his head for a long, significant moment.

"When I have witnessed our Führer standing before the tomb of Napoléon . . ." He paused to look up at me and I thought he might start crying. "It was a moment full of poignancy. Full of significance. Full of . . . history." He smiled to himself and rolled his French cigarette in the ashtray.

"What next?" I said, and Catela shifted uneasily in his seat. Ritter smiled broadly and reached across the table to fill my glass from a bottle of very old cognac he was hoarding. I didn't say no.

"An excellent question, Mr. Teller," he said, filling Catela's glass, too. "The Wehrmacht has done in three weeks what Hindenburg and Ludendorff could not do in four years. Those days of the trenches are happily over and you have now witnessed the birth of modern warfare. So your question is exactly right. What next? I believe there are no limits." He raised his glass. "Heil Hitler."

I raised mine. "Being from a neutral country, maybe I should add Churchill to that." Ritter paused with his glass halfway to his lips.

"Churchill is a fool," he said.

I shrugged. "To conquerors and fools, then."

I knocked the drink back and it burned sweetly. Ritter laughed heartily and threw his back, too. Catela took a gentlemanly sip, looked at his watch, and nervously surveyed the room.

"Don't take it personally," I said. "She's always late. It's compulsory star behavior."

"I am happy to wait all night," he said with undisguised enthusiasm.

"Good, because that's not out of the question," I replied.

"What brings the great Lili Sterne to Lisbon?" Ritter asked bluntly.

"Sightseeing," I said, and he laughed.

"There are many people doing many things in Lisbon at this time," he said. "Sightseeing is not one of them."

"She's a big history buff, and it seems that Lisbon has quite a history," I said. "Did you know that Portugal is the oldest nation-state in Europe?"

"No, I wasn't aware of it." Ritter yawned.

"Sure. It was founded in 1139. Three hundred and fifty years before Spain."

"Fascinating," he said, settling back into grimness.

"But it goes back a lot further than that," I went on. "Legend has it that Ulysses himself founded the city, although there's no evidence of that. It was probably the Phoenicians, I forget what century, but they were tossed out by the Greeks, which gives you an idea. The Carthaginians got rid of them and stayed until 200 B.C. when the Romans took over. They were here for a couple of centuries, until the Moors came up from Morocco. They held the city for a while until the Christians laid siege for four hundred years until finally . . . I hope I'm not boring you, Colonel. I just thought with your interest in history . . ."

"Major," he corrected me. "And I'm sure Lisbon has a fascinating history, but I must leave you now."

He stood up and Catela sprang to his feet, too. It had nothing to do with Ritter, though. He'd spotted Lili gliding toward the table, in full flow. She was stunning in slinky sequins and I found myself standing up, as well, as though royalty was approaching. Everyone in the room was trying hard not to look starstruck, without much success. Lili left a trail of whispers in her wake. Even Ritter looked impressed. I noticed a slight break in her concentration when she spotted him, but no one else did.

"I've kept you waiting . . ." She offered her hand to Catela, who promptly smothered it with his lips.

"A pleasure," was all he could bring himself to say.

"Thank you for sending the flowers, Captain. It was very thoughtful of you."

Catela could only nod his head up and down. I think he was literally struck dumb. Lili turned to Major Ritter and gave him a dubious look.

"Allow me to present—" Catela began, but Ritter stepped forward and took her hand without it being offered.

"Guten Abend, Fräulein. Sturmbannführer Heinrich Ritter." Lili pulled her hand away and he performed a well-executed bow instead. *"Ich hatte das Vergnuegen, eine Vorfuehrung von Ihnen 1922 in Berlin zu sehen. Eine schoene Erinnerung."*

"Berlin was a long time ago," she said. "The world has changed."

"Zum Besseren. Wuerden Sie dem nicht zustimmen?"

"I'm sorry, Major," Lili said, ice-cold. "I've forgotten my German, and it's rude to speak it when no one else understands what is being said."

The major sniffed and turned noticeably red, as if she'd slapped him in the face. He finally smiled awkwardly and tried to answer in a jocular tone.

"Vielleicht waere es eine gute Idee, wenn die anderen es lernen wuerden— Und fuer Sie, sich zu erinnern."

I pretended not to understand, but, of course, I did.

4

I never told Lili that I was born in Berlin. I'm not sure why—you'd think that growing up within a few miles of each other would be worth mentioning, but I guess I didn't have anything to say about it. My childhood was remote, unfamiliar, as if it was a collection of borrowed memories—fleeting images of my mother before she got ill, my brother's face at the window on the day I left. But they were just snapshots. They didn't move and they didn't speak to me. I didn't feel any more German than I did Chinese.

It hadn't been a conscious effort. I think when I hit New York, I was trying so hard to be just another kid from the neighborhood—taking on a new name, a new look, a new way of talking—that in the process I wiped out my past, without really meaning to. Or maybe it wasn't as profound as that. Maybe I was just so busy surviving that I lost track. I suppose if you don't visit a memory from time to time, it eventually dies of neglect. Or gets buried so deep that it might as well be dead. At any rate, I didn't delve into my childhood, and this wasn't the place to start, so I pretended not to understand that the major had said, "Perhaps it would be wise of them to learn—and for you to remember."

. . .

A s soon as Ritter took his leave, Catela started snapping his fingers at every waiter in the room, spouting off a series of commands in rapid-fire Portuguese. Each waiter nodded dutifully, bowed, and backed away from the table, scurrying off to do whatever it was he'd been charged with. Copious plates of food and bottles of wine and champagne started arriving shortly thereafter, allowing Catela to turn his attention to Lili.

He started with a rehearsed speech:

"May I say what an honor it is to be sitting here, with you, at this table?" He raised his glass. "You are even more beautiful than I could have thought possible."

"Please, Captain," Lili said, puncturing his bubble. "This will be a very long dinner if you're going to gush all the way through it. Let's have a drink while you tell me how you can help me find Eva Lange." She withdrew a cigarette from her sparkling bag, tapped it a couple of times, then placed it between bright red lipstick lips.

Catela sat there for a beat with a silly grin on his face before fumbling for a light. He probably expected a couple of hours of flirting before getting down to business. Lili wasn't in the mood for flirting.

"Yes," he finally said, clearing his throat a couple of times. "Yes, of course. I hope we can find this woman . . ."

"Eva Lange," Lili repeated.

"Yes, Eva Lange. I hope we can find her. But, as I have said this morning to Senhor Teller, these things can be very difficult in Lisbon at this time. I'm sure you understand that there are many—"

"You've checked the records?" she interrupted coolly.

"Yes, yes, of course," he said, making it obvious that he hadn't even considered it. "I'm afraid there is no information that anyone of that name—"

"Eva Lange," Lili reiterated. "Her name is Eva Lange."

"Yes. Eva Lange. No information that she has ever entered or departed from Lisbon." He shrugged sympathetically. "It is possible, of course, that your information is incorrect and your friend has never been here."

"She was here," Lili said emphatically, exhaling smoke. "I'm sure of it."

"Is it not possible that your employee, Mr. Grimes, has made an identification error? There is a great deal of confusion in our city at the moment . . ."

"That's why I need your help," Lili said flatly, before abruptly changing gears. "Surely a man of your importance can cut through all the confusion."

Catela basked in the compliment. "Let me assure you that I will do all that is in my power. If she is in Lisbon, I promise you, she will be found. In the meantime, I hope you will allow me to be your host." The captain seemed to think that he could palm us off with French champagne and double-talk.

"It would help if we could see Eddie Grimes's notebook," I interjected, seeing my opening.

Catela smiled patronizingly. "As I told you, Senhor Teller, we have found no notebook."

"I'd like to have a look in the car," I said.

He looked at me like I was nuts. "Even if you are correct, this car has been in o Boca do Inferno for more than two weeks. Do you really believe these papers will be worth something?"

"You never know," I said, realizing how feeble it sounded, adding, "We'd be happy to pay whatever cost is involved, if that's the problem."

"Cost is not a concern," he said, dismissing my bribery attempt with a sneer.

Lili frowned. "What the hell is 'o Boca do Inferno'?"

"Eddie Grimes drove off a cliff, a couple of miles up the road," I said. "A place called o Boca do Inferno."

"The Mouth of Hell," Catela helpfully translated.

"And you want to get the car out?"

"We don't have much else to go on." I shrugged.

Lili swung around on Catela. "Can you arrange it, Captain?"

"Of course," he said without a hint of hesitation. "I will be most happy to have it done, as a service to you. You see? I am your servant. You must only ask, and I will do."

That kind of treatment was nothing new to Lili. She thanked him, then picked over her food while we listened to a long-winded account of the captain's fascinating and inevitable rise to power and influence. I excused myself after the main course, to Catela's obvious delight and Lili's look of betrayal. The captain informed me that if I wanted to see Grimes's car come out of the water, I should be at the cliffs at dawn when the tide was at its lowest point. I told Lili that I'd check it out and return directly to the hotel to let her know what, if anything, we'd found.

The Estoril Casino seemed to be the after-dinner spot, so I went along to mingle with the money and soak up the atmosphere. Located just across from the Palacio, the large, modern building was perched atop a small hill, facing the sea, its clean white walls bathed in a spectrum of soft-colored lights. It was a fine, balmy evening, and I enjoyed the taste of the salt air as I wandered up the slope.

I'd been surprised at how quickly Catela had folded, but I shouldn't have been, not after spending time in Hollywood. Something about being up there on that silver screen transformed everyday flesh and blood into modern-day deities, immortals who constantly found, and came to expect, humble offerings being laid at their feet. I guess they didn't call them matinee idols for nothing. Still, I felt kind of sorry for Lili. It looked like our story was heading for a sad ending and it was obvious that her childhood friend meant something to her. As far as I could tell, aside from her star status, she didn't have much else that did.

I entered the casino and was stopped by a thin rake of a man with a beak for a nose and thick glasses that made his eyes look like they were bulging out of his head. He was standing behind a counter that ran the length of the lobby.

"Excuse me, senhor . . ."

"Me?" I said, even though it was obvious who he was addressing.

"Yes, senhor. If you please . . ." He gestured me over. "May I see your membership card, please."

"I haven't got one."

"I'm afraid, then, that I cannot allow you to enter . . ."

"Nobody else has one," I noted, indicating the dozens of well-dressed heels that were passing through on their way to the tables.

"I know them," he said with a smirk.

"All of them?"

"Yes, sir."

"I see," I said. "Do I look that scruffy?"

"Excuse me, senhor?"

"Never mind." The only reason I'd been going in was to pass the time, but now I was determined. "How do I get a membership card?"

"I will need to see your identification documents . . ." I reached for my passport. "And you must pay five hundred dollars."

"Five hundred dollars?" I repeated.

"Yes, senhor."

"Five hundred American dollars?" I said, just to be sure.

"That's correct. Five hundred American dollars."

I was about to swallow my pride and beat a retreat when a voice came up behind me—

"Este é Senhor Teller, Luis! Está viajando com Senhorita Lili Sterne e teve apenas o jantar com capitão Catela . . ."

I turned to see the grinning face of a slightly rumpled middle-aged man, late thirties, I guessed. He was a portly fellow with a twinkle in his eye and an unmistakable English accent, even when he was speaking Portuguese. He winked at me.

"I just told him who you are."

"Desculpe!, senhor," the rake pleaded. "Please forgive me, I have not known . . . Please, you must accept my apology . . ." I thought

I'd better let him off the hook before he got down on his knees.

"Forget it," I said. "No harm done."

"*É muito zangado!*" the smiling Englishman said as he led me away. "I just told him you're furious. Won't sleep a wink tonight, the bastard. Quite right, too. Harry K. Thompson, the *Times*. You've seen my byline. Happy to be of service."

"Jack Teller," I said.

"That's right," he confirmed. "Bit of luck, really, isn't it? Now you can give me an exclusive on what the devil Lili Sterne is doing in Lisbon when Europe's on the verge of collapse. Just kidding, of course. I mean about the exclusive, not about Europe being on the verge of collapse. It is. What *is* she doing in Lisbon, anyway?"

"What makes you think she's in Lisbon?"

"Don't blame you, old chap," he laughed. "Not a bit. I wouldn't trust me either." He led me into the main gaming room and to a long circular bar in front of the roulette tables. The sound of the wheel turning, diamonds clinking, and money changing hands was accompanied by a lonely pianist playing Rachmaninoff on a baby grand in the far corner.

"What are you having?" Thompson asked and I ordered scotch, neat. He ordered brandy and ginger. "Well, here's to the fiddlers on the *Titanic*. If you're going down, you might as well have background music."

"To Nero," I said.

"Quite!" We downed them in one and I called for another round.

"So . . ." Harry smiled mischievously. "What's my lead, then?"

"How about 'Englishman Fiddles About While Europe Collapses'?"

"Don't like that one much," he sneered. "How about 'Hollywood Star with German Origins in Clandestine Meeting with Gestapo Major'?"

"I wouldn't recommend it," I said. "Besides, I thought the *Times* was a serious newspaper."

"Freelance, actually," he confessed. "I'll be anybody's whore. And that includes *Variety*."

"That sounds like a threat, Harry."

"I wouldn't do that to you, Jack. Not without pictures." He took a healthy swallow of the incoming brandy. "The truth is I couldn't give a rat's ass about Lili Sterne, but I'm a bit desperate. This warcorrespondent stuff doesn't suit me. I'm more of a human-interest kind of guy."

"There are plenty of humans in Lisbon," I said.

"Debatable, old chap. Highly debatable. But let's not get carried away with my troubles! Tell me about yours! What about this chap Eddie Grimes?"

"Eddie Grimes?"

"Come on, Jack, let's not be silly. Everybody in Lisbon knows he was working for Lili Sterne. What was he up to?"

"Off the record?"

"Absolutely!"

"Never heard of him."

"Bastard!" He smiled. "All right. How about an exchange of information. It's a popular pastime around here."

"What would you have that'd interest me?"

"That's it, you've got the hang of it already. How about the fact that your good friend Capitão Catela isn't pulling that car out of the sea because you want him to. Not even because Lili Sterne wants him to."

"You're well informed," I said, genuinely impressed.

"That's the job, old boy."

"Okay, I'll bite. Why's Catela pulling the car out?"

"You have to promise to give me something," Harry said, popping his empty glass on the bar for a refill.

"Like why Lili Sterne is in Lisbon?"

"That's how the game is played."

"Okay," I agreed. "You show me yours and I'll show you mine."

"Right! Captain Catela is pulling Eddie Grimes out of the drink because . . ." He leaned over and finished in a mock whisper. "Sturmbannführer Heinrich Ritter asked him to. Or should I say told him to?"

"Ritter?"

"That's right. Your friendly neighborhood Gestapo officer."

"Why would Ritter care about Eddie Grimes?"

"I'm sure he doesn't. But he cares very much about Hans Kleinmann."

"Who's Hans Kleinmann?"

"Ah, ah, ah," he scolded, collecting his third drink. "Your turn."

"Okay. Lili's trying to locate a childhood friend, somebody she grew up with in Berlin. Eddie Grimes found her here, or thought he did, anyway. He was supposed to take her back to the States, but he drove off a cliff instead."

"And you're taking his place?"

"Up to a point," I said. "I don't plan on driving off any cliffs."

Thompson nodded thoughtfully. "Touching, but hardly front page, is it?"

"I'm glad you think so."

"That it's touching or that it's not front page?"

"If it got into print, I might end up going over that cliff, after all. What about this Kleinmann character?"

"Ah, yes! Dr. Hans Kleinmann. He's attached to the German embassy here. Some sort of state secretary, I think, whatever that means."

"What's he got to do with Eddie Grimes?"

"He disappeared a couple of weeks ago. Same night as your detective friend. That's why Ritter's here. To get to the bottom of it." Harry swallowed the last of his brandy, but I could see that he was watching me over the lip of the glass.

"Why would Ritter think this guy's disappearance had anything to do with Grimes?"

"Haven't the slightest," Harry said. "Care to hazard a guess?"

"Not really."

"He's probably just fishing—so to speak." He slid off his chair, catching his balance on the bar. "You'll have to let me know how it turns out. Nice talking to you, Jack, but I think I'll go home now. I feel I'll be falling over soon and I'd like to be near my bed when it happens."

"Don't miss," I said.

"Ta-ta." He winked and wove his way toward the exit. Likable guy, I thought. For a reporter.

"**W**ould you like to play, senhor?"

I wasn't sure that I'd understood the man in the elegant gray suit. He spoke in a polished, but almost inaudible baritone voice.

"Excuse me?" I said.

"Would you like to draw chips?" he clarified. I was about to politely decline when he added, "You may sign for them on Miss Sterne's account."

"In that case," I said, "why not?"

"Will one thousand be sufficient?"

"A thousand?"

"Yes, senhor. Will that be sufficient?"

"I guess it'll get me started," I said.

"Very well. What is your preference?"

"Sorry?"

"Your game. Which game do you prefer to play?"

"Oh, I guess I'll try my luck at the wheel."

He nodded and placed a voucher and a gold pen on the bar. "Sign there and I will have the chips ready for you at this table." He nodded toward a table in the far corner, and I signed on the dotted line.

"I wish you good luck, senhor," he said as he pocketed the chit and disappeared.

I polished off my drink and wandered over to find an empty chair and two neat piles of fifty-dollar chips waiting for me. There were six players around the table. An old broad dolled up in a Victorian evening gown was the only one to acknowledge me with a nod and a wisp of a smile. She must've had ten grand sitting in front of her, and twice that decorating her earlobes. I guessed she was a local and a regular customer. Next to her was a banker type—bald, midfifties, fat, and boring. He had a sour look that said he was losing big-time. Not much of interest there, aside from the five-star bimbo he had waiting in the wings. On my left was a fidgety fellow who stayed on his feet, leaning across the board, dropping chips like they were too hot to handle. To my right was a man in sunglasses who was leaning back in his chair, ignoring the action. Asleep maybe, but I wasn't sure. A more-than-middle-aged Russian countess, or so I imagined, rounded out the group.

I lit a cigarette and dropped a couple of chips on numbers twenty-one and twelve, for no particular reason. I soon remembered why I never spent time at the wheel. It's a guessing game, no better than playing the numbers. My chips started disappearing as quickly as they'd appeared, and by the time Lili snuck up behind me, I was down seven hundred and change.

"First you abandon me to Don Juan, then you throw away my money like it's pennies from heaven. Tell me again why I brought you with me." She'd apparently consumed enough Dom Pérignon to get me out of that doghouse.

"Must be my irresistible charm."

"I'm managing to resist."

"Lover boy go home?" I asked. Lili raised an eyebrow and tossed her head back over her shoulder to have a peek.

"I think I lost him." She ignored the man in sunglasses, who was awake now and ogling her.

"Shall we go out the back way?" I suggested.

"You'd know all about that, I suppose."

"It has its advantages."

She picked up a chip, fiddled with it. "What about Eva?"

"Nothing definite," I said. "I might know more tomorrow." She gave me a look that I ignored, then handed me the chip.

"Put it on twenty-seven," she said, and I did.

The croupier spun the wheel and gently released the ivory ball onto its track. There was some activity at the door—a party of six or so entering the casino, heralded by a discreet buzz of excitement that spread rapidly across the floor. I immediately recognized the couple at the center of the commotion. Three and a half years earlier he'd been king of England, Scotland, and Wales, crowned head of the British Empire, defender of the faith, and emperor of India. He had a reputation for being charming, urbane, witty, and he wasn't half bad-looking, either. With those kind of credentials, it's safe to assume there was no shortage of females flinging themselves at his feet, for marriage purposes and otherwise, but he fell head over heels for an American, of all things, and from Baltimore, of all places. Not exactly queen material, either, since she'd been married twice already. And not what you'd call a great beauty. More like one of the evil sisters than Cinderella. Who knows? Maybe that was the attraction. Anyway, she must've had something going for her because he gave it all up so he could marry her, and as a result he became one of the most admired men on the planet.

Edward and Mrs. Simpson, love story of the century. I wondered what the hell they were doing in a casino in Portugal.

"They're waiting for a boat back to England," Lili whispered in my ear, as if she'd read my mind. I noticed a look on her face that I'd never seen before. Even she was impressed.

"Numero vinte-sete!" the croupier called out. "Twenty-seven black."

"What d'you know," I said. "Looks like you're a winner."

"Let it ride," Lili purred.

"It's only money," Lili shrugged as a small fortune in chips went back to the croupier's side of the table. It wasn't so much the stupidity of the comment that pissed me off as the stupidity of the bet. I've never had much sympathy for a loser who's just thrown in a winning hand.

"Yeah, easy come, easy go," I said, but she wasn't listening. Captain Catela had spotted us and was making a beeline for the table.

"Where's that back door?" she said.

"Too late." I smiled. "You're trapped."

"I despise you."

"I'm heartbroken."

She shot me one last scolding look before Catela descended on her. He seemed to be in a state of considerable agitation and couldn't straighten out his tongue for a minute.

"Calm down, Captain," Lili sneered. "Take a deep breath." Funny enough, Catela took her advice and it seemed to work.

"The Duke and Duchess of Windsor have asked to meet you," he exhaled in a whisper. "They are awaiting us . . ." Lili raised an eyebrow and pretended to look bored, but I could tell she was a long way from bored.

"Why not?" she said indifferently. "How often do you get to meet a man who's given up everything for a woman?"

"Every day," I said. "They're called husbands."

"You're a hopeless cynic, Mr. Teller," Lili scolded as she took the captain's arm and led him away.

"Isn't everybody?" I said, but I was talking to myself by that time. I didn't mind not being invited to the command performance, but I would've paid a lot of money to be a fly on the wall when Lili Sterne came face-to-face with Wallis Simpson. I had another drink and went to work on losing the last couple hundred of Lili's dough. It didn't go as planned, and when I found myself ahead I decided to take my own advice and quit before the streak came to an end. Besides, I was beat and ready to call it a day.

The cashier counted out twelve crisp one-hundred-dollar bills which I folded neatly into my pocket. As I turned to go I collided with the skittish fellow who'd been playing at my table.

"Sorry," I said. "Didn't see you."

"Please ... Is my fault." He spoke in an accent that I couldn't quite place. Russian or Polish or something along those lines. He was a slight man, with angular features and deep-set dark eyes. His smile, if you could call it that, was tentative and edgy.

"I have not been looking where I am going," he apologized, backing his way toward the exit.

"Jack Teller," I said, offering my hand.

"Pleased to met you," he replied tentatively, eager to move on.

I held his hand for a moment, which seemed to make him more than a little anxious. "Sorry, I didn't catch your name."

"Popov," he said. "Roman Popov ..."

"I can't quite place your accent." I was still clasping his hand.

"Belgrade." He pulled out of my grip. "Please again accept my apologies ... I wish you a pleasant evening."

"Sure, a pleasant evening," I said. "And by the way ... Roman, wasn't it?"

"Yes?"

"I put my winnings into my pocket, so you might as well give me back my wallet. It's empty, but I'd like to have it back all the same."

Popov put on a blank face. "Your wallet?"

"That's right. The one you lifted when you bumped into me."

"I'm afraid you are mistaken," he said. "You have misplaced your wallet."

"That's possible, of course," I conceded. "I could be mistaken. But I don't think I am."

"That is unfortunate, but—"

"How are we gonna find out?"

"Please, you must excuse me now." He tried to slip away, but I blocked his path to the door.

"I know what we can do. I've got this friend. His name is Captain Catela—you probably know him. We just had dinner together. Why don't I call him over and he can help us figure out what happened. I'm sure he'd be happy to."

Popov was silent for a long moment, then he shrugged, smiled sheepishly, and produced the wallet. "I'm having a bad night," he explained.

"It might've just got a lot worse," I pointed out.

"So you won't inform Catela?"

"No."

"You are a gentleman."

"Just tired," I said, heading for the door. Popov caught up with me.

"May I walk with you?"

"Suit yourself," I said, and he followed me out into the soft night air. The sky was inky black and teeming with stars that melded on the horizon with the lights of Cascais, the little fishing village that sat on a bluff a bit further up the shoreline.

"May I tell you the truth?" Popov said out of nowhere. Somehow I didn't think the truth was what I was about to hear, but I said sure, go ahead.

"It was not my intention to steal your money."

"You were just gonna borrow it, right?"

"In a way, yes, that is true."

"You'll have to excuse me, Roman, but where I come from that's called bullshit."

"Yes, I quite understand. I would be somewhat of the same belief if it was I in your position. But I tell the truth nonetheless. Let me explain."

"I'm all ears," I said wearily.

"It was my intention to follow you out of the casino and return to you your billfold, acting as if it had fallen from your pocket."

"Well, thanks for explaining that. I feel a whole lot better now."

"I understand your doubt, of course. But, you see, my purpose was not to steal from you. It was to meet you."

"You a Lili Sterne fan, too?"

"Of course, who could not be? But this was not my reason. I have wanted to speak with you, not Miss Sterne."

"Maybe you'd better cut to the chase."

"Excuse me?"

"What d'you want, Roman?" I was getting tired of this.

"I want nothing. Only to help you."

"What makes you think I need help?"

"Everyone needs some help of one kind or another."

"And what kind do you think I need?"

"You'd like to find this Eva Lange, would you not?" I stopped walking and faced him.

"How do you know about Eva Lange?" He smiled cagily and waited. He had my attention now and he was gonna milk it.

"This is Lisbon," he said, somewhat cryptically.

"Do you know where I can find her?"

"Perhaps."

"Do you or don't you?"

"I can find out."

"Roman . . ."

"Yes?"

"Are you selling information or services?"

He thought about it for a moment. "Everything has its price," he finally said, avoiding the question. "But I'm not a greedy person. I'm certain we will come to an acceptable agreement regarding my fee."

I forced a smile, but my patience was wearing thin. "If you think you're gonna go on some sort of payroll on the off chance that you come up with something, you can forget it," I said.

"And if I have already some information?"

"Then you'd better give it to me. If it leads somewhere, I'll make sure you get well paid."

"Why do you wish to find this girl?"

"None of your business," I said. "Now don't think I haven't enjoyed our little chat, but it's late and I'm tired."

"Please excuse my intrusion."

"Sure," I said, and turned toward the hotel entrance. I think Popov stood there for a minute, watching me go in, but I didn't look back. I headed for the desk, where I could ask the concierge to arrange for Alberto to pick me up in the morning. He'd given me the number of a neighborhood bar where messages could be left.

"Yes, Mr. Teller, I can phone him, of course, but . . ." The concierge coughed uncomfortably and nodded toward a bench in the corner where he'd installed a young girl who was wearing too much lipstick and not enough skirt. She was no more than sixteen, probably less. "She claims you are expecting her," he said.

I looked at the clock behind the counter—twenty minutes after midnight. I'd completely forgotten about my appointment.

"That's right," I said, not interested in explaining myself. "Does she speak English?"

I stood my ground while I was treated to an extended look up the man's nostrils. He finally gave up and beckoned the girl with his index finger. She skulked over to the desk.

"*Fala inglès?*" the concierge demanded.

"*Pouco,*" she whispered softly.

"What's your name?" I asked her.

"Fabiana," she said, turning big brown eyes on me.

"Okay, Fabiana," I said. "Come with me."

I thanked the concierge for his help and felt the sting of his look in the back of my neck all the way across the lobby to the elevator.

Fabiana was well practiced in her routine. I hardly had the door closed before she was in the bedroom, unclipping her bra and stepping out of her skirt. She was confused and a little concerned when I stopped her, and led her back into the suite's small living room.

"I just want to talk to you," I said.

"*Sim,* senhor," she replied, sitting down to await further instructions. She really was just a kid, and I hated to think what kind of further instructions she was used to getting.

"Don't worry," I said. "There's nothing to worry about. Do you understand?"

"*Sim,* senhor, I understand."

I took the newly acquired roll of bills out of my pocket, peeled a hundred off the top, and showed it to her. She looked at me like I was crazy, probably wondering what the hell she was expected to do to earn this.

"Just some questions," I said. "About the man at the Imperial Hotel. Do you know who I'm talking about?"

"*Sim . . . o Americano.*"

"That's right. Do you remember what happened that night?"

"*Sim. A senhora entra—*"

"In English, please."

"*Sim.*" She nodded and collected her thoughts. "The lady comes in."

"That's right. And what happened then?"

She shrugged. "I go."

"You left?"

"*Sim . . .* I left."

I handed her the photograph of Eva. "Is this the lady?" Fabiana took the picture in her hand and studied it very carefully for quite some time.

"*Sim . . . Creio que sim.*" She gave the photo back. "I think yes, this the lady."

"Did she say anything to the man?"

Fabiana thought for a moment. "She say to stop . . ."

"Stop what?"

"What he does . . ."

"What was he doing?"

Fabiana looked down at the floor, embarrassed.

"Never mind," I said, getting the idea. "Let's skip over that part. What happened next?"

"I go."

"Did the lady say anything else?"

"No, senhor."

"Did the man say anything?"

"He tells me to go . . . 'get lost,' he say."

This didn't seem to be going anywhere, but I thought I might as well get my money's worth.

"Did the man say anything to the lady?"

She thought about it again. "No . . ."

That seemed about all there was to tell. Nothing new, but at least I could be slightly more certain that it was Eva who had visited Grimes on the night he died. I was about to dismiss Fabiana when she offered something more.

"I think he is too afraid to say something."

"Afraid?"

"Yes . . . *assustado.*"

"Why would he be afraid?"

She hesitated. "Because," she said. "Because the . . . um . . ." She formed a V shape out of her thumb and forefinger and pointed it at me.

"Gun?" I said.

"*Sim. Pistola. A senhora tem uma pistola.*"

"The lady had a pistol?"

"*Sim . . .*"

"Are you sure it was the lady and not the man who had a pistol?"

"Yes, I sure. The lady, she point it to the man and so he is afraid. Then he say to me 'get lost' and I go."

She looked up to see if that was going to earn her the hundred. I put it in her hand and sent her on her way, hoping it might mean she wouldn't have to screw any more creeps like Eddie Grimes for a while, even though I knew it didn't. I called down and told the concierge to put her in a taxi and to put it on my bill.

I poured myself a nightcap and examined the picture of Eva. It was hard to imagine the pretty young girl in the boat with a gun in her hand. Must've been quite a surprise for Eddie Grimes when he looked up to find her standing there holding a pistol in his face.

The gun was an interesting twist, all right, but it didn't really change anything. A sensible precaution on her part, that's all. She'd been running since Berlin, keeping a half step ahead of the Nazis, probably traveling under a false name. Naturally she would've been alarmed when, almost home free, some jerk showed up out of the blue asking questions about her and trying to arrange a meeting. The fact that she wanted some insurance in hand when she confronted him just showed that she'd developed good survival instincts.

No, the gun didn't change anything. From the sound of it, she burst into Eddie's room, and once she'd figured out who he was, she turned around and took off, with Eddie in pursuit. The odds still favored an unlucky accident on a dark road in the middle of the night.

Of course, if you could always count on the odds, it wouldn't be much of a game, would it?

My eyes shot open, but I didn't move. I lay there on my pillow, holding my breath, listening closely. Had I been dreaming?

No . . . There it was again. The soft rattle of somebody trying to jimmy a lock. I slipped out of bed, felt my way past the bedroom door, and stood in the dark living room, half-asleep, wondering who the hell was trying to break into my suite, and why. I didn't have time to ponder it, though, because the latch gave way and the door eased open, allowing a thin shaft of ghostly light to fall across the floor. I glanced around for a weapon, spotted a bottle of malt whiskey, and reached for it—too quickly, because I misjudged the distance and knocked it over, straight into a set of glass tumblers. It all hit the floor with a resounding *crash!*

I waited a beat, and so did the intruder. Then the door slammed shut and I could hear footsteps escaping down the hall. I shot across the room, fumbled around in the dark, found the door handle, and was halfway up the corridor before the pain hit. I fell against the wall, saw the trail of blood I'd left behind, and lifted my bare foot to find a cluster of crushed crystal embedded in the heel. I let out a low whistle.

Christ, it hurt!

I retreated to the bathroom, where I sat on the toilet and plucked the larger fragments of glass out. After flushing the wound with warm water and wrapping it in a towel, I limped out onto the narrow balcony that overlooked the hotel pool. The predawn air was fragrant and still, the only sound the waves crashing onto the beach in the dark distance.

That was no hotel thief, I thought. Those guys work the day shift, when the guests are busy lolling around the pool. And besides, with all the fat cats in residence, no decent second-story man would take an interest in me. No, I couldn't say what this guy was after, but it sure as hell wasn't the family jewels. I'd have to watch my back from now on.

A hazy pink light started to emerge on the eastern horizon. You could almost smell the heat of the day coming on. I decided to get dressed and go down to the lobby.

It was too early for breakfast, so I headed to the bar where a stone-faced waiter set me up with a pot of coffee. I lit the first Lucky of the day and picked up a dog-eared copy of the London *Times*. It was a week out of date, but so was I.

The front page looked like this:

LARGEST DEFENCE ARMY IN
HISTORY READY TO HOLD ISLAND

LONDON, JUNE 29—While Britain's fleet has been distributed for a complete continental blockade, German submarines and air force are undertaking to isolate this island as a prelude to invasion. The British, however, in their island fortress, with the largest defending army in history awaiting attack, face the future confidently, certain that supplies and determination are sufficient to withstand any assault . . .

And so on. More of a pep talk than news, which was about what you'd expect under the circumstances. I flicked through more of the same until I came across a more intriguing item buried on page twelve:

APPEASEMENT MOVES ARE FEARED

LONDON, JUNE 29—Along with the military aspects of the war, Great Britain was said by informed spokesmen today to be experiencing a hidden political battle. There is a widespread concern in Whitehall, according to these spokesmen, that if Germany should invade England and score early successes, there are those in Parliament, and elsewhere, who would seek to overthrow the Churchill government and form a "peace" cabinet which would not hesitate to deal with Germany.

In a related development, the German radio station DJL last night declared that Britain was "making well-camouflaged, undercover moves toward approaching the Axis powers for the purpose of ascertaining under what conditions Germany might be willing to enter negotiations with England." The statement went on to say that Germany was in possession of information indicating that the royal houses of Europe would play the principal role in the "hoped for" negotiations. The broadcast, which was in English and possibly intended for the British public, said that royal houses close to the British Crown would be used as a channel for the feelers.

Advices from London last night stated that there was absolutely no truth in reports from abroad that Sir Samuel Hoare, British ambassador to Spain, had broached the question of peace or armistice terms in Madrid. On the contrary, it was said, he has emphasised the determination of this country to continue the struggle.

Meanwhile, Labourite J. J. Davidson declared that he would ask Home Secretary Sir John Anderson tomorrow if he was aware that "former members of the pro-Nazi organisation, The Link, met in London last week and discussed the question of peace terms under a sympathetic government."

Interesting. Not so much that there was a faction in Britain that wanted to make peace with Germany—I would've been more surprised if there hadn't been one—but interesting that an item like that would appear in the *Times* at all. Treason isn't the sort of thing you want to be peddling to a jittery public on the eve of an invasion, yet the "informed spokesmen" source in the lead sentence suggested that the item had been planted by the government itself. If Whitehall was concerned enough about the rumors to plant a denial, then there must've been some truth to the "undercover moves" claim on German radio. In fact, the denial went a step further than the report by implying that the ambassador in Madrid was the go-between. It looked to me like a public warning to the plotters, a "we know who you are" kind of thing.

Not surprising that Churchill would be worried about his rear flank. Sure, the Brits were defiant now, but "blood, toil, tears and sweat" might not sound so good when the panzers were rolling through Kent. Even if the British people were willing to fight on, you could be sure that there'd be more than a few Honourable Members of Parliament—not to mention Lords and Ladies—who would happily jump ship rather than go down with it. Churchill would be out the door as quickly as he'd come in and the great British public would wake up to find their morning papers featuring snapshots of Herr Hitler sightseeing in Piccadilly.

I poured a second cup of coffee and put the paper aside. Like pretty much everyone back in the States, I saw the war in Europe as tragic and crazy but, most of all, far away. And nothing to do with me. The tragedy was a bit closer now—the faces of those refugees had done that—but it was still crazy and it still had absolutely nothing to do with me. I was sorry that Europe was going to hell in a handbasket but they'd have to make the trip without me.

I knew a kid named Andy Dent, a horse wrangler on the Warner lot, who went over to Spain in '36 to fight the good fight. He couldn't have been more than twenty years old, a nice, quiet cowboy from Wyoming and nothing short of a genius with horses. I don't know if he wanted to save the world or if he was just looking for adventure, he never said, but all he got was shot in the head the second week he was over there. Not much of an adventure and the world didn't get saved. Sure, I thought Hitler was a nutcase and every time I saw him in a newsreel I shook my head, but the bottom line was that it wasn't my fight. And if I'd learned anything in my first twenty-five years on this crazy planet, it was that only suckers get involved in somebody else's fight.

That was how it looked to me that morning, anyway, as I sat alone in the bar at the Palacio, drinking coffee and contemplating the fate of the world.

The wind had picked up by midmorning, pulling the sea onto the rocks, making the job of the small fishing boat next to impossible. Catela wasn't on the scene yet when we arrived, so I joined Alberto on the hillside with a loaf of bread, a wedge of hard cheese, and a basket of fruit that he'd brought from home. Across the way, I noticed that the Cape Cod–style villa on the promontory overlooking the cliffs looked a bit more lived in today. The shutters were open and there were a number of cars parked in front of the main building.

Below us, a couple of teenage boys were making dives into the Mouth of Hell, trying to attach a line to Eddie's car, which was lying just below the surface. Once the line was secured, the idea was to float the car with buoys and let the navy trawler that was waiting offshore tow it a couple of miles west to the beach at Cascais, where it could be hauled ashore. That was the plan, anyway. The divers were having a tough time of it, though, disappearing under the waves for long periods of time, only to surface twenty or thirty yards away, dangerously close to the rocks. They'd fight their way back to the boat, clamber aboard, and, after a few minutes' rest, go through the whole routine again.

I was beginning to have my doubts about the whole operation

when a long black car pulled up behind us, accompanied by a half-dozen motorcycle cops. After a moment, Catela stepped onto the road, followed by a very somber-looking SS Major Ritter. I'd been wondering if he would make an appearance and wasn't surprised that he had.

"*Seig Heil,*" I muttered to Alberto, who gave me a very nervous look as we stood up to greet the uniforms.

"Good morning, Senhor Teller," Catela offered with a strained smile. "A fine day, yes?"

"If you're going sailing," I said, looking out to sea. The sky was clear cerulean blue and there were whitecaps as far as you could see.

"Do you enjoy sailing?"

"Not particularly."

"I see," Catela said curtly, confirming that the small talk was over. "Major Ritter has expressed an interest in seeing o Boca do Inferno, so I suggested that he accompany me this morning." Ritter hung back and eyed me suspiciously.

"Sure," I said. "Plus he wants to find out if his missing diplomat is down there with my missing detective. That right, Major?"

Ritter cracked a smile that I thought might crack his face. "You have adapted to the ways of Lisbon in a short period of time, Mr. Teller."

"Information is power, isn't that what they say?"

"My interest is strictly casual."

"I would've thought a missing state secretary would rate more than a casual interest."

"You misunderstood me," Ritter said with a patient sneer. "I'm quite interested in locating Dr. Kleinmann, of course I am. What I meant to say was that I have no reason to believe that he has been involved with your detective. I am, however, obliged to investigate every possibility. I'm certain you understand."

"Sure, I understand," I said. I understood he wasn't out there on a hunch any more than he was on a sightseeing tour. I wondered what connection he thought there was between Eddie Grimes and

Dr. Kleinmann, and if Eva Lange had anything to do with it. I considered mentioning her name in passing to see how he'd react, but decided against it. If it turned out she was still alive, then she was in hiding and this was the guy she was hiding from.

Catela excused himself in order to dispatch one of his motorcycle cops along the bluff, presumably to threaten the men in the fishing boat, but I could see that they'd already spotted Ritter's car and didn't need any additional incentive. A couple of the older guys were already stripping off, ready to make the dive.

"Well, I hope your man's not down there," I said, which was true enough. Ritter was staring intently down at the boat and for a moment I thought he hadn't heard me. When he finally looked up, he smiled.

"And I hope also that Eva Lange is not down there. For Fräulein Sterne's sake, of course. I understand they have been lifelong friends together." He let it hang for a moment and I didn't say anything, only because I didn't know what to say.

"Captain Catela is always very forthcoming with me," the major added.

"I'll have to remember that," I said.

"You needn't worry. I have no interest in this woman," Ritter stated flatly. "Unless, of course, she has knowledge of Dr. Kleinmann's whereabouts."

"Why would she?" I said.

He shook his head slowly. "I can see no reason that she would."

Catela reappeared and assured Ritter that he wouldn't have to wait long. He was right because the new divers had the car secured and floated in a matter of minutes.

An hour later, we stood on the beach in Cascais as they pulled Eddie Grimes out of his rented red coupe and laid him out on a blanket in the sand. I'd seen dead men before, but Eddie was worse off than most. Swollen by two weeks in salt water, his skin a shriveled pasty white, he looked more like a beached walrus than a human corpse. A long open gash across the top of his head revealed a shattered skull and there were so many broken bones that his limbs twisted around like a plate of fat spaghetti. Most of his front teeth were missing and his eyes were open but rolled up inside his head. But as bad as he'd been knocked around in the fall, Eddie wouldn't have felt a thing because it was obvious that he'd been very dead before he took the plunge. Two nice neat bullet holes in his chest testified to that.

There was no Eva Lange in the car, and I wondered how long it would take Catela to get the story of the lady and the gun out of Fabiana. I also wondered how much it would take to buy him off. It should be easy enough, I thought. No one was gonna raise a fuss if Eddie Grimes was quietly laid to rest in an unmarked grave, and with Lili working on him, maybe it wouldn't even cost a fortune.

Ritter, who'd been standing back, chain-smoking his French cigarettes while he kept an eye on the proceedings, came up behind me.

"Curious," he blurted out.

"What?"

"That this woman would shoot the very man who has been sent to save her. It has been this man's mission, has it not? To save Eva Lange?"

"What makes you think she shot him?" I said.

"Who else?" Ritter's eyebrows flitted up.

"There are some pretty desperate people around here," I said. "An American driving around in a flashy car. Maybe somebody looking for money."

"What is your view, Captain?" Catela stood up from his inspection of the body, carefully folded the handkerchief he'd been holding over his nose, and placed it into his pants pocket.

"He was murdered," he shrugged, stating the obvious.

The major scowled. "And your suspect is Eva Lange?"

Catela looked at me apologetically. "I'm afraid it must be."

"That's ridiculous," I scoffed, wondering if this was the opening of negotiations. "There's no evidence that she—"

"She did threaten him with a gun," Ritter interjected. "Is that not correct, Captain?"

Catela shrugged a powerless yes. "It's a matter between our two governments," he apologized, nervously adjusted his sidearm. "A missing diplomat is a serious matter and I have been instructed to offer every possible assistance."

"Why didn't you tell me about the gun?" I said.

Catela frowned. "Please, Senhor Teller . . ."

"What?"

"I could ask the same of you."

"What are you talking about?"

"The young whore has surely told you about the pistol when she visited your room last night . . ." He paused for a smirk. "That was the purpose for her visit, was it not?"

Here I thought I'd been a step ahead and it looked like I wasn't even in the game yet.

"*Capitão!*"

One of Catela's men waved us over to the water's edge, where the car was being examined. Several cops were staring into the open trunk, and a moment later, so were we.

Dr. Kleinmann was in pretty much the same shape as Eddie was, except for the fact that instead of getting two in the chest, he'd been killed with a single bullet to the brain. The hole was almost exactly in the center of his forehead

"Don't be ridiculous, darling. Eva wouldn't hurt a fly. She wouldn't be capable of it." It was said with such finality, as if that should be the end of it, that I thought I'd better drive the point home.

"She was seen pointing a gun at Grimes on the night somebody put two slugs in his heart. If I was Catela, I'd think she did it, too." I was trailing Lili around her suite, watching her pull the place apart in an increasingly desperate search for smokes, billowing beige silk pajamas fluttering in her wake as she swept from one room to another.

"We could probably buy her out of that," I continued, ". . . if it wasn't for the dead German in the trunk." She stopped in the middle of the bedroom, put a hand on her hip, and made a sour face.

"I can understand why she'd want to shoot a Nazi, but why Eddie Grimes? . . . Help me find my damned cigarettes, will you?" She resumed the search.

"Want one of mine?" I said, and she threw a look of disdain over her shoulder. I shrugged and pretended to look around the bedroom while she checked out the en suite. I heard bottles of perfume and whatever else being ruthlessly shoved aside, then she reappeared in the doorway, smokeless.

"Who was it?"

"Who was what?"

"Who saw Eva? With the gun?"

"Oh. A girl Grimes had in his hotel room. Eva paid him a surprise visit and found them together."

"A prostitute?"

"Right."

"The girl you had in your room last night?"

"Depends on what you mean by 'had.' Is everybody keeping tabs on me?"

"You weren't exactly discreet, darling. Monsieur le concierge had a big stick up his ass this morning." She eased across the room and picked up the phone on the bedside table.

"I'll bet he enjoyed that," I said, and she couldn't help giving up a smirk.

"Send up ten packages of Rothmans," she said into the receiver, hanging up without further ado. "Have you eaten?"

"I could use a coffee."

"It's probably cold."

I followed her through to the lounge, where an untouched feast of a breakfast was laid out on the table. Lili poured a coffee and handed it over. I added sugar.

"What are the options?" she said. It was a good question and I wished I had a better answer.

"We could try the bribe, anyway, but I don't think it'll fly. Not with Kleinmann involved."

"Who's Kleinmann?"

"The dead German." She was right about the coffee, it was stone cold. I put it down and dug out my smokes. "Sure you don't want one?" I said as I lit up.

"Well, I'm not going to stand here and watch you," she scowled. I obliged and lit her up. She took a huge lungful of smoke, which seemed to settle her, then she flopped onto the sofa, suddenly exhausted. She flicked an ash into a flowerpot and looked out the

French window toward the sea. We didn't speak for a long minute.

"We have an engagement this afternoon," she finally said, offering up a jaded smile. "Tea with the duchess."

"We?"

"I'm not going alone, and I'm certainly not going to take the Latin lover. Don't worry. You won't have to curtsy."

"If you say so." I wasn't being coy and I wasn't worried about which fork I should use, either. Meeting the former king and his new wife might be entertaining, but if I was going to have any chance of staying ahead of Ritter, I couldn't afford an afternoon with the chattering classes.

"Be downstairs at three," Lili said, effectively dismissing me. "Your driver can take us over." There was no point arguing, so I nodded and headed for the door. I hesitated on the way out.

"Is there something else?" Lili said.

"Maybe it wouldn't be such a bad idea if you put the chain on your door at night."

"Isn't that a bit dramatic?"

"Probably. But do it anyway."

I took her silence to be acquiescence, and started out the door again. She called after me.

"Jack . . ."

"Yeah?"

"What can we do about Eva?"

"Find her. Before anybody else does."

"And then?"

"Let's find her first."

"Easier said than done, old chap."

Harry Thompson was looking down the barrel of a tall gin and tonic, the first of the day. I'd located him at the central bar in the sleepy town of Cascais, soaking up his early-afternoon breakfast, pen and blank notebook set out on the table in front of him, ready for inspiration when it came. Dark sunglasses hid the worst of the damage, but the wrinkled white suit gave him away.

"I thought you might be able to point me in the right direction."

"What made you think that?" He dug the lime out of his glass and squeezed it out onto his tongue. It made my back teeth cringe.

"You seem to know things."

He gave me a long look. "You're right about that. How'd you know where to find me?"

"You don't exactly keep a low profile. I asked over at the casino." He grunted and looked longingly into his empty glass. I signaled the barman for another.

"I have to come up with something in ..." He looked at his pocketwatch. "Christ. Less than two hours. I hate my life. No, I hate my editor." The G&T arrived and Harry helped himself to a healthy dose.

"How about an interview with Lili Sterne?" I said.

"Are you serious?"

"Why not?"

"It's not front page, but at least it's something," he ruminated. "It'd keep them off my back for a few days, anyway. Would she do it?"

"No chance," I said.

"Oh, well, then ... up yours." He saluted me with his glass and threw it back.

"You write what you want, and as long as she comes out looking okay, there won't be a problem."

"Jack, boy, if she gets onto the paper, they'll have my nuts for lunch."

"No problem," I assured him. "I'm signing off on it."

"Can you do that?"

I shrugged. "She won't see it anyway."

He weighed the idea. "I suppose I could do the 'good German' angle. She could say lots of nasty things about Hitler. Repulsive little man with a Napoléonic complex, that sort of thing."

"There you go," I encouraged him. He picked up the pen and scribbled the thought onto the pad.

"Be a good chap and order another one, will you?" he said, pushing his empty glass across the table. "I write much better when I'm sloshed and I'm not even close yet."

I signaled the barman and waited while Harry sketched out his article. It only took a couple of minutes.

"How's this for an opening? . . . 'Teutonic film legend Lili Sterne was in Lisbon last night and this reporter was privileged to sit down for an exclusive chat with her, not about her towering film career, but about the state of the world and, in particular, the way in which Herr Hitler and his—quote—band of brutish bullies—unquote—have brought ruin and disgrace to her former homeland."

"Is that one sentence?"

"Sure. Editors like that. Makes it look like you worked on it."

"I'm not too sure about the 'Teutonic' bit."

"Mmm, maybe. 'German film legend.'" He made the correction. "Sacrifice flair for clarity. That's life these days. Want to hear more?"

"I'll wait for the early edition," I said. He looked a little hurt, but I was pressed for time.

"What about Eva Lange?" I said.

Harry furrowed his brow. "What makes you think she wants to be found?"

"I don't know if she does or she doesn't, but that's not the point. The point is that *I* want to find *her.*"

"Think she killed Kleinmann?"

"Again, I don't care one way or the other."

He nodded. "If I were you, I'd tell Lili Sterne to forget about her friend and go back to Hollywood, where the sun shines twenty-four hours a day. Lisbon's a cesspool, and if you go snooping around a cesspool, you're going to find yourself knee-deep in other people's shit."

"Thanks for the advice, but I'm looking for information."

"Okay. Don't say I didn't try, though."

"Come on, Harry."

"There's a chap who might be able to help you out. At a price, of course."

"Of course."

"He's a Slav. I don't know how or why he got here, but he makes it his business to know everybody else's business. Not a very pleasant chap, but he gets around."

"Is his name Roman Popov?"

Harry looked mildly surprised. "You've had the pleasure, then."

"He tried to pick my pocket last night and said it was because he liked me so much."

"That's Popov."

"I wrote him off as a leech."

"Quite right."

"But you think he might know something?"

"As I said, he makes it his business to know what's going on. And he did go out of his way to meet you last night."

"If he had something, why didn't he say so, then?"

"One has to proceed with caution in Lisbon if one hopes to survive, let alone do business. A snake like Popov deals with both sides, so he has to be sure he doesn't get caught in the middle. In fact, it wouldn't surprise me if he was chatting up Major Ritter right now. At any rate, whether he knows something or not, it's better to have him on your side. I'm afraid it won't be cheap, though. Hollywood and all that."

"You know where to find him?"

"He moves around a lot. Like a rat. But you can try here. Don't tell him I sent you." Harry scribbled an address on his notepad and tore the page out. "It's in the Alfama. Not the most pleasant of abodes."

"Thanks, Harry," I said, and got up to leave.

"What's the hurry?" He smiled broadly. "Have one for the road."

"I've got an appointment with a former king," I said. "Probably shouldn't keep him waiting." I signaled the barman to pour Harry another, but he already had it waiting.

"I've got to hand it to you, Jack. You do get around."

"See ya, Harry."

"Count on it." He winked and disappeared into his glass. I dropped a few escudos onto the bar and headed out.

I'd been staring vacantly out the car window, so I didn't recognize the villa until we were well inside the gate, and I could see the cliffs off to the west, waves crashing against the distinct profile of o Boca do Inferno. The estate was considerably larger than it had looked from across the estuary, much of the grounds hidden by a grove of tall pines. Alberto pulled into a semicircular drive, where a number of impressive cars were parked, and cut the engine.

"Who does it belong to?" I asked.

"Is the house of Doutor Espírito Santo," Alberto explained.

"Must be some doctor," I said. The house was bigger than it had seemed from a distance, too. An entire wing was hidden behind the main structure, almost doubling the size of the place. It looked as though it'd been given a fresh coat of white paint recently.

"He is no *doutor* for medical," Alberto explained. "He is own a big bank of Portugal. Too much money."

"There's no such thing as too much money, darling," Lili announced from the backseat, where she was doing a final face check in a hand-held mirror. She was in red carpet mode, waiting for someone to open her door. I got out and did the honors, beating a Japanese-looking butler who'd appeared from inside the house and was heading our way. He bowed respectfully as Lili stepped onto the gravel, then indicated for us to follow.

Alberto joined the other drivers, stretched out under a tree while Lili and I were led around to the side of the villa and along a hedge just high enough to screen the source of the voices that were coming from the other side. All the ground-floor windows were shuttered, maybe to keep the rooms cool, more likely to frustrate prying eyes like mine.

We turned a corner where there was a break in the hedge. The butler stopped just short of it and waited for a moment, maybe letting us collect ourselves before the big entrance, then he ushered us through to a pleasant grassy area set in the shade of the pines. A table of tea and cakes, manned by a couple of young waiters, was set up on the far side of the rectangular lawn while a couple of dozen guests gathered in small groups, the men mostly standing while the ladies tended toward the garden chairs.

"Lili, dear!"

The duchess strode across the grass, arms extended, face lit up by a welcoming smile. She wasn't what you'd call a natural beauty— high, broad forehead, wide cheekbones, and long, dominant chin, with small, birdlike brown eyes and razor-thin red lips. Her flat black hair was pulled back so severely that it looked like she was wearing a helmet. But she moved with grace and she had charisma, the kind that you don't learn. As she got closer, it occurred to me that the stress of the abdication and the wedding had taken its toll. She looked older than she had in the papers. More lived in

She placed her hand on Lili's arm in a gesture of intimacy. "I'm so pleased that you've come!" she said. "You'd have disappointed quite a few men if you hadn't!"

"That wouldn't do," Lili purred.

"Of course he is the greatest fan of all. I've heard about nothing else since last night." She leaned closer and lowered her voice. "He was so miserable that he wasn't able to have a proper chat with you. He didn't perk up until I suggested we invite you for tea." The duchess always referred to her husband as "he," as if he was some kind of deity.

"He's attending to some business at the moment," she continued. "Though I'm certain that when he hears you've arrived, he'll be straight down."

"Very kind of you to think of us," Lili smiled disingenuously, picking up on the tone of the afternoon.

The duchess turned on me. "Hello," she chirped, extending a hand. "Who are you?"

"Jack Teller," I said.

"Jack and I are traveling together," Lili explained.

"I don't blame you." The duchess kept her eyes locked on mine and gave my hand a suggestive squeeze. "He's quite handsome."

"I suppose so," Lili allowed. "If you like the type."

The duchess smiled coyly. "But, of course, I'm a married woman."

"So I've heard," I said.

She let go of my hand and turned back to Lili. "Look how much of an effort they're all making not to look at you. Let's go over and put them out of their misery." She locked arms with Lili and guided her toward the party. I was about to follow when I was tapped on the shoulder.

"Hey, Teller."

I swung around and found myself face-to-face with the golden boy. He looked a bit awkward standing there in a dark suit, cup of tea in hand.

"Hello, Brewster," I said.

"How are things going? . . . If you don't mind my asking, that is." He flashed the million-dollar smile.

"Could be better," I admitted.

"So I've heard."

"Don't look so damned happy about it."

"Look . . ." He took a step toward me. "I'm sorry that we got off on the wrong foot yesterday. If I was out of line, I apologize." It sounded genuine enough, even though I knew it was nothing more than a career move. It didn't matter, though, because I needed a Brewster more now than I had a day earlier. Even if I managed to find Eva before Ritter did, I'd have to find a quiet way to get her out of the country and some timely help from Uncle Sam would be the fastest and most reliable ticket.

"Don't worry about it," I said. "I was probably a bit out of line myself."

"Friends, then?"

"Sure," I said. "Friends."

He nodded and glanced over at the crowd Lili was drawing a few yards away. "I don't know what's caused more of a buzz around here, the Windsors or Lili Sterne hitting town . . . What did you think of the duchess?"

I thought about it for a second. "Friendly."

"That's a good way of putting it," he chuckled. "Very diplomatic."

"So it's not just me, then."

"Sorry," he grinned. "Pretty much anything in pants. It's all tease, though. No follow-through."

"I guess I'll live."

"Oh, I think she'd give you a good run for your money, all right. If you know what I mean . . ." Brewster got a kind of faraway look in his eye as he sized the duchess up from across the garden. I wondered what his imagination was up to. "She's had some pretty exotic training, you know."

"Training?"

"Sure. When she was in China, back in the late twenties, with her first husband—the duke is number three, you know . . ."

"Yeah, I read that."

"Well, her first used to spend a lot of time at the brothels around Shanghai. I mean like day and night. Apparently she got tired of waiting around and decided to join in the fun. They used to go regularly."

"They went to a brothel together?"

"According to the Brits, anyway. They have a file on the whole thing. They think she might've picked up a trick or two out there that helped her snare the king."

"Maybe," I said, pretty sure there would be more to it than that. On the other hand, the mighty orgasm—or lack thereof—has undoubtedly had a hell of a lot more influence on the course of human history than the books credit.

"Cup of tea, sir?" The freckle-faced kid looked and sounded like a refugee from Buckingham Palace.

"Is that all you're offering?" I said.

"At the moment, sir, I'm afraid so, sir."

"Thanks anyway."

"Yes, sir." He performed a perfectly executed shallow bow and turned on his heel.

"I heard about Kleinmann," Brewster said, switching gears. "Can't say I'm brokenhearted. It'll make your job a lot tougher, though."

"You know him?" I asked, suddenly interested.

"Met him a couple of times. An arrogant SOB, but aren't they all?"

"Diplomats?"

"Funny," he said, not laughing.

"What do you know about him?"

"Kleinmann? Not a lot. A party guy."

"What kind of parties?" I was thinking along the lines of Eddie's interest in the seedy side of life and wondering if there was some kind of perverted connection between them.

"You've been in Hollywood too long, Jack. I'm talking about the Nazi Party."

"Oh," I shrugged. "Right." Maybe I had been in Hollywood too long.

"You see, there are two kinds of Germans at the embassy these days. The lifelong diplomats—educated, old-money, establishment guys . . . They've got a touch of class and they actually know what they're doing. Then there are the party guys. Hitler's crowd. They think they have class, but all they've got is clout. Like von Ribbentrop himself."

"Who's that?"

Brewster gave me a look. He was enjoying this. "Joachim von Ribbentrop, foreign minister for the Third Reich, and close friend and confidant of Adolf Hitler. You've heard of Hitler, right?"

"It rings a bell."

"Talk about arrogance, Ribbentrop is it. Notice I didn't use the *von*. It isn't real. He got it ten years ago. Paid to get himself adopted by the widow of some distant cousin who'd married into the aristocracy. Even the money's new. He was a wine salesman until he married the boss's daughter."

To Brewster's country-club mind, a bourgeois wine salesman pretending to be an aristocrat was just about the greatest Nazi crime yet committed. And dropping the *von* from the offender's name was, to him, a severe, but just, penalty.

"What did Kleinmann do?" I asked.

"At the embassy?"

"Right."

"No idea," Brewster said, shrugging it off. Didn't matter in the slightest to him. "The guy you should ask is over there. The one with the thick glasses." He nodded toward an unexceptional accountant type who was standing inconspicuously among a half-dozen men involved in a deep discussion about something.

"His name's Griffin Stropford," Brewster informed me. "Financial attaché at the British embassy. That's his cover, anyway. In fact, he's MI6."

I gave him a look. "MI6 . . . ?"

"See how helpful I can be?" he gloated. "British intelligence. His Majesty's Secret Service."

"Not *too* secret, I guess."

"Hey, I'm giving you top-level stuff here, Jack. Between you and me."

"How do you know I'm not a German spy?"

"Fuck you," Brewster smiled, but he looked a little worried for a second. "Stropford's the guy who showed me the 'China file' on the duchess," he added.

"That was nice of him," I said. "I thought we were neutral."

"Well, there's neutral and there's neutral. Anyway, he wanted to know if we had anything on her. As she's American."

"Do we?"

"That's not something I can talk about," Brewster said solemnly. In other words, he didn't know.

I was about to ask for an introduction when my attention was drawn to the other end of the garden, where the former king of England was entering. He was accompanied by a tall, urbane-looking gentleman who wore a polka-dot bow tie.

The best thing about the duke joining the party was that they started pouring real beverages. The former monarch had a taste for good whiskey, and I took full advantage of the thirty-year-old malt that suddenly appeared. After two or three I even started enjoying myself.

Lili was in full flow, treating the crowd to her trademark performance of sexual innuendo punctuated with suggestive looks and knowing smiles. The duke happily played straight man in an impromptu double act that went down very well with the would-be courtiers. I was a bit surprised that the duchess was so willing to give up center stage, but she kept a close eye on things. I had the feeling that she could keep a close eye on things from pretty much anywhere on the planet.

Brewster drifted off to ingratiate himself with the high and mighty, leaving me to my own devices. I was hovering in the background, trying to catch the eye of a dark beauty who'd been abandoned by her silver-haired husband when I realized that the man in the polka-dot tie was standing over me.

"The wife of the Spanish ambassador," he said in my ear. "Thoroughly devoted to her husband, I'm afraid."

"Was I being that obvious?"

"Ricardo Espírito Santo," he said, offering his hand.

"Jack Teller."

"Yes, I know. Lili has been telling me all about you."

"I hope you didn't believe her."

"Not to worry." He smiled affably. "Your secrets are safe with me."

Santo was an impressive figure—over six foot tall with a lightly tanned complexion, a prominent jaw, and a penetrating look. I put him in his late thirties, maybe forty. He oozed money. Big money.

"Do you like dogs?" he said.

"Not really."

"You'll like mine. Come, I'll show you."

"Your first time in Lisbon?" he asked casually as we strolled through the grounds toward the kennels at the back of the house.

"That's right."

"As you can imagine, we haven't seen many Americans this year. Most are avoiding the crossing."

"Probably something to do with those torpedoes that keep bumping into ships."

Santo swept the idea away with a wave of his hand. "It would be quite foolish of the Germans to sink an American vessel."

"Yeah, well, I guess some people aren't too comfortable betting their lives on Hitler's good sense."

Santo smiled, but he didn't mean it. The dogs could sense his approach and were going wild with anticipation.

"Here are my beauties!" he exclaimed as we turned the corner and the caged beasts came into view. There were three of them, each in a separate cage, all big and mean with huge heads that contained long sharp teeth. The kind of creatures you'd expect to be guarding the Mouth of Hell. Bull mastiffs, I'd say, but I'm not much of an expert. Whatever they were, I kept my distance and hoped they'd be keeping theirs.

"Highly bred," Santo said, the proud father. "From the best blood." He got down on one knee and admired them, although I noticed he kept his distance, too.

"Surely, you can appreciate the beauty."

"Adorable." I humored him.

One of the trio—a bitch—swiveled her oversized head and took a long hungry look at me while emitting a low rumbling sound from the back of her throat.

"She senses your fear." Santo laughed as he stood up and extracted a leather cigar case from his breast pocket. He removed the cover and offered me a hand-rolled Cuban.

"No, thanks," I said, digging out my Luckys. "I'll stick to these."

Santo shrugged and turned away. "Let's walk," he said, pointing us toward a wooded area behind the kennel. The dogs watched and whined for a minute, then gave it up and settled back into prison life.

We walked in silence while Santo prepped his stogie, meticulously rolling it in his palms to warm the tobacco, neatly clipping the top, then carefully punching a hole in the bottom before firing it up with a solid-gold lighter engraved with the initials *R.E.S.* The afternoon sunlight caught the smoke as it wafted up, turning and twisting into the pine-scented atmosphere.

"Lili tells me that you are the man to discuss business with," he finally said.

"Depends on the business, I guess."

He paused, as if reflecting, but I had the feeling that he knew exactly where he was heading and the space was just for effect. "Lili places a great deal of trust in you, in spite of your youth, if I may say so. She is clearly not a foolish woman, so you must be a reliable sort of person . . . Discreet."

"I try not to disappoint my friends," I said.

"A good policy," he smiled. "Do you believe in coincidence, Jack?"

"I never really thought about it," I said. "But, sure, I guess so."

"I'm not so certain." Santo slowly shook his head. "Sometimes things seem to occur by happenstance when, in retrospect, there is a sense of inevitability about them. As if it was meant to be."

"Fate?"

"Or destiny. Whatever you choose to call it. For instance, it may seem coincidental that Lili Sterne is in Lisbon at this particular moment . . . But perhaps there's a reason for it. Perhaps a very significant reason."

"Such as?"

Santo frowned and looked at the end of his cigar to see if it was still burning. It wasn't, but he didn't do anything about it.

"Are you free for dinner tomorrow evening?"

"I suppose—"

"Good. My car will pick you up at the hotel. Be ready at half past eight."

We must've been walking in a big circle because when I looked up I saw that we were right back at the entrance to the garden party, which was breaking up. The duke and duchess had disappeared into the house, along with Lili, who, I was told, would be wining and dining with the royal couple. Santo excused himself and I headed for the car. On the way out, I saw the Spanish ambassador with my dark beauty on his arm, and I could've sworn that she flashed me a smile.

"Pardon me . . ."

"Yeah?"

"My name is—"

"I know who you are," I said. "And I'm guessing you know who I am, so we can skip the introductions."

Griffin Stropford rocked back on his heels, examined me through a pair of thick, round horn-rims, and produced an unexpected chuckle.

"Quite!" he said emphatically.

Though he must've been in his midthirties, Stropford had a

schoolboyish look—round face with chubby cheeks, a shock of sandy-brown hair that fell arbitrarily across his forehead, and an ill-fitting blue suit with a tie that came up about three inches short. Alberto had spotted his car as we were driving back from Santo's place. The English spymaster couldn't have been trying to hide the tail; at least I hope he wasn't, because it would've been tough to miss a black Rover with diplomatic plates riding six feet off our bumper. He'd followed us into the hotel, parked up behind us, and jumped out from behind the wheel so he could be waiting for me at the entrance.

"So?" I said, after he'd had his chuckle.

"Richard Brewster . . ."

"What about him?" I headed inside and he followed.

"That's how you know who I am. I daresay he told you about me?"

"As a matter of fact, he did," I said.

"Quite . . ." he repeated, a little less forcefully this time. I kept moving across the lobby toward the reception desk.

"I, er . . . I thought you might like to have a little chat." He was still smiling, but it was a bit strained now.

"About what?" I retrieved the room key.

"I daresay, you'll find it quite interesting."

As he stood there, hat in hand, clumsy smile spread across his face, I thought if this was the best England had to offer, they were in real trouble.

"Okay," I said. "Follow me."

"So what do you wanna know?" I threw my jacket on the back of a chair and loosened my tie.

"Perhaps you misunderstood me," he said, looking a bit baffled. "I have information which I believe may be of interest to you."

"Where do you live?"

"Pardon?"

"Near the embassy?"

"Near enough," he confirmed, suspicion growing.

"In Lisbon?"

"Correct."

"Well then."

"I'm sorry, I'm afraid I—"

"You came forty miles out of your way because you can't wait to help me out with some information?" I opened the balcony door to let some air into the room.

A smile crept across his face. "Oh, I see . . . Yes, very good."

"So . . . What do you want to know?"

"Well . . ." Stropford took his glasses off, carefully cleaned the lenses with a crumpled handkerchief, then checked them in the light before replacing them on the bridge of his nose.

"You disappeared for quite some time with Espírito Santo."

"That's right."

"May I ask what the topic of conversation was?"

"He wanted to show me his dogs."

"I see. Do you have a particular interest in dogs?"

"Can't stand them," I said truthfully.

"I presume, then, that it would be fair to say that the animals were not the principal topic of discussion?"

"That would be fair to say, yes." I flopped into a big armchair, kicked my shoes off, and stretched my legs out across the coffee table. Stropford was waiting for an invitation, so I motioned for him to sit down. He slid into the seat across from me but kept his wing tips firmly planted on the ground.

"So, you're a spy, huh?" I said, taking him by surprise. "I think you might be the first one I've ever met. But then I guess you don't always know with spies, do you? That's the whole point . . . Although you don't seem to make much of a secret about it."

"The cloak-and-dagger side of things is somewhat exaggerated in the public's mind," Stropford said. "The result of overzealous authors, no doubt."

"What do you do, then?"

"I write a great many reports."

"Interesting," I said, and left him hanging. There was a lull in the conversation while he thought about how to get back on track.

"I, er . . . I understand that you have an interest in learning more about Dr. Kleinmann."

"I'm curious how he ended up in the trunk of Eddie Grimes's car with a bullet in his head," I said. "But I don't suppose you know the answer to that."

He shook his head. "I'm afraid not. But, as I said earlier, I believe you'd be quite interested in what I do know."

"Try me."

He cleared his throat. "Perhaps we can effect a mutually beneficial exchange of information?"

"Why are you so interested in what Santo and I talked about?"

Stropford leaned forward in the chair. "How much do you know about him?"

"Just that he's got money. Banker, isn't he?"

"Amongst other things."

"Such as?"

"Wolframite."

I gave him a look.

"Wolframite is a raw material found in abundance in the Serra da Estrela mountain range to the north. It's the source of tungsten."

"Sorry," I said. "Still doesn't mean much to me."

"Tungsten is the ingredient used to harden steel. Quite handy for manufacturing tanks and artillery and that sort of thing. Espírito Santo has been making a great deal of money by selling it to the Germans. At highly inflated prices, I might add."

"So you've got the former king of England rooming with a guy who's in bed with the Nazis," I said. "Yes, I can see your problem."

"Quite," Stropford confirmed.

"Does he know?" I asked.

"Pardon?"

"Does the duke know about Santo's business dealings?"

"One must presume not, but one can never be sure."

"Why don't you tell him?"

He chuckled nervously. "Hardly my place, is it?"

"It must be somebody's place."

"Indeed, but not mine. My place is to learn as much as I can about the situation and to relay it to London. Which, in answer to your previous question, is why I'm so interested in what Santo had to say."

"You want me to spy on him?"

"Not in so many words, no."

"What then?"

"Well, if you could tell me what you discussed at the garden party this afternoon . . ."

"Sounds like spying to me."

"If you like," he said, straining to smile.

"What's in it for me?"

"Well . . . er . . . What do you have in mind?"

"How about a knighthood?"

"Well, I . . . er, I don't—" He realized I was pulling his leg. "I see," he said with a chuckle. "Very good." Stropford was growing on me. At least he knew how to laugh, even if it did take him a minute.

"Truth is I don't know what Santo wants," I said.

"I see . . ."

"Not yet anyway."

"Oh? . . . How so?"

"I'm supposed to have dinner with him tomorrow night. I guess he'll lay it out for me then."

"Hmm . . ." Stropford stared into the table. "You'll go?"

"I said I would."

"Good . . . Tomorrow night, you say?"

I nodded.

"Right . . . It's Monday today, so that'll be Tuesday."

"Makes sense."

"Why don't we meet up Wednesday morning, early . . . Someplace out of the way . . . I know just the spot . . ."

"Hold on a second," I said, sitting forward. "I don't know what Santo wants to talk to me about, but whatever it is, it'll be with the understanding that it's private." Stropford started to say something, but I kept going. "Now, I understand that you've got a job to do and that's fine, maybe I'm even sympathetic, but I work for Lili Sterne. She pays the bills and I take care of her business. It's an exclusive arrangement, just like yours is."

He leaned forward and folded his hands together, interlocking his fingers like he was about to say a prayer.

"Let me say this," he began. "There are, well . . . questions . . . questions about the duke. Important questions about his . . . his . . . judgment." Stropford was choosing his words so carefully that he could barely get them out. "Can we agree at least on the following? That if Santo's proposal has anything to do with the Duke of Windsor, you will let me know . . ."

"I can't promise anything," I said.

"But you'll consider it?"

"Sure. I'll consider it."

"Good!" Stropford stood up sharply. "I won't take any more of your time, then." He headed for the door.

"Aren't you forgetting something?" I said. He gave me a quizzical look, then remembered.

"Oh, yes, Dr. Kleinmann. Sorry. Yes . . . Well, we'd been keeping a close eye on him for some time. I've no doubt he was Abwehr."

"Abwehr?"

"Military intelligence."

"The SS?"

"Heavens, no . . . The SS is Hitler's private police force, whereas Abwehr is a legitimate intelligence service, an arm of the Wehrmacht. In fact, there's quite a rivalry between the two agencies."

"Major Ritter . . . ?"

"Gestapo through and through."

"Isn't he investigating Kleinmann's death?"

"They smell blood. He'd love to be able to report to Berlin that Dr. Kleinmann was up to no good."

"Kleinmann was Abwehr?"

"Correct. We're almost certain that he was running the Lisbon unit. It's quite an important posting at the moment, probably the most important in Europe."

"Did you have him killed?"

Stropford chuckled. "No, I'm sorry to say that as much as I would have liked to, I didn't. You see, both sides operate under a sort of unspoken cease-fire here in Lisbon. Salazar is quite adamant about that."

"Somebody wasn't honoring the truce."

"Indeed."

"Aren't you curious who?"

"It's of some interest . . ."

"But you're more interested in the duke's friends . . ."

Stropford gave me a scolding look. "I have many interests at the moment, Mr. Teller."

"I understand," I said. "Sorry . . . Any idea who did kill Kleinmann? Or what he was doing with Eddie Grimes in the first place?"

"Afraid not, on either score."

"Well, it's interesting, him being a spy, but I'm not sure how it helps me."

"There's more," Stropford said.

"Like . . . ?"

"You've expressed an interest in one Eva Lange, I believe?"

"That's right."

"A personal friend of Miss Sterne?"

"They grew up together," I explained.

"In Berlin . . ."

"Right."

"Yes, well," he said, shifting his weight as he considered how to put it. "Miss Lange was in touch with Dr. Kleinmann."

"In touch?"

"She was observed in his company, several times. Their relationship was of a . . .well, of a personal nature." He emphasized the word, making sure the meaning didn't escape me.

"She was sleeping with him?"

"We're quite certain of it. And while we can't be as sure about this, the inevitable conclusion, of course, is that she was in Dr. Kleinmann's service ... Er, on a professional basis as well as a personal one."

"You think she was a spy?"

"That would appear to be the case."

"A German spy?"

"Does it surprise you?"

"I guess it does," I said. "Although I'm not sure why. I don't know much about her, outside of what Lili's told me."

"She spent some portion of her life in England?"

"Her mother was English," I confirmed. "Her father brought her over to Germany after her mother died."

"That would certainly fit the profile."

"Profile?"

"Abwehr has been attempting to send recruits into London for some time, but on a significantly increased basis since the fall of France. Many come through Portugal under the pretense of being refugees. We've intercepted a number of them, both men and women of various nationalities, but the one thing they have in common, unsurprisingly, is a complete command of the English language. If they were to get through, they would be able to quickly melt away into the British landscape."

"You think Eva killed Kleinmann?"

"Can't say, I'm afraid. Though if she was working for him, I'm not sure what the motive would be."

"Maybe she had a change of heart."

"Anything's possible," he said. "Do you intend to inform Miss Sterne?"

"I guess I'll have to. I'm not sure how she'll take it."

"Mmm," he grunted, buttering it with significance.

"What?"

"Well, perhaps it's not my place to say it, but . . .well, can you be certain of Miss Sterne's loyalties?"

"Lili?!" I almost choked.

"She is, after all, of German origin."

"German, yes, but—"

"A number of American citizens of German heritage have returned to the fatherland since the war began. Many are being used as agents."

"Forget it," I said. "Lili's a lot of things, but she's not a Nazi sympathizer."

"I'm sure you're right. Still, that's how we're forced to think these days." He opened the door to go but stopped short.

"One other thing . . ."

"Yeah?"

"It may be of interest to you that Dr. Kleinmann and Mr. Grimes were shot with two different weapons . . . It follows, of course, that they were likely murdered by two separate individuals."

The phone rang.

"Yeah?"

"La senhora, she has just gone to her suite," the voice informed me.

"Thanks," I said, and hung up. I owed Javier the desk clerk ten bucks.

I flicked the bedside lamp on and looked at my watch. Almost midnight. After Stropford left, I'd retreated into the bedroom to lie down and must've drifted off while mulling over his revelation. There was no reason to doubt it, but I wished there was. It would've been easier to tell Lili that Eva was dead than to tell her she was a Nazi spy. I thought about letting it go until morning, but I knew that would be a mistake. If she still wanted to locate her friend after hearing what I had to say, I'd have to get moving. Ritter would have Catela's Guarda Nationale looking under every rock in Lisbon until they found her. I couldn't be hanging around until noon while Lili got her beauty sleep.

I scraped myself off the bed, went into the living room, found my shoes, and slipped into my jacket. Taking the stairs up the two flights, I wondered what kind of mood I'd find her in.

She appeared quickly after I rang the doorbell, wearing her bath-robe, but still in makeup.

"Hello, darling!" she practically sang. "Come inside!" I stepped in. Feeling a bit on edge and not quite awake; it probably showed. "You look like you need a nightcap," she said.

"Sure," I said. "I'm not interrupting anything, am I?"

"What would you be interrupting, darling? Do you think the King of England is hiding under my bed?"

"Former king," I corrected her as she handed me a large snifter of brandy.

"That's right," she said, raising her glass. "To former kings and aging movie stars!"

"You had a good night, then."

She made a face. "You were supposed to say something banal like I don't look a day over twenty-nine."

"You don't look a day over twenty-nine."

"Thanks so much, darling." She lifted the crystal to her lips, but kept her eyes locked on me. "You know something about Eva, don't you?"

"Yes . . ."

"Is she dead?" Lili held her breath.

"No. At least, not as far as I know."

"Then you haven't found her?"

"No . . ."

"What then? . . . Come on, darling. If she isn't dead and you haven't found her, what could it be?"

"You won't like it."

"For God's sake, Jack . . ."

". . . It, ah . . . It looks like she's been working for the Germans. As some kind of spy."

A curious look came over Lili's face, and I wasn't sure what would happen next. After a long moment, she forced a snicker, turned her back to me, and crossed the room. She swung around and faced me again from a distance, leaning precariously against the drinks cabinet.

"You can't be serious . . ." She laughed nervously. "If it's a joke, it's not at all funny."

"It's not a joke."

"Then what are you talking about?"

"She was seen by the Brits."

"Seen doing what?"

"With the head of German intelligence—"

"Nonsense!" she scoffed.

"They're pretty sure."

"Pretty sure?! It's quite an accusation to make if you're only pretty sure!"

"I'm telling you what they told me."

"That they saw her with someone?"

"With Kleinmann."

"Who?!"

"The guy they found in the trunk of Eddie Grimes's car. He was head of German intelligence in Lisbon."

"It's absurd!" she snapped. "They saw her with a man and suddenly she's a Nazi spy?!"

"They saw her more than once."

Who's saying this?!"

"Somebody who has no reason to lie."

"Everyone has a reason to lie, darling." She started pacing back and forth on the far side of the room, like a caged panther.

"Maybe she killed him," I said, trying to look on the bright side.

"I hope she did!" Lili's eyes flashed.

"Sure, why not?" I continued, trying to be helpful. "They could've had a falling out, a quarrel . . ."

She stopped pacing and threw me a look.

"What does that mean?"

"Nothing . . ." I tried to backtrack. "It's not important."

"But not nothing . . ."

"It's just that . . . well . . ." I wished I'd kept my mouth shut, but it was too late now. "Eva was sleeping with this guy. With Kleinmann."

Lili just stood there, eyes fixed on me. There was a very odd expression on her face and I felt I'd better say something.

"So maybe it didn't have anything to do with him being a Nazi. Maybe it was just good old-fashioned sex . . ."

In one swift, spontaneous move, Lili exploded across the room and threw her brandy hard in my face. I stood there, frozen in shock, taking in the look of utter contempt that was on her face.

"You're talking about someone who—" She clammed up.

"Look, Lili, I—"

"Get out!" she said in a voice that sent a shiver up my spine. *"GET THE HELL OUT!"*

There was no point in trying to sleep, even if I'd wanted to. After rinsing my face and taking a few laps around the rug, I decided to get some air. I walked down to the lobby, slapped Javier's ten-dollar bill onto the front desk, and headed out into the night, away from the casino lights. I couldn't really see where I was going, but that didn't matter. The point was to be moving.

I wondered if the storm would blow over or if that was gonna be it for Lili and me. I'd seen her explode a couple of times before, but I'd never been on the receiving end. It was unsettling, those piercing eyes flashing with honest-to-goodness rage. Maybe it would pass, probably not. From what I'd seen, there was no going back when she got like that. Oh well. I was fond of Lili and I enjoyed the perks, but if that was how she wanted it, I wasn't gonna cry any tears. I only had to pack my bag.

Eva Lange had some kind of powerful hold on her, that was for sure. Or at least the memory of her did. It was as if she was the last vestige of something Lili didn't want to lose and saving her was the last hope she had of salvaging it. The past, I guess. Her youth. It was fading fast and now history was steamrolling over the remnants. Everything had changed, she'd said, even the people. But Eva wasn't just anyone. She was the shy protégée who she had taken under her wing, the beautiful cellist who'd played like an angel on their last night in Berlin. How could she be recast as a Nazi agent, much less a Nazi's lover? It just wasn't in Lili's script.

That's the problem with the past. You have this picture of what it was, but, of course, it's nothing more than an illusion, a series of flickering images playing out on the back of your brain, like a Saturday matinee. Made to order in your very own dream factory, with all the filters and soft focus you care to add, and all the bad takes left on the cutting-room floor. It's whatever you want it to be. Or need it to be. Comedy, romance, adventure, tragedy, it's all rolled up in a neat little package that you can play whenever the sharp edges of the day get too pressured or frightening or downright boring. The problem is that it's all light and shadow, with no substance. Expose it to the outside world and it disappears, washed out by the harsh reality of the midday sun. Lili existed in the moving pictures, and when they started to fail her she found refuge in the past. If the past failed her . . .

I felt myself slowing down. I must've been cruising at a hefty clip because when I turned around the lights of the casino and the hotel looked a mile away. I stood there in the dark looking back at them. I had to laugh. I could still smell the forty-year-old cognac I'd taken up the nose. Only Lili would come up with that. It was like a scene out of one of her films.

Damn!

I shook my head and started back toward the hotel. There was no walking away, of course, even if I'd wanted to, which I didn't, not really. The thing was under my skin now and I guess the real truth was that I cared more about Lili than I'd realized. Anyway, I'd have to be a real jerk to leave the lady in the lurch over a spilt drink.

A set of headlights appeared in the distance, puncturing the darkness of the empty highway. Nothing sinister about that, I thought, but still—something didn't feel right. The road was wide open, yet the car was crawling along at ten, maybe twenty miles an hour. A bit late to be taking in the scenery. I moved onto the left shoulder and stood there, watching the vehicle approach.

The driver spotted me at thirty yards. He flicked on his brights, gunned the engine, and veered sharply to the right, burning rubber as he cut across the asphalt, coming straight at me. It was too late to get out of the way, so I sprinted toward the oncoming car. Vaulting up and over the hood, I rolled onto my shoulder and came up against the windshield, which cracked under my weight. The momentum carried me over the top, across the trunk, and down hard onto the pavement. I rolled into a ditch, and lay there, face down, head spinning and heart pounding.

The car pulled onto the verge about twenty yards along, and sat there, idling. I tensed up, wondering if I could move if I had to. I was about to try when the car suddenly spun out across the gravel, found third gear, and accelerated up the road. Its red taillights quickly receded into the distance, then vanished into the night.

I stood up, brushed myself off, and checked for damage. My right shoulder was pretty sore, but it was functioning. Other than that, and a few scratches, I was in good shape for a guy who just went head-to-head with a speeding Buick.

When I got back to the Palacio, I had Javier phone Alberto, in spite of the hour. I was in the mood to get to the bottom of this.

The Alfama was spooky at this hour, the narrow streets still and silent and full of shadows. My steps bounced off the empty cobblestones and echoed into the distance, where a dog barked at the unwelcome trespass.

I'd left Alberto in the car while I walked the hundred paces up the hill to find the crumbling edifice that Popov called home. Harry Thompson had said he moved around a lot, like a rat, and from the look of things he lived like one, too. The place needed a wrecking ball.

I took the scrap of paper out of my pocket, turned it toward the light and examined it again:

RUA DAS TAIPAS, N. 35
TOP FLOOR

This was it, all right. I stepped back and checked the uppermost floor. Dark, like the three levels below it. I wondered if coming down here in the middle of the night had been such a good idea after all, but it was too late to worry about that now.

The entranceway was a few steps below street level, an old door decorated with a hundred years of peeling, faded paint. It appeared to be out of use until I got closer and saw it had been padlocked from the outside. A new fitting, recently installed. Apparently my rat was in residence but was out on the scrounge at the moment. I'd come this far, I might as well wait, I thought. If Popov didn't show in a couple of hours, I'd go to Plan B. In the meantime, I'd try to figure out what the hell Plan B was.

Alberto came to life with a start when I opened the door and slid into the backseat.

"*Sim*, senhor . . .?" he grunted.

"Go back to sleep," I said, and he happily complied, pulling his cap down over his eyes and falling into a noisy snooze almost immediately.

The stiffness in my shoulder was setting in. I didn't doubt that the asshole in the Buick was the same asshole who'd tried to break into my room the night before, and it was pretty clear now what he had in mind. He was almost certainly a hired hand, but whose? My first thought was Ritter. If Eva was really a German agent, like Stropford said, then maybe he . . .

Ridiculous. Even if the major wanted to get rid of me, the Gestapo didn't hire guys to run you down in the middle of the night. They weren't that subtle. It was possible, of course, that Eva herself wanted to bump me off, but that didn't make much sense, either. She might not want to be found, but I wasn't the only person in Lisbon looking for her, and I certainly wasn't the one she needed to worry about.

I was tired and out of ideas. Guessing was a waste of time, anyway. There was nothing to go on. I settled back into the seat and began my vigil. I'd find out soon enough who had it in for me. Assuming, of course, that I didn't turn up dead first.

. . .

It was starting to look like dawn when I spotted Popov rounding the corner. Alberto peeked out from under his cap, but he didn't seem bothered when I stepped onto the sidewalk. He grunted softly and turned over.

The Slav was walking quickly, head down, hands stuffed into the pockets of a dark raincoat, even though there hadn't been the slightest hint of precipitation since I'd arrived in Lisbon. Aside from an Arab-looking man who was opening the metal shutters on his shop while his wife washed and swept the pavement, we were the only two on the street. I kept a reasonable distance up the hill, even though Popov didn't seem to be aware of anything but his feet. He was furtively removing the padlock from his door when I caught up with him.

"Remember me?" I said.

"Sure, sure," he said. "Of course I remember. Jack Teller. How you've found this place?"

"Tough to keep anything a secret around here," I said. "Shall we go up?" I had my fist jammed into my jacket pocket so he couldn't be sure if I was asking or telling. It wasn't lost on him.

"Why not?" Popov tried a smile and failed. He looked terrible. White as a sheet and wrung out, he was suffering from some kind of skin rash, especially around the eyes, making them red and puffy. Pulling the door open, he led me into a pitch-black hallway that smelled of damp plaster and, for some reason, onions. I held the door open as he struck a match against the wall and used it to light an oil lamp that was hanging on a rusty nail. He pointed me toward a dark stairwell.

"After you," I insisted.

The steps moaned and creaked under our weight and the wooden banister was hanging by a thread, but we made it to the top landing. Popov removed another padlock and pushed the door open. It was too dark to see much of anything, so I waited by the door while he crossed the room and opened the rear-window shutters, allowing the soft early-morning light to filter in.

The first thing I saw was the paintings. Dozens of them, all shapes and sizes, stacked against the dingy, crumbling walls. I was no expert, but I'd wandered through enough museums to be able to spot a Rembrandt, and I saw two of them right away, matching portraits of an old man and his wife. There was a Frans Hals, too, and what I thought was a Cézanne still life. The space itself, a large rectangle with high ceilings and long, shuttered windows, looked like some forgotten old museum attic. Antique furniture, gold-plated clocks, porcelain figures, stacks of fine china, rolls of carpet, a half-dozen bronze statuettes, and even a medieval tapestry were strewn around the place like so much junk. A mountain of silver picture frames—minus the family photos, of course—was heaped carelessly in a corner. It was Popov's private warehouse of plundered treasure.

"Impressive," I said.

"People want sell, I buy," he said defensively. "If not me, somebody else does."

"What do they get in return?"

He thought about it a moment. "A chance."

"I guess that don't come cheap," I said, and he shrugged it off.

"Do you intend to rob me?" Popov cast a suspicious glance at my fist, which was still impersonating a gun. I laughed out loud, which he didn't appreciate, then revealed my bluff. I took aim at him with my index finger, cocked my thumb, and fired.

"Bang!"

"Very amusing," he sneered.

I wandered over to the stack of paintings and started flicking through them. Most were unexceptional family portraits or nondescript landscapes, but there were a few gems, like the Pissarro landscape that depicted an apple tree in full snowy blossom against a vibrating blue-and-violet sky.

"I can make you a good price." Popov sidled up beside me. It was a handsome painting, but taking it with me was out of the question. I'd never stop wondering what had happened to the rightful owner. Besides, I certainly didn't need a lifelong reminder of Popov.

"No, thanks," I said, setting the painting aside. "You shouldn't stack them up like that, you know. They'll get scratched."

Popov made a face, indicating that he didn't much care. "You have come because you reconsider my offer?" he said. "Regarding this girl."

"I heard that sometimes you can do more than bullshit."

"The situation has changed since we spoke," he said, ignoring the compliment or insult, whichever it was. "Now she is suspected in the murder of—"

"A thousand bucks," I interrupted, not wanting to waste time. I could see that Popov was impressed. He'd probably been hoping for half that, but he tried to play it cool anyway.

"What will you expect in return?"

"Eva Lange."

"She is quite valuable," he said coyly. "There are others who would like to find her . . ."

"If you've got a better offer, take it. Otherwise, I'll give you twenty-four hours."

"May I ask of what importance is she to you?"

"No."

He folded his arms tightly across his chest and paced back and forth a couple of times before stopping abruptly and turning to face me.

"If certain parties were to learn that I have given assistance in this, I would be forced to leave Lisbon very quickly. This would be quite inconvenient . . ."

I removed the roll I still had in my pocket and peeled off a crisp bill. "A hundred now, the rest when I have her." I could almost hear his greedy little heart beating in anticipation.

"And if she is reluctant? What level of force may I use?"

"I'd go for persuasion if I were you," I said. "I don't know about this Dr. Kleinmann character, but Eddie Grimes was no pushover. And you know how it turned out for him."

"You have a suggestion?"

"Tell her you're taking her to see Lili Sterne. Say that she's arranged safe passage out of the country."

"This is true?"

"Do you care?"

"No," he shrugged. "Of course not."

"Good," I said, offering him the hundred. He reached out and, with a skulking grin, wrapped it up in his palm.

Alberto tapped his horn, swung into the opposite lane, and floored it, punching past the slow-moving tram that was struggling to make it up the hill. A lady bicyclist swerved to avoid us, but I saw in the back window that she managed to stay upright. This part of Lisbon reminded me of San Francisco, with its steep cobbled streets and colorful trolleys. Of course, I'd never been to San Francisco, so I could've been off the mark.

The black sedan carrying the two not-very-secret secret police that I'd spotted outside Popov's place wasn't behind us anymore, so I figured we'd lost them. They looked to me like local guys, probably Catela's, and Alberto agreed. I must've led them right to Popov, which was kind of inconvenient. I didn't know if the Slav could really deliver Eva, but if he did and Catela's guys were in the picture, they'd snatch her right out from under my nose. I had to get them out of the way for twenty-four hours.

We found the German embassy on a quiet, tree-lined street at the top of the hill, an unimposing white Neoclassic building two stories high with black wrought-iron balconies outside the upper-floor windows. I left Alberto parked by a small square at the end of the road and approached on foot. Entering through a heavy wooden door with shiny brass handles, I found myself in a tiny anteroom with a window that looked onto an entrance hall of pristine white marble. A uniformed guard, probably in his forties, looked up from behind a table that he could barely get his legs under.

"I'd like to see Major Ritter," I said in German.

He smiled politely. "Document?"

I handed him my passport and he carefully copied down the name and number in his logbook before picking up the phone and dialing through. After a brief exchange with a secretary, he hung up and told me to take a seat, someone would be with me shortly. He explained that I could pick up my passport on the way out.

The only seating was a hard wooden bench set off to the side. I sat down, lit a smoke, and tried to look comfortable, without much success. It seemed a long time before a dwarfish woman in a gray suit and a personality to match appeared and motioned for me to follow. She led silently through the entrance hall and up a broad staircase to a corner office where I found Ritter posing behind a big desk.

"Where did you learn to speak German, Herr Teller?" He didn't bother to get up.

"I was born in Berlin," I said.

"Fascinating," he said insipidly. "I wouldn't have guessed it."

"It's been a long time."

He motioned me into a chair, leaned back in his, and offered up a sickly smile. "So, then . . . What may I do for you?"

"Actually, I thought there might be something I could do for you."

"Such as?"

"Well . . ." I paused, putting on a worried look. "May I speak frankly?"

"Please."

"The truth is that I . . . Well, I had a falling-out . . . an argument . . . with Miss Sterne."

"I'm so sorry to hear of it," he said, perking up. "But perhaps she will forget it. It is often so with a woman."

"She tossed a brandy in my face."

Ritter couldn't help chuckling. For a moment I could imagine him out of uniform, as a husband or father or lecherous uncle. It made him seem almost human. Almost.

"Did you deserve it?"

"I told her something she didn't want to hear," I explained.

"A cardinal error. You must always tell a woman exactly what she wants to hear. Especially a beautiful woman." He clearly considered himself an expert on the subject and I was happy enough to play along if it was gonna make things easier.

"Next time I'll know." I smiled.

"But you didn't come here to take my advice regarding the female sex," he said, a few degrees above freezing now.

"No," I agreed. "I came to offer my services . . . Now that I'm a free agent."

"Services?"

"Yes."

"What type of services?"

"You want to get hold of Eva Lange, right?" Ritter leaned forward ever so slightly without realizing he was doing it.

"Do you know where she is?"

"Yes," I said, then let it hang there for a moment. The major searched my eyes, as though, if he looked hard enough, he'd be able to see into my head and determine if I was lying.

"It is a matter for the local authorities," he finally said. "This woman is suspected of—"

"Sure," I interrupted. "I can talk to Captain Catela if you want. I was just worried that he might, well . . . If you have confidence in him, that's fine. Who am I to say?" Ritter furrowed his brow and stubbed out his cigarette.

"Do you have her in your custody at this moment?"

"Tomorrow morning."

"You are one hundred percent certain of this?"

"Yes."

"How can you be sure?"

"It's been arranged. She thinks I'm going to take her to Lili, who will use her friends at the American embassy to get her out of the country."

"This is true?"

"That depends on your answer, Major."

Ritter gave me a lengthy look, then stood up, went to a window, and studied a passing cloud.

"In welchem Statdteil sind Sie aufgewachsen?" He was asking me what part of Berlin I grew up in.

"The address was Schonestrasse, number forty-seven," I responded in English. He turned to face me.

"Ah, yes, I know the street. In Siemensstadt, is it not?"

"Weissensee," I corrected him. "Just off Rennbahnstrasse. I remember there was an ice-skating rink on the corner. I used to go there every Saturday afternoon."

"Yes. I recall it now." He sat against the edge of the desk, arms crossed, and looked down at me.

"Have you still family in Berlin?"

"My father was killed in the last war and my mother died in 1927."

"No other family?"

"I was an only child," I said. There was no point in mentioning Josef. I hadn't seen my younger brother in sixteen years and I hadn't heard from him in almost as long. I couldn't say if he was dead or alive, let alone where he was now.

"Tell me." Ritter leaned forward slightly and narrowed his eyes. "What is your feeling about Germany?"

"In what sense?"

"If you were forced to choose between your mother country and your adopted one, where would your allegiance lie?"

"In Switzerland, where they have all those banks."

Ritter cracked a smile. "A very good answer. Because I wouldn't have believed you if you had told me that you want to help due to love for the fatherland."

"Five thousand dollars is what I had in mind," I said. The major stopped smiling and retreated back behind the desk. "That's how much Lili was going to pay me," I added.

"Of course, I don't believe you," he said. "But I will not bother to negotiate with you. If you are telling the truth, it will be worth the cost. I will pay the equivalent amount, in deutsche marks, and only when I have Eva Lange in my possession."

"How about an advance?"

He grinned. "Certainly not."

I didn't expect one, but I thought he'd expect me to ask, so I did. Then I snuck in the real reason for my visit.

"I'll need you to call Catela off for twenty-four hours," I said. "I don't want him to scare her away."

"I have no authority over Captain Catela," Ritter said with a straight face, quickly adding, "but I don't expect he will present a problem."

"Fine." I got up and offered my hand across the desk. "Then we have a deal."

Ritter stood and gripped my hand, a little too vigorously I thought. Making a point, I guess.

"I'll be in touch," I told him.

I was dead tired, but I was hungry, too. I asked Alberto to take us somewhere for a hot meal and he knew just the place on the way back to the hotel. It turned out to be his cousin's small olive and fruit farm, which was a twenty-minute detour up the side of a mountain, but that was fine with me. The food was good, Fabio and his wife, Rosalina, were friendly, and the afternoon drifted pleasantly away. On the way back to the hotel, Alberto swung by his own small house to tell his oversize wife that he would be home for dinner after all, but I think he really wanted to show off his four-year old twin daughters. I gave them each a dollar and we set off again. By the time I walked into my room, it was late afternoon. Still time for a snooze before Santo's car turned up.

I kicked off my shoes and loosened my tie as I went to pull the drapes across the balcony doors, which I'd left open to air the room. I saw a movement out of the corner of my eye and before I could move . . .

POP! POP! POP!

I dropped to the floor, spun away, and lay there, hugging the carpet while I got my bearings. There was plaster dust on the floor and three bullet holes now decorated the ceiling above my bed. The shots had come from outside, in the garden. Edging back toward the door, I took a deep breath and leaned across to have a peek outside. The half-dozen or so guests who were gathered around the swimming pool seemed unaware that anything had happened, and the only other person in sight was one of the hotel gardeners, who was scurrying across the lawn toward the back gate.

Bastard!

I stepped onto the balcony, and before I knew what I was doing, I'd climbed onto the iron railing. I teetered there for a couple of seconds—just long enough to realize that three stories is a long way down—then I pushed off. Looks like the deep end, I thought as I sailed through the air, but as everybody knows, water can distort things, make distances—and depths—seem bigger than they are. I hit bottom hard.

Pushing off, I bounded out of the pool and raced toward the back gate, leaving behind a very startled group of sunbathers. I stepped onto the narrow service road just in time to see a late model Buick sport coupe pull away and disappear down the bottom of the lane.

The concierge with the stick up his ass wasn't too impressed when I squelched through his lobby in my stocking feet, walked up to the front desk, and asked for a spare key. He gave me a long, sickly look, but I wasn't in the mood, so I gave it right back to him. He got the message and looked the other way.

I went upstairs, got undressed, and toweled off. I didn't expect to be able to sleep now, but I got into bed anyway. It felt great to have my eyes closed, and it wasn't long before I found myself sailing across the ice on a bright winter afternoon at the old rink on Rennbahnstrasse. Everything was vivid and clear and full of detail—except for the faces. I couldn't for the life of me figure out who the hell anybody was.

I didn't notice that the car wasn't heading toward Santo's place until the driver made a left turn off the coast road and we began a steep ascent into the mountains. I was about to ask where we were going but changed my mind. I'd know soon enough.

The road wound its way north up the slope until we reached a peak that provided a soaring view across the Atlantic, pink-and-yellow sky reflecting off the calm waters of the Tagus estuary, Lisbon's lights sparkling through the silky dusk beyond. We continued to climb, making a series of hairpin turns, through the cobbled streets of a quiet old hill town, then onto a narrow lane that cut a straight line through a lush wooded area. I felt refreshed after my nap and the cool mountain air was like a drug. Settling back into my seat, I wondered what Santo had in mind for our meeting. He'd certainly picked an out-of-the-way spot.

A few minutes later the car slowed to a crawl and made a left turn through a stately iron gate. It was pretty dark by now, but I could make out the lights of a large estate at the end of a very long approach, although as we got closer I could see that the word *estate* didn't quite cover it. Palace was more like it, with a capital *P*. I thought I'd seen lavish, but this place made the biggest, most overdone Hollywood pretense look like the wrong side of the tracks.

The facade, painted a pale coral, featured imitation Corinthian columns, flowing floral cornices, a classic Greek pediment, and a gallery of pure white marble gods and goddesses posing along the roofline. It looked like a giant pink wedding cake that had been decorated by a band of mad pastry chefs.

The car followed the road around to the left, along one of two single-story wings that unfolded from the main body of the building, extending outward at right angles to embrace a formal garden of patterned hedgerows, tall cypress trees, and myriad ornately carved fountains. There was even a canal, lined with brightly lit lapis tiles that glistened out across the darkness. We pulled up in front of a grand staircase where a young man in a green jacket and feathered cap was standing at attention. He stepped forward, opened the door, and performed a deep bow as I descended onto the gravel.

"Nice place you got here," I said, but he was poker-faced.

"Follow me, please, sir," he said. I complied, trailing up the steps onto a vast empty terrace lit by a series of gas torches, flames flickering gently in the summer breeze. We continued through a decorative arch, where the air was steeped in the perfumed scent of night-blooming jasmine, and then along a lengthy colonnade that deposited us in front of a discreet entrance at the back of the palace.

My impassive guide was apparently not house-trained because he was very careful not to cross the threshold as he opened the door and ushered me inside. I stepped into an expansive hallway that was a bit like entering one of those "House of Mirrors" at the local carnival, except that those mirrors aren't framed in twenty-four-karat gold. Waiting for me was another escort, this one in black tie and tails but equally deadpan. He mutely led the way along the mirrored corridor for a while, our images bouncing back and forth between the walls, then we changed course and entered a series of interlocking rooms that seemed to have little or no function other than to display objects of art, mostly from the Far East. Chinese vases, silk tapestries, that sort of thing. Several twists and turns later we came upon a set of double doors that seemed to be our final destination. Yet another domestic was waiting there. Silver-haired, with ridiculously good posture, he gave me the once-over and wasn't very impressed.

"Call him 'sir,'" he instructed in the King's English, "... and remain standing until he invites you to sit."

"And keep my elbows off the table," I added, but Jeeves didn't appreciate my brand of humor. He stepped aside and let me pass without comment, unless you call a sneer a comment.

The door closed, leaving me alone in a small private dining room, oval-shaped, with red velvet walls, no windows, and soft, subdued lighting. An egg-shaped table, echoing the shape of the room, was set for three. Very elegant, from the silver candelabra to the ivory napkin holders. It hadn't hit me that I'd be dining with the Duke of Windsor until somewhere along the hall of mirrors, so I hadn't been able to think it through. I'd listen politely, nod a lot, and say as little as possible.

"Hello, Jack." Espírito Santo entered through a door I hadn't noticed because it was covered in the same red velvet as the wall. I was about to respond when the familiar royal figure appeared, cigarette in limp hand, traditional bemused smirk on his face. Santo pulled me forward.

"Your Royal Highness," he said. "Allow me to present Jack Teller . . ."

"Hello, Jack." The duke smiled affably and offered a warm handshake. "Thanks so much for coming."

"My pleasure," I said, remembering at the last minute to add a "sir" on the end of the sentence.

"I do hope we haven't kept you waiting."

"No, sir, I just got here."

"Good," he said. "Excellent. Well then . . . Shall we?"

He slipped into his place at the head of the table. Santo and I waited behind our chairs, facing each other until the duke was settled, at which point he impatiently waved us into our seats.

"Sit down, for God's sake," he said, as if he hadn't noticed our deference. "We needn't stand on ceremony."

We took our seats and Santo turned to me.

"I apologize for the secrecy, Jack, but it is important that His Royal Highness is not compromised in any way. I'm sure you understand."

I told him I did, but it occurred to me that if the duke was going to be compromised, it would be because he was hanging out with a guy who was doing business with Adolf Hitler, not because he was having dinner with Jack Teller.

The hidden door opened again and a waiter in white gloves appeared with a bottle of chilled white wine in hand. Assuming the manner of a matador about to face the most celebrated bull in the land, he ceremoniously planted himself at the head of the table and presented the bottle to the guest of honor. The duke had a good long look before giving the go-ahead, at which point the matador, with great aplomb, produced a corkscrew from his vest pocket and extracted the cork. Snapping to attention, one arm fixed rigidly behind his back, he poured a measure of wine into the duke's crystal goblet. The duke took equal care with his part of the performance, holding the drink up to the light, swirling it around a couple of times, and giving it a good sniff before finally bringing the glass to his lips, gently sucking air over the top of the liquid as it decanted onto his tongue. After a moment of intense gustatory scrutiny, the duke nodded and pronounced the vintage "very nice indeed." The waiter took a bow in the form of an almost imperceptible nod of the head, then proceeded to fill the remainder of the glass. After making his way around the table, pouring mine and Santo's with a lot less aplomb, he made a smooth exit.

"I understand it has quite an interesting history," the duke said, sipping the Chablis. Santo hesitated for a moment, not sure what he was talking about. "The palace," Windsor clarified.

"Ahhh, yes . . ." Santo stumbled to catch up. "Yes, yes indeed . . . It does have quite a history. In fact, it was no more than a modest hunting lodge, perhaps ten rooms, when Dom Pedro the Third commissioned it as his summer palace . . ."

"A wedding gift for his fiancée, I believe," the duke interjected.

"Exactly so," Santo confirmed.

The duke shot me a knowing look and raised a strategic eyebrow. "Who also happened to be his niece," he said. I wasn't sure if he was making a comment on the good old days when kings could marry whoever they pleased, but I took it that way. "That's the sort of history one can get their teeth into," he added with a thin smile.

"I'm impressed with Your Royal Highness's knowledge," Santo soft-soaped. The duke batted the compliment away with a flick of the royal wrist and turned back to me.

"Tell us about yourself, Jack."

"There's not much to tell," I said, hoping I could leave it at that.

"I don't believe it, not for a minute," the duke grinned. "Any man with the good fortune to accompany Lili Sterne halfway round the globe must have a story to tell."

"Lili and I are just friends," I explained.

"She's an extraordinary woman. Absolutely extraordinary."

"Yes, sir, she certainly is."

"How did you two meet?"

"A couple of years ago," I explained. "On the set of one of her pictures . . ."

"Which one?"

"A very bad western called *Ride the Wild Wind* . . ."

"Starring Errol Flynn," the duke proudly declared.

"Yes, sir, that's right," I said, more than a little surprised that he was familiar with a movie that even the critics had mercifully forgotten. "Now I'm the one who's impressed."

"Oh, I've seen all of Lili's films," he said.

"I'm not sure she would've wanted you to see that one."

"Mmm, she was given rather short shrift," the duke mused in all seriousness. "And the film was the worse for it, too. But then I'm a terrific fan, you see. I love all her pictures, no matter how dreadful.

There's something about her that I find hard to describe. Something quite magical. Very elusive . . . Perhaps it's our shared ancestry."

He glanced over, checked my reaction before continuing. I smiled and nodded.

"Of course I'm even more besotted now I've met her in the flesh . . . I'll have to be careful not to get carried away, though . . . Being a married man, as I now am."

"A very fortunate married man," Santo chimed in. The duke smiled graciously, and I thought I'd better second the opinion. I said something about the duchess being every bit as charming as she was beautiful.

"Yes, she is an exceptional woman," the duke affirmed. "Unlike any I've met . . ." He seemed to go distant for a brief moment, but he came back quickly with a smile.

"I propose a toast to exceptional women . . ."

He raised his glass and we followed.

"To Lili Sterne and my wife . . . Not necessarily in that order, you understand." He started to drink, but pulled up short. "What about you, Santo? Is there an exceptional woman you'd like to add?"

"Several," Santo grinned mischievously.

"Touché!" the duke laughed. "Well, good luck to you. I fear those days are gone for me . . . And do you know, I don't envy you a bit!"

As we drank, a pair of waiters appeared from behind the hidden door with our first course of poached fish under a creamy white sauce. It smelled delicious.

"Interesting that you should mention Errol Flynn, Jack," Santo said casually as they started serving. "I met him several years ago, at a cocktail party in Mayfair, and then again, here in Lisbon. Do you know him well?"

"I was his stunt double on six or seven pictures," I said, and the duke's ears perked up.

"You were Errol Flynn's stunt double?"

"Yes . . ."

"How fantastic! And here I was thinking you were just another Hollywood hustler."

"That, too," I assured him.

"Well, hats off to you, on both accounts. We ran across Mr. Flynn ourselves, a couple of years ago, in Paris. Charming fellow, absolutely charming. Wouldn't you say, Jack?"

I didn't think it would go over too well to say what I really thought—that he was an arrogant pig—so I shaded the truth a bit, Hollywood style.

"I couldn't agree more," I said, cutting into my fish. "Charming fellow."

Dinner proceeded along those lines, the conversation pretty much limited to Hollywood gossip, Portuguese cuisine, and the wines of Europe, until we hit dessert. As I bit into a piece of honey-soaked sponge cake with caramelized pears on top, Santo and the duke exchanged a glance. The duke waited until the servants had left the room before getting down to business.

"Have you been to London, Jack?"

"No, sir, I haven't," I said. "I hope to someday."

"Yes, you must see it. I only hope it will still be standing." He put on a worried puppy look. "I hate to think what will happen. I fear it will be devastating, absolutely devastating."

"It must be difficult for you," I said, which seemed to strike the right chord. He put down his fork and turned to show me the pained expression on his face.

"I've been desperate, absolutely desperate . . . My wife and I were in Antibes when news came of France's surrender. Shocking turn of events, but there you are, it's happened. We've had to abandon our house in Paris, with all its possessions. Not an easy thing to accept, but we must all take a good hard look at reality now, and someone . . . *Someone* must put an end to this, this . . . insanity before thousands more are killed and maimed. And for no other reason than to save the faces of a few stubborn politicians . . ." His voice trembled with emotion and his hands balled up into tight fists. Santo took over, his voice as smooth as silk.

"The English are in a hopeless position," he said. "It's only a matter of time before they are forced to come to terms with the new reality of Europe. The only question is how long it will take—and how much must be destroyed before they come to the realization."

"It should be obvious to all"—the duke took over again—"that modern warfare no longer allows us to speak in terms of victors and vanquished. The world is at a critical juncture—this cannot be put too strongly, Jack. The course of the next hundred years will be decided in these coming weeks. If Germany and England are allowed to continue along the current path, Europe will be left in ruins, ripe for the taking by the bloody Bolsheviks . . . It may sound silly to put it this way, but the time has come when someone needs to say, you two boys have fought long enough and now it's time to kiss and make up."

The duke turned to Santo, cueing him to take over. The banker leaned forward and looked me square in the eye.

"You understand that our conversation must remain strictly confidential," he said. "It must not go beyond this room."

"Jack can be trusted," the duke assured him. "I'm certain of it." They looked to me for confirmation and I nodded.

"Of course," I said.

"At some point in the very near future . . ." Santo began slowly, tasting each word before letting it slide off his tongue, "His Royal Highness's voice will be heard around the world, in a live radio broadcast. At that time he will propose a plan for an immediate and permanent end to hostilities between Germany and England. It will not be an empty plea, but will contain specific points that can be accepted by both sides . . . No one else is in the position to make such a proposal. Because of His Royal Highness's continuing popularity among his people, and the enduring respect they have for him, his declaration will rally the country to his side, and enable those who support peace—some of whom are in the British cabinet—to come forward. There is good reason to believe that the German government will be favorably disposed to the plan, allowing for an early end to the war." He paused for effect. "You are being entrusted with something very important, Jack. This will be a speech to change the course of history. One that will be remembered for a thousand years to come."

Santo sat back and awaited my reaction. I tried hard not to have one. I don't know what I was expecting, but it sure as hell wasn't that the former king of England was negotiating with Hitler behind Churchill's back in order to initiate a revolution among his former subjects. He might see it as a historic peace mission, but most would see it as high treason. I'd just been thrust onto some very dangerous ground and I knew that I had to step carefully.

"What is your view of that idea, Jack?" the duke said, quiet gaze fixed firmly on me.

"I think you'd be doing the world a great service, sir," I answered without hesitation, and he smiled humbly.

"Well, somebody must step forward." He offered me a cigarette, which I accepted. "I'm sorry to say that the British ministers of the day are not up to the task. I fear they're no match for the likes of Hitler and Mussolini. These are strong, decisive men who know how to lead."

I nodded sympathetically.

"I'm counting on your help, Jack."

"Yes, well, to be honest, sir, I'm having a tough time seeing how I figure into this."

The duke smiled cryptically and turned to Santo again.

"His Royal Highness would like Miss Sterne to carry a personal message to President Roosevelt," he said. "A letter."

"I see," I said, swallowing hard. "What would the letter say?" I didn't really expect a straight answer, but the duke seemed eager to give me one.

"I believe that Roosevelt has an inaccurate understanding of the strategic situation in Europe," he said. "I suspect that he is receiving bad advice from men who profess neutrality but, in truth, wish to see America enter the war. They are convinced that Hitler must be defeated, no matter the cost. It is, of course, understandable that Roosevelt might be susceptible to those voices—England is the mother country, after all, and when the mother is attacked the natural instinct of the child is to come to her aid. But, in this case, the child must stand aside. Should the United States become involved, it would extend the war by ten years, perhaps longer. Western Europe would be reduced to nothing more than a pile of rubble and we know what would happen then. The armies of Russia would simply march in. Communism would be victorious."

He paused to take a long drag on his cigarette and slowly exhale the smoke.

"My letter to the president," he said, "will outline those points—in a slightly more circumspect manner, of course—and it will request that the United States support my plan for peace when it is announced. The best way to save England, Jack—probably the only way—is to force her to make peace. It may be accomplished now or it may be accomplished after she has been bombed into oblivion by the Luftwaffe. But, one way or another, it must happen."

Christ, I thought. He makes it sound like a goddamned threat.

11

"THE GERMAN AIR FORCE HAS MOUNTED A SERIES OF ATTACKS ON SHIPPING CONVOYS OFF THE SOUTHEAST COAST OF ENGLAND . . . IT IS THE FIRST MAJOR ASSAULT BY THE LUFTWAFFE IN WHAT THE PRIME MINISTER HAS DUBBED 'THE BATTLE OF BRITAIN . . .'"

The crowd—mostly Brits—had grown in number as word spread through the hotel of the report coming in on the World Service. They gathered around a radio that had been placed on the bar and listened in transfixed silence:

"THE BOMBING RAIDS BEGAN AT DAWN WHEN A FORMATION OF GERMAN PLANES STRUCK AIRFIELDS ALONG THE SOUTH AND EAST COASTS OF ENGLAND. THE ATTACKS HAVE CONTINUED THROUGH-OUT THE MORNING WITH REPORTS OF ENEMY RAIDS ALONG THE WEST, SOUTH, AND EAST COASTS . . . EXPLOSIONS HAVE BEEN RE-PORTED AT GUISBOROUGH, CANEWDON, HERTFORD, COLCHESTER, WELWYN, AND ELY . . . THERE HAS BEEN SPORADIC ACTIVITY OVER THE SCOTTISH COAST BETWEEN FIRTH OF TAY AND BEACHY HEAD . . ."

The broadcast paused, leaving only static to fill the room. People exchanged looks with each other, but no one spoke. After a moment, the announcer returned, with a hint of urgency in his voice.

> "WE TAKE YOU NOW TO A LOCATION IN MANSTON, NEAR RAMS-
> GATE, WHERE OUR CORRESPONDENT, CHARLES GARDNER, WILL
> PROVIDE AN EYEWITNESS ACCOUNT OF ... WE TAKE YOU THERE
> NOW ..."

More static, for quite some time. People didn't move, just stood there in uneasy anticipation, knowing they were caught in a moment they would never forget. Then, abruptly, Gardner's voice came in—agitated, excited, but in control:

> "... NOW THE GERMANS ARE DIVE-BOMBING A CONVOY OUT AT SEA
> ... THERE ARE ONE, TWO, THREE, FOUR, FIVE, SIX, SEVEN GERMAN
> DIVE-BOMBERS, JUNKERS 87S ... THERE'S ONE GOING DOWN ON ITS
> TARGET NOW ... AND BOMBS AWAY ... NO, MISSED THE SHIP. THERE
> ARE ABOUT TEN SHIPS IN THE CONVOY, BUT THEY HAVEN'T HIT A
> SINGLE ONE ... AND ... THERE YOU CAN HEAR OUR ANTIAIRCRAFT
> GOING AT THEM NOW ... OH! ... OH! ... NO, WE THOUGHT THEY
> GOT ONE, BUT IT GOT AWAY ... BUT NOW THE BRITISH FIGHTERS ARE
> COMING UP ... HERE THEY COME ... YOU CAN HEAR OUR OWN
> GUNS GOING LIKE ANYTHING NOW ... I'M LOOKING ROUND NOW,
> I CAN HEAR MACHINE-GUN FIRE, BUT I CAN'T SEE OUR SPITFIRES ...
> THEY MUST BE SOMEWHERE THERE ... OH, HERE'S A GERMAN AIR-
> CRAFT COMING DOWN NOW ... IT'S COMING DOWN IN FLAMES
> ... HE'S COMING DOWN COMPLETELY OUT OF CONTROL, A LONG
> STREAK OF SMOKE, HE'S ... AH ... THE PILOT'S BALED OUT BY PARA-
> CHUTE. IT'S A JUNKERS 87 AND IT'S GOING SLAP INTO THE SEA, AND
> THERE IT GOES! SMASH! ... TERRIFIC PUMMEL OF WATER AND THERE
> WAS A JUNKERS 87 ... POSSIBLY THE FIRST GERMAN AIRCRAFT TO BE
> SHOT DOWN OVER BRITAIN ..."

I wondered if the duke was listening, and if so, what he was think-ing—he seemed to almost relish the idea of his countrymen being bombed into submission. There was an underlying bitterness in him that you didn't see in the newsreels, a sense that what he wanted more than anything was to get even. I'd always had my doubts about "The Love Story of the Century" angle, and now I was convinced that there was more to the abdication of Edward VIII than met the eye. While he was clearly in love (or some version of it) with Wallis Simpson, he didn't strike me as the type of guy who'd easily walk away from all that power and glory. Who knows what kind of palace plotting had dethroned the king, but it was clear that he wasn't quite finished with the intrigue.

I felt a tugging on my sleeve and looked around to find a dirty face looking up at me. He must've been eight, maybe nine, one of the kids that hung around the hotel entrance hoping to catch a handout as the big cars came in and out. I was surprised that he'd been able to make it through the lobby and was about to reward him with a coin when he produced an envelope.

"Senhor Teller?"

"That's right."

"For you."

I reached for the envelope, but it disappeared, replaced by an empty palm. I covered it with a dollar bill, got a devious smile and the envelope in return.

"Who—?" But the kid had already vanished.

I walked out into the lobby to have a look around, hoping to get a clue about the source of the letter, but aside from the desk clerk, the place was deserted.

I wandered into a private corner, unsealed the envelope, and removed the thin piece of folded brown paper it contained. In the middle of the page was a scribbled message:

RUA ESPERANÇA, 66
2 P.M.—P

"Hello, old chap!"

Harry Thompson appeared out of nowhere, looking unusually bright-eyed and bushy-tailed in a crisp white cotton suit with a splashy red tie to match his complexion.

"Looks like the curtain's finally come up, eh?"

"Curtain . . .?" I stuffed the letter into my pocket.

"The fate of the world, dear boy. Or haven't you heard? The Jerries are giving us a good old pounding this morning."

"Oh, right . . . Yeah, I was just listening . . ."

"Although I expect this will look pretty tame by the time we're through."

"You're probably right," I said. "Well, good to see ya, Harry." I gave him a pat on the back and headed for the door. He followed.

"What news of Hollywood? Have you found the legend's little friend yet?"

"Afraid not."

"Was our elusive rodent of any help?"

"Not yet."

"Not to worry. I have a feeling he will be."

"We'll see," I said.

"How about a drink? I'm buying today . . ."

I swung around to face him. "What do you want, Harry?"

"Just being social, old boy . . . I thought I owed you a round . . ."

"Cut the shit, will ya?"

He smiled. "Well . . . Since you put it like that . . . A little bird told me about an intimate little dinner up at the Palacio Queluz last night . . . A threesome, I understand. I thought you might like to comment. Off the record, of course."

"Why would I want to do that?"

He shrugged. "Because you have a soft spot for me?"

I laughed. "Try again, Harry."

"Just tell me what you want to hear, dear boy."

I paused, gave him a look. "You wouldn't know anyone who drives a late-model Buick with a broken windshield, would you?"

"Sorry, old man, but I'm hopeless when it comes to motorcars. They all look the same to me."

"Well, thanks, anyway," I said, heading outside, where Alberto was waiting.

"Hold on, Jack." Harry kept pace. "I can certainly look into it . . . Or perhaps there's something else I can offer . . . Perhaps we could come to some sort of financial arrangement . . ."

"How much?"

"Well . . . I don't know. What if we were to say—"

"A thousand dollars."

Harry looked startled. "Look here, old chap . . ."

"A thousand bucks to find out what your former king is up to. It'd be worth every penny, I promise you."

Harry looked me over, trying to decide if I was serious. "I'll, ah . . . I'll have to see what I can do," he said, and that was enough to clinch it for me.

"You know, Harry, up until a minute ago I bought the act."

"I'm not sure I follow you, Jack. What act is that?"

"The washed-up-newspaperman-at-sea-on-a-bottle-of-whiskey act."

"I'm not that good an actor," he laughed. "That's me, I'm afraid, for better or worse."

"Forget it, Harry." Alberto opened the back door for me, but Harry grabbed me before I could get in.

"Hold on," he said.

"What?"

"I think I can get the money . . . In fact, I'm sure I can . . ."

"Forget it."

"For Christ's sake, Jack, what—?"

"Look, Harry, I'm sympathetic. I hope you guys beat the shit out of the Nazis, but, in the end, it's your war, not mine."

"I'm just looking for a story."

"Sure you are . . . You can tell Stropford I had a very nice dinner with the duke, but, as much as I enjoyed it, I don't plan on seeing him again. I've got other things to do."

"What are you talking about, Jack?"

"Don't bother to deny it, Harry."

He paused and finally gave in with a shrug. "All right, then. Let's not play games. But this is important, Jack. Very important. If you could just—"

"If you ask me, you guys should forget about the Duke of Windsor and start worrying about Hitler."

"Yes, well, thanks for the advice, old chap, but forgive me if I say that you don't have a fucking clue what you're talking about."

"I'm sure you're right, Harry," I said, slipping into the backseat. "But that's because, like I said, it has nothing to do with me."

I pulled the door shut and we drove away, leaving Harry standing there on the sidewalk, in a substantial huff.

Popov was leaning against a patch of cracked and faded blue tiles that hadn't yet fallen off the exterior wall of Rua Esperança 66, a scruffy three-story building on the fringes of the Alfama. I told Alberto to pull the car up short, not wanting to attract any more attention than necessary. Popov tossed his cigarette aside and watched me as I made my way up the incline.

"Is she here?" I said, looking the building over.

"No, but not far."

"Lead the way."

He hesitated. "I, of course, have complete trust in you, but—"

"But not really?"

He shrugged and grinned nervously. "After I show you, maybe you'll think you don't need to pay."

"You're confusing my scruples with your lack of them," I said.

"Still . . ." he said

I reached for what was left of my bankroll. "Here's four hundred," I said, peeling them off. "With the hundred I gave you yesterday, that's half. I'll give you the other half when I see her." He shrugged and happily stuffed the bills away.

"Come," he said. "I take you."

The shops were closed for lunch, the streets more or less deserted. Popov took his time, leading us on a twisted route through a maze of cobbled lanes and fragrant alleyways. He kept glancing over at me, like he was building up to something.

"This woman . . ." he finally ventured. "Eva Lange . . ."

"What about her?"

"The interest is personal or—"

"It's private," I said.

"Sure, sure," he nodded. A woman hanging laundry out a second-story window watched us closely as we passed. "Lili Sterne . . ." he persisted. "She knew the girl in Berlin . . . ?"

"That's right."

"They were friends . . . ?"

"Like I said, Roman, it's—"

"Yes, private, I know. But I wonder . . . Why does a big star like she make such a big effort now to find her friend? Why not before?"

"What difference does it make?"

"Only curiosity," he mumbled.

"I wouldn't worry about it," I said. "You get your money and she gets her friend. Everybody's happy."

"I'm not so sure of this," he said uneasily.

"Why not?"

He stopped walking and looked up, across the narrow street. Following his gaze, I realized that I knew this place. I'd been here three days earlier, standing in the same spot in front of the same dreary facade of the Imperial Hotel, the place Eddie Grimes called home in his last sleazy days, where Eva Lange found him in a state of sweaty perversion on the night he fell into the jaws of hell. It took me a minute to get it. Then I realized why Lili wouldn't be happy— Popov wasn't looking at the hotel. He was looking at the building next to it.

"She's dead," I said, and he nodded. "I understand now why you wanted to be paid in advance."

"You don't pay the rest . . ." It was more of a statement than a question, but I answered anyway, just to be sure there wouldn't be any misunderstandings.

"No, I don't."

"You didn't say that she must be alive."

I wasn't interested in arguing the point, and he didn't really expect me to give him another five hundred for handing over a corpse. "How did she die?" I asked him.

"You can talk with Senhor Baptista. He expects you." Before I could object, Popov had slipped away, disappearing into an alleyway.

As I walked through the door of the funeral parlor, I felt sick to my stomach. Maybe it was the sweet perfumed air mixed with the bitter taste of formaldehyde that made me want to gag, but it didn't help knowing that I'd have to face Lili with the news.

"I wasn't sure that I'd see you again," she said, looking uncharacteristically chastened.

"Here I am."

She produced a half smile and opened the door to let me in. The room was a mess, stale from old smoke, and I wondered if Lili had been out at all in the thirty-six hours since we'd fought. It didn't look like it.

"Want a drink?" she said. "I promise not to throw it in your face." It was as close as Lili would get to an apology, and it was more than I'd expected.

"Believe it or not," I said, "it's not the first time that's happened to me."

"You must be doing something right." She passed me a scotch on the rocks and looked me straight in the eye. She knew why I was there.

"You found her . . ."

"Yes . . ."

"She's dead, isn't she?"

"Yes."

Lili didn't react at first. Nothing. She just stood there looking at me, stuck in the moment. She looked tired and alone and vulnerable. I wished there was something I could do for her, but Lili wasn't the type you could wrap up in your arms and make everything all right.

"Did you see her?" she said, the edge back in her voice.

"Yes."

"Are you certain it was Eva?"

"She was using her own passport."

Lili nodded and dropped onto the sofa.

"How?"

This was the tough part. I stalled and Lili gave me a look. "How did she die, Jack?"

"She, uh . . . She killed herself."

"What?"

"She killed herself."

Lili shook her head back and forth. "How?"

"She jumped . . . from a window."

"When?"

"Last night."

"Last night," she repeated in a whisper, then lowered her head, supporting it with her right hand as it massaged her brow. I was standing over her, wondering what I should do, when the phone rang.

I picked it up. "Yeah . . . ?"

"Capitan Catela would like to see Miss Sterne." It was the concierge.

"Is he here?"

"Standing in front of me."

"He'll have to come back," I said. "Miss Sterne is—"

"I'm afraid he is quite insistent, senhor."

I drew a deep breath. It didn't take Catela long to get here, I thought. I wondered how much Popov had made on that end.

"Send him up in ten minutes." I replaced the receiver and turned to Lili. "Catela's here," I said. She pulled herself off the sofa and found herself looking into a mirror.

"I need a new face," she said softly.

Standing in the hallway, hat in hand, commiseration plastered across his worried brow, Catela wasn't too happy to see me. He dropped the sad countenance and pushed his way in.

"Where is she?" he said curtly.

I offered him a drink, which earned me a sharp look.

"Please inform her that I am here."

"She'll be out in a minute . . . Scotch?"

He didn't try to hide his pique at finding me in the middle of his big scene. "I've come on official business."

"Well, I'm gonna have one," I said. Heading for the bar, I refilled my glass while Catela stood in the center of the room.

"Hello, Captain . . ."

Catela's face lit up as Lili swept in, once again the image of beauty and grace, in complete control of the room. It was a remarkable transformation.

"You should have given me some warning," she said, breezing past to retrieve a cigarette from the rosewood box that sat on the coffee table. "Instead of surprising me like this."

"I'm sorry, I . . ." His face fell back into mourning. "I'm afraid I have the unpleasant duty to inform you of some very unfortunate news . . . I have information regarding your friend . . ."

"You really must remember her name, Captain. It's Eva. Eva Lange."

"Yes, of course . . . I . . ."

Lili placed a cigarette between her lips. Catela reached for his lighter, but she turned to me.

"Give me a light, darling."

I lit her up and she swung back around on Catela.

"Jack's already told me that she's dead," she said, turning a sneer into a cold smile. Catela threw a look my way. He must've trusted Popov more than I did.

"But thank you for coming all this way to deliver the news," she continued. "I'm sure you must have more important things to occupy your time. Now, if you'll excuse me, I must make arrangements to leave Portugal . . . As soon as possible."

"Please accept my condolences," Catela whined. "I have come myself because I would like to consider you a friend and of course, as such, I am concerned of your feelings . . ."

"How very sensitive of you," Lili mocked.

"But there is another reason, as well," he confessed. "I . . . I'm afraid I must ask that you come with me . . ."

"For what purpose?" she said, taken aback.

"As you know, your friend . . . er, Eva Lange . . . was wanted for questioning in the murder of a diplomat at the German embassy. I'm afraid, therefore, that I must ask you to identify the body."

Lili froze.

"Is that really necessary?" I said, stepping forward.

Catela gave me a butt-out look and addressed his response to Lili. "You are the only person in Lisbon who knew her. If there was any way in which to avoid it, I assure you—"

"All right," Lili cut him off. "When?"

"If you please, I will take you with me now . . ."

"Jack will take me."

"I would prefer . . ."

"Thank you, Captain, but Jack will take me."

"Of course," he relented. "I can meet you there in one hour."

"As you wish," Lili said, dismissing him with a puff of smoke. Catela performed an awkward bow and backed his way out the door.

"Bastard . . ." she snarled as the door closed. I was sure he heard it, and I was even more sure that Lili meant him to.

• • •

We were two hours late. Lili made sure of that by ordering room service and sending it back twice—once because the steak was undercooked and then because it was overseasoned, which was a pretty good trick on her part because she didn't even pretend to taste it. I nibbled around the edges and flipped through magazines while she soaked in the bath to the mournful sounds of Billie Holiday on the Electrola. When Lili finally reappeared she was stunning in black from head to toe.

It was a long, silent drive into Lisbon. Lili stared out the window at the gathering dusk, lost in her past, I presumed, while I mulled my future. There wasn't much to think about, really. I was free to go anywhere and do anything I wanted, but I had no real desires on either score. Hollywood had come to an end, that was clear, and it wasn't because I was afraid of Charlie Wexler, either. I figured that I'd fallen off enough horses for one lifetime, and it was time to move on. But where? Damned if I knew. Hell, I thought, I hadn't planned anything in the first twenty-five years of my life, why start now? The future would find me soon enough.

"She wouldn't have . . ." Lili whispered.

"What?"

She turned to face me.

"She wouldn't have jumped. Eva would never do that."

Senhor Baptista and his parlor had undergone a makeover, too. A small, nervous man in his midfifties with jet-black hair forming a perimeter around a shiny bald top, he'd changed from his day wear into a trim black suit and tie with a white carnation carefully displayed in the lapel. The previously drab room, which Eva had shared with four other unfortunate souls when I first saw her, was all hers now and decked out with an arrangement of fresh white orchids and a couple of dozen candles. Her pine box had been replaced with a polished oak casket lined with white satin.

Lili betrayed no emotion as her eyes fixed firmly on her dead friend's face. Baptista had used all his talent—along with a fair amount of lipstick and rouge—to put some life back into the poor girl, but his efforts had produced the opposite effect. She was like a porcelain doll, with features painted on cold, hard glass, and thick auburn-colored hair that looked dull and brittle. It was hard to imagine this lifeless form, cold and empty, as the spirited young girl whose picture had been taken in a rowboat on a sunny, summer afternoon fifteen years earlier.

Lili approached the body. As she stood there, head bowed, gazing onto the casket, time seemed to stand still. Baptista lowered his head, too, and folded his hands over in prayer, but he kept glancing up at Lili, unable to keep his eyes off the famous actress. Catela simply watched. After some time, Lili pulled her veil back, leaned forward, and kissed the girl's forehead. When she turned toward us her eyes glistened in the candlelight, and a tear fell across her cheek.

"Yes," she said softly. "This is Eva Lange."

"I extend my most heartfelt condolences," Catela said, stepping forward. He tried to take her hand, but she pulled away, meeting his plaintive gaze with a sharp, penetrating look. You could sense the venom rising inside her and for a moment I thought it would spill out in a blistering rage, releasing all the bitter contempt and worldly scorn that she kept bottled up behind her matinee idol smile. But it didn't come. Instead, Lili drew a long breath and, in a little-girl-like gesture, wiped the tear off her cheek.

"She deserved better," she said. "I only wish . . ." She trailed off, unwilling to reveal a quivering voice.

"You must not blame yourself," Catela said gently. "It is a sad result of the times, I'm afraid." He seemed genuinely moved by Lili's tears. She nodded and offered her hand now, which he held tightly.

"If there is anything I can do . . ." he said. "Anything at all . . ."

"Thank you," she said. "It's very kind of you." She dabbed her eyes with a silk kerchief. "Please accept my apologies if I was harsh with you earlier . . . It was . . ."

"There is no need to explain." He bowed chivalrously and kissed her hand. "I am forever your servant."

She nodded and looked to me. I took her by the arm and escorted her to the car, which was waiting outside.

"I'll look into the next passage to New York," I said once we'd put some distance between us and the funeral parlor.

"Not yet," she said as she lifted her veil and provided me with an impish smile. "How was I?"

"What . . .?"

"Do you think I overdid it?"

"Overdid it?"

"I was going to do angry, but my instincts took over and led me into heartbroken. I was worried that the tears would be too much, but I think it was quite effective, don't you?" She leaned back and smiled. "Yes, I was good. I was very good."

"Lili . . .?"

"But damn it, Jack!"

"What?"

"The best performance of my life and there's not a camera within miles! That should have been my Oscar!"

"Lili . . . Are you saying . . .?"

She handed me her purse. "Light me a cigarette, will you, darling?" I removed the pack of Rothmans, lit one up and gave it to her.

"Let me get this straight," I said. "Are you saying that that woman—"

"I've never seen her before in my life."

I fell back into my seat, grinned, and shook my head. "I'll be damned," I chuckled. Lili was right. It was an Oscar-winning performance. I'd certainly gone for it. Hell, we'd all gone for it. Hook, line, and melodramatic sinker.

I told Alberto to stop the car.

Senhor Baptista wasn't expecting company. The front door was locked with the shades drawn, so I slipped down the back alley and in through an open window. I found the undertaker, along with his doltish assistant, in the middle of moving the Eva stand-in (so to speak) from her temporary eternal resting place back into the more modest accommodation of a pine box. Baptista gasped when he saw me and threw his arms up, letting his end of the poor lady hit the floor with a *thud*. The auburn wig tumbled across the tiles, revealing the impostor's short black hair.

"Senhor . . .!"

I stepped into the room and picked up the wig. "I guess she won't need this anymore," I said. The assistant was dumbstruck, standing there with a empty look on his face, hanging on to the dead lady's thighs while the top half lay splayed out across the floor. It would've looked risqué if she hadn't been so dead.

"Please, senhor . . ." Baptista retreated toward the wall as I moved toward him. "I can to explain . . ." He was starting to sweat.

"Don't you think you'd better pick her up first?" I said.

"*Sim, Sim* . . .yes, of course, senhor . . ." He gingerly moved forward and, after some fumbling around, was able to slip his hands under the lady's armpits and gather her up off the floor. He looked to me for further instructions.

"Put her away," I said.

He nodded, passed the instruction on to the dolt, and they carried her over to the waiting box. Baptista was grunting and sweating so badly now that the dye in his hair was starting to run down his forehead. Pitiful.

Once they'd finally dropped her into the coffin, Baptista wiped his brow with a silk handkerchief, staining it black, then turned to the dolt and mumbled something. I didn't get the specifics, but I understood enough to know that it wouldn't be a good idea to let the guy disappear, so I grabbed him by the back of the shirt as he tried to pass and yanked him back into the room. His legs flew out from under him and he fell into a heap of gangling knees and elbows.

Baptista tugged on his collar, cleared his throat, and let out a nervous chuckle. "How may I be helpful, senhor?"

"Who was she?" I said, looking over at the anonymous corpse.

"Er . . . No one in particular . . . Just a lady . . ." He flinched at the sudden movement of my arm coming toward him. I was just offering him the wig, which he accepted once he realized that he wasn't under attack.

"You did a good job," I said. "Fooled me, anyway." He accepted the compliment with a nervous smile. "You must've been well paid, to risk lying to the Guarda Nationale . . . What do you think would happen to you if Captain Catela found out?"

"Oh, senhor . . . That would be—"

"Were you paid in advance?" If they'd made arrangements to meet afterward, there was still a chance I could get my hands on the weasel. But Popov had covered that base.

"*Sim,* senhor . . . In advance."

My first instinct, after putting Lili in a taxi back to the hotel, had been to go after the little shit, but I told Alberto to change course when I realized it was pointless, he'd be long gone. You had to give the guy credit—the idea of using a corpse to pose as Eva showed a creative flair that I couldn't help admiring, in spite of wanting to wring his scrawny little neck. It was a simple enough ruse. All he needed was a passport and a cooperative mortician—which was why I'd decided to drop in on Baptista.

"Let me see her passport," I said.

I'd checked it out the first time, but I wanted to take a closer look. A fake passport wouldn't have presented a problem for Popov—the forgery business was booming in Lisbon and he certainly would've had his greedy fingers in that pie—but if it was a phony, it was a damn good one. It was one thing to be fooled by a heavily made-up corpse lit by a few candles, but the photo I'd seen sure as hell looked like the girl Lili had photographed in a boat fifteen years earlier. If the passport was for real, the conclusion was inevitable—Popov had actually found Eva and I'd been outbid by Ritter. If that was true, she would already be on a train to Berlin, or worse.

"Senhor?" Baptista looked perplexed.

"The passport."

"I'm sorry, senhor," he trembled. "I . . . I . . . I . . ."

He got stuck as I moved closer and placed a helpful hand on his shoulder. I hadn't had to strong-arm anyone for quite a few years, but Senhor Baptista made it easy, almost fainting at the mere suggestion of physical coercion.

"I . . . I . . . I . . ." he continued.

"Take a deep breath," I said. He took my advice and it settled his nerves enough to allow him to continue.

"I no longer have the passport, senhor."

"You no longer have it?"

"Yes, senhor . . . I mean, no, senhor . . . I . . . I . . . I no longer have it, senhor."

"You're not lying to me, are you?"

"I promise you . . ."

"You lied before."

"Yes, senhor . . ."

"So why should I believe you now?"

"I lied before . . . But not now."

I was pretty sure that he was telling the truth. Catela would've taken Eva's passport in order to hand it over to Major Ritter, but I wanted to be positive, and besides, the undertaker deserved to be roughed up, just a little. I grabbed his wrist, spun him around, and pulled him into an easy half nelson.

"Please, senhor!" he screamed. "I tell you the truth!"

"Are you sure?" I tightened the grip.

"*Sim, Sim!* . . . I give passport to Senhor Popov! . . . Please! I can give to you money, senhor! Please, it hurts! Aiiee!"

I released him. "What did you say?"

He gave me a pained look and nursed his arm. "I say I give you money."

"Not that . . ."

"Senhor?" He brightened.

"You said that you gave the passport to Popov."

"*Sim,* senhor . . ."

"Why would you do that?"

Baptista shrugged. "Is part of the agreement."

"I don't follow," I said. "Didn't Popov give you Eva Lange's passport?"

"*Sim* . . . Yes."

"Then you gave it back to him?"

"No, senhor. Capitão Catela takes this passport."

"Catela took it?"

"Yes."

"Then why did you say you gave it to Popov?"

Baptista furrowed his brow. He was as confused as I was. "I give to Captain Catela the passport of Eva Lange," he explained. "I give to Senhor Popov the other passport. The one of this dead lady . . ." He gestured toward the woman in the coffin.

"Popov took *her* passport?"

"Yes, senhor . . . It has been most important to him to have this."

• • •

I was feeling upbeat as I headed out into the night air to rejoin Alberto. It was clear now that Eva was still alive, and that Ritter didn't have her. There was even a reasonable chance that, with the right kind of help, I could get my hands on her before she could make her exit. I was so buoyant, in fact, that I almost missed the Buick sport coupe with a cracked windshield that was parked a bit further up the road. On first glance, the car looked empty, but upon closer inspection, I could see that my would-be killer was hunkered down behind the wheel. Waiting until I passed, no doubt, so he could step out and shoot me in the back.

I ducked into the nearest doorway, which landed me in a gloomy little tavern called Paraiso. The barman, who looked like he hadn't seen daylight in a while, gave me the once-over as I stepped up to the counter and ordered a bourbon. It was a dank, cheerless place, empty but for me and my sullen host. The wall calendar was stuck on March 1934.

I was sipping my drink and considering my options when the answer walked out of the back room, looking for a fresh bottle of whiskey. He was big and ugly, and had a tattoo of a giant python running up one arm, across his shoulders, and down the other arm. He gave me a look—like the one you'd give a slug while you were deciding whether or not it was worth stepping on—then he took possession of the booze and disappeared back to where he came from. I followed.

The snake man was just sitting back down at a table, where a serious game of cards was in progress. He and his fellow players—three equally ugly hulks—wouldn't have looked out of place unloading cargo on the Jersey docks, so I approached with caution.

"Boa tarde," I said, and got a round of grim looks in return. I decided to get right to the point. "Anybody speak English?"

The snake man, who had started dealing the hand, placed the deck back down on the table, lifted his head, and narrowed his eyes at me. I thought he was about to stand up again, so I quickly reached into my pocket, removed a hundred-dollar bill, and tossed it into the ante. The snake man gave me a second look, then reached across the table to pick it up, giving it a thorough inspection before returning his gaze to me.

"I speak English," he rasped.

"Good!" I smiled. "Ever hear the expression *easy money?*"

The grayish piece of soap that sat on the side of the sink wasn't too inviting, so I made do with a splash of cold water on my face. The greasy hand towel wasn't very appealing, either, so I dried off on my sleeve and headed back downstairs, arriving just in time to see my stalker being airlifted onto a bar stool by my newly hired employees. A couple of them held him in place while Ramiro—which turned out to be the snake man's name—patted him down and came up with a .38 Smith & Wesson, which he handed over to me.

I couldn't help laughing when I got a look at the guy—he was a two-bit hood, straight out of central casting. The only thing missing was the toothpick.

"What's the big joke?" he said. Christ, he *was* out of central casting. Then the penny dropped . . . Of course!

"The joke is that with all the money in the world, and with all that power, you're the best that Charlie Wexler could come up with."

"Charlie who?" He sneered. I shook my head and turned my attention to the .38.

"You know," I said. "A pistol like this is no good from a distance. You'd have to get pretty lucky to hit somebody three stories up."

"I got no idea what you're talkin' about."

"You have to get in close. The closer the better." I pushed the barrel up against his nose and cocked the hammer. "Like this."

"Hey, listen, pal . . . I . . . I'm just doin' a job. This is between you and Wexler."

He was right, but I enjoyed watching him sweat a little. Once he looked sufficiently chastened, I uncocked the hammer and removed the gun from his nostril. "I guess I should consider myself lucky that

Wexler doesn't know the difference between a real killer and a dime-store hood. What's your name?"

"Joe."

"Joe what?"

"Joe Bolognese."

I laughed. "Is that your real name? Joe Bolognese?"

"What about it?"

"Nothing. Nothing at all. It's perfect."

I asked for a phone, which the barman produced from under the counter. Bolognese started to look worried when I told him I was going to talk to my friend, the deputy chief of the National Police.

"What're you gonna do?" he said.

"It's not what I'm gonna do, Joe, it's what you're gonna do. I thought two years—no, on second thought, let's make it three. One for every time you tried to kill me. And I wouldn't count on time off for good behavior. They don't go in for that sort of thing around here. In fact, they might just forget all about you in there. It's not like home, you know, where they keep track."

Bolognese looked a bit sick to the stomach as the party broke up. The boys decided they'd call it a night when they heard that Catela's men were on their way, so I left the barman holding the gun on Joe and said my good-byes.

Climbing the hill to meet Alberto, I composed the wire that I decided to send off to Wexler the next day, explaining why he hadn't heard back from his hit man. I thought I'd end the telegram by asking him to convey my very warmest regards to the missus.

I found Brewster in a dark corner of an out-of-the-way bistro, sharing a table with a stunningly attractive blonde—a woman of a certain age who sparkled with diamonds from every angle.

"Hiya, Dick," I said, sliding onto the banquette beside her.

"Teller . . . ?" He almost dropped his fork. "What the hell . . . ?! What are you doing here?" He was more amused than angry, which was a pleasant surprise. The lady, on the other hand, was a long way from amused.

"Some coincidence, huh?" I turned to her and smiled, but the icy response told me not to bother. Brewster was starting to look a little less jolly himself.

"I'm kind of busy at the moment, Jack, in case you didn't notice."

"As a matter of fact, I did notice," I said. "Aren't you going to introduce me?"

"She doesn't speak English."

"That's convenient," I said.

"What's that supposed to mean?"

"It means that I can tell you to get rid of her without hurting her feelings."

Brewster squinted across the table at me. "How the hell did you find me?"

"Your butler."

"Luiz?"

"I didn't get his name."

"I'll have to have a word with him."

I shrugged. "He tried to tell me that he didn't know where you were, but it was obvious that he did."

"What did you do?"

"I scared him a little, that's all. Nothing serious."

"You really take the cake, Teller, you know that."

"So I've heard."

"What do you want?"

"Your country needs you."

"My country will have to wait until tomorrow morning, in my office."

"Your country needs you *now*, Dick."

"Get the hell out of here, Teller," he said. I thought I noticed a hint of a smile on the ice queen.

"You mean that?"

"From the bottom of my heart."

"Okay," I said, getting to my feet. "I can take a hint. It's just that you seemed so eager to help, that's all. Can't say I blame you, I guess. I'm sure it'll be worth it." I looked the lady over. She didn't mind, but Brewster did.

"Well, thanks for stopping by," he said.

"Sure. And I wouldn't worry. You can always get a job as a banker . . . or in the insurance business. It can't be as boring as it sounds."

He gave me a long, desolate look. "Can't it wait?"

"Would I be here if it could?"

He sighed. "What do you want?"

"Do you have a car?"

"My driver will pick us up in an hour."

"You'll have to call her a taxi, then."

"Jack . . ." He shook his head, tossed his napkin onto the table, and excused himself in French. I followed him into the restaurant's small lobby.

"She's a Hapsburg," he whispered loudly.

"No shit?" I said. "A Hapsburg?"

"That's right. And Hapsburgs don't take taxis."

I laughed.

"I'm serious, Jack."

"Look, Dick . . . I don't care if you put her in a goddamned golden carriage drawn by six white stallions. Just get rid of her."

He wanted to punch me, but he swallowed his pride. "This better be damn good. I've been working on her for two months."

A few minutes later, Brewster slid into the backseat and offered me a smoke. I already had one going. "So what the hell's so goddamned urgent?" he said.

"I need to find someone."

"Sure, Eva Lange. So what else is new?" He lit himself up.

"I'm looking for somebody else now."

"What happened with Eva?"

"She's dead," I said. "At least officially."

He blew a cloud of smoke in my direction. "Just tell me what you want, Jack."

I gave him the bare bones of the story, about Popov's ruse with the dead girl and Lili's quick-thinking performance that fooled Catela. I also told him that I thought it had been set up to get the heat off Eva for Kleinmann's murder.

"Okay," he said. "So she's off the hook. What's the big emergency?"

"She'll try to leave Lisbon before anyone can figure it out," I said.

He shrugged. "Maybe. But what makes you think you can find her now when you couldn't before?"

"I know what I'm looking for now."

"And that is . . .?"

"Lisa Foquet."

"Who the hell is she?"

"The lady at the funeral parlor."

"What lady?"

"The dead lady," I said. "Thirty-two years old, medium height, short, dark hair, carrying a Belgian passport."

Brewster thought about it for a moment. "You think Eva Lange is going to use it?"

"So you're not just a pretty face, after all."

He shrugged it off. "It doesn't make sense."

"What?"

"Popov had two good buyers for Eva—you and Ritter. Why would he go out of his way to help her escape?"

It was my turn to shrug. "I don't care about the why. What I need is the when and the where." Brewster impatiently flicked an ash onto the floor. "I need passenger lists. Ships, planes, anything that's leaving the country. Can you manage that?"

"Sure. First thing tomorrow."

"Not good enough."

"Just what the hell did you think I could do at"—he checked his watch—"nine forty-five on a Wednesday night?"

"Make some calls."

"Make some calls? At this hour?" He snickered. "It doesn't work like that, Jack."

Strangely enough, I didn't really dislike Brewster, but I was moving in that direction. "Let me explain it to you again, Dick," I said, trying to keep cool. "I'm handing you a golden opportunity here. A once-in-a-lifetime offer."

"Knock it off, Jack . . ."

"I'm serious. This is your chance to get noticed by the top guy. How often does an opportunity like that come along? Give me a couple hours tonight and you can save years of kissing ass and scheming your way up the ladder. Come on, Dick, be smart. Once you're on top, you can fuck all the princesses you want." I let it sink in for a minute. "So how about it? You can either sit here all night, listing the reasons why there's nothing you can do, or you can use your brain and make something happen."

There was a fairly long silence before Brewster cleared his throat and said, "There is one guy I could call."

I leaned against the back of the car and peered into the darkness. There wasn't much to see. The black sedan carrying Jesós Chaves, a fat detective in Catela's Guarda Nationale, had pulled up some time ago. I'd watched from my perch above the docks as he and the two uniformed cops he'd brought along approached Brewster, who'd been waiting alone on the quay. After a short conference, they'd all boarded the SS *Avoceta*, whose departure had already been delayed for an hour.

It hadn't been easy—or cheap—to find Detective Chaves. A sergeant at Guarda headquarters had been willing to provide his home address in return for twenty bucks. Mrs. Chaves directed us to the local bar for five, and the bartender there soaked us for ten just to bring the detective's brother, Jorge, into the discussion. Jorge made out with fifty bucks for taking us to an apartment around the corner, where we finally found our man sharing a bathtub with his triple-D-cup mistress. It took a hundred to convince him that it was worth drying off and heading into the office to check the passenger lists. We'd agreed that if he found Lisa Foquet on one of them, he'd phone Brewster at his apartment.

After two whiskey sours, served by the wary Luiz, the phone rang. Lisa Foquet was on a list all right, but, of course, she wouldn't come cheap. The *Avoceta* was scheduled to sail for Liverpool in roughly twenty minutes and Chaves felt that stopping her was worth five hundred. I only had two bills left on my roll, which was scoffed at, but Brewster got him to accept three as a take-it-or-leave-it proposition, and donated the extra hundred himself. Brewster was all right, in the end.

I checked my watch—almost midnight. My name was too bound up with Eva Lange's to tag along, so I'd decided it would be better to stay in the background, a decision I was starting to regret. They'd been on board the better part of forty minutes. What the hell was taking so goddamn long? She was in a first-class cabin. All they had to do was knock on the door, grab her, and bring her ashore. Five minutes, in and out. What could go wrong?

Someone called out. A man's voice, deep and resounding, echoing around the wharf. Then all hell broke loose—the ship's engine burst forth with the rumbling explosion of vibrating metal, heavy chains scraping against the ship's hull, men yelling back and forth across the darkness . . .

I took a step forward, straining to see any movement. Nothing at first, but then I saw them, coming down the ramp. Three, four men and—yes, another silhouette, a woman's figure, hidden behind one of the larger figures. As they stepped onto the concrete berth and passed under a dim lamp, I got my first shadowy look at her. I couldn't make out much more than the short black hair of her disguise, but there was something about the way she walked—the way she held herself—that made me know it was Eva. There was a grace about her that just fit, though I couldn't say why.

I thought she looked up at me, but they were still a good hundred yards away and I was standing in total darkness. She couldn't have known that I was waiting there.

At fifty yards, the group stopped moving and one of the uniformed cops removed a set of cuffs from Eva's wrist. Chaves shook Brewster's hand, then followed his men back to the coupe to be driven away, a much richer man than he'd started the evening. Brewster said something to Eva, then took her arm and started walking her toward me.

For some inexplicable reason my heart started beating like crazy. It was totally unexpected and the closer she got the harder it beat. I couldn't control it. When she got close enough that I could see her face, I realized she was looking straight at me. Or maybe straight through me was more like it. Her expression said everything about her. Tenacious, compassionate, smart, combative, playful . . . it was all there, all in that one look.

"Meet Lisa Foquet," Brewster said as he set her in front of me. I wasn't sure that I could get any words out, so I just stood there looking at her. She returned the gaze for a moment, soft brown eyes meeting mine head-on in the darkness. Then she allowed a hint of a smile to cross her lips.

"You almost let me get away," she said in a rich, warm, gently mocking voice.

Once I got my heart out of my mouth, I turned to Brewster and grumbled, "What took you so damned long?"

"The ship's captain," he shrugged. "Said we couldn't take her without paperwork."

"They took me anyway," Eva chafed.

"So I see." I met her implacable gaze again. It was more than a bit unsettling. I'd never felt tongue-tied or awkward with a woman before, and I didn't much care for the feeling.

"I'm Jack Teller," I managed.

"Yes, I know who you are," she said in a refined English accent. "I'd like to say what a pleasure it is to meet you, but I'd be lying."

"Do you know why I've been looking for you?"

"Yes," she said simply. "I do."

"Lili would like to help you."

Eva cocked her head and looked at me sideways. "To do what?"

"You'll have to talk to her about that."

"Ah . . . You're just doing your job."

"Something like that."

"Well, then, I suppose congratulations are in order. You've bagged your quarry."

I wasn't sure if she was angry or teasing. Maybe both. I never could figure out how to read Eva—there was too much going on. And as soon as you thought you had her pegged, she'd change direction on you.

"Are we done here?" Brewster chimed in. "Because, as interesting as this is—"

"We'll drop you off," I said, opening the car door for Eva.

"Where are we going?" she said, standing firm.

"Don't worry—"

"Easy for you to say! The Gestapo isn't looking for you!"

"Everyone thinks you're dead."

"For the moment they do."

She was right, of course. The body swap had been an effective deception, but there were too many ways for the story to fall apart to be sanguine about it. Popov might get talkative, Baptista could run scared, or our fat detective might even put two and two together. Eva had planned her exit very well and I had just wrenched her back into the very danger that we were supposed to be saving her from. No wonder she wasn't gushing with gratitude.

The ship's horn blew off a parting shot. A look of quiet distress flashed across Eva's face as she watched her escape vessel pull away, but she didn't dwell on it. Swinging quickly back around on me, she gave me a hard, measured look, then calmly slipped into the backseat.

"I hope you know what you're doing," she said.

W e dropped Brewster off and continued on in silence, leaving the city and driving west, into the dark, pine-scented mountains. I was aware of Eva's soft breathing beside me and I sensed her staring out the window into the void, but she didn't stir until the car pulled onto the bumpy dirt track that led to the farm. It was pitch-black, but I remembered the layout from our visit the previous day. The road curved around to the right, along a steep ridge that opened onto a clearing where the small stone-and-tile house stood overlooking a long, green valley. It had occurred to me while I'd been waiting at the dock that Alberto's cousin's place would be the perfect spot to stow Eva for a few days. Aside from a goat, a donkey, and a couple of pigs, no one would be the wiser.

Alberto was barreling along when, out of the blue, he hit the brakes. The car swerved left and I went right, bouncing my forehead off something hard. It hurt like hell and I came up cursing.

"Jesus Christ!" I yelped, which was met by heartfelt laughter from Eva.

"You think that's funny?" I snapped.

"Don't you?"

"No, as a matter of fact, I don't!"

"You don't have much of a sense of humor, then."

I was deciding how to respond when my vision came back into focus and I saw what she was laughing at. Standing in front of the car, bathed in our headlights, was a man pointing a two-gauge shotgun at us. The funny part was that, aside from a pair of unlaced black dress shoes, he was buck naked. I recognized him as Alberto's cousin Fabio. He took a step toward the car and squinted into the light.

"Quem é?!" he demanded.

"Não dispare!" Alberto cried out from his position on the floor below the dashboard. "Don't shoot! . . . *É o teu primo, Alberto!"*

Fabio lowered the weapon. *"Alberto? . . . Que está fazendo aqui nesta hora?"*

Alberto grabbed the steering wheel and pulled himself back onto his seat as Fabio's face appeared in the driver's-side window. "I bring my friends to stay with you," he said, gesturing toward us.

"Olá." Eva smiled.

"*Olá,* senhora," Fabio politely replied.

"Desculpe que fizemos esta surpresa," she said, in what sounded to me like reasonable Portuguese.

"Nada, senhora. É o meu prazer."

Fabio looked over at me and smiled with recognition. "Ah, good evening, senhor!" he said. I was about to respond, but before I could get the words out, a quizzical look came over him.

"Why is this blood all across your face?" he said.

Fabio's agreeable wife, Rosalina, was reticent about dousing my injury with a painful dose of iodine, but Eva had no such qualms. In fact, she seemed to enjoy watching me squirm as she administered the caustic torture.

"It's just a scratch," she reassured me as she deftly wrapped my head with a strip of old linen. Fabio had quickly disappeared back to bed (never mentioning his state of undress) while Rosalina provided Eva with a cup of tea and medical supplies, then said good night, too. Alberto was fast asleep in the next room.

Eva had removed the black Lisa Foquet wig, revealing dark, chestnut hair that swept past her cheek with a stylish kink before falling lightly onto her shoulders. Her face, lit by a single candle on the kitchen table, where my treatment was taking place, had changed surprisingly little in the fifteen years since the boat photo. More defined, perhaps. Certainly less naive. She leaned forward to pin the bandage, close enough that I could feel her breath on my face and smell the lilac-scented soap she'd used to wash that morning. The top two buttons on her shirt were undone and I could see the white line of her bra pressing against her breast.

"How does that feel?" she said.

"I guess I'll live."

"You're lucky you have such a hard head." She stepped back to review her work. "It's a bit overdone, but at least you won't bleed all over Rosa's pillow."

"That's a relief."

She rolled the remainder of the towel into a ball, placed it and the scissors she'd been using onto the table, then sat down beside me. "I don't suppose you told them how much trouble they'll be in if I'm found here."

"We'll have to make sure that doesn't happen," I said. She nodded, but I wasn't sure she'd been listening.

"You should have let me go, you know."

"Lili wants to—"

"Save me?" She gave me a dubious look. "I'd have been safe in England."

"You probably said that about Amsterdam and Paris."

A delicate crease appeared in her brow. "I haven't heard from Lili in thirteen years. Why now?"

"You can ask her tomorrow," I said. "Alberto will have her here first thing in the morning."

"I will ask her," she said. Then, cocking her head, she gave me a coquettish look and served up a mischievous smile. "I suppose that makes me your prisoner tonight . . . Would you like to tie me up?"

I opened my mouth to say something, but nothing came out. Eva threw her head back and laughed, a full, throaty, honest laugh, and it made me smile, too.

"Well, if I have to be someone's prisoner, I suppose I'd just as soon be yours. But I'm too tired to be tied up tonight." She got to her feet, placed a hand on my shoulder, leaned over, and kissed me on the cheek. "Pleasant dreams," she said, then she picked up the candle, smiled sweetly, and swept out of the room, leaving me in the dark.

She was playing me. I knew she was playing me. Of course she was. And she was doing a damn good job of it, too. Why else would I be sitting there with an aching head and a silly grin plastered across my face? I got up, stumbled into the next room, and curled up on a bed of ceramic tiles, where I eventually drifted off to the melodic strains of Alberto snoring like a pig.

• • •

I sat up with a start, thinking that someone was coming toward me, but there was no one there. Just Alberto, mumbling something unintelligible. I wasn't even sure if I'd been asleep or awake. Probably somewhere in between. My head was throbbing, but it was more than that and the hard floor that kept me turning over. It was Eva.

Women were never far from my mind, and they'd had various effects on me, never predictable. Glamorous movie stars had left me stone cold, while a well-placed smile from the Sunday-school teacher in Davenport, Iowa, had once given me a new sense of religion. I sat through a month of very long Sundays before I finally snapped out of it.

But my reaction to Eva was a new one. I was pent up, that's for sure—it had been over two weeks since my last encounter with Mrs. Wexler—but there was more to it than that. Hell, I hadn't even set eyes on Eva before I started going loopy. And what I really wanted—what kept going through my mind as I lay there not sleeping—was to kiss her. That's all. Just a kiss. Not a hard, passionate, give-me-everything-you-got kiss, either. Just a soft, brush-against-the-lips kind of kiss. Strange. Not my usual brand of fantasy. Clearly, I wasn't thinking straight.

I couldn't shake the image of her eyes. The way they looked at you, thoughtful, wary, self-assured, but with tenderness and, I thought, some sadness, too. And the lovely curl of her upper lip when she—

I was smiling again. That would have to stop. There were too many questions hanging over Eva Lange to wade into those waters, let alone to go off the deep end.

Questions like—*Who the hell is she?*

An artist escaping the repression of Nazi Germany, or a loyal party member dispatched to prepare for the Reich's imminent invasion and occupation of England? Was she no more than a talented musician who found herself in the wrong place at the wrong time, or a cold-blooded killer who shot Eddie Grimes twice in the heart, then pushed his car off a cliff? And what about Hans Kleinmann? Had she been mistress to the murdered head of German intelligence in Lisbon? Had she been working for him? Or had she been playing him, too? Playing him right up to the moment that she put a bullet between his eyes. The only thing I knew for sure was that, whoever she was, and whatever she was, Eva Lange wasn't a lady that you'd want to underestimate.

I realized that I wasn't smiling anymore.

The sound of a car approaching roused me from a deep sleep. I opened my eyes and was met with bright, midmorning sunlight streaming in through the open front door. I poked my head out just in time to see Alberto pull up in front of the house. He leapt out from behind the wheel and raced around to open the passenger door, but Lili didn't wait. Dressed in tan slacks, an emerald-green scarf tied over her head, and oversize sunglasses to hide her face, she stepped onto the dusty track and stood there, looking nervous and out of place.

I saw Eva before she did. Standing in a field away from the house, she'd been feeding carrots to a donkey. She didn't move at first, covertly watching the arrival from a distance for as long as she could. It wasn't until Lili started to turn in her direction that Eva fixed a smile to her face and began striding toward the car.

Lili froze. I don't think she was even breathing as she watched Eva glide through the long grass, sunlight striking her gracile form, a smile radiating out to greet her long-lost friend. When she was within a few feet of the car, Eva stopped. The two women shared a long look that seemed to say whatever it was that needed to be said, then Eva opened her arms and accepted Lili into a close embrace. They stayed that way for a very long time—lost, motionless, holding firmly on to each other.

"We've heard all sorts of stories about you."
Lili smiled nervously and reached into her bag, fishing for a

fresh pack of cigarettes. She'd been chain-smoking all through lunch, which had been served in the shade of a big oak tree at the edge of the mountain. The view was spectacular, across a lush river valley that wound its way down to the sea about four miles away, but I'd been watching the two women circle each other, playing with childhood memories while carefully avoiding anything that might shed light on all the questions that hung in the air. Now, finally, Lili seemed ready to broach the subject.

"What did you hear?" Eva inquired with an easy smile.

"A lot of nonsense, really." Lili waved it off as insignificant. "I refused to believe a word of it."

"Some of it might be true."

Lili gave her a look but softened quickly. "It doesn't matter," she said, reaching across the table for Eva's hand. "All that's over. The only thing that matters now is that I've found you . . . We're together again."

"It's lovely to see you, Lili." Eva squeezed Lili's hand, but only so she could withdraw hers. Lili covered by putting a cigarette between her lips.

"Jack will arrange passage to New York as soon as possible," she said, getting down to business. "We'll spend a few days there—you'll adore New York—then on to Los Angeles. You'll stay with me, of course. For heaven's sake, I have twelve bedrooms, eleven of them empty! . . ."

Eva looked to me, but I was staying out of it.

"I know," Lili continued as I lit her up. "You're thinking, Hollywood, how dreadful! But there's more to it than you might think. There are even signs of culture starting to take hold. Do you remember Bruno Walter? Of course, you do. Director of the Städtische Opera until he left Berlin, two years ago. That's when I should have got you out, but there's no point in worrying about that now. Well, he'll be conducting the Philharmonic this season. I know him quite well. We'll give him lunch as soon as we get back so he can meet you. I'm sure he'll be delighted—"

"Lili . . ." Eva moaned.

It stopped her cold. She must have known that she'd gone too far. "Yes, darling?"

"I know that you want to help, and I appreciate it, really, I do, but I won't be going with you. I can't . . ."

"Of course you can." Lili flicked an ash onto her plate. "You can if you want to."

"There are things I have to do here."

"Eva . . . darling . . ." Lili tried a lighthearted laugh, but it fell flat. "Be sensible. There's no reason for you to stay here. It's—"

"You shouldn't have come," Eva said flatly. "I don't know why you did." I could see that she was struggling to keep her emotions in check. Lili leaned forward and spoke in a whisper, the way a mother would speak to a child.

"I want to help you, darling. I want to help you get away from all this . . . this insanity."

"You don't belong here."

"For God's sake, Eva! Who does?!"

"I do."

Lili hesitated, frustrated with Eva's obstinance, unsure what to say next, but unwilling to give up. "You need time. Time to think it over. It's all very sudden, I know, but—"

"Stop it!"

Eva exploded onto to her feet, causing Lili to recoil. She was frozen, unable to so much as blink. Eva stood her ground for a moment, then exhaled, her anger dissipating.

"Go back to Hollywood, Lili. Please. You can indulge your fantasies there. There's no place for it here."

Then she turned and walked away, without looking back. Lili just sat there, in shock, unable to move. She'd exposed her dream, laid it out on the table in a moment of unguarded enthusiasm, and in an instant, it was gone, evaporated. She had nothing to hold on to now, no ridiculous fantasy to shield her from that heartless enemy, reality. I felt sorry for her. She looked sad and defeated and, suddenly, so much smaller.

I found Eva lying in the tall grass on the other side of the farm-house, hands behind her head. She sensed me standing over her, and opened one eye.

"I was pretty tough on her, wasn't I?"

"She got the message." I crouched down beside her, and Eva met me halfway by propping herself up on one elbow. She picked a blade of grass and absentmindedly stripped the stalk as she spoke.

"I didn't want to leave any ambiguity." She looked me in the eye. "I don't want to be saved, Jack. I intend to fight this war, in whatever way I can."

"I understand."

"Do you?"

I shrugged. "Probably not."

"I need your help," she said. "And I think you owe it to me."

I didn't answer right away because I was preoccupied with the way she twisted the stripped blade of grass around on itself, then tied it in a knot. She lowered her head so she could catch my eye.

"Will you help me, Jack?" she said softly.

"If I do, it won't be because I owe you."

"I must get to London," she said.

I hesitated. "Maybe I want to help you, but I don't want to think of myself as a pushover. I'd like to know who and—more importantly—what I'm helping."

Eva searched my face for a moment. "Does it matter?"

"I'd like to think so," I said.

She broke into an unexpected smile. "All right then, go ahead. Ask me anything. I'll tell you whatever you want to know."

"Well . . ." I decided not to beat around the bush. "You've been accused of being a murderer and a Nazi spy . . ."

"Guilty, your honor," she said. "I plead guilty on both counts."

I nodded, tried to think where to go from there. "Did you kill Eddie Grimes?"

"No."

"Kleinmann?"

"Yes, I did kill him."

She said it so matter-of-factly, like she was talking about buying a loaf of bread, but I couldn't help recalling the neat little hole that had been made in the middle of the German's forehead.

"Were you working for him? Before you killed him, that is."

She sighed. "It's not as simple as that."

"Either you were or you weren't."

"I wasn't working for *him*, precisely. I was working for Abwehr—"

"German military intelligence?"

"Yes."

"Is that why you were going to London? To spy for the Germans?"

She shook her head slowly. "You'll have to sit down if you want to hear it all."

I lowered myself onto the grass and waited. Eva was quiet for what seemed like a long time, eyes lowered, focused on her hands, which were folded in her lap. When she finally spoke, it was in an even, unflinching voice, devoid of any detectable emotion.

• • •

"In the spring of 1938—just over two years ago—a man appeared at my door. A nice enough man, harmless-looking, very polite. He showed me his credentials and explained that he was conducting a census of the area and would need to ask me some questions. It was the usual sort of thing, so I didn't think anything of it. Not until later, anyway, when he started delving into my past, particularly my childhood in England. He pretended it was just curiosity, but I could see that there was more to it. At any rate, he soon left and I forgot all about it—until a week later, when a second man came to my apartment. This one wasn't like the first man. This one was very serious and he came right to the point.

"My profile had been noticed, he said. Noticed by some very important people who believed that I could be of great service ... Service to the fatherland."

Eva raised her eyes to meet mine. "I wish I could say that they threatened me or coerced me in some way. But it wouldn't be true. I signed up quite happily.

"It would be difficult for you to understand. I don't even know if I understand it myself. It was a strange time. Everything was changing. After those dark days, people were finally smiling again. There was a sense that things were getting better, that we had a future ..." A bitter smile found its way onto her lips. "I suppose the truth is that I thought it would be fun. A game. Some sort of grand adventure ..."

She lingered for a moment, the only sound the overhead leaves rustling in a gentle afternoon breeze.

"I was sent to school in Hamburg—a school for spies. It was really quite something. Very exciting. I was meeting all sorts of people, from all walks of life. A few days earlier, I'd been struggling with Vivaldi's Sonata in B-Flat Major, and now I was about to become a secret agent.

"They started me in an English course. Most of us were proficient in at least one other language, but we had to be absolutely perfect. There were several classes, each with an instructor from a different part of the country, so we could learn the correct accents and idioms. I was put in the London class, which I was glad of. The idea of being in London, living a secret life ... It seemed a very romantic future.

"Our education was soon expanded to include other skills. How to operate a radio transmitter, how to photograph documents in the dark with a camera no bigger than a cigarette lighter, how to read and write in code, the use of firearms ... Everything you'd expect to learn at spy school, and some you wouldn't." She smiled. "There was one course called How to Behave Like the English. The men learned about cricket and rugby, while the women were taught how to cook roast beef and Yorkshire pudding.

"In August of 1939 our class was graduated and we were sent off to various postings around Europe—a few even went to America. I was disappointed that instead of being assigned to London, I was given a position as an instructor at the Amsterdam conservatory, under my own name. It was rather an anticlimax. My orders were to bicycle out into the countryside every weekend and see what I could see. Well, I didn't see much of anything, and I didn't feel like a spy at all. I felt like a music teacher with a bicycle.

"Then, in May, the invasion came. It was as much a shock to me as it was to the Dutch. Oh, I knew we were at war, but I—" She paused to push a stray lock of hair back behind her ear. "I didn't expect it to be so brutal. First the bombings, and then, when the Gestapo came ... It was terrible, Jack. Unspeakably cruel." Eva's eyes flitted away and she swallowed hard before continuing.

"A week later, I was instructed to enter France, traveling by train through Belgium, Luxembourg, and Switzerland, again using my own name. I was to make my way to Paris, where I would contact an American businessman called Charles Bedeaux. He was sympathetic to Germany and, apparently, quite well connected. He would introduce me at the British embassy as someone who might be 'of interest' to their intelligence service ... It was quite an honor, I was told, to be one of the few chosen to be a double agent for the Reich. A great trust had been placed in me.

"It was expected that I would be sent to England for training, then placed back in Germany as an operative for MI6. There would be a number of benefits to the Reich, of course. I'd gain valuable information about how British agents were trained, as well as how they were inserted into Germany. But, most importantly, I'd be able to relay all sorts of deceptive information across the Channel. Very useful when the invasion came. And I think it would have worked, if not for one problem—me.

"I was never really sympathetic to the Nazis. In the beginning, like all my friends, I'd simply ignored them. We'd shake our heads and wonder how anyone could take them seriously. Then one day, I woke up and found that they were in power, and no one was shaking their heads anymore. I listened to Hitler's speeches and, like everyone, I was exhilarated. Not so much by what he said, but by the way he said it. He was strong and bold and you felt you could trust him. He cast a spell and we were all swept along. Perhaps if I'd been in Berlin still, I would've been among the crowd, cheering the awe-inspiring victories of the Third Reich, but in Amsterdam it didn't feel at all like victory. It felt sickening. It was no longer just words. I saw what they did.

"Why? I asked myself. Why did we have to do this? There was supposed to be a reason, but for the life of me, I couldn't remember what it was supposed to be. Had it ever existed, or had it been conjured up, a trick of Hitler's black magic? I hated myself. For being part of it, yes, but even more than that, for being so gullible. So blind. *What had I been thinking?* How had I not seen, not understood, what these men were? What they were capable of? . . . Those were the questions that went through my mind on the train to Paris. The answer, of course, was simple. Painfully simple, and even more disturbing.

"I did know. That was the sad answer. Of course I knew. How

could I not? How can anyone not see what the Nazis are and how they intend to use their power? They haven't tried to hide their hate, or their brutality. Quite the contrary, it's there for all to see. But I closed my eyes to it because to recognize it for what it was, and to do nothing about it . . . That would be inconceivable, wouldn't it? So, like so many others, I went along."

I became aware of Lili, standing in the grass a few yards behind us. I couldn't be sure how long she'd been there, but when she realized that I'd seen her, she stepped forward. I jumped to my feet.

"I'm sorry, Lili. I—"

"Don't apologize, Jack," she said. "It doesn't suit you."

"We were just—" Lili waved me off.

"You stay," she said. "I'll send the car back for you."

She sounded genuine enough, so I said I would see her back at the hotel for dinner. Lili nodded, then she stood there for a moment, looking uncharacteristically ill at ease. She looked to Eva, who was still sitting in the grass.

"I'm sorry, Eva, for being so stupid."

"You weren't, Lili."

"Of course I was. But I suppose we all have the right to be stupid now and then. Even rich and famous movie stars." She offered up a wry smile, then made a graceful exit across the field.

15

It had cooled off considerably and looked like an afternoon shower was on the cards, so Eva and I moved inside, finding a welcome fire in the hearth. Rosa delivered a tray of coffee and cakes, which was left untouched on the table as we stretched out in front of the flames, and Eva picked up where she'd left off.

"When I arrived in Paris, I went straight to the address I'd been given for Charles Bedeaux, and that afternoon he introduced me to an official at the British embassy. A gentleman named Geoffrey Stevens, who seemed to be quite important. The three of us met in a quiet bistro off the Champs-Élysées, and after the wine had been poured, I told him my cover story.

"My father, I explained, had been working for Mr. Bedeaux's company in Berlin when, six months earlier, he'd disappeared. I'd learned from the neighbors that the SS had come in the middle of the night and taken him away. I had no idea why they would take him, I said, making my lip quiver as I'd practiced, and that was Bedeaux's cue to step in.

"'Your father was working with me,' he said. 'With me, and

others, against the Nazi regime. He didn't tell you because he didn't want to put you in danger.'

"It was part of the cover story, but I took a moment to act shocked before continuing with my account. I described to Mr. Stevens how I found out where my father was being held and how I went to the prison every day, demanding to see him, and how every day I was refused. I begged them to tell me why he was being held, but I was told to go home and wait for word. Finally, after several weeks, word came, in the form of a letter. Just two sentences. We regret to inform you that Rudolf Lange has died in prison. His death was the result of complications due to pneumonia.

"I choked back a tear and Bedeaux picked up the story from there. He told Stevens he'd sent for me to come to Paris, as my father had asked him to do in the event of his death. He was to arrange a visa to the United States. But when I arrived, Bedeaux told Stevens, I refused to accept the passage to America. Instead, I'd asked him to help me find a way to fight the Nazis . . . I would do anything, I added dramatically. Anything to avenge my father's death.

"Stevens seemed to take the bait. After all, on the surface, I was the perfect intelligence candidate, and I had been introduced by a man whom he clearly trusted. A room was arranged for me in a nearby hotel and I was told to be at the embassy the next morning at eight o'clock. When I arrived the following day, I was taken to a small, windowless room where two men were waiting to interview me.

"I didn't waste time. Before they could ask me a question, I confessed everything. About my training in Hamburg, about Amsterdam, and about my mission to become a double agent. Naturally, they got very excited and called Mr. Stevens into the room. He sat there, calmly puffing on a pipe, as I repeated my confession in more detail. When I'd finished, he just nodded and spent a long time looking at me. Finally, he stood up and said, 'Thank you, Miss Lange. As you might expect, we'll want to discuss this further with you.' Then he left. The two men escorted me to the basement, where I was locked inside a very small room.

"Over the next two weeks, I was interrogated for eighteen hours a day, every day. It was all very polite, with tea and toast in the morning and a cup of hot milk before bed, but it was like torture going over the same material day after day. I'd be thrilled when the interviewers would change, because it meant that we were going to start a new subject. If a woman appeared, I'd know that the questions would be of a more personal nature. They left nothing untouched.

"Most often, we'd talk about technical issues, or they'd ask me for names, descriptions, anything I knew about my fellow students and teachers in Hamburg. They created a profile for each one. Even the tiniest piece of information was of interest—birthmarks, demeanor, likes and dislikes, that sort of thing. I answered all the questions as fully and honestly as I could, describing everything in brain-racking detail.

"Then, one afternoon, Mr. Stevens walked into the session. I hadn't seen him since the first day and he seemed a bit on edge now. Less unflappable. After dismissing my interrogators, he sat down across the table from me.

"'We're not sure that you can be trusted,' he said.

"'I'm telling the truth,' I answered.

"'Oh, yes, we're quite certain of that,' he said. 'But if you were trying to take us in, that would be an excellent tactic, wouldn't it?'

"I told him that if he didn't want to use me, there was nothing I could do about it. I'd find another way to fight the war. I told him that, if necessary, I was prepared to give my life, and again, it was the truth.

"Stevens looked at me for a long time, as though he was trying to decide what to do. Then he said, quite calmly, 'The Wehrmacht is within fifty miles of Paris. The city will be occupied inside of two days.'

"I was horrified. If France had fallen in two weeks, how would they be stopped?

"'I can't get you to London now,' Stevens said. 'For obvious reasons. I'm not even sure how I'll get back.' He threw an envelope onto the table. 'Inside are five hundred francs, thirty pesetas, and thirty escudos, along with your passport. If you can manage to get to Lisbon, you might find a way to London from there. If you do, find me.'

" 'I'll get there,' I assured him.

"He told me that there was a man in Lisbon who might be able to help me. 'He's with a special section of intelligence that's just been set up,' he said. 'I'm afraid I don't know much about it or him, but I managed to get his code name and an address for you.'

"His code name was Bicycle," Eva said, looking up at me. "And the address was Rua das Taipas, number thirty-five . . . The top floor."

"Popov?!" I laughed. *"Popov* was your contact?"

"That's right."

"That weasel works for British intelligence?" I shook my head. "If that's how far England has sunk, I can't say I fancy their chances in this thing."

"It's not a horse race, Jack."

"Somebody's gonna win and somebody's gonna lose."

"And you'll be there on the sidelines, adjusting the odds."

I shrugged. "I don't go looking for fights."

"It's one thing to avoid a fight, quite another to run away from one."

I gave her a look. "You're trying to bait me."

She laughed. "Is it working?"

"I like the lure, but I'm not too sure about the hook."

"I'm afraid that you can't have one without the other."

"In that case," I smiled, "go on with your story."

"When I arrived in Lisbon, I went straight to the address Stevens had given me, where I found Roman. I don't think he'd been expecting me, but when I told him my story, he promised to do what he could. Passage to England was next to impossible at the moment, at any price, he said, so he arranged for a room in a small hotel overlooking the port. When things calmed down, he'd find a way out for me. I'd used all my money, so Roman gave me enough to buy some food and a couple of English books. I spent the next three days reading Thomas Hardy and watching the ships sail.

"Roman appeared on the morning of the fourth day and told me there would be no way to get me to England, perhaps for weeks. But, he said, as I was stuck in Lisbon, there was something I could do for him.

"As far as the Germans knew, he said, I was still working for them. I'd gone to Paris, and following their instructions, I had volunteered for service with British intelligence. MI6 had interrogated me for two weeks, then instructed me to come to Lisbon in order to go on to England, just as Abwehr had hoped would happen.

"It was true, I agreed, that the Germans still thought I was on their side, and I expected the Brits to use that to their advantage, but how would that help him in Lisbon?

"Roman explained that he had been hearing things that led him to believe that important information was being passed to the German government from 'a high-level individual.' He suspected that the intelligence was being sent to Berlin through the head of Abwehr in Lisbon."

"Kleinmann," I said, and Eva confirmed it with a nod.

"If I could get close to him, Roman said, I might be able to confirm the stories that he had been hearing. I would contact Kleinmann, explain that I was on my way to London to fulfill my assignment, and suggest that he be my link back to Berlin. It was a plausible scenario because, in fact, I'd been instructed to find my own means of communication, depending on my circumstances. I'd been given a code name and a password, which Kleinmann could verify with Berlin.

"Roman wouldn't tell me what he hoped I would find, but he said that if his suspicions were confirmed, it would be a very important discovery—one that might 'change the dynamics of the war.' I agreed to the proposal and, that afternoon, went to the German embassy.

"Kleinmann was cautious at first, but once he'd contacted Berlin, he became very friendly. We spent the next day in his office, planning our future communications. I could see that he was attracted to me and I led him to believe that, if he played his cards right, ours could become something more than a professional relationship. So he set about wooing me, taking me to expensive restaurants and fancy nightclubs and even giving me an emerald brooch. It was horribly ugly, and, in fact, so was he, but I encouraged him nonetheless. It wasn't easy smiling as he pawed me under the table with his fat fingers.

"I noticed that on some nights Kleinmann would leave his office with a locked black case under his arm. If he carried the bag home at night, he would be driven to the airport early the following morning, where he would deliver the bag into the hands of a courier, who would fly it directly to Berlin. There, a motorcycle from the Foreign Office would carry the consignment directly to von Ribbentrop, who had the only other key. If information was being passed to Berlin through Kleinmann, this was how it would travel. I had to look inside that case.

"An opportunity presented itself one night when Kleinmann decided to take me to a performance of *Don Giovanni* at the Teatro Nacional. He'd learned from my file that Mozart was my favorite composer and wanted to surprise me. When he collected me, I noticed that the bag was on the front seat of the car, beside the driver, and I knew that this would be the night. During the performance, I did everything I could to arouse him, which wasn't difficult. I was shameful, really. By the time Don Giovanni was dragged off to hell, Dr. Kleinmann was putty in my hands—so to speak. I suggested that rather than join his friends from the embassy, we have a nightcap at his residence. He was beside himself, believing that all his romancing was about to come to a dazzling climax. Once we arrived at the house, it was just a matter of holding out for as long as I could—I managed to get the better part of a bottle of cognac inside him before I finally had to give in . . ."

The thought of Eva being manhandled by the likes of Kleinmann gave me a shot of angry adrenaline, but I was careful not to show it. I tried to console myself with the knowledge that she'd slept with him in the line of duty.

"He didn't last long," Eva continued. "After such a buildup, I suppose he just couldn't hold out. Before I knew it, it was over, he'd rolled onto his back and was snoring like a pig, with his trousers in a twist around his knees. I finished undressing him, then waited—it must have been a full hour—before getting up. There was no light in the bedroom, so I went slowly, one foot in front of the other, hoping that I remembered correctly where the door was located. I walked into a table and something—maybe a picture frame—crashed to the floor. He stirred, but after a moment, his heavy breathing began again.

"I found my way out of the bedroom and into the study, where I'd seen him leave the bag. I turned a lamp on and found it on the desk—locked. I'd been stupid. His keys were in the trousers that I'd left hanging on the bedpost. I had to go back.

"This time I woke him. He sputtered and snorted and grumbled that I should get back into bed. I slipped under the sheet, and after he'd fumbled around for a few moments, he dozed off again. I was pinned under his arm, but managed to slide out from under him, retrieve the keys, and get back to the study without making any noise. By this time, there were signs of morning and I was getting anxious. I knew that his driver would soon be knocking on the door.

"Most of the papers were diplomatic exchanges. Standard bureaucratic chatter. But then, in the midst of all the typewritten memos, I found a large manila envelope addressed to the foreign minister. It wasn't sealed, so I reached inside and took out a single, plain white envelope. There was nothing written on it, but I could see that there was a handwritten letter inside. Easy enough to steam open—if I had time.

"I carried the envelope to the kitchen and put some water on to boil. It seemed to take forever. What is the expression? 'A pot—'?"

"A watched pot never boils," I said.

"Yes, that's it." Eva smiled a thank-you. "But it finally did boil, and I was able to unseal the envelope and remove the letter. It was written on fine linen paper in a very tight, very precise script. As I read it, and realized what it was, my heart started to beat. I understood now what Roman had meant about it changing the dynamics of the war. When I'd finished, I read it again, to be sure I'd understood correctly. I started to memorize it, but I was too nervous and I had to have the words precisely right. I found a pen back in the study, slipped out of my panties, and copied the letter, word for word, into the inside."

Eva closed her eyes, took a deep breath and said, "It read like this:"

26 June 1940

Dearest Friend,

I write to you from the most recent of the seemingly endless parade of temporary abodes we've suffered since leaving Antibes, this one situated on the fringes of an undistinguished village at the border between Spain and Portugal. It is our intention to cross over in the next few days, in the guise of visiting a nearby friend, then to make our way to Lisbon, where we will await further developments. I intend to send this letter ahead so as to give you an opportunity to make arrangements for our stay.

I will not bother you with all the details of our recent tribulations, but suffice it to say that our lives have not been made any easier by the powers that be. (I'm certain that you will know to whom I refer.) What upsets and, I must say, angers him more than anything is that not only have they not bothered to offer assistance, but they seem to be going out of their way to make our situation even more difficult than it already is. The reason, of course, is clear. They know the sway he holds over his people and, for this reason, they feel they must, at all costs, keep him quiet. This strategy will not succeed.

As you well know, my husband is a man of action. He could not—

and will not—stand idly by to watch these absurd declarations of defiance be carried out to their illogical conclusion. He has taken the suggestions you made in your last communication to heart and is currently formulating a plan that might achieve our mutual goal of peace. He understands the unique responsibility that history has presented to him and, with your support, he will not fail in it.

It is critical that we make our move at the right moment. He feels, I think astutely, that the people must first taste some of the "blood, toil, sweat and tears" that they have been so cavalierly promised with such quixotic bravado. When the time is right, there are others in positions of influence who can be called upon, and he has even talked about bringing to bear the influence of my former country in his plan. This, I believe, is something that he is in a unique position to achieve.

Above all, it is his desire to minimize the destruction that must occur (and which we can justly lay at the door of the present occupant of Number 10). To that end, he would like AH to know that there are sensitive documents that would help shorten the time and extent of the destruction. These papers can be made available once we are in a more settled position.

Finally, if I may speak openly (as I know I can), we find ourselves in a desperate situation. The powers that be are using the purse strings, as they are prone to do, hoping that this will compel him to toe the line. Anything you can do to relieve that pressure would be most appreciated and will, of course, be a debt that will be fully repaid when we are again in charge of our own destiny. I feel foolish making this request, but I'm afraid that we have been put in that position.

My greatest wish is that I could see you again. It has been far too long and so much has happened. But I feel we will be reunited soon. Until that time, I remain, as always,

Yours,
Wallis

Wallis Simpson's letter fit right in with what I knew about the Duke of Windsor's so-called peace plan, though it certainly cast it in a new light. Not only was the former king plotting against his brother's government, he seemed to be doing it at the suggestion of Hitler himself! And his assertion that England might have to suffer a few Luftwaffe bombs before seeing the wisdom of surrender wasn't just table talk—he was actively encouraging the Germans to give his countrymen a taste of the Blitzkreig. And, most amazing of all, *he was offering to provide documents that would make the job easier!*

For a price, of course. There's always a price.

I don't know if the duke was a true believer in National Socialism or not. Perhaps he saw himself as a natural candidate for membership in the brotherhood of "strong leaders," joining Hitler, Mussolini, and Franco in the elite pantheon of Europe's most recent despots. But—as with most people willing to betray their country—his motive wouldn't have been ideological. His Royal Highness could talk about the perils of communism until his face was as blue as his blood, but the bottom line was that he wanted another shot at the title, and the Führer was just the guy to give it to him. No, the duke and his lovely wife weren't ideologues. They simply saw the war as a wonderful opportunity to get back on top.

"There were rumors that von Ribbentrop and Mrs. Simpson were lovers," Eva explained. "While he was ambassador to the Court of St. James."

It didn't shock me, but the rest of the world might've been a bit taken aback. To them, Edward and Wallis were the twentieth-century version of Romeo and Juliet. Star-crossed lovers whose undying passion could not be denied; the noble king who relinquished his realm in order that he might wed his true love, a commoner. If their adoring public knew that Mrs. Simpson had been fooling around with a Nazi on the side, it might've taken some of the shine off the fairy tale.

I didn't see any reason to let Eva in on what I knew about the duke's plans, so I asked her what happened after she'd copied the letter.

"I put the key back in Kleinmann's trousers and slipped into the bed," she said. "I pretended to be asleep, which wasn't easy with my heart pounding like a hammer, as it was. I lay there, going over each word of the letter, committing it to memory. When the driver rang the bell, about twenty minutes later, I got up and dressed as quickly as I could. I was nervous, and made all the more so by the way Kleinmann watched me, never taking his eye off me as I pulled my clothes on. I thought he knew, and was playing with me.

"My heart stopped when he walked over and slipped his hand inside my panties. I closed my eyes and held my breath, believing I was as good as dead." Eva smiled bitterly. "But he interpreted my reaction as the inevitable result of his magic touch. He smiled like a conqueror, kissed me on the cheek, and whispered that he had a dinner appointment that evening, but if I came to the apartment at ten o'clock, I would find him there. He thought I would be grateful. I played along, of course, acting delighted that I would have another opportunity to experience his manhood, whereas all I really wanted was to wash him off me. I couldn't even breathe properly until he stepped into his car and drove away, on his way to the airport, the black case with the letter inside sitting safely on his lap.

"I thought about going directly to Rua das Taipas, but Roman had been adamant that I was to wait for him in my room, so I made my way back there. But as I approached the building, a strange feeling came over me—a sense that I was being watched. I couldn't say why, but it was palpable and I became quite anxious. What if Kleinmann had been aware of what I'd been doing after all? He wouldn't have confronted me then and there. He would have had me followed, hoping to discover who I was working for. I was afraid that I would put Roman and his entire operation in jeopardy.

"I wasn't sure what to do. Perhaps it was just my nerves and I was imagining it. But, if it was real—if someone was watching me—it could only be one of Kleinmann's agents. Aside from Roman, no one else knew where to find me. I ducked into the local bar, where I could gather my thoughts. It was dark and cool inside, and empty, except for an old man seated by the door. I'd seen him there before, leaning against his cane, observing the world through a pair of rose-tinted glasses.

"'Does he find you?' he said to me as I entered.

"'Does who find me?'

"'The man who looks for you.'

"'What man?' I asked him.

"The old man signaled for me to come closer. 'He comes here last night and shows a photograph of you to all the people. It is an old picture, but I can see it is you. He offers big money, this man, but I don't like his face, so I say no, I don't know you.' The old man frowned. 'But Ricardo, the bastard, I see he takes the money and then this man, he goes to his car and he waits. He waits still.' The old man lifted his cane and pointed across the street. 'There he is. He still sits in his big red automobile.'"

"Eddie Grimes," I said, recalling the red coupe that had been extracted from the jaws of hell.

"Yes," Eva nodded. "Though I didn't know it at the time. I

couldn't imagine who it would be. Surely an operative for Abwehr wouldn't be using a car like that. I went to my room, making sure that my stalker could see me. Then I waited, watching from my window. After a few minutes, he got out of the car and started walking toward the building. I ran downstairs, to the basement, where I knew there was a back exit. When I heard the front door open and footsteps on the stairway, I slipped out the door and circled around to his car as quickly as I could. The door wasn't locked, so I slid into the driver's seat, keeping my head down so he wouldn't see me if he looked back. I didn't know what I was looking for—anything that might give me a clue as to who he was. A hotel receipt in the glove compartment had his name on it, but it meant nothing to me.

"I decided that I'd better find Roman before he walked straight into my mysterious pursuer. I hurried to Rua das Taipas and found him asleep. At first he was surprised to see me, then he became angry that I'd ignored his instructions. I didn't tell him about the man in the red car, but when I showed him the letter, he calmed down and became very quiet. It was a rather disappointing reaction, to be honest. I wanted him to tell me how well I'd done and how important my discovery would be, but he didn't say anything at all. He just took a piece of thin blue paper and, using a code that I didn't know, slowly copied the letter onto it. Then, without a word, he struck a match and set fire to my panties.

"When the fire had burned out, he asked me if Kleinmann had arranged to see me again. I told him about my instructions for that night, and he said that I would have to go. I detested the idea, but I knew he was right. If I didn't appear, Kleinmann would become suspicious, and Roman needed time to transmit the letter to London and await instructions. As I left the warehouse, Roman slipped a small pistol into my handbag.

"'You never know,' he said, and I didn't argue.

"I couldn't go back to my room, so I spent the day wandering the streets. The anticipation of seeing Kleinmann again made me feel physically ill—empty and cold—so I concentrated on the man in the red car. Who was he and what did he want from me? I was certain that he had nothing to do with Abwehr. I'd seen from the hotel receipt that he had an American address—San Francisco—but that didn't help. By the time darkness came, I was possessed with curiosity and decided that I would have to find out.

"The proprietor at the Imperial Hotel wasn't at all forthcoming, but he didn't mind letting me go up to the room. In fact, he seemed to quite relish the idea, though I didn't understand why until I got up there. The room was on the second floor, with a cheap lock that was easily opened. After removing the pistol from my bag, I threw open the door. I won't describe the scene that I encountered— suffice it to say that Mr. Grimes was not, in any sense of the word, a gentleman. It took a great deal of restraint not to shoot him then and there . . ."

I recalled the look of resignation I'd seen on Fabiana's young face and felt a surge of disgust. I guess as much as anyone, Eddie Grimes deserved to end up in the jaws of hell.

"I didn't know what to do," Eva continued. "So I just stood there, frozen, my pistol pointed at the bastard's head. If he was afraid or embarrassed, he didn't show it. He casually disengaged from the girl, untied her, and told her to 'get lost,' which she did with considerable haste. I asked him who he was and what he wanted with me.

"'Eddie Grimes is the name,' he said, displaying a repugnant smile. 'Pleased to meet you.'

"I told him that I already knew his name, but he just kept smiling. He seemed to be laughing at me, in spite of the fact that he was naked with a loaded gun pointing at him."

"'You asked me who I am,' he said. 'That's the answer.' He stood up. 'If you wanna know why I'm here, how about I get dressed and we discuss it over a drink?'

"I told him that I didn't want a drink and that he could explain his business just as well without getting dressed. Aside from not wanting to stay any longer than I had to, I thought he might have a weapon hidden away in one of his pockets. When I asked him again why he was looking for me, he pointed to his jacket and said that he was just delivering something."

"Lili's letter . . ." I said.

"I was dumbfounded. After all those years. Lili . . ." Eva shook her head in disbelief. "I read the note quickly, and told him to relay my thanks to Lili, but I wasn't interested in accompanying him to New York, or anywhere else. Then I told him to stop following me. He just stood there, leering at me, but I didn't care. I had what I'd come for, so I left.

"I was late, so I found a taxi and gave the driver Kleinmann's address. The building was dark and I hoped that he might not have returned from his dinner engagement, in which case I could leave a note saying how devastated I was, and disappear. I was about to turn around when his maid came to the door. She led me to the sitting room, leaving me in the dark without a word. I thought it odd that she didn't turn on a light. Even the drapes were drawn. I tried the lamps, but all the bulbs had been taken out . . .

"Does the darkness frighten you?" His voice came from somewhere across the room, but I couldn't see him.

"'Darling?' I cried out in a poor attempt to sound lighthearted. 'That's very naughty of you . . .' I could only hope that he was playing some sort of game, but of course I knew better.

"'But you are the naughty one,' he said.

"'I don't know what you mean, darling . . . Is something wrong?' He went quiet, but I could hear him moving around the room, as though he was circling me. I thought about the pistol in my handbag, but I hesitated and it was too late. He grabbed me from behind and pulled me in, holding me tightly, pressing the barrel of his Luger against my ribs.

"'If you pretend innocence, I'll pull the trigger right now and throw you onto the street. You can die in the gutter, where you belong.' I felt his warm breath against my cheek as he embraced me tighter, jamming the barrel into me, driving it with enough force to make me moan. I said nothing, and neither did he. Nor did he move.

He just stood there clutching me for what seemed like a very long time, breathing hard into my ear.

"'Berlin knows that I've made contact with you,' I said. 'If I turn up dead, they'll send someone . . . Gestapo.'

"'You're not going to turn up dead,' he said. 'You'll simply disappear . . . And I will be as mystified as everyone else as to what happened to you.'

"He took me to a car that was parked outside and told me to drive. I placed my handbag, with the gun in it, on the floor by my feet, within reach if I had the opportunity. Kleinmann seemed preoccupied, sitting silently, speaking only to give me directions that took us west, out of the city and along the estuary.

"I asked him, after some time had passed, how he had found out.

"'I keep the key in my right pocket,' he responded, in a flat, lifeless voice. 'You replaced it into the left one. I only noticed when I made a final check of the documents at the airport.'

"'That was stupid of me,' I said, and he grunted his agreement. 'But aren't you concerned that I've already given the information to the British?'

"'Not really,' he said. He was clearly more worried about his own skin, and quite rightly. If it was discovered that I'd stolen his secrets while he slept in the next room, his future in the Reich would be limited, to say the least. The Gestapo saw Abwehr as an unwelcome competitor and would be more than happy to place Kleinmann's head on a platter and serve it up to Hitler.

"As we climbed higher along the cliffs, a fog descended on us and it was increasingly difficult to see. There were very few other cars on the road, just the occasional headlight in the distance behind us. Kleinmann seemed to be watching the road ahead very carefully, looking for something. Then he saw a sign for a tourist attraction—"

"O Boca do Inferno," I interjected.

"Yes," Eva said. "He told me to stop there. I pulled the car onto the verge and he got out, instructing me to slide across the seat and exit on his side. I knew this would be my last chance, so, before I moved, I reached for my bag. But it was too obvious. He grabbed it from me and tore it open. When he saw the pistol, he looked up at me with the strangest expression. Like an injured puppy, as if this was the ultimate betrayal. When he was moments away from shooting me and tossing my body off a cliff into the sea!

"He was angry now. Throwing the bag back onto the seat, he dragged me onto the road. I tried to get my bearings, but the fog made it difficult to see beyond a few feet. I could hear the waves crashing against the rocks below us, but I wasn't sure how far away it was, or in which direction. I can't run, I thought. I must keep him talking.

"'You don't have to do this,' I said. 'We can work something out.'

"He laughed, but it came out strained and tense. In spite of everything, when it came to the moment, I think he was having difficulty.

"'What I did had nothing to do with my feelings for you, Hans,' I said, struggling to sound sincere. 'It was just a job.'

"'You'd say that now, wouldn't you? You'd say anything.' He lifted the gun slightly and I felt the moment was at hand. I could hardly breathe, but I had to keep him talking.

"'If you let me live . . . Just for tonight . . . I'll give you something to remember. Do you understand what I'm saying? I can do things that you'll never forget . . .' He looked at me sideways and I thought there was a chance. 'Why not?' I pressed. 'You can get rid of me afterward, if you still want to. Why not see what I can do?'

"A smile slowly crept onto his face, then he reached down with his free hand and started to unbutton his trousers. 'Get on your knees,' he said. 'And give me a demonstration.' I looked down at him—he was all excited—and then at his grinning face. It was all I could do to keep from vomiting.

"'On second thought,' I said. 'Perhaps you'd better go ahead and shoot me. I'd prefer it. Please, go ahead and pull the trigger. I really would rather die.'

"He was about to do just that when a car's headlamps appeared from around a bend in the road. Kleinmann grabbed me and pulled me down behind his car. The oncoming vehicle was moving quickly, but instead of passing, it came to an abrupt stop about thirty feet ahead of us. The driver cut the motor and turned off the headlights.

"Kleinmann was panicking, unsure what to do. He had to see who this was, but he couldn't leave me alone. After a moment, he grabbed me by the arm and pulled me over toward the mysterious car, keeping the Luger pushed against the small of my back. As we approached I could see that this was the American detective's red car. He must have been following me since I left his hotel.

"In the fog, I don't think he saw us approaching until it was too late. He had just opened the door, causing the car's interior light to come on, when he looked up to see Kleinmann pointing the Luger at his chest. I think he wanted to say something, but his words were cut off by the shot. I saw the gun's flash, then Grimes fell back into the car. He was still alive, clinging to the steering wheel, desperately trying to remain upright, a look of utter shock on his face. He must have known that he was about to die.

"I don't know what he'd expected to find. Perhaps he thought he was about to interrupt a lovers' tryst. He looked back at Kleinmann, his eyes pleading for mercy, but, of course, there was none. The Luger fired a second time and Grimes fell back onto the seat. His body twitched a couple of times, then it went completely still.

"It was my Hamburg training that saved me. Without thinking, I made a small, tight ball with my fist and pivoted on my left foot. As I swung my hips around, I drove my knuckles into the sciatic nerve, just above Kleinmann's left buttock. He gasped for air, and as his legs buckled, I pulled free. I didn't know if he'd been able to hold on to his gun, so I ran back to his car and retrieved my pistol.

"I had no qualms about killing him. In fact, I was eager to do it. I found him unarmed and helpless, on the ground, scrabbling around in the dark, trying to find his pistol.

"'How ironic,' I said. 'That you're the one who's ended up on his knees.' Then I placed the pistol a few inches from his head and fired."

Eva lifted her eyes to meet mine. Her expression was thoughtful, but her voice was surprisingly buoyant. "Have you ever killed anyone, Jack?"

"No," I answered truthfully. "I never have."

She nodded. "I was surprised at how calm I felt. He was a horrible man, of course, but he was a human being. You'd think that killing a human being would make you feel some sort of distress, wouldn't you?" She pursed her lips and slowly shook her head.

"But I felt quite satisfied."

"Why in God's name would you want to go to London?"

Harry Thompson was sounding grumpier than usual, an effect, no doubt, of the dangerously low level of alcohol in his system. He shot a vexed look across the counter, where the bartender was busy filling a waitress's tray.

"It's not for me," I said.

Harry peered over my shoulder, highlighting his unequivocal disinterest in my problems. The casino was flush at this hour, jammed with after-dinner chumps whose idea of a good evening was giving their money away. It was the only action in Estoril, and the first place I'd looked for Harry.

"Who's it for, then?" he finally said, curiosity getting the better of him.

"A friend."

"A female friend, I take it?"

I shrugged. What else?

"Jack the lad, eh?" He turned his attention back to the bartender. "That man is jeopardizing his best tip of the night." His palm came down hard on the bar.

"*Whiskey, senhor! Por favor!*"

The barman produced a smile and a shrug, put his finger in the air, pleading for another *minuto*.

"It's urgent," I said.

"It's always urgent, dear boy. Someone special?"

"Not particularly," I said. "But I told her I'd help and I'd like to keep my word."

"Very noble," Harry scoffed.

The bartender finally arrived with a couple of scotches on the rocks. Harry gulped his down before I could remove the swizzle stick from mine. He took a moment, eyes closed, to feel it spread, then rejoined me with a shiver and an almost congenial smile.

"Correct me if I'm wrong, Jack, but the last time I saw you, you were informing me that I could fuck off because my problems had nothing whatsoever to do with you. So, tell me, please, why I should give a tuppenny toss about yours."

"I'd be willing to pay."

His face went sour. "Perhaps you should see our friend, the rat. That's more his area of interest."

I leaned in and lowered my voice, more for effect than anything else. "I could pay with information."

His interest went up a notch. "Such as?"

"Still want to know what the duke's up to?"

"Is he up to something?"

"Where's my ticket to London?"

He scowled. "If you have something to say on the subject, I assure you that a ticket will be forthcoming."

"We'll talk when it's already come forth," I replied.

"Friends must sometimes rely on trust, Jack."

"I trust you, Harry. But I'll trust you a lot more when I have the ticket in my hand."

He couldn't help smiling. "All right. If you want to be that way. What's the young lady's name?"

"Lisa Foquet."

"Foquet?" He took out his reporter's notebook and jotted the name down. I had to spell it out for him.

"She's traveling on a Belgian passport," I said, in case it mattered. Harry nodded and put the pad back into his pocket.

"You remember the little bar in Casçais?"

"Sure. Your breakfast spot."

He grunted. "Shall we say teatime?"

"What the hell is teatime?"

"You really are an uncivilized lot, aren't you? Teatime is four o'clock—P.M."

"Four it is, then," I said, slipping off the bar stool. "And listen, Harry . . . Why not bring your friend Stropford along? He might as well hear it direct." Harry was a drunk, but he was also a newspaperman, and I didn't trust a newspaperman to get the story straight. He got the implication.

"Bastard," he snarled.

"I knew you'd understand, Harry."

I gave him a friendly pat on the back and headed for the door. I was looking forward to a few hours in a real bed.

"Herr Teller!"

I'd almost slipped past unnoticed, but Ritter spotted me and jumped to his feet. "Come, sit here beside me! We will have a drink!" He beckoned me to the table, where a band of well-tailored fascists were treating themselves to a night of good champagne and bad women. They all ignored me, except for one, sitting across the table, who stole a look. Small and blond with a boyishly round face, he would've been the spitting image of Mickey Rooney if it wasn't for the scar that ran from his right temple, across his cheek, all the way down to his chin. His look didn't linger, but it was more than just an idle glance. I slipped into the empty seat beside Major Ritter.

"I see you are alone," he said. "Have you still problems with your mistress?"

"If you mean Lili, she's not my mistress, in any sense of the word. And, no, we patched things up." I had no intention of accounting for her whereabouts, particularly as she'd left a note telling me that she was dining with the Windsors and would see me in the morning.

"Please, take some champagne," the major said, snapping his fingers at a nearby waiter, even though the bottle was right in front of him.

"Is it somebody's birthday?"

He cast a wry look in my direction. "We celebrate Germany and the Führer, of course. But let us make a toast with which you will feel more comfortable. To your safe journey home!" He raised his glass.

"And to yours," I said.

The major smiled sardonically and sized me up as he sipped the bubbly. "I've not yet decided how to analyze you, Herr Teller."

"I'm a complicated guy."

He laughed. "Not so much, I think. In fact, you seem to be quite a shallow individual, with no personal conviction whatsoever. You possess a misplaced sense of your own value and your character is defined by frivolity and impertinence."

"Personal conviction can get you into a lot of trouble."

"You see. A perfect example. You seem unable to take anything seriously."

"Maybe it's just you I can't take seriously."

He flinched, but decided to let it ride. He was having too much fun to go into storm-trooper mode.

"You're not a coward, I give you that," he said. "And you seem to be capable of great loyalty—not to a cause, or an idea, perhaps, but to a person. I suspect that no amount of money or persuasion would deflect you from a duty you feel for a friend. Am I correct?"

"I've probably never been sufficiently tested," I said, lighting a smoke. "But you're welcome to try me. With the money, that is, not the persuasion. I have a feeling that you'd be too good at that."

"But I have already tried you, Herr Teller. Did I not offer to pay you five thousand dollars if you supplied Eva Lange to me?"

"And did I not accept?"

Ritter shook his head. "You said that you did, but you were not sincere. You hoped only to distract my efforts while you found the girl and stole her off to America, for your—what shall we call her if not your mistress? Would you say benefactress? Or perhaps you consider Lili Sterne a friend? In any case, you would not betray her for five thousand dollars. Am I correct?"

"I guess we'll never know," I said.

"Yes, of course. We could not know because Eva Lange is dead. Is this your position?"

"Well?"

He frowned. "But . . . Are you certain of this?"

"Of what?"

"That Eva Lange is dead."

"Sure I'm sure," I said, starting to feel a bit queasy. "I saw her . . . Lili identified her."

"Yes, I heard about it." Ritter displayed a genuine smile now. "I understand that she gave quite a convincing performance. Or should I say conniving?"

Now my gut was starting to contract. "I'm not sure I follow you, Major . . . Captain Catela—"

"Is a vain imbecile. He would jump from a cliff if Lili Sterne told him to do so."

"I'll be sure to let her know that," I said, forcing an uneasy smile. Ritter leaned in to me, a look of drunken glee on his face.

"Perhaps, Herr Teller, you would be well advised to take me more seriously after all."

I inhaled a lungful of smoke and blew it out slowly. "Then you're still looking for her?"

Ritter smiled cagily. "But, Herr Teller. Why ever would you think that I would be looking for a dead woman?"

It was too dark to see my watch. I flipped the switch on the bed-side lamp: 3:28. No point lying there, I thought. I slipped into the light cotton bathrobe that the hotel provided, went into the living room, and poured myself a scotch and water. I didn't really want it, but it gave me something to do. I lit a smoke that I didn't want, either.

Ritter's performance had been disquieting, to say the least. There was no doubt that he knew Eva was alive, in spite of his coyness. Somebody had sold us out. But who? There were a dozen candidates, with Popov at the top of the list, closely followed by Senhor Baptista. The only one I could eliminate completely was myself, and Lili was pretty much out of the question, too. That left Brewster; the fat detective and his two sidekicks; Baptista's doltish assistant; Alberto, and his cousins, Fabio and Rosalina.

It could've been any of them, but that would have to wait. The question of the moment was how to get Eva out of the Gestapo's reach. Ritter would have Catela's entire force out looking for her. If somebody was talking, then it was just a question of time before—

I put the scotch aside. How could I be so stupid?

. . .

"I need a car."

"A car?"

"That's right. A motor vehicle."

"You would like one?"

"Yes."

"Now?"

"That's right, Javier. Now."

"But, senhor . . ." The usually helpful desk clerk checked the clock on the wall behind him. "It is four o'clock in the morning. Where can I—?"

I slapped a hundred-dollar bill on the counter. "I'm sure you'll figure it out."

The road was pitch-black and empty. No one could've been following without me knowing, but just to be sure, I doused the headlights and pulled Javier's old Opel onto the verge as I approached the turnoff. I sat there for a couple of minutes, long enough for a smoke, then eased my foot onto the accelerator and made the turn before hitting the headlights again.

There were only a couple of dirt tracks intersecting the winding gravel road that traversed the face of the mountain, so I was pretty sure I hadn't missed the entrance to the farm, but it seemed a lot farther than I remembered.

I found the turn and slowed to a crawl, recalling that the track ran along a very narrow ridge, falling off steeply to the left as it curved around to the right. I was on full alert, keenly aware of the engine's low rumble and the crack of dry twigs as they were caught under the slow turn of the wheel. The car's headlights tore through the night with a sudden intrusion of harsh white light, shadows flitting through the brush, escaping into the inky depths beyond. I knew what was coming. Death doesn't hide in the dark. It permeates the air and announces itself with a sickly feeling in the pit of your stomach.

The body lay across the path, facedown, arms folded underneath the naked torso. If I had any doubts about who the dead man was, they were eliminated when I saw the black dress shoes. I pulled the car up close, bathing Fabio in light, then killed the engine. The sudden silence was a bit unnerving, causing me to peer out into the void as I stepped into the night air and approached the corpse.

His face was immersed in a deep pool of dark red blood. As I approached I could see why. His throat had been cut so deeply that his head was nearly severed from his body. I paused, tamped down my emotions, then crouched beside the body to get a closer look. He hadn't been lying there long. Steam rose off the gaping wound and the blood was just starting to congeal around his ears. I noticed that the barrel of his shotgun was poking out from under his considerable frame. Stepping around to the other side, I took hold of it and pulled gently. It didn't move. I tried with both hands, giving it a good yank, but still no movement.

Christ, I thought, I'm gonna have to roll him over.

I took a deep breath, shoved my hands under Fabio's chest, and lifted. I almost had him over when I looked down and discovered that I was the object of his fixed gaze. It was disconcerting, to say the least, but I was able to hold on long enough to kick the shotgun out from under him.

It was a relic of the nineteenth century—two rusty twelve-gauge barrels fired with external hammers, and a handle that was held together with electrical tape. It would probably blow up in my face if I tried to use it, but it was better than nothing. I turned toward the house and steeled myself for what I might find.

The door was open. As I stepped into the murky stillness, a dim, flickering light drew me through the front room, where I'd spent the previous night, toward the back of the house. The light grew in intensity as I approached, a soft orange glow emanating from inside the bedroom, dancing across the undulating gray plaster of the back wall. I went slowly, listening for any sound, any movement. There was none.

As I rounded the corner, her blood-splattered hand came into view. She was reaching out, pleading—maybe begging for mercy from her killer, or perhaps attempting to call her husband, who already lay naked and dead on the road. Or maybe it was Rosalina's last desperate plea to God that He not let her die there, in wretched anguish, on the cold, hard tiles.

The flame in the oil lamp hovered over the scene, flitting and jumping behind its glass casing, casting a nervous illumination onto the horror that I faced. An innocent young woman had been sliced open—not with cool precision, but with a savage brutality that made every fiber in my body contract in revulsion until I could scarcely draw a breath. I fell back against the door. The sheets were smeared with deep crimson, her cotton nightgown saturated with blood emanating from her stomach, where the blade had penetrated, and there were bloody handprints across the white walls. She'd been attacked in the bed, then tried to make it out of the room, using the wall for support. She hadn't made it, collapsing before she reached the door. That's where she'd realized that she was going to die, and all she could do was beg for help. From her husband, her executioner, or from God, it didn't matter. None came.

All the constricting pain I felt suddenly came together to form a ball of agony in the pit of my stomach. I doubled over, and in my body's attempt to expel the ache, I retched everything I had, coughing and sputtering until I was empty and gagging on my own bile.

I straightened up and took a shaky breath. It was impossible to avoid looking at the poor girl's face again. I hadn't exchanged more than a polite smile with this gentle soul, but seeing her there in that state was enough to make me want to cry like a baby. My physical reaction to the grisly scene was certainly understandable, but it wasn't just the blood that had made me sick. It was the fact that this was a case of mistaken identity. It was the thought that this could have been Eva.

The dawn's silky light seeped into the night sky, lifting the black veil that had draped the mountain in darkness. The world was taking shape again. I leaned into the doorway, absorbing it all as I lit a smoke and tried to get my bearings. I knew now who had sold us out, but that was for later. First, there was Eva. Where the hell was Eva?

Something caught my eye and made my stomach tense up again. About thirty yards from the house, a dark object, in the grass. The light was too faint yet to give it definition, but something was definitely there, something of substance. I tossed my cigarette aside, picked up the shotgun, and ran. My legs felt heavy and numb, as if I was running in one of those dreams where you have to get away from something, but you're weighed down by some invisible force of nature, and the more effort you make, the harder it is to break free.

As I neared the object, it began to take on the form of a human. A man, flat on his belly, limbs fixed in a crawling position. I stood over him, breathing harder than I should've been for such a short sprint, feeling sorry that the bastard was beyond the pain that I would've liked to inflict on him, and that he deserved. It was some comfort to know that he hadn't died quickly. I counted three places where the bullets had torn through the black leather jacket before they ripped into his lungs. Behind him was a twenty-foot trail of matted grass that showed the path he'd crawled in his escape attempt, starting where the first shots felled him, finishing where his life had been ended with at least one point-blank bullet to the brain. The top right side of his head was pretty well missing.

I kicked him over onto his back. The lifeless face of an assassin. It didn't say much. Just that I'd never seen him before. That didn't matter, though. I already knew where he'd come from and why he'd been sent.

"Don't turn around."

Eva's voice was muted, flat and cold.

"Okay," I said.

"I've killed three men. A fourth won't make any difference to me."

"If you thought there was a reason to do that, you would've already done it," I said, hoping like hell that I was right.

"Did you come with him?"

"No."

"Why did you come?"

I needed to talk to her face-to-face, so I didn't answer. "I'm going to drop the shotgun, Eva," I said calmly. "Then I'm going to turn around. Okay?" I waited for a response, but none came, so I let the gun fall out of my hand, put my arms in the air, and started rotating around.

I could see that Eva was on the edge. She held the Luger tightly in both hands and stood firm, ready to absorb the kick when she pulled the trigger. I considered myself lucky that my skull was still intact.

We stared at each other for a moment.

"I thought they'd killed you," I said, but she ignored the implication.

"You weren't supposed to be here until later. Why did you come?"

"I saw Ritter last night."

"And?"

"He was drinking champagne and talking too much."

"What was he saying?"

"That he knew you were still alive. Somebody sold us out."

Eva laughed. "I'm still not sure that it wasn't you, Jack."

"I think you know better," I said.

She stared at me for what seemed a very long time, then she dropped her arm to her side, as if the pistol was too heavy for her to support any longer. She shook her head.

"Why, Jack?" I wasn't sure what she meant, and I don't know that she did, either.

"You said you've killed *three* men . . ."

"There's another one over there." She gestured up the field. "The same as this one. Gestapo."

"There's nothing we can do here," I said. "My car's on the drive."

She nodded and slung her handbag over her shoulder. I didn't feel right about leaving Rosa and Fabio, but it would have to wait. Eva glanced back at the house as we walked toward the car and I thought she was thinking the same thing. But neither of us said anything.

I slowly reversed down the drive, passing the killers' vehicle, which was stowed in the brush just a few yards from where I'd stopped. I guessed that the driver had pulled up to keep Fabio busy, allowing his partner to come up from behind, then they'd gone on to the house on foot.

We hit the main road at the bottom of the mountain. Lisbon to the left, Estoril and the Palacio to the right. I turned right.

Alberto was in his pajamas, watering the line of potted plants that sat on the doorstep of his two-room stucco home. He smiled as I pulled up, put down the watering can, and came toward the car. Then he saw my face and froze.

"Senhor . . . What a big surprise. Why—?" When Eva stepped out of the car, he went quiet and pale.

"Maybe we should do this inside," I said. There were a number of similar dwellings scattered along the dusty road and I didn't want to wake the neighbors.

"I . . . I don't understand. Has something happened?"

"Yes, Alberto. Something's happened."

He started backing away and stumbled over the watering can, hitting the ground squarely on his back. He flailed around for a moment, trying to find his legs, then resorted to covering his head when I leaned in. I wasn't sure what I was going to do with him, but I started by grabbing him by the collar and dragging him to his feet. I pushed him up against the wall of the house, my clenched fists pressing hard against his throat. He tried to say something, but couldn't get it past his windpipe, so I eased up slightly. I didn't want him passing out on me.

Before I could open my mouth, Alberto's extra-large wife came barreling through the ceramic beads that hung in the doorway, launched herself onto my back, and started pummeling me, while screeching the Portuguese equivalent of *Help! Killer!* at the top of her lungs. Anyone within a half mile who wasn't deaf would've heard it, but the locals all decided against playing hero.

Eva got the big lady's attention by pressing the Luger up against her cheek. The screams ended abruptly, replaced by a series of long, equally annoying moans. Then the tears started. I was half hoping that Eva would just go ahead and pull the trigger when I noticed the young twins standing in the doorway, two looks of identical terror on their bookend faces.

"Tell her to take the kids inside," I said to Alberto. He relayed the message with a nod, and his wife didn't argue. She scooped the girls up and retreated into the house to await her husband's fate.

"Let me see the gun," I said, and Eva handed it over without comment. Alberto was starting to sweat, but staring a bullet down kept him focused.

"I am innocent," he said defiantly.

"Of what?"

He frowned. "Have you come to kill me?"

"I'm not sure yet," I said. "But it's a possibility."

He swallowed hard, and I pushed the pistol up under his chin. I wanted him to feel the metal.

"I'll count to three before I pull the trigger," I said. "Ready? . . . One . . . two . . ."

"They make me do it!"

"Do what?"

He was hyperventilating and got stuck. I removed the Luger and gave him a moment to catch his breath, but it didn't help much.

"They have made me to tell . . ."—he panted—". . . about the senhorita Eva . . . They want to know . . . where is she."

"Who wanted to know?"

"The Guarda . . . Catela . . . He comes in the night and he says if I don't tell, he takes me to jail . . . Please, senhor . . . I have my family . . . When I go to jail they don't see me again . . . What happens for them?" He waited for a sign of understanding, but got none. "But is okay, yes?!" He tried to lighten things up. "The senhorita, she is okay! They don't find her . . . Good! Good! To hell with them!"

I'd had enough. I cocked my arm and whipped the butt of the pistol hard across his head. There was a loud *crack!* and he went down again. I think even Eva was startled. Alberto cried out and held the wound, which wasn't producing much more than a trickle of blood, but it was already starting to swell up.

"*Bastardo!*"

He spat on the ground, but it was meant for me. I stepped up and, straddling him, placed the gun next to his ear and calmly fired off a shot. Alberto cried out and rolled himself up into into a fetal ball. I shoved the gun into his ribs.

"Tell me the truth, Alberto!"

"I have told to you—!"

"The truth, Alberto! How much did the Gestapo pay you?!"

"It's not like this! I swear!"

"The truth!" I prodded him. "No one came in the night and threatened you, did they?!"

"Yes! They came—! Capitão Catela—"

"Why would Catela come looking for Eva when he thought she was dead? Everyone thought she was dead—until you told them otherwise!"

"No . . . !"

"You saw a chance for some money, and you took it! That's right, isn't it?! You went to the German embassy and you told Ritter!"

"No!" I fired off another round.

"Didn't you?!"

"Please, senhor . . . !"

"DIDN'T YOU . . . ?!"

"YES! . . . Yes . . . I did . . ."

He looked up at me, wondering what I would do now. I stood there for moment, unsure myself. In spite of everything, I guess I pitied the poor bastard. He didn't deserve it, but I did anyway.

"How much did they pay you, Alberto?" I said, softly now. "What's the going rate in Lisbon for betrayal?"

He sighed, shook his head slowly back and forth, then looked to Eva for absolution. "I have to take care for my family . . ."

Eva gave him a steely look. "Go see Fabio and Rosa. You'll see exactly how well you took care of your family."

"What—?" Alberto looked from Eva to me and back to Eva again. "Is something happen to my cousins?"

I took Eva's arm and led her back to the car. Alberto pulled himself to his feet and followed.

"Please, senhor . . . !" He called after us. "I was wrong to do it. But please tell me . . . Nothing has happened to Fabio and Rosalina! They are innocent . . . !"

I gave him a look that stopped him in his tracks. He knew what it meant. As Eva and I pulled away, I looked into the wing mirror and saw that Alberto had fallen to his knees.

But it was too late for praying.

The persistent *clackety-clack* of the wheels bouncing along the track, accompanied by the gentle rocking of the carriage, should've been enough to lull me into a much-needed slumber, but I had too many thoughts knocking around in my head to allow for sleep. Paris was still fourteen hours away—plenty of time to do what I had to do—but I'd have to make my move soon, in the early hours of the morning, after we'd crossed the Spanish border. There would be no room for mistakes.

I was pretty sure that "The Angel of Darkness" hadn't spotted us at the station. He'd been too busy watching Madame Moulichon waddle aboard and settle herself into the compartment she occupied three cars behind the first-class accommodation that Eva and I were sharing. The German had a face that would be striking under any circumstances— the boyish Mickey Rooney looks, spoiled by the permanent scowl that somebody's knife had carved into the right profile—but the black eye and the bandage across his left cheek, courtesy of Eva's boot, made him impossible to miss. I'd watched him from behind the glass as he loitered on the platform, waiting until the very last moment to jump onto the train as it pulled out of Lisbon's main station.

I didn't like what lay ahead, but there was no other choice. Even if the Gestapo didn't yet know the importance of the mission that had been entrusted to the duchess's housekeeper, they'd figure it out once we hit Paris. We'd have to be very thorough with the cleanup, though. The German would have to simply disappear, with no telltale traces of blood left behind.

Eva murmured something unintelligible, slid her arm across my bare chest, and nestled onto my shoulder. I could feel the soft warmth of her breast through the thin cotton T-shirt she'd worn to bed, and the steady pulse of her heart seemed to match mine, beat for beat. An unfamiliar sense of sublime contentment engulfed me for a moment, but it was soon replaced by a foreboding for what was to come. I stared into the darkness and turned my thoughts back, toward the events of the last forty-eight hours.

"What a lovely surprise . . ."

Harry Thompson displayed a perplexed smile, looked over to me, and nervously cleared his throat. "You didn't tell me that you'd be bringing Mademoiselle Foquet, Jack . . . Er, perhaps she'd like to wait for you out here?" He made a sweeping gesture around the empty bar. "Inasmuch as we have a variety of matters to—"

"This is Eva Lange, Harry," I said, stopping him midsentence. He stood there, staring at me for a beat, then had another look at Eva.

"I see," he said. "Then she's not dead, after all."

"Harry's a reporter," I explained. "Nothing gets by him."

"So I see." Eva smiled.

"Yes, well . . ." Harry fumbled. "This is unexpected."

"Is he here?" I said.

Harry nodded and ushered us into a back room, where Stropford was seated at a small wooden table, plunging a tea bag in and out of a cup of tepid water. He looked up as we entered, broke into a broad smile as he rose to his feet.

"Hello, Jack," he said warmly, offering a hand. "Good to see you again. Glad we could make this work."

He stole a glance at Eva and didn't skip a beat when I introduced her. "Yes, I've heard all about you, of course," he said. "Please, sit down. Can't say as I can recommend the tea, I'm afraid. These wretched bags—another laborsaving device from America, I fear. It wouldn't be so bad, I suppose, if they'd just allow it to brew in a proper pot, but they seem to think it a good idea to allow one to do one's own dunking. Perhaps you'd like something with a bit more bite?"

"Whatever Harry's having," I said, knowing that was a safe bet.

"Canadian blend," Harry informed me. "Not bad, actually."

"Miss Lange?" Stropford offered.

"Nothing, thank you."

Harry headed back into the bar to fetch my drink.

"So . . ." Stropford grinned across the table at Eva. "Everyone's been looking for you, and here you are."

"Here I am," she echoed.

"You don't seem surprised," I said to Stropford.

He paused, scrunched up his forehead, and shifted his gaze toward me. "When Harry told me that you were inquiring about passage to England for a single female, my natural skepticism was aroused. I checked, and found that Lisa Foquet had already sailed, Wednesday night, on the *Avoceta*. When I wired the captain, he informed me of the last-minute arrest by the local authorities. They, of course, have no record of any such incident."

"That was me," I confessed with a grin.

"So I assumed." Harry reappeared with the whiskey, and Stropford paused long enough to watch me sample it before turning back to Eva. "I take it, then, Miss Lange, that you've decided against a life in Hollywood."

"You take it correctly."

He nodded his head sympathetically. "Most people would view the chance to leave Europe for the sunny climes of California as an opportunity not to be missed. Particularly when the offer comes under the auspices of the likes of Lili Sterne."

"I don't want to live under anyone's auspices."

"I quite understand." He smiled. "Still, one can't help wondering why you would choose to give up the safe haven of America in favor of an uncertain future in London."

"I think I understand what you're implying, Mr. Stropford," Eva said. "And, given my background, I know that I must be subject to a certain amount of scrutiny before I'm to be fully trusted, but surely I've already gone some way in proving myself."

Stropford cocked his head. "I'm not sure I follow you. Are you referring to the death of Dr. Kleinmann?"

"And the surrounding circumstances . . ."

He frowned. "My understanding is that his murder—if you will—was the result of a disagreement of a personal nature. Is it not true that you and he—"

"Excuse me," I broke in. "But we didn't come here to get the third degree."

"Of course not." Stropford nodded sympathetically, then leaned forward and frowned. "Why exactly did you come?"

"So you could—"

"—arrange entry into Great Britain for a German agent without asking any questions? I must say, I think you're being somewhat naive if that's what you expected."

Eva shifted in her seat. *"Former* German agent," she said.

Stropford gave her a contemptuous look, reached into his coat pocket, and removed a pipe. He looked her over as he took the stem between his teeth, struck a match, and fired up. "Perhaps," he said, leaning back on his chair. "And perhaps not."

Eva exhaled a short, sharp breath, and tried to smile. "I spent two weeks locked in the basement of your embassy in Paris, being thoroughly interrogated—"

"Yes, I'm aware of those interviews," Stropford interrupted

dismissively. "But just two days ago you were attempting to sneak into Britain using a false identity. What am I to make of that?"

This was headed nowhere good and I was losing patience. "Look," I said. "We can sit here playing 'what if' games all day long, but we're just gonna go around and around in circles. So how about we jump to the bottom line? Are you going to help her get to England or not?"

Stropford gave me a weary look, leaned forward, and dropped his spent match into a dirty ashtray. "I must consider all the facts before making any sort of decision along those lines."

"Then how about considering the fact that every German in Lisbon is trying to kill her?"

He shrugged. "She looks very much alive to me."

"For Christ's sake," was all I could say.

"What about Bicycle?" Eva said softly.

"Bicycle?"

"Didn't you see his report?"

Stropford was stumped. "I'm sorry . . . Which report is that?"

Eva stared at him from across the table. "You don't know what I'm talking about, do you?"

"I must confess that I don't."

Eva sat there for a moment, gathering steam, then sprang to her feet and started pacing the room. We all watched for a moment, then she stopped as suddenly as she'd started and swung around on Stropford.

"Then you don't know about the letter?"

"What letter is that?"

"The one from the Duchess of Windsor to von Ribbentrop."

Stropford needed a moment to take it in. He looked to Harry, who shrugged, and then to me. "There exists a letter from the Duchess of Windsor to the German foreign minister?" He spoke slowly, clearly enunciating each syllable, ensuring there would be no communication errors.

"Yes," Eva said.

Stropford narrowed his eyes at her. "You've seen it?"

She nodded.

"And the Gestapo know she saw it," I said. "Which is why they want her dead."

"What exactly did the letter contain?" Stropford asked warily.

"Would you like me to recite it word for word, or just give you the gist?"

"The gist will do, for now." He laid his pipe upside down in the ashtray, sat back in his chair, and crossed his arms.

"Well . . ." Eva closed her eyes and looked upward, as if she was reading from an image that she'd burned into her memory. "The duchess begins by saying that her husband wouldn't stand idly by and watch England be destroyed . . . And that he's working on a peace plan which has the support of—'others in positions of influence'—is the way she put it."

Stropford shifted in his seat. "She said that to von Ribbentrop?"

"Bloody hell . . ." Harry exclaimed.

"It gets better," I said.

"Go on," Stropford instructed Eva.

"She said that the duke would like 'AH' to know that there are documents that would shorten the war, and that they could be 'made available' once their 'affairs had been settled.' Then she asked him for money."

Stropford went pale. He reached for his tea, but changed his mind and replaced the cup in its saucer. "Anything else?" he said.

"He's asked Lili to carry a letter to Roosevelt," I explained. "Asking America's support for the peace proposal. That's what my dinner was all about."

"I see." Stropford nodded his head slowly up and down for what seemed like a very long time, then he turned to Eva. "Do you have any proof of this letter's existence?"

"No physical proof, no. I wasn't in a position to—"

"Where is the actual letter now?"

"In Berlin, I suppose. It was sent over two weeks ago."

"Hmm . . ."

"What's that supposed to mean?" I said.

"It means that it would've been helpful to have had this information sooner."

"I thought you did have it," Eva said.

"Yes. This Bicycle chap . . ."

"Who the devil is Bicycle?" Harry sputtered.

"He's the Lisbon contact that Geoffrey Stevens gave me," Eva said.

"Geoffrey Stevens?" Harry looked perplexed.

"Our man in Paris," Stropford explained, adding, "When we had a man in Paris."

Eva continued. "Stevens told me that Bicycle was a British agent who would help me get to London. He gave me an address, that's all. He didn't even know his name."

Stropford sat forward. "I presume that you've learned it since?"

"Yes," Eva replied. "His name is Popov. Roman Popov."

"Let me be clear about this," Stropford said, once the stunned silence had worn off. "Roman Popov is not, never has been, and never will be an agent of His Majesty's government."

A look of dismay spread across Eva's features.

"Are you sure about that?" I said, and Stropford bristled at the implication.

"I assure you that he could not be operating in Lisbon without my express knowledge and consent."

"Then why would this guy Stevens steer Eva to him?"

"I have only her word that he did."

"Why don't you check with him?"

"Indeed," Stropford responded coolly. "I would certainly do so if that were possible. Unfortunately, Geoffrey Stevens was killed in an artillery attack in northern France as he made his way back to England."

I stole a glance at Eva. She looked exhausted and, not surprisingly, on edge. Her situation was painfully clear. The British government had never heard of Bicycle, let alone about the von Ribbentrop letter, and they believed that Eva was a German agent who had walked into the Paris embassy in an attempt to infiltrate British intelligence. They explained her shooting of Dr. Kleinmann, the head of Abwehr in Lisbon, as the result of a lovers' spat, and the fact that she claimed Roman Popov as her contact in British intelligence made her all the more suspect.

"Even if she was still working for the Germans," I said, "why would she invent something like that letter?"

"Any number of reasons." Stropford shrugged. "As bait, to draw us in. Or to make us think the German High Command knows more than they actually do. They might believe that if we feel our defenses have been compromised, we'd be more likely to come to terms."

"Sounds pretty far-fetched," I said, noticing Eva move back around the table toward the seat she'd vacated.

"Possibly," Stropford allowed. "Clearly, the only acceptable course of action is for both of you to accompany me back to—"

He stopped there, his face frozen. I wasn't sure why until I looked sideways and saw that Eva had removed a Luger from her handbag and was pointing it across the table at the two Brits.

"Eva . . .?" I said.

"I've decided against going to London." She moved a couple of steps toward the door. "You can come with me or you can stay, Jack, but you'll have to decide quickly."

I stood up, but didn't move. Harry piped up.

"You're a bloody fool, Jack, if you go along with this. If there was ever any doubt about what she's up to, it's gone now. Look at her!"

I did look at her, and she looked back. It couldn't have been for more than a couple of seconds, but it was enough for me.

Eva handed me her bag. It was heavier than it should've been, and when I looked inside I saw why. She'd been collecting guns. Five, in all. Three Lugers, including the one in her hand, a Colt .38 Special, which must have been Eddie's, and a little Glock, which I took to be the weapon Popov had given her, the one she'd killed Kleinmann with. I chose the .38 and trained it on Harry, who just shook his head ruefully.

"Oh, Jack," he moaned. "She's not worth it."

"Be quiet, Harry."

"You're an American," Stropford said. "None of this has anything to do with you."

"I guess it does now," I said.

"It's not too late. If you put the gun down, you can remain neutral, but once you go through that door—"

"Get their wallets," I said to Eva.

"Their wallets?"

"I don't know about you, but I'm broke."

Eva nodded, moved around the table, and slipped her hand into Harry's jacket. She came up with a sad, empty piece of leather.

"Skint." Harry smiled, looking embarrassed. "As usual."

Eva tossed the wallet onto the table, then performed the same operation on Stropford, resulting in a much healthier-looking billfold. She flipped through the bills.

"About seventy escudos and a ten-pound note," she reported.

"Take the escudos," I said. Eva nodded, removed the notes, and replaced the wallet. "Give them to the bartender and tell him to go home. We'll lock the place up for him." Eva nodded and headed toward the front room.

"And ask him for some rope!" I called after her.

"Are you sure about this, Jack?" Harry said.

"Of course not." I shrugged. "But you know, Harry, sometimes you just have to close your eyes and take the plunge."

"Welcome to the war," Eva said as I threw the car into gear and punched the gas.

"Just one question."

"What's that?"

"Which side are we on?"

She gave me a look. "I'm not sure we have a side anymore."

"Okay," I said. "You and me against the world."

She smiled and turned toward the window, watched as I swerved to avoid a young boy who was leading his fully laden mule along the side of the dusty road.

"It doesn't make sense," she said quietly.

"What?"

"Why did Geoffrey Stevens send me to Roman? If he isn't a British agent, what is he?"

"Let's ask him."

I pulled the car onto the main road, gunned the engine, and headed east, toward Lisbon.

• • •

The warehouse had been swept clean—not a speck of dust left, let alone a Rembrandt or a Cézanne. "Looks like he flew the coop," I said, pushing the door open. "And took it with him."

Eva crossed to one of the long windows at the far end of the loft, and stood looking out across Lisbon's rooftops, tinged with the pink and yellow of the western sky. The light cast her face in a deep, rich, radiant glow, and I stood there taking it in. She felt me watching and turned, leaving her right side drenched in sunlight as the left slipped into shadow.

I moved toward her.

"Jack . . ." She sounded hesitant.

"Yeah?"

"I hope you didn't do this just for me . . . Just so we could be together."

"Why the hell else would I do it?"

We stood there for a moment, defying the laws of gravity, staring into each other's eyes. When we finally succumbed, we didn't so much fall, as slide into each other. Holding her sent an unexpected shudder through my body, which she must have felt, because she pulled me tighter, and then we kissed. I don't know how long we stayed there, lost in each other, but by the time we resurfaced, we were standing in total darkness.

And somebody was standing there with us.

We sensed it at the same moment. A figure, just inside the door, peering into the darkness. He wasn't aware of us yet.

We didn't move, didn't breathe.

Eva let her arms fall slowly to her side, then she stepped back and held herself flat against the wall. There was just enough ambient light filtering through the window to illuminate her eyes, which were locked onto me, waiting to see how I'd react.

I watched the intruder.

He took a couple of steps—heels echoing off the hard wooden

floor—then he stopped again. He sensed us, too, now. Eva reached out, tried to take my arm, but I avoided her grasp. I was tensed, waiting for my moment. I couldn't get entangled.

A movement—a fleeting shadow, or perhaps just the intuition of one—then a shaft of crisp white light cut through the darkness. The flashlight's beam swept across the floor and flitted up the walls, crossing the room like a prison searchlight, moving steadily closer to our exposed position.

I looked back to Eva. Her face was flushed, head tilted back, heart beating as wildly as mine. I couldn't be sure, but I thought the trace of a smile spread across her parted lips, and it sent a shiver up my spine. Was she enjoying this?

Was I?

I exploded out of my stance and raced toward the light. BOOM, BOOM, BOOM . . . My footsteps shook the hollow floor and reverberated through the building.

I counted . . .

ONE . . . TWO . . . THREE SECONDS . . .

The spotlight found me.

FOUR . . . FIVE . . . *FLASH . . . CRACK!*

A bullet ripped through the air, and sailed past my ear like an angry wasp. I didn't react, didn't adjust. He wouldn't miss again . . . I had to get there first . . . A glimpse of cold gray steel made me feel the point-blank emptiness of a gun aimed at your face. Then white light burst into my eyes . . .

CRACK!

The gun discharged again. I leapt forward, tucked my chin into my collar, and rolled over my shoulder. I hardly touched ground, finding my feet again before I knew which way was up. Swiveling around quickly, I located the light, pushed off my right leg, and buried my shoulder into the man's lower spine. He was smaller, lighter than I'd expected, and he came sailing off the floor—I could hear his neck snap backward as I drove him at full speed into the wall. We came down in a heap, and I quickly pulled myself up to a sitting position. The guy was facedown, lying perfectly still. I thought for a moment that I'd broken his neck, but then he grunted and started to come to. Unable to find the gun, I crawled back to pick up the flashlight which lay on the floor, its beam scraping the surface of the warehouse's old wooden floorboards.

When I swung the light back around, I found Eva standing over the guy, a Luger gripped tightly in her hands, pointing at his back. The intruder groaned and squirmed, but he wasn't aware of his surroundings yet. Certainly not that he was about to be shot in the back. Eva stood taut, ready to fire, but undecided. I turned the flashlight onto her face.

"You gonna do it?" I said.

No answer. She remained fixed, unable to stand down, but unable to pull the trigger. I pulled myself onto my feet, walked over, and gently removed the pistol from her grip.

"If you were gonna shoot him, you would've done it by now," I said. She sighed and let her arms fall to her side. The man on the floor was slowly coming around. He made a move to push himself off the floor, but didn't get far because his face met Eva's boot on the way up. The force of the blow flipped him over onto his back and he was out for the count this time. I moved the light to his face and recognized him right away.

"Tell me something," I said.

"What?"

"Does he look like Mickey Rooney to you?"

It really wasn't a fair question, because the blood that was gushing out of the guy's cheek was blurring any resemblance to the lovable movie star.

"His name is Engel," Eva said slowly. "Walter Engel. They call him *der Engel der Schwärzung*. The Angel of Darkness."

ili was packing. At least, she was standing over two maids, telling them how to pack. Every hat, shoe, silk stocking, and sequin had to be checked, logged, and rechecked before it could be carefully placed in one of the five large trunks that would be making the return crossing to New York and then on to Hollywood. It didn't help that neither of the ladies-in-waiting spoke a word of English, including the one I'd pushed past to get into the room. Lili was in fine form.

"Good God, darling! You look like hell!"

I caught a glimpse in the mirror and saw that she was right, I did look like hell. I felt like it, too.

"It's been an interesting day," I said.

"You'd better clean up and start packing. We leave first thing in the morning. I must be in New York by the twenty-second and this is the only hope." She cast an impish look over her shoulder. "It's been an interesting day for me, too."

"I won't be making the trip back," I said.

That got her attention. She stopped in her tracks, gave me a look, then allowed a tight smile to form on her lips. "I see. Well, I should have guessed it, I suppose. You don't deserve her, you know."

"You can't leave either, Lili," I said. "Not yet anyway."

"The hell I can't."

"You'll have to wait for the next boat."

The smile fell off her face. "Do you know who phoned me this afternoon, Jack? Von Sternberg, that's who. He wants me to meet him for lunch in New York. He has a part—"

"It's important, Lili . . ."

Her voice went up a notch. "—a part that every leading lady in Hollywood would give their firstborn child to play, and von Sternberg is going to offer it to me! Unless, that is, I stand him up for lunch! So you can see that this is rather important, too! Do what the hell you like, but I'll be sailing for New York at ten o'clock tomorrow morning!"

She fixed me with a steely glare, daring me to speak.

"Why the hell did you come here, Lili? What was the point?"

"Don't be stupid, Jack."

"Want to know what I think?"

She frowned. "Do I have a choice?"

"I think you didn't like what you saw in the future, so you decided to go off on some pathetic misty-eyed search for the past. And now that the future is looking a bit more promising, you're ready to pack up and move on, leaving the one person who seems to mean something to you high and dry."

I prepared for the worst, but it didn't come. She stood there for a moment, staring at me, then she deflated and dropped onto the bed. She shook her head a couple of times, then fixed me with grim, plaintive eyes.

"You're a bastard, Jack," she said. "A real fucking honest-to-goodness bastard."

The sea air reached down into my lungs and gave me a much-needed burst of energy. The sound of the waves rumbling in off the Atlantic made conversation superfluous, so we made our way up the beach without words. At one point Lili stopped and placed her hand on my shoulder while she removed her shoes, then she wandered into the surf, allowing the salt water to slide up under her bare feet. We'd slipped out of the hotel using the basement employees' entrance, the same way I'd come in, then around the back of the tennis courts, and over to the shoreline. I think Lili was enjoying the intrigue.

We found Eva sitting in the sand by the car, which I'd pulled onto a deserted section of the beach about a mile up from the Palacio. She stood up when she saw us and a soft breeze blew through her hair. I liked the way she held it back off her face with one hand as we approached.

"Hello, Lili," she said, a darting glance at me trying to discern the state of play.

"Hello, darling," Lili said warmly, but with a nervous edge in her voice. "I hope you know what you're doing with Mr. Teller here. He has something of a reputation, you know."

"I'll let you know if he lives up to it," Eva laughed.

"I'd prefer to remain in the dark, thank you."

Lili crossed her arms and looked off toward the western horizon, barely visible in the soft light of the waning moon. She could have been waiting for her close-up. I suppose Lili was always waiting for her close-up. After a wistful moment, just the sound of the surf crashing onto the beach, she sighed and turned back to us.

"All right," she said. "Tell me how we're going to save England."

I checked my watch as the duke's Bentley pulled into the parking area behind the hotel. Eight o'clock sharp. They were right on time.

The limo rolled to a stop in front of the service entrance, where I was waiting with an umbrella, ready to shield the royal couple from the light rain that had been falling since midafternoon. I stepped forward, but the gray-uniformed driver was faster, jumping out from behind the wheel and popping his own umbrella as he took up a position beside the passenger door. He stood at attention, waiting for the black Austin sedan to park up a few feet behind the Bentley. Two men dressed in brown suits and matching fedoras exited, and, after a cursory glance around, gave the driver the all clear.

Espírito Santo was the first to emerge. He gave me a nod, then turned back to offer his hand to the duchess, who stepped onto the pavement looking like a crow in drag. She glanced my way—I wasn't sure if she smiled or sneered—then the duke himself decamped, displaying his usual wrinkled brow. Judging by the odd look he gave me, he didn't have the slightest idea who I was.

"Hello, Jack." Santo greeted me warmly, then stepped back to allow the duchess to come forward. "May I present Mr. Jack Teller, Your Grace?"

"Yes, we've met. Very nice to see you again, Mr. Teller." She extended a regal hand, which I took, but stopped short of kissing.

"My pleasure," I said.

"You remember Jack Teller, Your Grace," Santo said as Windsor himself stepped forward.

"Ah, yes, of course. Jack." He nodded. "Good of you to arrange all this."

"It's Lili's party, sir," I said. "And I have to say that I've never seen her so nervous." I knew that I couldn't go wrong with flattery, and the duke proved me right, breaking into a wide, vain grin.

"Nonsense," he protested. "Nothing to be nervous about. We're all friends."

Santo was eager to get me alone. He pulled me aside the first chance he got, over cocktails, while Lili was entertaining the royal couple with tall tales of Hollywood.

"I presume, Jack, that we'll be able to discuss the matter which the duke and I raised with you the other evening," he said in his silky voice. "You were somewhat ambiguous on the telephone."

He was right, I had been vague, deliberately so. I wanted to make sure they turned up, but I didn't want them to know what to expect once they got there. It kept me in the driver's seat.

"The truth is," I said, beginning the speech I'd been rehearsing all day, "that I talked to Lili about your proposal, and she's nervous about getting mixed up in politics. As you can imagine, she's very protective of her relationship with the president." I let the disappointment sink in for a moment, then dangled the hook. "But I think we can get her to come around if we just take it slowly."

"Yes, of course," he said eagerly. "We must take it slowly."

"Lili doesn't expect me for dinner," I said, and Santo didn't bat an eye. He saw me as a useful go-between, but, ultimately, as an employee who wouldn't be expected to get a seat at the table. Counting on the arrogance, I'd had Lili arrange for six courses to be served, which would take close to three hours. Enough time for me to go to the villa, have a good look around, and get back without being missed.

"Stay off the subject of war and peace and give her plenty of champagne," I said. "I'll turn up later, for a brandy, and we can work on her then."

Santo smiled approvingly and patted me on the back. "A fine plan, Jack. Very well thought out."

I hoped that he was right. Of course, the part of the plan that I hadn't mentioned—the part that involved breaking into his villa and stealing top secret documents—that would be the tough part. I wasn't especially worried about getting onto the grounds, or even into the duke and duchess's apartment. I had enough breaking-and-entering experience under my belt to be confident on that score. It didn't even concern me that there was bound to be some security minding the fort. My guess was that the guys in the Austin were the first string, and whoever was left behind would be thinking of it as a night off. They certainly wouldn't be expecting a cat burglar. No, it was the second part of the plan that I was skeptical about. If the papers were there, I'd have a pretty good chance of finding them, but these were the documents that the duke had told Hitler would "shorten the war." It was unlikely that he'd have them tucked away in his underwear drawer. I'd made that point when Eva proposed the idea, the previous evening on the beach. We'd all piled into the car to talk, me in the front seat, the two girls in back.

"I don't mind the risk," I'd said. "But it seems kind of pointless. They'll have those papers stashed away in some bank vault somewhere."

"Where?" Eva responded. "Think about it. The duke and duchess are refugees—"

"Really, darling," Lili interrupted. "Refugees?"

"They're just as displaced as the people you see wandering the streets of the Alfama. They have no home, they don't know where they're going next, and they're willing to trade everything for a future. Those documents—whatever they contain—are their future. I don't think they'd trust anyone with them, certainly not a bank."

It was hard to argue with the logic—and it was also futile. It was clear that if I didn't go along, Eva intended to do the job herself. Besides, I didn't have any better ideas.

Once we'd agreed on the plan, Lili headed back to the Palacio while Eva and I drove up the coast about thirty miles, where we found a desolate guesthouse that provided a couple of spartan rooms for a few escudos. Eva was quiet in the car, staring blankly out the window the entire time, and went straight to her room once we'd checked in.

As I lay there, alone on my musty pillow, an uneasy feeling came over me. I'd just agreed to steal secret documents that could help Germany win the war, and put them in Eva's hands. What if she'd been stringing me along, after all? There was a corner of my mind that still held the images of the three men she'd killed—two of them shot in the back.

I was pretty sure that I'd fallen in love with Eva, and I thought maybe she felt something for me, too, but that didn't necessarily rule out becoming victim number four. It was one thing to risk your life for love, even to die for it, quite another to play the chump. Anyway, why take a chance? I could sneak out early, drive back to the Palacio in order to set the plan in motion, and have the duke's papers in hand before Eva could find her way back. Once I handed the documents over to the Brits, Eva would be in the clear, and we'd all live happily ever after.

Or something like that.

"I say, Jack . . . Hold on a moment, would you?"

I was halfway to the elevator when I heard the duke calling out. I spun around and saw that he was heading my way, his arm around the duchess.

"So sorry to trouble you, Jack, but my wife isn't feeling terribly well. She won't be able to stay for dinner, after all. Would you mind very much seeing her to the car?"

"No . . . no . . . I . . . sure, of course I will." I turned to the duchess. "I'm sorry you're not—"

"A migraine," she said woefully. "I get them quite frequently, I'm afraid."

"Come on very suddenly," her husband added. "Bloody awful."

The duchess turned to her husband. "I'm so sorry to ruin the dinner party, darling. And Lili's gone to such an effort."

"You mustn't worry about that." The duke took her hand and held it in both of his. "What you must do is lie down in a dark room with a hot compress over your forehead. And take two aspirin, no more. I'll explain to Lili."

She smiled and planted a kiss on his cheek. "Thank you, darling. I feel dreadful upsetting everyone's evening."

"Nonsense! You haven't upset anyone's evening. Has she, Jack?"

I smiled and concurred, but of course it wasn't true. She'd just put a serious dent in mine.

The duchess's headache seemed to subside as soon as I pulled the elevator doors closed. She raised her head and didn't just look at me—she eyed me like a vulture sizing up a piece of red meat sprawled out across the road.

"You know, Jack," she said. "You don't need to stand on ceremony with me. In fact, I'd rather you didn't."

"All right." I smiled, hoping we could leave it at that.

The lift moved slowly past the fourth floor on its way down to the basement. We were using the service elevator, as we had on the way up, so the royals could come and go unseen.

"Why hasn't Lili absolutely devoured you?" she chirped. "I really don't know how she could resist. In fact, my imagination is running quite out of control at this very moment."

I was more than a bit dumbstruck, which the duchess seemed to enjoy. She displayed an inverted smile, her dark red lips curling down at the corners of her mouth, her eyes narrowing until they disappeared entirely. She leaned forward slightly.

"Am I shocking you?"

"Isn't that the idea?"

She laughed, almost a giggle. "I could do a lot worse."

"I can imagine," I said.

"Can you, Jack?"

I tugged at the lever and we came to an abrupt stop. The duchess just stood there, a wicked smile locked onto her face, waiting to see what I was going to do. I stepped forward to pull the doors open, but she still didn't move. She didn't even blink. Finally, she let forth a forlorn sigh and reached into the small handbag she'd been clutching under her arm.

"Imagination is fine, up to a point," she said. "But we have to live a little, too. Don't you think?" She extended her hand and there, in the center of her palm, was a small, brass door key.

"Take it," she ordered.

I slammed my hand down hard on the steering wheel. Damn! But I couldn't help laughing at the same time. At least I wouldn't have to worry about how to get inside the villa. The problem was what I'd have to do to get back out again!

The thought of being "devoured" by the Duchess of Windsor was enough to turn my stomach in several different directions at the same time. I could skip the whole thing, of course, which was tempting, but there wouldn't be another chance like this. No, I'd have to go ahead with it. Maybe I could fend the lady off and find a few minutes alone to look around. Not likely, though, I had to admit. She'd have her claws in me the minute I walked through the door and she wouldn't let go until . . . Well, I didn't want to think about it.

I guess the duchess never really got the Shanghai whorehouse out of her system, and the duke, it seemed, just wasn't up to the task. It certainly wouldn't surprise me, with that limp hand . . .

I tried to recall a similar circumstance, with an equally unappealing female, who I'd managed to perform for. None came to mind. Not even Betty Hooper of Louisville, Kentucky, measured up, although I'd been so tanked up that night that it would be impossible to say for sure just how low I'd sunk.

Hell, I'd just have to grit my teeth and use my imagination. I turned the engine over and was about to slip into gear when I sensed a movement behind me—somebody tucked down below the back-seat, lying on the floor. I froze. The .38 was in the glove compartment, three feet away . . .

Go easy, I thought, no sudden movements.

Slowly lifting my right hand off the gear stick, I extended it out across the darkness, revving the engine slightly to drown out the noise as I took hold of the latch, twisted it around, and let the door fall open with a soft *click*. Grasping the handle of the gun, I slipped my finger around the trigger, took a deep breath, swung around sharply, and pointed the gun at the stowaway . . .

"Jesus Christ!" I yelled. "I almost shot you!"

Eva pulled herself up into a sitting position. "Yes, I noticed that."

"What the hell are you doing back there?!"

"Coming with you." She climbed over the seat and settled into the front.

"How did you get here?!"

"By donkey!" she shot back, shutting me up. "Why did you leave me stranded?"

"Well . . . I . . ."

She scowled. "What happened to you and me against the world?"

"Nothing . . ."

"Then why did you abandon me?"

I shrugged. "I feel better doing this on my own."

"Two of us have a better chance of finding something."

"Yeah, well . . . it's dangerous," I said, unable to come up with anything better. She just laughed.

"I'm not sure if you've noticed, Jack, but I'm not exactly help-less." I felt a bit foolish and decided to change tack.

"It's good that you're here, anyway. We've got a kind of a . . . well, a situation."

"What kind of a kind of situation?"

"The duchess went back to the villa. Claimed she had a headache."

"I see. That is awkward."

"More awkward than you think." I produced the key. "She gave this to me."

It took a moment for it to sink in, but once it did, Eva started to laugh. "Oh, no . . . Do you mean to say that . . . The Duchess of Windsor . . . Oh, Jack! . . . Can't you see how comical that is?!"

"I'm having a little trouble with it," I said, stony-faced.

"All right," she said, getting control of her funny bone. "Fine. It's fine. In fact, it works out perfectly."

"You think so, huh?"

"Well, it must mean that she'll be alone."

"Just the housekeeper, who'll be asleep, and the driver, who lives over the garage."

"Good. That's good . . . I can look around while you keep the duchess occupied."

"Occupied?"

"Yes. In the bedroom."

"I keep her occupied in the bedroom?"

"Yes."

"While you look around?"

"That's right."

"That doesn't bother you?"

"What?"

"Me and the duchess . . . In the bedroom . . ."

Eva looked over at me. She was trying not to smile, but not doing a very good job of it. "Jack . . ."

"Forget it," I said, trying to sound breezy, which is pretty tough when you feel like an idiot.

"Jack . . ."

"No, you're right. Why should it bother you? I'm the one who has to—" I shook my head. "Something about that lady gives me the creeps."

"It has nothing to do with how I feel about you."

Eva slid over, pulled my arm around her shoulder, and leaned into my chest. As she turned her face toward mine, the soft light caught the curve of her lips just right, and her brown eyes pulled me into their deep, dark depths. I felt I had an angel in my arms, and I wanted to tell her so. But, for one reason or another, I didn't. I kissed her instead. I kissed her long and hard. But it was something more than a kiss, too. It said what I hadn't been able to say out loud. And Eva said it back to me.

The key slipped effortlessly into the lock, and with a turn of my wrist, the door fell open. I'd left Eva and the car in a scenic view area about a hundred yards up the road—not far from o Boca do Inferno—and entered the grounds through the unlocked back gate, as the duchess had instructed. Aside from a faint light coming from the room over the garage, there wasn't a sign of life anywhere. The duchess had thought of everything, including a route through the garden that kept me downwind of the kennels, ensuring that the monsters wouldn't pick up my scent and start raising unholy hell. She had it so meticulously planned, in fact, that I wondered how well trodden the path to her back door was.

Stepping into a dimly lit vestibule, I shut the door behind me—making sure it stayed unlocked for Eva—then turned left along a short corridor, and through a swinging door. Once my eyes adjusted to the darkness, I saw that I was standing in an elegant dining room that opened through a wide arch onto a spacious living room with high ceilings. I passed under the arch and, as promised, spotted the stairway that would lead me to the duchess's boudoir. I paused to look around. At one end of the room was a gathering of large sofas and snug armchairs arranged around a big stone fireplace. The other end featured a fully stocked bar, with a half-dozen stools lined up along the counter. In between were Persian rugs, objects of art, and a mix of old master and contemporary paintings. The place smelled like money.

Something on the far wall caught my eye. It was too dark to be sure from a distance, but as I picked my way across the room I could see that it was indeed the Pissarro landscape that I'd admired in Popov's warehouse. I stood in front of it for a moment, absorbed by the light and color of the apple blossoms set against the vibrating violet sky, wondering who else had received a piece of the stolen treasure trove.

"Like it?"

I swung around to find the duchess posing seductively at the bottom of the stairs. Kitted out in a long, red-and-gold dressing gown that was tied loosely at the hips, her pasty-white skin, deep red lips, and black hair pulled back in an impossibly tight bun, made her look like a ghostly china doll.

"You should," she said. "It's a Monet."

"Pissarro," I corrected her.

An eyebrow shot up. "Well, now, isn't that impressive? You know art." She tossed her head and gave me her best provocative smile. "What else do you know?"

Then she turned and sashayed it back up the staircase, throwing a glance over her shoulder at precisely the right moment. She was well practiced in her art, that's for sure.

The mood in the bedroom had been set with a couple of red silk scarves thrown over standing lamps, a cozy fire on the hearth, and a whiff of incense in the air. The duchess herself was on display in the center of the room, arms falling limply at her side as she rotated her hips to some crazy music that was playing on the Victrola. It sounded like Indian snake-charmer music, which seemed appropriate enough.

I stepped inside, closed the door firmly behind me, and took up a position against the wall. Digging a Lucky Strike out of my pocket, I lit up and waited for the show to begin. The duchess took her cue and, keeping an alluring eye on me, began turning in a slow circle, hips gyrating to the music as she allowed the robe to slide slowly off her shoulders and down her back. Coming around for a second rotation, the gown plunged dramatically to the floor, leaving me with the demoralizing vision of this Cinderella sister bound tightly into a low-cut black leather corset with matching garter belt and stockings. I cupped my hand to my mouth, faking a drag off my smoke as I choked back a laugh, transforming it into a smile of delight.

Nothing seemed to be expected of me at that point, so I stayed put and waited for more. She wriggled around for a couple more minutes and, I had to admit, she had a certain hypnotic style that might've been erotic if it hadn't been so damned funny. I was having serious doubts about how I was going to manage this when her eyes led mine over to the bed and I saw the equipment that was spread out across the satin sheets.

I'd been on the receiving end of a cat-o'-nine-tails on *The Buccaneer*—Paramount's excellent picture starring Fredric March as the famous French pirate Jean Laffite, who saved New Orleans from the Brits in the War of 1812—but that was a make-believe flogging and the look in the duchess's eye made it clear that she wasn't kidding around. She started slithering toward me and I pulled myself off the wall.

"Look, Duchess . . ."

"Perhaps you should call me something else."

"Such as . . . ?"

"What would you like to call me?"

I had a couple of ideas, but I let them go. "Look, I'm not really . . . This isn't something that I have a lot of experience with . . ."

A wicked smile crossed her lips. "Don't worry. I can show you. You might even like it."

"I'm not really . . ."

"Shush . . ." She was on me now, face-to-face, winding herself around me. "You see, Jack . . . My husband is a very powerful man, but he has a great deal of self-doubt. He needs a strong hand to guide him, and I provide it for him. It gives him satisfaction. But we all have our needs, don't we . . . ?"

She slipped her her hands up underneath my jacket, pushed it back across my shoulders and down my arms, letting it fall into a heap on the floor.

"Because with all those self-doubts, my husband finds it impossible to . . . well, to meet my needs. You don't have any self-doubt, do you, Jack? No, I can sense that you don't, and that's why I think you'll be able to give me what I need."

I wasn't really sure what she was talking about until, instead of stripping off my shirt, she started to roll up my sleeves. "I want you to do whatever you like to me, Jack. I'm entirely at your disposal."

She shot a meaningful glance toward the bed. There was quite an array of equipment to choose from. Laid out beside the whip was a riding crop, a collar and chain, a wooden paddle, some silk bindings, a pair of leather gloves, a black satin mask, and a few things I wasn't too sure about. I looked back at the duchess, who tipped her head to one side in a coquettish expression of hope.

"Anything?" I said.

She smiled submissively. "And everything."

The *CRASH! BANG! THUMP!* coming from downstairs must've had the same heart-stopping effect on the duchess as it had on me, but two very different images flashed through our minds. In her scenario, the Duke of Windsor—considerate and loving husband that he is—was coming home early to check on his poor wife's condition and, being a bit tipsy, had tripped over a piece of furniture. At the same moment, my head was conjuring up a picture of Eva, stumbling around in the dark and knocking over a lamp.

I made a move for the door.

"Stay!" the duchess barked, and I did. She twisted her head around as best she could, given her position on the bed. "Untie me!" she ordered.

I stood there for a beat, considering my options, and quickly realized that I had none, not really. If I left her there, I'd have to keep going and never come back. I crossed to the bed and started fiddling with the knots that bound her wrists to the headboard.

"For God's sake, can't you do it any faster than that!"

"You said you wanted it tight."

She gave me a look. "Do you realize what my husband would do to you if he found me like this!"

"Chop off my head?" I joked, but she didn't appreciate it. I finished unraveling her and she came off the bed like a shot. After pulling her dressing gown on, she stuck a stiff index finger in my face.

"Don't move!" she hissed. "Don't even fucking breathe!"

She stopped at the door, took a deep breath, put on a "slightly scared, and in a great deal of pain" look, then swept out of the room. I glanced down at the riding crop in my hand, and regretted that I probably wouldn't get another shot at her.

Unable to hear anything through the solid wooden door, I cracked it an inch. Nothing at first. Complete silence. I'd given Eva plenty of time to stow herself away, but there'd been no doubt that something was down there. I hoped the duchess would get scared and come back once she realized that it wasn't the duke.

Then voices. Two women. The second voice didn't sound like Eva, but I couldn't be sure, it was too muffled, too far away. I let the door swing open and stepped cautiously into the hallway. The conversation was less garbled, but I still couldn't make heads or tails of it. I moved along the wall until I was standing at the top of the stairs, where I could hear what sounded like a middle-aged woman speaking French.

I knew enough to pick up that the woman, who I took to be the housekeeper, had heard a noise and fell down the back stairs on her way to check it out. The duchess, not showing much sympathy, said something about her headache, then tried to get the maid, who she called Marguerite, to go back to bed. After that, I lost the thread, but Marguerite seemed to be saying that she couldn't sleep because she was afraid of something. Maybe she thought there was still someone in the house, but that was just a wild guess on my part.

I slipped back into the bedroom, picked up the crop, and sat on the bed, doing my best to look innocent. The duchess came through the door looking like she'd been sucking on a lemon. Figuring that our playdate was over, I stood up, placed her key on the bedside table, and flashed the most charming smile I could muster.

"Well," I said. "Thanks for a memorable evening."

All I got back was stony silence, and I let it go at that.

"I really must thank you, Jack." The duke was standing in Lili's doorway, gripping my hand and dripping with sincerity. "For all you've done tonight."

"We all do what we can, sir," I said.

"Quite right, quite right." He was ready to move on now, eager to get back to his doting wife, no doubt. Santo appeared from the living room, where he'd been saying his farewells to Lili, and greeted me as a new member of the brotherhood. He literally patted me on the back.

"Well done, Jack," he grinned. "Extremely well done. I promise you that your efforts tonight will not be forgotten." He leaned forward and lowered his voice. "I'd like to arrange for a more substantial token of our gratitude . . ."

"A handshake will do," I said, and I got an enthusiastic one, along with a big grin.

"If you decide to stay in Europe, please let me know." Santo winked as he exited to join the lonely-looking duke in the hallway. "I could use a man like you. Your powers of persuasion are quite impressive."

I was glad he thought so. Lili and I had worked on the scene for a couple of hours that morning, when I showed up at the hotel after skipping out on Eva. We hadn't actually scripted anything, but we'd bandied enough lines back and forth that we had a pretty good idea about how to play it. It was the kind of improvised rehearsal that I'd seen Howard Hawks run, which was one reason his pictures were so watchable.

Espírito Santo had been confident enough of success that in his breast pocket he carried the letter, which he handed over to Lili once she'd finally come around. She had no intention of giving it to Roosevelt, of course, but we'd convinced Santo and the duke that she would not only hand it over, but would also argue their case with the president. Why they thought he would pay more attention to a German-born actress than the British government, I don't know. I suppose Churchill couldn't flutter his eyes like Lili Sterne could, but it still smacked of wishful thinking.

I found Lili puffing madly on one of her Rothmans as she paced the living room. She was firing on all cylinders.

"Well?!" she said, watching me flop onto the sofa.

"It was interesting."

She put hands to hips. "Come on, Jack. You didn't break into the villa while she was there, did you?"

"Not exactly, no."

"What the hell is that supposed to mean?"

Lili's eyes widened as I told her the story of the backdoor key, and how I almost shot Eva when she surprised me in the car, and the plan for me to keep the duchess busy in the bedroom while Eva looked around downstairs. When I described the duchess's costume and what she had in mind for me, her mouth dropped.

"I don't know why I should be shocked." She smiled gleefully. "It's quite clear that she's a tramp. But, really, can you imagine?" She tossed her head back and laughed. "He must be the most foolish man on the face of the earth! And I can tell you from experience that there is some significant competition for the title!"

Lili wanted all the gory details, of course, but I managed to get her off the subject by suggesting that we read the duke's letter to Roosevelt. She liked that idea, quickly tore the envelope open, and read it out loud:

Lisbon, 13 July, 1940

Dear Mr. President,

It is with a heavy heart and grave concerns for the future of my country, and Europe as a whole, that I put pen to paper today. I feel a

*sacred duty to do whatever can be done to avoid the impending
catastrophe that surely awaits us if there is no intervention in the
current, dire situation.*

*I turn to you in this crisis, Mr. President, because I know you as a
man who can be relied upon for rational thinking, even as others fly in
the face of reason. You are a man of honour and discretion, and, above
all, I believe that you are a man of peace.*

*It is my intention to act as a mediator between these two great
nations. I have already received assurances from responsible parties on
both sides of this dispute that they would be open to such discussions.
Mr. President, I humbly ask for your support in these critical efforts. I
am certain that a statement from you at the right moment could prevent
further conflict in Europe, and thereby avoid a war of ruinous
proportions for the entire world. Let us work together toward peace.*

I eagerly await your reply.

Sincerely,

Edward, Duke of Windsor

Lili frowned and folded the letter back into its envelope. "He *is*
the most foolish man on earth. 'These two great nations,' indeed . . ."
She sighed, dropped onto the sofa beside me. "Do you know that
tonight he invited me to visit him in Buckingham Palace once this
nonsense, as he put it, has ended?"

"He's confident, I'll say that for him," I said.

"And do you know what he talked about all evening?"

"What?"

"All the friends we have. *WE!* As if I'm one of them!"

She flew off the couch and went back into caged-lioness mode. I
thought she could use a drink—and I knew I could—so I went over
to the bar and filled a couple of snifters with brandy.

"All his lords and ladies. Lord Halifax, Lord Redesdale, the Mar-
quess of Graham, the Duke of Hamilton, Wellington, Westminster . . .
I can't remember them all! And this isn't the only letter he's written.
He has one for his little brother—that's what he calls the king—sug-

gesting that he sack Churchill and replace him with someone who would take a more reasonable stance toward Hitler!"

She paused long enough to accept the brandy.

"It's not just them, either," she said, gaining steam again. "He wants to put me in touch with other 'like-minded' people in America. Like Charles Lindbergh and Joe Kennedy. That Irish pervert, I should have known that he was a Nazi."

She sipped at the brandy, and shook her head.

"I guess they can come from anywhere," I said.

Lili looked me in the eye, and I saw a sincerity that I hadn't seen in her before. In fact, I'm not sure I'd seen it in anyone before. Whatever the case, it was disconcerting.

"I feel ashamed, Jack," she said.

"Why would you feel ashamed?"

She shrugged. "Because while the future of mankind is hanging in the balance, my only concern was getting a part in a movie. So I could hold on to—" She stopped. "I don't even know what it is I'm trying to save. Is it the fame? Am I really that pathetic?"

"It's not pathetic, Lili," I said. "You're an artist. A great one. You don't need to be ashamed of that."

She smiled gently and placed a hand on my shoulder. "I think you're a good friend, Mr. Teller."

"I hope so."

I thought I saw a tear forming in the corner of her eye, but she managed to pull it back. Or maybe it was just a piece of dust.

"All right, then," Lili said cheerily. "What next?"

"Paris?" I repeated.

Aside from the furious *swish-swash-swish-swash* of the car's wipers, we'd made the drive back from the villa in total silence. I chalked it up to the failure of our mission, but it crossed my mind that maybe my bedroom time with the duchess was bothering Eva more than she'd expected. It turned out that I was wrong on both counts. She'd been plotting.

"I'm going tomorrow morning," she said. "I'd like you to come, but I'll understand if you don't."

I thought for a moment. Not about whether I'd go or not. Of course, I'd go. I was working on the why. It didn't take long for the penny to drop.

"Marguerite?"

Eva nodded. "She's taking the eight o'clock train. She's to go straight to their house on Boulevard Suchet, empty the contents of the safe, and return to Lisbon the following evening."

I recalled the duke telling me that he and his wife had been in Antibes when France fell, and had had to drive straight to Spain, abandoning their house and its contents in Paris. Apparently, one of the things they'd left behind was their ticket back to the throne.

"They're sending their housekeeper on a mission that could determine the outcome of the war?" I said.

Eva shrugged. "They can't very well go themselves."

"Does she know what she's doing?"

"She knows that she's to get the documents, but I doubt she knows what they are. She knows they're important, though. She's afraid. The duchess promised her that she'd be perfectly safe."

Neither of us said anything more, but we both knew that it was a promise that the duchess might not be able to keep.

"I'd love to stand on the platform, waving a handkerchief . . ." Lili forced a smile. "But I think that might be pressing our luck."

It seemed like another person sitting behind the wheel of the car, dressed in an old gray sweatshirt, baggy slacks, and a faded scarf pulled over her head. But it wasn't just the costume. I sensed that something had changed about Lili, as though a weight had been lifted from her shoulders.

"But you can step out long enough to give me a hug," Eva said. I stood back and watched as Lili got out of the car and the old friends fell into a long embrace. It was a clear, bright morning, the city's air purified by the previous day's rain, and life seemed almost normal as people made their way in and out of Lisbon's main railway station. I checked my watch: 7:40. Twenty minutes to buy tickets and get onto the train.

"When all this is over," Eva said to Lili as they separated, "don't be surprised if I show up on the doorstep of that big mansion of yours."

"I consider that a promise." Lili smiled, then turned to me. "Take good care of her."

"Count on it," I said.

We embraced, then Lili got back into the car and drove away. Eva and I smiled when the arm came out of the driver's-side window, madly waving a white handkerchief in the air.

I never saw Lili again after that. She went back to Hollywood, where she arranged another meeting with von Sternberg, but he'd already given the part to Gene Tierney. The picture, ironically titled *The Shanghai Gesture,* was interesting enough, but could've been a classic had Lili played the role of the decadent thrill seeker, Victoria Charteris. Over the coming years, Lili's career steadily shrank and, eventually, disappeared. As most people know, she became something of a recluse, closing herself off in her Upper East Side penthouse, seeing no one but the small staff that looked after her. The only glimpse the world got of the aging actress was an interview she did for a TV documentary in the late sixties, and the kindest comment from the critics was that she came off as a "distracted eccentric." A couple of years later, the papers made a big deal out of the fact that she died virtually penniless, but I happen to know that, over the decades, many good causes had received generous endowments from a mysterious organization called the Fallen Star Foundation.

The man at the ticket counter looked up and perused Eva's face. The passport was a good forgery—it damn well should've been at those prices—but he looked suspicious, anyway. Maybe he always looked that way.

I'd realized pretty quickly that we wouldn't get far traveling as Lisa Foquet and Jack Teller. Either the Brits or the Germans—probably both—would've had Catela put out arrest warrants, and they'd certainly be checking the trains. Eva thought we could buy our way out of Portugal, and then we'd be okay, but I wasn't so sure. It must've been around three in the morning that I woke up with the words *"I get you big money for American passport"* ringing in my ears. It took a moment to place them with the waiter who'd propositioned me on that first morning in Lisbon.

Fortunately, Miguel—which turned out to be his name—started work early. When he showed up just after six to open the café, he found Lili, Eva, and me waiting on his doorstep. After getting over the initial shock of coming face-to-face with a Hollywood icon, his eyeballs lit up with dollar signs. He ushered us into the back room and within an hour he'd taken our pictures, developed the film, pasted the photos into two genuine French passports, made the necessary changes, and soaked us for two hundred bucks. He also picked up my American passport and an autographed picture of himself and Lili, which he said would hold the place of honor over the bar, which, unsurprisingly, he'd just purchased from his erstwhile boss.

Eva and I walked away as Henri et Joséphine Barreau, of 14 Rue Clément, Paris. Joséphine looked a lot like Carole Lombard, thanks to Lili, who'd cut and colored Eva's hair the previous night. Henri, on the other hand, bore an unhappy resemblance to Harold Lloyd, thanks to a pair of round tortoiseshell spectacles that were requisitioned from the room-service waiter at the Palacio. The girls had disappeared into a twenty-minute fit of laughter when I'd first tried them on.

We'd spent an interesting night in the penthouse. Eva had waited in the hotel's boiler room until the duke and Santo left, and when I returned with her, after reading the Roosevelt letter, Lili had uncorked a bottle of Mumms.

"If it's to be our last night together, it might as well be a good one," she'd said. An unscripted, buoyant mood took hold after a couple of glasses, and we'd laughed several hours away, acting like kids on the night before a big holiday. At some point Eva had gone off to curl up with Lili while I dozed on the sofa.

"Cem setenta três," the ticket man announced. Eva counted out the escudos and handed them over in exchange for two first-class tickets to Paris. One way, of course.

Our cover story was that Monsieur et Madame Barreau had been vacationing in Estoril when France fell, and were now on their way home to Paris. I was a successful businessman, and my wife, Joséphine, was a primary-school teacher. We wanted to keep things simple, but because of my limited skills with the French language, we took Lili's suggestion that I play a mute. It seemed a stretch, but I didn't have any better ideas. We had Miguel put the condition on my passport, so if I kept my mouth shut—literally—maybe we could sell it.

I spotted Walter Engel—the Angel of Darkness—leaning against a wall opposite the platform entrance, pretending to read a Portuguese newspaper. He might have blended into the background better without the black eye and the bandage across his cheek, but as it was, he stood out like a sore thumb. I signaled Eva with an elbow to the ribs.

"Yes, I see him," she whispered as we passed by, seemingly unnoticed.

I shot a glance his way and saw that he was peering over his paper at something behind us. Eva sensed what I was doing and tugged on my arm, pulling me along. We turned onto the platform and she started chatting away in French—nothing too obvious, just a wife fretting over something or another. I had no idea what she was saying, so I just nodded my head up and down, like any speechless husband would do.

The cabin was small and elegant, though a bit faded. A high-backed seat, which folded down at night to become the bottom bunk bed, was decorated in a lush burgundy herringbone material, and the walls were covered with highly polished teak and cherry-wood tiles. The furnishings consisted of a small table in front of the window, with just enough room for the lamp and the single rose that stood on it, a washbasin in the corner, and a narrow, curved closet with a full-length mirror on the door.

As the porter handed Eva the key and explained, in French, about the water closet down the hall, I hurried to the window and tried to locate Engel. I spotted him a bit further down the platform, following a few steps behind a middle-aged woman who was struggling along under the weight of a fairly large suitcase.

"Is that her?" I asked Eva once the porter had closed the door.

"You shouldn't be speaking while you're sitting in the window," she said. "You can be seen even if you can't be heard. Yes, that's her."

Madame Moulichon, who the duchess had called Marguerite, stopped in front of one of the carriages, placed her valise on the platform, and looked around for someone to help her heave it onto the train. For a moment, I thought she was going to ask Engel himself, but once she got a good look at him, she flagged down a harmless-looking young man instead. Eva and I simultaneously sat back from the window as Engel strolled past. He came to a stop a few yards away and lingered there until the train lurched to a start, when he quickly hopped aboard.

"You think they know what she's up to?" I said.

Eva shook her head. "If they knew the documents were in Paris, they would have taken them already. No . . . I suspect they're watching everyone who has anything to do with the duke. As far as they know, she's going home to see her family."

"He'll figure it out pretty quickly when we get to Paris."

She was about to respond when the door burst open and the conductor stepped in. I turned to gaze out the window as he punched our tickets. He and Eva exchanged a few words in French—something about dinner—then he disappeared with a polite smile. As the train pulled away from Lisbon, following the Tagus River Valley north through the peaks of the Serra da Montejunto, my eyelids felt heavy and I let myself drift off into a deep sleep.

"That was quite a nap," Eva smiled as I resurfaced. The sun was high in the sky and the train was sitting in a small station with a faded sign on the platform that identified our location as FATIMA.

"How long?" I yawned.

"A couple of hours." She produced a small paper bag. "Are you hungry? I'm starved."

I groaned and pulled myself upright.

"I was dreaming," I said, trying to hold on to the images before they dissolved into the daylight.

"Good, I hope."

"Uhhh . . ." I shook my head as it came into focus. "More like a nightmare. Involving the duchess."

"Oh, really?" She removed two rolls and some hard cheese from the bag, unfolded a camping knife from her pocket, and started preparing sandwiches. "She made quite an impression, then."

"She was wearing jackboots and had a little black mustache like you-know-who. I'll spare you the rest."

Eva threw her head back, exposing her long graceful neck, and laughed wholeheartedly. It was a wonderful sight to wake up to.

"Poor boy," she said. "You've been traumatized."

The train grunted a couple of times, rocked back on its heels, and heaved forward. Eva handed me a roll.

"Where'd you get this?" I asked, not yet ready for food.

"An enterprising young man on the platform. He couldn't have been more than seven or eight." She produced a bottle of unlabeled wine from the bag. I retrieved a couple of glasses from the sink area, cleared the table for them.

"See anything along the way?"

"Madame Moulichon is three carriages back, sharing a cabin with a family of four."

"Better her than me," I said.

"Our angel has the cabin two doors up." She pried the cork out of the bottle.

"I'll have to steer clear," I said. "He'll recognize me from the casino."

Eva focused intently on the bottle as she poured. Keeping her hand perfectly steady as the train picked up speed, she managed to fill the glasses without spilling a drop. She replaced the cork, tamped it down, and slipped me a sweet smile.

"We're going to have to kill him, Jack," she said, as if I'd missed the obvious.

I handed her a glass, picked one up for myself, and tasted the homegrown tipple. It was thin, but drinkable. "Isn't shooting people starting to get a bit routine for you?"

"I thought you could take a turn," she said, sipping the wine.

"But you can't use a gun. It would make too much noise." Her eyes moved across to the table, and landed on the cheese knife.

"You want me to—" I drew my finger across my throat. "With that?"

"While he's asleep. These locks shouldn't be much of challenge for you."

She was right, the lock wouldn't be difficult, but to murder a man while he slept . . . Well, it gave me pause. Eva read my mind.

"You have to set any sense of fair play aside, Jack. It doesn't exist any longer. Not with these people."

She was right, of course, it had to be done. Once Engel realized what Madame Moulichon was up to in Paris, he'd raise the alarm and Hitler would have the duke's papers on his desk by the end of the day. No, Engel couldn't be on the train when it rolled into Paris, and if we were going to kill him, we might as well stack the odds of success and do it while he slept.

"It'll be messy," I said.

"Then we'll have to clean up."

"What about the body?"

Eva nodded toward the window. Fortunately, Engel was small enough that he'd probably just fit.

"The conductor's going to wonder where he disappeared to," I said, trying one last stall.

"Maybe that's all he'll do," Eva said, adding, "After all, he's French and Engel is German."

"And if he raises the alarm?"

"Let's take it as it comes," she said, and I nodded.

"When do we get to Paris?"

"Tomorrow afternoon, at two-thirty."

I picked up the knife, turned it over in my hand, and tried it on a piece of hard cheese. It would do the trick all right.

"Okay," I said. "Tonight."

We left it at that. I sampled the sandwich and, after a couple of bites, realized that I was hungry, after all.

. . .

After lunch, Eva retrieved a pillow from the overhead compartment, stretched out on the seat, and fell asleep. I stared out the window for a while, then got up to check the lock on our cabin door. It was British-made, a simple five-pin tumbler design with a spacer that allowed for the conductor's master key. Easier to open because once the master pins were lined up, the others would fall into place.

Like any decent hack, I knew where to find a pick, and sure enough, I found a bobby pin in Eva's hair. After gently removing it, I straightened it out, pulled the plastic tip off one end, and bent it to a forty-five-degree angle. I used the cheese knife as a tension wrench, and after a half dozen attempts, I'd managed to get my time down to twenty seconds. I hadn't lost the touch.

Getting in would be the easy part, though. I presumed that the setup in Engel's cabin would be the same as ours, and being alone, he'd almost certainly sleep in the lower bunk, to the immediate right of the door. It would be too dark to see much of anything, and I didn't want to start blindly stabbing at the guy, so I'd have to raise the window shade just enough to allow some ambient light in. I'd be at my most vulnerable then, with my back to him.

I'd never killed a man before. It was something to think about. Yes, it was war, like Eva said, and I certainly had no qualms about this guy coming to an ugly end. But it was one thing to justify killing him, another to plunge a knife into his throat as he slept. Would he wake up before he died? Would he know what was happening? Would he put up a fight, or would he try to cry out? Think it through now, I told myself, because there would be no room for questions, no time for hesitation, once I was standing over him. I'd have to be quick and clean, prepared for anything, with no peripheral thoughts to distract me from what I had to do. I'd have to be as cold-blooded a killer as my victim was.

. . .

We had dinner in our cabin—tender steak, creamy potatoes, and fresh asparagus, with a bottle of vintage Bordeaux. Afterward, the conductor knocked on the door to collect our passports—so we wouldn't have to be disturbed when we crossed into France—then the porter arrived to turn down the bed. We had to vacate, so we walked toward the back of the train and stood between carriages rather than risk waiting outside our door, where we might run into Engel. I was jumpy and Eva, sensing it, slipped her arm into mine and squeezed. Surprising what a difference it made.

"Ever been to Paris?" she asked as I lit a smoke.

"First time," I said. "Is it as beautiful as they say?"

"Yes, it is," she answered wistfully. "Though I can't imagine how it will look swathed in swastikas." She sighed and glanced sideways at me.

"I love Germany, Jack, with all my heart." Eva didn't owe me any explanations, but she seemed to want to say it, so I listened. "I try to think of it as a loved one who's been infected with a terrible disease—a parasite that worked its way into the brain, causing a kind of insanity. Because it's been left so late, the treatment will be harsh, and perhaps, in the end, it will even kill the patient. But without it, all hope would be lost. Does that make any sense to you?"

I opened my mouth to respond, but before I could get a word out, she leaned over and, lips parted, ambushed me with a warm, passionate, lingering kiss. It caught me off guard, but only for a moment. I took her by the shoulders, and pulled her toward me. She gave way, but without ceding the initiative. Eva was never a passive participant—not in life, and certainly not in kissing.

"Give me five minutes," she said, slipping out of my arms and quickly disappearing through the carriage door. I reached for another Lucky and smiled. I'd known, of course, that this would be our night. We'd both known. But knowing didn't make the prospect any less thrilling.

• • •

TML? No.

TOM GABBAY

238

OM GABBAY**

238

The cabin lights were dimmed when I entered and Eva was nowhere in sight. The newly made bed was untouched.

"Looking for me?"

I glanced up and found her smiling down from the upper bunk, a playful glint in her eyes. "I hope you don't mind that I took the top bed," she teased. I noticed that the ladder had been pulled up.

"Wanna throw me a rope?"

"Oh, no, I couldn't do that. You'll have to find your own way." And she disappeared under the sheets.

"Okay," I laughed. "If that's the way you want it ..." I quickly stripped down, stepped onto the lower bunk, and heaved myself up and over, landing squarely on top of her.

"That's rather forward of you, Mr. Teller ..."

I hovered for a moment, holding myself over her with locked arms, savoring the look of breathless anticipation on her face, her lips parted and ready.

"You think so, huh?"

"Yes, I do ..."

"Well, then ... I wonder what you'll think of this ...?"

I lowered myself onto her, kissing her deeply as I ran my hand along the curve of her spine until I touched the small of her back. I flattened my palm and toyed with the elastic band around her panties, tugging at them with my fingertips.

"I might have to scream," she whispered.

"Please do." I smiled.

I pulled the lingerie down across her hips, then along the long curve of her leg, until they disappeared into the bed. She wrapped her arms around my neck and pulled me into a frenzied kiss, each of us exploring the other with impatient hands. I lifted her T-shirt and lowered my lips onto her breasts, kissing the soft, pink flesh of her nipples. She tensed up with anticipation as I moved down, letting my tongue glide across her satin skin. She groaned and gave way as I kissed and fondled her, gently at first, then deeper, sensing her expanding pleasure and wanting to bring it to a shuddering climax.

I looked up, along the length of her torso, and could see that her head was thrown back and to one side, eyes tightly shut. She gripped the pillow in her fist and moaned softly, her body swaying back and forth with the movement of the train as it sped headlong into the night.

She reached down, pulled me back into her arms, and the world melted away, leaving just the raging fever of our lust.

Eva stirred and opened her eyes as the train rolled to a gentle stop. We shared a look through the darkness and listened as French customs officials boarded the carriage, stamping up and down the corridor, interrogating the conductor about each of the cabins' occupants, occasionally knocking on a door and asking for papers. Engel would be awake, too, I thought. I'd give it an hour after we got under way, just to be sure he'd gone back to sleep. I looked for my watch, but my wrist was bare. Eva showed me hers: 3:40. There would be time, but none to waste.

We didn't speak until the inspectors had disembarked, the train had let off a burst of hot air, and we'd rolled out of the station. As we headed into occupied France, Eva snuggled up to me.

"Lili told me you were quite a ladies' man in Hollywood."

I laughed. "Lili's been known to exaggerate from time to time."

"She said that all you had to do was look at a girl, and she'd fall at your feet. That no woman could resist you."

"She managed to resist pretty well."

Eva lifted her head, looked at me cockeyed, and let loose a wholehearted laugh. "You're joking, right?"

"Sure," I said. "I'm joking . . ."

She laughed again. "No, you're not. You don't know, do you?"

"Know what?"

"About Lili . . ."

"What about her?"

"She isn't interested in men, Jack. In fact, I think she finds them rather repulsive. At least as far as sex goes."

I let it sink in a minute. "You mean she—"

Eva nodded. "I thought you knew."

"I'll be damned," I said, shaking my head. I hadn't felt so guileless since—well, ever. How could that one get by me? Lili had often referred to all the foul men she'd had to bed on her way to the top—tossing off comments like "Thank God I'll never have to look another penis in the eye and say, 'Please, Mr. Producer, I was born to play this part!'"—but I'd never suspected that her aversion extended to the entire gender. I'd just assumed that she'd been discreet about her indiscretions. Apparently, she'd been very discreet.

"We were lovers," Eva said, surprising me again. I gave her a look, saw that she was serious.

"You and Lili?" was all I could come up with.

"Does it bother you?"

I thought about it a second. "No, it doesn't seem to."

"It only happened once," she continued. "It was the last time we saw each other, just before she went off to America . . ."

"The night of the concert."

"That's right. Did she tell you about it?"

"Only that you played like an angel, then you both got drunk on champagne."

Eva smiled. "I don't know about playing like an angel, but we certainly got drunk on champagne. It was one of those nights, you know, when everything is just right. Lili sparkled, the way only Lili can. She was going off to Hollywood to become a big star, and I was going to travel the world, playing music. The future seemed so filled with promise.

"It was lovely to see her. We'd been so close as children and suddenly there we were, together again, as if we'd never been apart. There were no barriers between us, no masks, no pressure, no need to pretend. We could just be ourselves. You don't often find people like that in life, do you?

"Anyway, we laughed about the past, and talked late into the night, and, well, one thing led to another . . . It wasn't until afterward that Lili confessed her undying love. I put it down to her overdeveloped sense of drama—she'd always been like that—but I also thought it was just as well that she was going away. We exchanged a couple of letters in the first year, but life moved on, as it always does. When Lili became a movie star, I assumed that she'd forgotten about me, or at least consigned me to the past. I heard nothing for years, then she showed up in Lisbon, with you."

Eva and I lay there side by side for a few moments, listening to the steady cadence of the train rolling over the track. I thought about Lili, and how empty she must have felt to have to reach back into her past in search of a fleeting moment of happiness. But maybe she'd been searching for something more. Eva was right, we don't find many people in life who allow us to let our masks down and be nobody but ourselves. After all those years in Hollywood, playing the role of the legendary film star, being the recipient of all that adulation, maybe Lili had lost the person whose heart went out to Eva on that perfect night in Berlin. Maybe finding Eva had been Lili's only hope of finding herself.

"How much time will you need?" When Eva finally broke the silence, it was in a very different voice. Detached. I didn't answer right away and she didn't rush me.

"Five minutes should be enough."

"Okay. Once you've done it, roll him up in his sheets and the blanket, tie him up with something, and wait for me. We'll push him out the window together. We'll look for a deserted spot ..." Eva paused, looked over at me. "Are you all right?"

"Sure," I said.

She turned onto her side and watched me through the darkness. I sensed that she wanted to say something more, but I let her come to it in her own time.

"When I was in Amsterdam," she began tentatively, "I received instructions from Berlin. They wanted me to make a list. A list of any German I could find who'd left the country since 1933. It turned out that there were quite a few. Many were teaching at the universities, but there were others, as well, doing all sorts of jobs ... There was one young couple who lived on my street. From Stuttgart. They had a little boy, nine years old. Very cute, very precocious. His name was Lukas. I didn't know the parents well, but I often spoke with Lukas as I walked past his house on my way home from the conservatory. He was a quiet child, perhaps a little bit lonely. He told me that his family had come the previous year, and that he missed his friends in Germany. I put them on my list.

"Then, one morning, a few days after Holland surrendered, the Gestapo came and took them away—the entire family. The father had been a journalist, and I assumed that he'd written something that the Reich found objectionable. He might be held, I thought, but surely the mother and child would be allowed home after a day or so. When, two days later, none of them had returned, I made inquiries. It took several days, but I was eventually able to find the Gestapo officer who had signed the arrest order. Do you know who it was?"

"Engel?"

"Yes. *Der Engel der Schwärzung.* I made arrangements to see him, concocting a story that I was interested in the family because I had been using the father as an informer on other Germans. I told Engel that he'd been quite useful to me and I would like him and his family to be released. It was clear that Engel wasn't at all interested in helping me—I was Abwehr, you see, and he was Gestapo. But I pressed him and he finally searched his records. When he found the information, he looked up at me and he smiled. He smiled for quite a long time, then he told me that the family had already been released—into the hands of God."

Eva paused to control her emotions.

"I was shocked and angry, and I didn't try to hide it. I don't think I could have hidden it. But Engel didn't understand. It didn't occur to him that I could be upset because an innocent family had been coldly murdered. He interpreted my anger as a reaction to his bureaucratic victory. The Gestapo had bested Abwehr by killing one of their assets. That was why he had been smiling.

"I asked him why they had been killed. Do you know what he said? They were 'enemies of the Reich.' A nine-year-old boy. The truth, of course, was that he had no idea why. But they had been on the list, so they had been taken out, told to kneel, and one after the other, they were shot in the back of the head. Engel said that he couldn't remember it, and I don't think he did, even though he had signed the paperwork. Perhaps he had even carried out the executions himself. Even if he didn't, he might as well have."

Eva's voice had never faltered through the story, and her eyes had never flinched. But now her emotions overcame her. She rolled onto her back and put both hands to her face. I pulled her closer and kissed her cheeks, tasting the tears that were coming now, in silent streams. She let me hold her for a moment, then she drew a long, shaky breath, and looked me in the eye.

"I can't remember the last time I cried, Jack," she said. "I honestly don't remember."

I tucked my wash bag under my arm and slipped into the empty corridor, sharing a last look with Eva before she pressed the door closed behind me. My heart rate increased with each step as I walked the thirty paces, knelt down in front of Engel's door, and removed the knife and hairpin from the pouch. The lock took me longer than I'd expected, thanks to the cold sweat that ran to the tip of my fingers, but after pausing to take a deep breath and starting over, I felt the pins drop into place.

As I turned the door handle, ready to step inside, something very odd happened. A wave of tranquility washed over me, engulfing me like a warm bath, soothing my jangled nerves. I didn't do anything to make it happen, it just did. My heart stopped pounding, the knot in my stomach evaporated, and my whole body relaxed into a peculiar sort of stillness—I felt alert and focused and entirely unencumbered. Perhaps "clear" is the best way to describe it. I would experience that same feeling many times in the future—in particular when I was about to face combat—but as I stood there on that train to Paris, preparing to kill someone for the first time, it was an entirely new sensation.

I carefully pushed the door open, slipped inside, and stood there, motionless, engulfed in darkness. I listened. For anything. Any sound at all. A movement, a stirring, a breath. But there was none. Nothing but the relentless beat of the train sluicing along the rails.

One . . . two . . . and a half paces across the cabin floor delivered me to the window, as I'd practiced. I reached out to find the wall with my left hand, steadied myself, and flipped around so I wouldn't have my back to the victim. I found the protruding wooden window frame, moved my hand up and around it to the shade's drawstring, and pulled gently, letting in only enough moonlight to give the room shape.

I could just make out the contour of a man lying in the bed. He seemed to be sleeping on his side, facing the wall, with the blanket pulled up around his head. There was no movement, no sign that I'd disturbed him, so I stood there for a moment, planning my attack. Slow and easy, I thought. No quick moves. Get close, but not so close that he'll sense something. Don't hesitate, and don't slice. The first cut has to be deep, into the jugular, severing it, if possible. Then be ready to hold him down, to cover his head with a pillow in case he cries out. If I do it right, he won't last long, I thought.

Tightening my grip on the knife, I stepped forward and stood over the bed where *der Engel* would meet his end. I held the blade over the spot I thought his head would be, and reached down to draw the blanket back. Some corner of my mind noted with interest how steady my hand was . . .

Then I was hit with a horrible, sinking feeling in the pit of my stomach. Something wasn't right. The blanket was the wrong shape. There couldn't possibly be anyone under there. I yanked the covers back and found nothing . . . Nothing but an empty bed. A sudden rush of adrenaline shot through my heart and one thought took over my whole being:

Get the hell out of here!

I hastily rearranged the bed into something approximating the way I found it, stepped away, and grabbed the door handle. *Christ, the window shade!* I couldn't leave it like that!

Crossing the cabin, I quickly lowered the shade, plunging myself into darkness again, then moved back toward the door. Halfway across the room, the train swung into a sharp left bend, sending me stumbling to the right. My hand went up to block the fall, and as I hit the wall I felt the hard steel of the knife's blade slice across the flat of my palm, unleashing a shooting pain up the length of my arm to my shoulder. I cried out and dropped the knife. Clasping my hands together, I could feel the warm blood pouring from the wound.

The door opened . . .

Engel entered with his back to me. In black silk pajamas with matching robe, he held a newspaper in one hand, a roll of toilet paper in the other. The Angel of Darkness had been taking a crap when he was supposed to be having his throat cut.

I planted my feet and stepped into a wide left hook, catching him squarely across the temple as he instinctively turned toward me. Falling backward, he bounced off the side of the bed and slid onto the floor. The cabin door kept banging open and shut, taking the room in and out of darkness, creating a strange, jerky quality to our movements.

I caught a glimpse of him on his knees, reaching for something under his pillow. Stepping up, I swung my leg around and kicked him hard in the ribs, propelling him back against the far wall. He groaned, shook it off, then lifted his right arm, bringing his Luger to bear on me . . .

The door fell shut again and the room went dark. There was a *LIGHTNING FLASH* and a bullet exploded into the mirror beside my head, showering the room with tiny fragments of razor-sharp glass. Then all hell broke loose. The door burst open and Eva started firing across the cabin. She got two shots off before Engel took slow aim and pulled the trigger.

She cried out and fell backward into the corridor.

There was a trace of a smile on Engel's face . . . though it could've been pain, too . . . as he swung his Luger back around on me. Something kept me from moving, and it turned out to be a good instinct, because I soon realized that he was having trouble focusing. He was fading. His extended right arm wavered, like he was struggling to support the weight of his gun. It sank steadily downward until, finally, his hand fell to the floor, his eyes rolled into the back of his head, and he passed out. A trickle of blood ran out from under his sleeve. Other than that, I couldn't see any sign of his wound against the dark material of his pajamas.

I rushed into the corridor and found Eva holding her left shoulder. "How bad?" I said.

"I don't know . . . I . . . I think I'm bleeding quite a lot." She was trying to be detached, but the fear was apparent. I could hear it in her voice and see it in her eyes. I knelt down to get a better look at the wound, saw that she was right. Her blouse was soaked in warm blood. I gently pulled the collar open, tried to get a better look.

"What about Engel?" she asked.

"You hit him."

"Is he dead?"

"I'm not sure . . . Maybe."

"We can't stay here . . . *Ah!*" She flinched as I pulled the shirt back off her shoulder. It was a clean shot, anyway. The bullet had threaded the needle, entering just below the clavicle and exiting above the shoulder blade. Still, she was losing a lot of blood.

"You need a doctor," I said.

She tried to laugh, but it came out as more of a grunt. "We're in occupied France, Jack, and we've just killed a Gestapo officer. A doctor isn't going to be much help . . . We'll have to jump."

"Jump?!"

"Yes . . ."

"We must be going fifty miles an hour."

"Help me up," she said, grimacing as she attempted to push herself up off the floor. I hooked my wrist under her good arm and, as gently as I could, lifted her onto her feet. She looked at me, smiled wanly, and swooned. I caught her and leaned her up against the wall.

"You're too weak to—"

"Let's worry about that once we're off the train," she said. I knew there was no point arguing, partly because she was Eva, but also because she was right. Dawn was looming outside, and people would start emerging from their cabins soon. With a dead or dying Nazi in his cabin, our survival odds were better with a flying leap off a speeding train. Not great, maybe, but better.

"Are you okay here for a minute?"

"Yes . . ." She nodded weakly.

I charged into our cabin, stripped the lower bunk of its top sheet, tore a piece away, and hastily tied it around my hand to keep it from bleeding. Furling the rest of it into a long roll, I knotted it several times along its length until it resembled a rope, then grabbed two pillows off the beds. On my way out, I removed the key from the door and double-locked the cabin from the outside.

Eva was looking pretty pale, but she was still standing.

"Stay with me!" I said, reaching across to close the door on Engel's cabin, which was still swinging back and forth. I looked up at the German and—I couldn't be sure. Was he still breathing, or was it the movement of the train? Had he moved?

I pulled the door shut, turned back to Eva just in time to catch her as she slumped toward the floor. Holding her upright with one hand, I gathered the bedding and her Luger with the other, then placed her arm around my neck and led her back to the platform between carriages.

Opening the exterior door, I leaned out and looked around. The ground was flat and open, but it was whipping by fast and the train showed no sign of slowing. Alone, my chances might've been reasonable. If there was one thing I'd learned in Hollywood, it was how to take a fall. But with Eva . . .

There was no point thinking about it. It had to be done.

"WE'LL GO TOGETHER!" I yelled above the din.

Eva nodded. She must've had a rush of adrenaline, or maybe it was the cold air rushing past, but whatever the reason, she seemed to have come alive. I pulled her forward, placed the two pillows on either side of her wounded shoulder.

"WHAT ARE YOU DOING?!"

"GIVING YOU A LANDING PAD!" I removed my belt. "GET READY, THIS WILL HURT A BIT!"

Wrapping the leather around the two pillows, I pulled it tight and buckled it up.

"MEIN GOTT!" she cried out.

"I'M SORRY!"

I wrapped my arm around her and drew her close, positioning her injured left shoulder on my right side, then I pulled the bound sheet around both our torsos and tied it as tight as I could, using a triple knot. I could see that it was causing Eva excruciating pain, but I had to be sure we'd stay together.

"OKAY, WE NEED TO GET DOWN . . . AS LOW AS POS-SIBLE!"

I had to yell even though she was right next to me.

"BEND YOUR KNEES!"

I pulled her down into a crouching position.

"WHEN I SAY JUMP, WE'RE GONNA GO STRAIGHT OUT, AT A NINETY-DEGREE ANGLE, AS FAR AS WE CAN! PUSH OFF WITH EVERYTHING YOU'VE GOT, AND DON'T TRY TO CONTROL THE FALL! I'LL DO IT FOR BOTH OF US! AND DON'T TRY TO LAND ON YOUR FEET! WE'RE GONNA ROLL, LIKE A LOG, WITH THE DIRECTION OF THE TRAIN! OKAY?!"

She nodded.

"COVER YOUR HEAD WITH YOUR FREE HAND!" I said. *"LIKE THIS!"*

She mimicked me, placing her right arm across the top of her head, covering her left ear with her palm.

"I'LL COUNT DOWN FROM THREE!"

I watched the approaching landscape, waiting for a clear spot, with no bone-crunching trees or rocks or telegraph poles to come up against.

"OKAY, READY?! THREE! . . . TWO! . . ." I could feel her tense up. *". . . ONE!"*

We went in unison and, it seemed, in slow motion, every fraction of a second making itself known as we arched upward and sailed through the air, unattached to anything but each other. I could see everything—every fold in the land, every slope, every blade of grass, all laid out in full, Technicolor detail. I threw our weight backward, staying at a right angle to the train while making us almost parallel to the earth, then I swung my hips left, positioning my body between Eva and a hard landing. I saw sky, then we hit with a punishing *THUD!*

Once you hit solid ground, there's no control, you go where the momentum takes you. All you can do is close your eyes, protect your head, and if you've got one in you, say a prayer.

The world was nothing more than a blur of shapes and colors, then, suddenly, we were still, lying side by side on our backs. I gasped for air, looked over, and saw that Eva had lost consciousness. I lay there, trying to catch my breath, listening to the fading rattle of the train as it disappeared into the distance.

There was a secluded spot a hundred yards away, under a group of tall elms that ran alongside a small river inlet. I laid Eva out in the soft grass and went to work on her. After cleaning both sides of the wound as best I could with a piece of bedsheet soaked in cool water from the canal, I put one of the pillows under her shoulder, placed both hands over the bullet hole—one on top of the other—and bore down hard, putting all my weight behind it. She groaned and tried to shift away from the pressure, but I kept her pinned. Just as well that she'd passed out, I thought.

I stayed that way for a long twenty minutes before easing off and taking a peek. The wound had stopped hemorrhaging, but I gave it another five minutes, just to be sure. Then I unknotted the sheet and ripped it into long strips that I bound as tightly as I could around her shoulder. I could do nothing more, so I rolled onto my back and took a deep breath. I winced. Bruised ribs. Could've been a hell of a lot worse, though. I couldn't help chuckling. It was like Lili's close-up at the funeral parlor. Best jump of my life and not a motion-picture camera within a thousand miles.

The morning sky was clear and bright, just a cloud or two floating by on a gentle breeze. Sunlight was starting to filter through the tree branches, warming the ground, and I became aware of a symphony of birdsong all around us. Closing my eyes, I drifted into a trancelike reverie, and soon lapsed into an uneasy sleep.

I woke with a start, aware of a shadow hovering over us. Sitting up sharply, I came face-to-face with a young girl. A delicate little thing, with dark eyes, silky brown hair tied back in a tangled ponytail, and bangs that cut straight across a perfectly oval face. Eight years old, I guessed—maybe nine—she was wearing a dark blue pleated skirt, a white blouse buttoned to the top, a navy cardigan torn at the elbow, beige ankle socks, and a worn-out pair of lace-up shoes. My sudden movement caught her off guard and she took a quick step back.

"Oh, pardon, monsieur!"

She looked like she was about to run.

"It's all right . . ." I said, showing my hands. "Don't be afraid . . ."

The girl stayed put, but kept her distance, watching me carefully, undecided about whether I should be trusted. When I turned away to check Eva, she took a tentative step forward.

"She is dead?"

I shook my head. "No. Just resting."

The girl nodded, moved another step closer, and leaned over Eva to get a better look, searching for a sign of life.

"What's your name?" I asked.

"Abrielle . . ."

"That's a pretty name."

She smiled shyly.

"I'm Jack."

She shot me a sideways glance. "Hello."

"Where'd you learn to speak English so well?"

"It's my best subject . . . But I don't go to school now."

"I see."

The blood rushed to my head as I hauled myself onto my feet. I waited for the dizziness to pass, then picked up a clean piece of the torn sheet, walked over to the river, and dipped it into the water. Abrielle maintained her vigil over Eva.

"You live around here?" I asked.

"Monsieur?"

"Nearby. Do you live nearby?"

"No, monsieur. It's very far away I live."

"What are you doing so far from home?" I asked, but she just shrugged, watching over my shoulder as I knelt beside Eva and dabbed her face with the moist cloth.

"What has happened of her?"

"Somebody shot her," I said, seeing no reason to lie about it.

"It was because of this war," she said matter-of-factly. A veteran, I thought.

"Yes," I confirmed. "It was because of this war."

She nodded thoughtfully and produced a frown. "My father is in this war, too. I don't know if he has been shot."

"I'm sure he's okay," I lied.

Eva's pulse was strong and she seemed to be resting comfortably, so my thoughts turned toward our next move. I checked my watch: 9:40. Dead or alive, they would've discovered Engel by now, and they would've realized that Monsieur et Madame Barreau were missing, too. It might take a while for the Gestapo to show up, but it wouldn't be long before the area was crawling with French cops, if it wasn't already.

"Is there a village near here?" I asked Abrielle.

"Yes, monsieur, not so far. There . . ."

She pointed across a field of long grass. I noticed that at the base of an old oak tree, about forty yards away, there was a nest of blankets that must've served as Abrielle's bed. I wondered what her story was—why she was on her own, far from home—but there was nothing I could do about it, and I had other things to worry about, so I let it go.

"Can you do something for me, Abrielle?"

"Monsieur?" She looked skeptical.

"Will you wait here with this lady until I get back? If she wakes up, tell her that Jack went to get a car and he'll be back as soon as he can."

She nodded, clearly happy with the assignment. "Yes, I can do it."

"Good girl. I won't be long." As I headed off across the field, I heard Abrielle calling after me.

"Monsieur!"

I turned around. "Yeah?"

"What is her name?"

"Eva!" I called back to her. "Her name is Eva!"

She smiled happily and took up her post at Eva's side.

There wasn't much to choose from in La Rocque, a sleepy little hamlet set alongside the River Adour, but I managed to find a faded yellow Renault parked behind the butcher's shop. It was an open top two-seater, with four bald tires and a rusty chassis, but the key was in the ignition. I opened the door, slid in behind the wheel, and was pleasantly surprised when it coughed into action right away. Not smooth, not by a long shot, but it ran. I could've just driven off, of course, but Lili had handed me an envelope stuffed with francs before we left, and we didn't need anybody running to the cops about a stolen car, so I removed the key, got out, and headed around to the front door.

A little bell rang when I entered the shop. It took a moment before a heavy man with a leery look on his face and a large meat cleaver in his hand emerged from the back room. He greeted me with a disapproving look. I smiled politely, removed the envelope from my jacket pocket, and, one by one, started placing one-hundred-franc notes onto the counter. I fanned them out so he would get the full impact of his impending wealth, and the image had the desired impact. His eyes grew larger with each bill. When I'd counted out thirty, I stopped and looked up at him. He narrowed his eyes, cocked his head, and waited. I gave it a moment, just for fun, then held out my palm, revealing the key to his car.

"*Vous voulez acheter la voiture?*" he grumbled.

I nodded. After performing a couple of eloquent grunts and a few meaningful sniffs, the butcher shrugged his massive shoulders and scooped up the cash.

· · ·

E va was sitting up when I returned, involved in what looked like a weighty conversation with Abrielle, who was seated beside her. They spotted me coming across the field, and both broke into broad smiles and waved, as if I was a late arrival for the family picnic.

"I hope you brought food!" Eva called out. "We're famished!"

I produced a couple of baguettes that I'd picked up at the patisserie to go with the chunk of pâté the butcher had thrown into the deal once his bulging pocket had elevated his mood. Eva broke off a piece of bread and handed it to Abrielle, who attacked it right away, while I lit one of the French cigarettes I'd picked up at the bar in town. Eva spotted the Renault across the field, where I'd left it on a dirt track.

"Is that it?" she said.

I nodded. "It's got four wheels and it goes."

"As long as it goes as far as Paris," she said, turning back to Abrielle. *"Ramasse tes affaires et attends-nous."*

The girl quickly ran off across the field, crust in hand, toward the oak. I watched her gather up her blankets, fold them neatly, and carefully place them into a small black suitcase that was lying nearby, then I turned back to Eva.

"What's going on?" I asked.

"Help me up," she said, and I gave her a hand. She was a bit stiff, but she could walk on her own. I followed her into the field of grass.

"We're taking Abrielle home."

"We don't have a lot of time to—"

"She lives in Paris."

I nodded and we took a few steps in silence while I figured out what to say about that.

"Look, I feel sorry for the kid, too, but—"

"The authorities will be looking for a couple. Having a child along will make us less suspicious."

"Maybe so, but ..." I hadn't expected this, and I didn't like it, though I couldn't really put my finger on why. "What are we going to do with her once we get to Paris? Assuming we get there, that is."

"She has an uncle in Montmartre. We'll drop her off and spend the night there."

"How do we know this uncle can be trusted?"

She shrugged. "I suppose we can't be certain. But there's a curfew in effect, and we can't very well check into a hotel. Anyway, he'll be grateful that we've rescued his niece, and we'll only need a few hours."

"It's dangerous," I said, searching for some valid reason to leave the child out of the equation. "Dangerous for her."

Eva gave me a sideways glance. "Is that the best you can do, Jack? That it would be much better for Abrielle if we abandon her here, to fend for herself?"

I shrugged. "Gimme a couple of minutes and maybe I can come up with something better."

A brielle had never ridden in a car before, and the look of sheer delight on her face as she sat in the jump seat, covered in blankets, pâté sandwich in hand, wind blowing in her hair, was enough to put a smile on anybody's face. Even mine.

"Enjoying the ride back there?" I called to her.

"*C'est magnifique!*" she cried out, grinning from ear to ear. I looked over at Eva, saw that she was smiling, too.

"How are you feeling?"

"Like I've been shot," she groaned.

"We had a lucky escape."

"Not just lucky." She put on an impish smile. "You must be a pretty good stuntman."

"The best." I grinned.

Eva laughed, pushed the hair off her cheek, and settled back into the seat. Closing her eyes, she sighed deeply and offered her face up to the midday sun.

I stuck to the secondary roads, making Paris a long ten hours away, at best. If all went well, we'd roll in before the eleven o'clock curfew, stay the night with Abrielle's uncle, and be at the duke's town house on Boulevard Suchet not much after six, when the streets reopened. Madame Moulichon was supposed to catch the evening train back to Lisbon, which gave us roughly twelve hours to do whatever it was we were going to do.

How's the kid doing back there?" I said to Eva when she woke up, a couple of hours later.

She leaned over and planted a kiss on my cheek. "Now don't go spoiling your tough-guy image," she said.

"Yeah, yeah. It's getting kind of chilly, that's all."

Eva laughed, then twisted around to rearrange Abrielle's blankets.

"She's had a tough time of it, huh?" I said.

"Yes, she has."

"So? You gonna tell me or not?"

"If you're interested."

"I'm interested."

"Well . . ." Eva began, stealing a glance at the sleeping child. "She left Paris with her mother, about a month ago—the day before the Germans arrived. Abrielle wasn't clear about where they were going, and I'm not sure that her mother knew, either. They were just escaping, along with the rest of Paris. There was a crush of people on the train, she said, taking up every available space in the carriage. She and her mother sat on the floor, in the aisle, unable to move, even to go to the bathroom. It was hot and humid, people moaning and babies crying, but after a few hours, Abrielle was finally able to fall asleep. When she awoke, the train had stopped and her mother had disappeared. Just vanished. Nobody could say where she'd gone, so, terrified that she'd been left behind, Abrielle panicked and jumped off the train just as it was leaving the station."

"With her mother on it."

"I would think so." Eva paused for a moment. "At any rate, she wasn't in the station, which turned out to be Bordeaux. Abrielle waited there for three days, until she was told that she'd have to leave. She wandered the streets for another couple of days, until the trucks carrying German soldiers started to appear. She just started walking then, and she's been walking every day since, with no idea where she's going."

I caught a movement in the rearview mirror and saw that Abrielle was waking up. Eva noticed, too, and turned around to give her a smile. There was something touching about the way the girl looked to Eva. Her face lifted and filled with hope—probably the first she'd felt in a long time. But there was something else in it, too, something much more than hope. Faith, I guess you'd call it. Faith and trust.

Ahead of us lay Paris, but for now we all sat back and took in the clean, fresh air and watched the western sky melt into a watercolor of purple and gold. It was a beautiful sight. You could almost believe that all was right in the world.

All was certainly not right in Paris. The "City of Light" was in mourning.

We left the car at the Porte d'Orléans and caught the last Metro, heading toward Clignancourt. On the surface, everything seemed normal. People sat on hard benches with open books and newspapers, or stood, swaying silently back and forth with the rhythm of the carriage, and they wore the same deadpan faces that you'd find on any subway system in the world. But it wasn't normal. It was far from that.

There wasn't a German in sight, but their presence was everywhere. In the slumping shoulders of the man who stared blankly at the cap he held in his lap; in the empty eyes of an old woman who fiddled nervously with a lace handkerchief gripped tightly in both hands; it was even in the students, who stood in groups of three and four, but had nothing to say to each other. It was in the deafening silence, and in the fallen faces of every Parisian we came across. It was the sound and the look of defeat. They couldn't believe what had happened to them.

Even the weather was gloomy. People wore coats in mid-July, and carried umbrellas. The mist that hung in the air seemed to cling to everything—buildings, sidewalks, it even attached itself to the people. Everything was obscured by the depressing fog that had descended on Paris.

We got off the train at Boulevard de Rochechouart and climbed the hill toward Sacré Coeur. Abrielle was unclear about the exact location of her uncle's apartment, but knew that the famous dome was visible from his front door. That didn't narrow our search too well, though, because the dome could be seen from pretty much every doorway in Montmartre. All we could do was hope that she'd find her way once we got to the top.

We wound our way through a maze of deserted lanes, our steps intruding on the languorous silence of a city in hiding. The only signs of life were the occasional twitching of a curtain and the packs of dogs that roamed the alleys—once-loved pets abandoned to the streets as their owners fled the approaching Wehrmacht.

I could see that the climb was taking its toll on Eva. She looked tired and I worried that she might start bleeding again, but she pressed on silently to the top. We avoided the church's main square, circling around the back instead, where we were less likely to be seen. I glanced at my watch, but it was too dark to see. I knew it was well past eleven o'clock, though.

"Do you remember anything?" I said. Abrielle pursed her lips and thought hard.

"A blue door."

"A blue door?"

"Yes."

"Anything else?"

"A pink restaurant."

I gave Eva a look, which she avoided.

"Which way do you think we should go, Abrielle?" she asked gently. "Don't think about it too much, use your first instinct."

"Mmm . . ." The girl cast her eyes around and chose a direction. "That way."

I was considering other options—all of which were pretty unappealing—when, a couple of blocks later, we came upon La Maison Rose, a little corner bistro that was unmistakably pink. I think even Abrielle was surprised. A minute later, we were standing in front of a blue door with a view of Sacré Coeur. It was an odd location for a residence, stuck in an odorous alley between Rue Saint-Vincent and Rue Cortot, but Abrielle had led us straight there, so I knocked—softly at first, then harder when there was no response. We waited, but still there was nothing.

"Are you sure he lives here?" I asked, thinking it looked more like the back of a restaurant and perhaps Abrielle had confused it with her uncle's workplace.

"Yes, it's right," she assured me.

I knocked again, loudly this time, and after a couple of minutes, I could hear whispers coming from inside. I hit the door again, banging it hard with the bottom of my fist.

"*Qui est là?*" A man's muted voice called out from behind the door. Abrielle stepped forward.

"*C'est moi, oncle . . . C'est Abrielle . . .*"

The door opened a crack, revealing only pitch-black inside.

"*Abrielle . . .?*"

"*Oui, c'est moi, Oncle Christien . . .*"

The door swung back, revealing a tall, slender figure in his early twenties. Younger than I'd expected. His pale skin and delicate, almost fragile frame, contrasted with strong, angular features and a shock of thick, wavy black hair that was brushed straight back off his forehead. He took a tentative step across the threshold, then stopped to look around.

"*Ici, oncle,*" Abrielle said softly. "*Je suis ici.*"

He turned toward the sound of her voice and she stepped forward, taking his hand in hers. Falling to his knees, he scooped his niece into his arms, and they clung to each other for several moments. When they finally separated, I could see that there were tears in both sets of eyes. Christien shook his head, laughed out loud, and planted a kiss on each of Abrielle's cheeks. Then he looked up and whispered, *"C'est qui, avec toi?"*

He was looking in our direction, but his gaze was distant and unfocused, as if he was looking straight through us. It wasn't until then that I realized that Abrielle's uncle Christien was stone-cold blind.

His accommodation turned out to be a couple of stark rooms in the back of a small jazz club, a place called L'École, where he'd been playing piano until the Germans closed them down, along with every other venue in France. The Nazis described jazz as "degenerate Negro Jewish music," which seemed to me to bestow undue credit on Irving Berlin, but I guess they thought it gave their denunciation a bit more punch. Anyway, the Reich's culture police didn't waste time putting lights out on the Jazz Age in Paris.

We'd interrupted something. Christien quickly herded us into his small kitchen, hoping we wouldn't notice the cloud of Gauloise-flavored smoke that was wafting in from the front room.

"You are American," he said to me before I'd made a sound.

"How'd you know that?"

"You walk like an American."

"Do Americans have a particular way of walking?"

He shrugged and produced a plate of boiled eggs, some soft cheese, and the better part of a baguette from inside a cupboard. Placing it all on the wooden table, along with a bottle of red wine, he motioned for us to sit.

"You must eat," he said.

Abrielle was the only one to take him up on it. She devoured everything in sight as Christien told us how he'd only recently learned of his niece's ordeal, through a desperate letter from his sister that had taken nearly a month to reach him. Apparently, she never got off the train in Bordeaux. She'd left Abrielle asleep as she pushed through the crowd to buy some bread and fruit from a vendor on the platform. When she got back to their place, her daughter had vanished and the train had left the station. She'd begged them to go back, but no one would listen. Unable to get off until the Spanish border, she had taken three days to make her way back to Bordeaux. She arrived just about the time Abrielle was leaving, and she'd been searching ever since, fearing the worst.

Abrielle started to come apart at this point. The poor girl, drained and exhausted, finally felt safe enough to cry. Eva pulled her into an embrace and gently stroked her forehead, whispering softly in her ear that they would write a letter to her mother first thing in the morning, and that Abrielle could draw a picture of herself on the letter, smiling happily, because that would make her mother feel happy, too. Abrielle nodded, wiped away her tears, and tried to smile.

"She needs to sleep," Eva said.

Christien suggested that she and the child use his bed, and seeing the strain on Eva's face, I seconded the idea. I asked Christien if he had any bandages and he provided a first-aid kit with enough gauze and tape that I was able to put a decent dressing on Eva's wound. Abrielle was asleep before I left the room, and Eva wasn't far behind. When I got back to the kitchen, Christien was waiting for me.

"Come," he said. "Meet my friends."

Claude played bass, Raymond was on drums, and the quiet one, Gérard, played tenor sax. Each offered a little smile and nodded as Christien went around the table, introducing them by name and instrument, as if they'd just finished playing a set and were taking a bow. A fifth chair was pulled up for me, and by the time I sat down, Claude had filled a glass with Armagnac and pushed it across the table.

"The whiskey, she is finished," he apologized with a shrug. "So, now it is begins, the hard time of war." Claude was like a big, friendly teddy bear, with tight black curls at the top of an oversize head, and big, chocolate-brown eyes. I hadn't seen him standing yet, but I would've put him at about six-foot-three.

"Here's to better times, then," I said, raising my glass. *"Vive la France."*

A rousing chorus of *"VIVE LA FRANCE!"* came back at me, and drinks were tossed back. As Claude went around the table with refills, I glanced around the darkened room. It was a smallish club—seating for about forty, with standing room for maybe another thirty. The tables were arranged around a low stage with a set of drums on one side and a shiny black baby grand on the other. In the back of the room, near the entrance, there was a small bar. The dark blue walls were hung with black-and-white photos of jazz players, including a signed one of Louis Armstrong blowing his horn so hard that it looked like his eyes were about to explode out of his head.

Claude finished pouring and raised his glass at me. "And now we drink to America," he grinned. The table echoed the toast, though with decidedly less gusto this time around. Then it was tobacco time. Everyone reached for their pack and we lit up in unison.

"America, she will come now into the war," Raymond said through rising smoke. "Yes?"

I leaned into the table and paused before answering. It would've been easy to be flip with it—something about John Wayne and the cavalry would've been my first instinct—but Raymond wasn't posing an offhand question. These were men who found themselves alone at the bottom of a deep, dark hole, with no way to climb out, and they wanted to know if anyone was going to throw them a rope. They deserved an honest answer.

"No," I said. "America's not going to come to the rescue. At least, not anytime soon. I'd be lying if I said otherwise."

That prompted a sharp exchange between Claude and Raymond, which seemed to boil down to an "I told you so," "Well, fuck you," sort of dialogue. I changed the subject.

"So you guys are jazzmen, huh?"

"We have used to be," Raymond said. "But the Nazis, they don't dig it so much." The guys had been around enough musicians—mostly black Americans who'd made Paris a haven for jazz since the last Great War—that morsels of swing-speak sometimes appeared in their otherwise basic English. "They like only the music for marching," the drummer added. "Pum, pum, pum."

It turned out that the four were partners in L'École, which had been open for about a year. They'd pooled their resources to buy the place, hoping they could make enough money to escape their day jobs, and it had just started to draw a crowd when the Germans showed up.

The conversation inevitably turned to New York and my days running the Kit Kat Klub. The guys listened intently as I told stories about legends like Gene Krupa, Lester Young, and Art Tatum, who'd used the Kat as a late-night drinking hole. I got the full seal of approval when they heard that, in '32, I'd given Billie Holiday her first gig outside of Harlem when I hired her to sing at the club. She was no more than seventeen at the time, but she had a lot to sing about, even at that tender age.

Christien had been sitting back up to this point, hands folded together on his lap, listening, and—in some sense—watching me. In spite of his silence, or maybe because of it, it was clear that he was the group's leader. When he was ready to speak to me alone, he didn't have to say a word. The boys somehow got the message, and disappeared into the back of the club.

Leaning across the table, Christien located his Gauloise and extracted a smoke from the pack. I struck a match and lit him up, keeping the flame alive while I readied one for myself.

"You know," he said, drawing on the cigarette. "On each night for a month, we have sat here together at this table—Raymond, Claude, Gérard, and myself—talking until early in the morning. And each time we face the same question: What will we do?" He paused to take a long drag on the cigarette.

"What will we do?"

"I wish I had an answer for you," I said.

"Perhaps you do."

I shifted in my seat. "I don't know who you think I am, Christien, or what I'm doing here, but—"

"I know that you are not a tourist." He let the silence hang for a moment, allowing it to make his point.

"Talking, of course, will not defeat the enemy," he said when he continued. "If we wish to live, we must fight."

"If staying alive is what you're after, then maybe you'd be better off not fighting."

"No, you are wrong about this. You see, if we fight, certainly they will kill some of us. Perhaps many. But in the moment that we accept this evil, then we will surely die, all of us. We may go on breathing, but we will feel empty and defeated, and this will be because our spirits have been extinguished. And when our spirits have died, we will cease to exist. We will become a part of them. It starts to happen already, with the police, the government. How long will it take for them to kill us all? So you see, we have not much time. In order to live, we must start quickly to die. This is perhaps one of God's playful ironies."

Christien must've been able to sense the expression I had on my face, which was probably somewhere between amused and annoyed, because he broke out laughing.

"You're right," he said. "This is just more talk. What I wanted to say is that we offer ourselves in whatever task you have come to Paris to undertake. We are ready to do anything, if it will begin us in our resistance."

I was roused at 5 A.M. by the gentle sound of a piano. Christien wasn't playing a melody so much as a series of melodic phrases, expressions of a color or mood that seemed to speak to each other, then melt together into a single statement. I sat up from the floor, where I'd finally found a couple of hours of sleep, propped myself against the wall, and listened as he swept up and down the keyboard. I hadn't heard anything like it before.

As if responding to a Siren's call, one by one, the other three musicians rose from the dead and took up their instruments. Claude first, on bass, then Raymond, softly brushing his snare. Finally, Gérard took up his sax and the sound transformed into a haunting interpretation of "Body and Soul." I saw that Eva had been lured by the music, too. She stood at the side of the stage, her hands on Abrielle's shoulders, a look of lost delight on both of their faces as the sound washed over them.

I've gone back to that image many times over the years, and still do, to this day. It was one of those unexpected moments in life—an instant that sneaks up on you and takes hold and won't let go. There was something magical about the way Eva looked over at me and smiled. It was as if the music had swept away all the dark guilt that she held in her soul, and allowed her a brief moment of genuine happiness, which she chose to share with me.

The measured *clip-clop, clip-clop* of the horse's unhurried steps was the only intrusion into the quiet elegance of Boulevard Suchet. The new day had brought a dose of bright, clear sunshine, filtering down through leafy elms to fall in pools of warm, dappled light across the stone mansions that lined the avenue.

Our early-morning journey had initiated me into the allure of Paris. Upon leaving L'École at dawn, Claude and I set out across Montmartre, traveling west through winding lanes that had been walked a half century earlier by the likes of Renoir, Sisley, Degas, and too many others to name. As the morning's first light burst forth from the east, strafing the spires and cathedrals that rose out of the cityscape below us, the streets started to come alive with Parisians. They ventured out on foot, and on bicycle, carrying the weight of their defeated spirits in wounded silence.

Claude left me inside the gate of the district cemetery and continued on to the depot, which was around the corner. I wandered through the gravestones, checking names and dates, until he reappeared, sitting atop his fully loaded milk wagon, wearing a royal-blue smock over spotless white overalls. I climbed aboard and slipped into a matching uniform he'd left on the seat for me. It must've been his spare because there was enough room in it for two of me. Claude raised his eyebrows, shrugged his big shoulders, and snapped the reins. As the wagon lurched forward, I rolled up my sleeves and moved Eva's Luger into the pocket of the smock, where I could get at it quickly if it was needed.

We clattered along the cobblestones for a couple of blocks, then turned left into a broad avenue, heading south toward L'Arc de Triomphe. As we neared the center of Paris, evidence of the occupation became more conspicuous. Newly printed road signs, in German, were placed at each intersection, marking directions to hotels, official buildings, and all the major sights. I noticed a poster, placed at one of the tram stops, that depicted a young French boy eating a piece of bread as he smiled lovingly at the congenial Wehrmacht trooper who held him in his arms. Two girls watched longingly from a distance, eager to join in the mirth. Printed along the bottom of the happy scene was the advice *FAITES CONFIANCE AU SOLDAT ALLEMAND!*

Place your trust in the German soldier.

Number 24 Boulevard Suchet was built in the Neoclassic style of Louis XVI, suitably grand, but a far cry from Buckingham Palace. Four stories high, with a gray slate mansard roof, its only security was a four-foot-high black iron railing. I was glad to see a tradesman's entrance on the side of the building.

Christien had suggested the milk-wagon approach. I hadn't given him any details about what we were up to, just that we needed a way to scout out a wealthy residence without being noticed. It turned out that—like most of Paris—he knew the duke's mansion, but he still didn't ask questions.

The idea was for me to stay with the wagon and have a good look around the area while Claude siphoned off a couple of pints of milk and carried them to the service entrance. He'd ask Madame Moulichon—or anyone else who answered the bell—if they wanted to restart their daily delivery, and be told, presumably, that his services weren't required. He would then ask if he might have a glass of water and, with a little luck, be invited inside. Although this wasn't his normal run, it was unlikely that anyone would be suspicious of a thirsty milkman, especially one with a face like Claude's.

Once inside, he'd engage the maid in conversation, try to ascertain if she was alone in the house, and if she was expecting anyone during the day. He might even be able to locate a safe access point— a window or door that wasn't overlooked by inquisitive neighbors. If he came back with the all clear, I'd jump off the wagon and slip inside while he continued on around the corner, to the edge of the Bois de Boulogne—the vast woodland on the western edge of central Paris—where Eva would be waiting. Claude would drive by without stopping, but he'd give her a nod to let her know that it was safe to walk back to the house, where I'd let her in. In the meantime, I would have "prepared" Madame Moulichon for a chat. Between Eva's French and my Luger, I had no doubt that we'd convince her to hand over the contents of the duke's safe.

"Don't stop," I said.

"Eh . . .?" Claude looked up and down the street.

"Keep going. And don't look around."

I'd spotted a black Citroën parked a few doors down from the residence. I don't know what made me suspicious—maybe it was the car's position on the street, or maybe I'd picked up a movement inside it—but whatever the case, it was a good instinct, because as we neared, I could see that there were two men sitting in the front seat. Chancing a quick sideways glance, I saw that the man closest to us, the one in the passenger seat, was Walter Engel. *Der Engel der Schwärzung* had survived Eva's bullet. The second man's face was blocked by Engel's head. I should have turned away, but something prevented me. Fixing my eyes on the interior of the car as we passed, coming within a few feet of it, I slipped my hand into my pocket and gripped the Luger. But Engel didn't look my way. Instead, he turned to say something to his partner, allowing me to see that the second man, the one in the driver's seat, was none other than the rat from Belgrade—Roman Popov.

Eva was sitting on a bench at the edge of the woods, an innocent Parisian reading the French equivalent of a dime-store novel as she soaked up the sunshine. I didn't have to look at her as we passed. My presence was enough to tell her that things hadn't gone as planned. I waited a block before slipping out of my overalls and jumping down from the wagon.

Eva had already stood up and was walking toward me when she veered off the sidewalk onto a gravel footpath that led into the woods. I followed for several minutes, maintaining the distance between us, until I lost sight of her in the thickening trees. I picked up my pace and found her waiting a couple of feet off the path, in a small clearing.

"What's he doing in Paris?" she said when I told her about Popov.

"Keeping questionable company," I replied. "Walter Engel was with him."

"You said he was dead . . ."

"I said I thought he was dead. I guess neither of you is a very good shot."

She frowned and looked back along the empty path. "Do you think they'll take the documents?"

"I don't know," I said. "But if I had to bet on it, I'd say no. They'll get them anyway, and Hitler won't want to get on the wrong side of the duke. My guess is they won't touch her, but they'll stay on top of her, all the way back to Lisbon."

"She can't get on that train, Jack."

"Yeah, well, I'm not too keen on another rail trip, either. Forget the house, though. We'd never get past those two."

Eva nodded, started pacing back and forth in the small space. She snapped a twig off a tree, broke it in two, and tossed it aside. "What if she were to go out? Shopping, or visiting friends . . ."

"One of them will stay with the house."

"We might be able to sneak up on one of them."

"Sure," I said. "Maybe we could get the jump on him, maybe even kill him and dump the car somewhere without anyone seeing us, but what then? The papers will be in the duke's safe. I don't know about you, but my skills stop short of safecracking, and if we wait for the maid, we're right back where we started, only worse because if Popov doesn't find Engel when he gets back, or vice versa, we'll have every storm trooper in Paris stopping by to say hello."

"Perhaps we could snatch her—"

"Off the street?"

"Why not?"

"Well, for one thing, she's not going to be carrying the papers on a shopping trip." Eva lowered her chin and frowned at me.

"You're not being very helpful."

"Sure I am. I'm pointing out all the ways we could get ourselves killed and still fail."

"How about pointing out a way we can succeed?"

"As a matter of fact, I do have an idea."

"You do?"

"Yes."

L'Église Saint-Julien le Pauvre had stood on the same ground, in one form or another, since the sixth century, making it the oldest church in Paris, a city that had no shortage of old churches. Hidden away on the Left Bank of the Seine, in the shadow of Notre Dame, it was a sanctuary, a tranquil escape from the undercurrent of fear and foreboding that permeated the occupied city. Christien attended classes a couple of blocks away at the Sorbonne, so when I phoned him at the club, he'd suggested that we meet there to discuss my plan.

As we passed through the church's west portal, the air became cool and dry, as if we'd walked into an underground cavern. The subdued light, reflecting off the ancient stones, was warm and welcoming, almost sepia in color.

Eva and I stood at the back of the chapel, looking down the aisle toward the altar. Instead of stalls, there were wooden chairs with straw seats set out in a dozen or so neat rows. We found Christien in the front, the lone worshipper in the church. He was looking up toward the ceiling, as if drawn by the soft light that was falling onto his face from above.

"Do you pray, Jack?" he said as we sat down in the row behind him.

"No," I said. "I don't."

"I didn't used to, either. But now I find myself doing it all the time. I do it without thinking."

"What do you pray for?" Eva asked softly. Christien turned toward her, his eyes meeting hers head-on, as though he could somehow see her.

"I pray for strength," he said. "For the strength to sacrifice every-thing, if this is what I am asked to do."

Eva nodded silently and we got down to business. We sat there for a few minutes, talking in hushed tones, then we left, one by one. Eva went first, and I noticed that she hastily crossed herself before she turned away from the altar.

Madame Moulichon would have had all sorts of potential dangers on her mind—carrying secret documents for the former king of England through Nazi-occupied France would be enough to make anybody wary—but she'd have no reason to be suspicious of a taxi. That was the hope, anyway.

Christien had contacted half a dozen car services before uncov-ering her reservation. Twenty-four Boulevard Suchet, at five o'clock, the dispatcher had confirmed, to arrive at Gare Montparnasse in plenty of time to catch the six-fifteen to Lisbon. Christien had apol-ogized to the man and told him that the car wouldn't be required, after all.

I glanced over at Claude. He looked a bit shaky, his knuckles white as he gripped the reins a little too tightly. I pretended not to notice, lit a couple of cigarettes, handed one to him.

"So you're a milkman," I said, to distract him.

"Like my father." He smiled, accepting the smoke.

"Do you work together?"

Claude shook his head. "My father was killed in the war . . . The first one . . . I was a baby." He paused, watched the smoke come off his cigarette. "Too much war," he whispered.

"Yes," I said, thinking about my own father, who'd died on the opposite end of the same battlefield. "Too much war."

I checked my watch again. Where the hell was Raymond? I'd had reservations about him from the beginning. After all, he was a drummer, and drummers were notorious for tempting danger. It made them feel alive. But Christien had had faith in him. He'd pointed out that it was Raymond who'd procured the taxi, a loan from his cabbie uncle, and he'd even driven it on a couple of occasions. He'd do well, I'd been assured, so I set my misgivings aside.

But it was almost five-thirty . . .

"*Les voilà,*" Claude breathed excitedly as the big yellow-and-black Peugeot rounded the corner at the far end of the narrow alley we'd been staking out. The horse, probably sensing the apprehension in Claude's voice, neighed and pulled on the bit.

"Easy," I said. "Hold her . . ."

The alley connected two modest residential streets that we'd found a few blocks from the duke's residence. It was on the route to the station, so the maid—and more importantly, Popov and Engel, in the car behind—would assume that the driver knew a shortcut. Once the taxi left the alley, Claude would swing the milk wagon into it, blocking the Citroën long enough for Raymond to get lost in the back streets of Paris. He'd stop a few blocks away to pick up Eva, who'd handle Madame Moulichon, then we'd all meet up later, back at the club. Simple enough—but it all depended on separating the two cars here.

Raymond gunned the Peugeot through the alley, as I'd told him to. He had to clear it and let us move in before the Citroën appeared.

"Okay," I said to Claude, patting him on the shoulder as I jumped into the back and slid out of sight, under the heavy green canvas that covered the wagon. I lay flat on my belly, facing out, my index finger wrapped delicately around the Luger's trigger.

Claude slapped the reins, called out *"Hue!"* for the horse, and I had to hang on to one of the aluminum milk cans to stay on board as the wagon jerked forward. I heard the taxi go by, then we quickly swung around to the left, the wagon's ironclad wheels meeting the alley's cobblestone surface with a jolt. The Citroën announced itself almost immediately.

HONK! HONK! HONK!

They got closer with each blow of the horn. The wagon came to an immediate stop, as we'd gone over. Raymond needed only a couple of minutes to disappear, and as long as it looked like Claude was no more than a bumbling milkman trying to get out of the way, they'd be in too much of a hurry to catch the taxi to make any trouble for us.

HONK! HONK! HONK!

They were on top of us now and the horse was getting flustered, balking as Claude tried to coax her backward while calling out *"Je suis désolé! Je suis désolé!"* in response to the tirade of angry German invectives that were being hurled at him . . .

"Aus dem Weg, Arschloch! Beweg' das Pferd oder ich schiesse es!"

Engel was threatening to shoot the horse, but of course he wouldn't do that. He might shoot Claude, though, if he didn't get the damned animal on the move.

"Je suis désolé! Je suis désolé!" Claude kept repeating as Engel continued to fire abuse at him. The wagon pitched to the left with Claude's weight, then bounced back when he jumped down to the pavement. His presence seemed to calm the horse. After whispering a couple of soothing words, he took her by the bridle and we started to move backward. I thought we were home free when the wagon rolled onto the smooth pavement of the main road, but it was too soon to breathe a sigh of relief.

The Citroën's engine revved a couple of times, then it screeched forward, probably heading straight for the horse at full speed. The frightened beast reared up on its hind legs, lifting the wagon with it, and spilled me—along with a few dozen gallons of milk—onto the street.

I rolled a few times, sprang to my feet, and found myself face-to-face with a startled Popov. He sat there, hands on the steering wheel, face frozen in shock. Under other circumstances, I would've laughed out loud, and maybe I did manage a little smirk before I raised the Luger and started firing rounds into the car. They both ducked—just in time, too, because all four shots hit the windshield. The glass held for a fraction of a second, then it shattered, exploding into a thousand tiny fragments.

Back on the wagon, Claude was struggling to control the terrified horse, who wanted no part of a shoot-out.

"VENEZ, JACK! VITE! VITE!"

The hulking Frenchman beckoned, which must have made him slacken the reins, because the mare took it as permission to bolt. She shot off like a Thoroughbred out of the gate, leaving me stranded in the road, facing two Gestapo thugs who I'd just tried to blow away. I could stand and fight, or I could turn and run for my life.

My legs didn't touch the ground. I exploded out of my stance and flew up the street, my entire being focused on outrunning the bullet that I knew was chasing me down. Somewhere in the far reaches of my brain, I recalled somebody saying that the worst thing you can do if you're trying to avoid getting shot in the back is to run in a straight line because it gives the killer too constant a target. To hell with that! I thought. I'm running as straight as I can—straight into the back of that goddamned wagon!

The old nag must've been making thirty miles an hour, but it felt like seventy. I managed to pull within a couple of feet of the gate, which had broken off on one side and was being dragged along the pavement, but I was running out of steam and starting to lose ground. Claude twisted around to urge me on, but he didn't slow the damned horse down. When he looked up at the street behind me, I saw in his eyes that this was it—now-or-never time.

I shoved the Luger into my belt, took one last, long stride, pushed off, and leapt across the closing couple of yards, hands outstretched, extending every inch of my frame toward the detached wooden gate.

I came down hard, knocking the air out of my lungs, but I was still moving. Hugging the timber as I bounced along the road, I pulled myself up to a more secure position before chancing a look around. What I saw were two chrome headlights and a metal grille bearing down on me. The Citroën was no more than a few feet away, and closing. The car surged forward and I pulled my legs out of the way a fraction of a second before the bumper crushed the bottom half of the gate. It splintered beneath me and scattered along the road.

The car slipped back a few feet, and I caught sight of Engel hanging out the window, trying to line up a shot. I was a sitting duck and had to make a move before he did.

Could I hold on with one hand? I'd have to. I let go with my right hand, reached for the pistol. Eight rounds, that's what a Luger holds. I'd just used four, and Eva—how many bullets had she fired at Engel on the train? Two? Three? If it was more than that, I was empty. Why the hell hadn't I checked the damn thing?!

There was no shot at either man—the angle was too high. But I couldn't wait. Locking my elbow, I held my arm straight out and took aim . . . Bouncing up and down with the road, I could hardly see for the vibrations, let alone draw a reasonable bead. But it wasn't going to get any better, so I squeezed the trigger.

POP!

The pistol kicked back in my hand and the car kept coming. I took aim again . . .

POP! . . .

And *BANG!!!*

The Citroën's right tire exploded and the car careened sideways off the road. It jumped the curb and piled headfirst into one of those cylindrical columns used to display posters around Paris.

I had to smile as we pulled away and rounded a corner. Not just because we'd gotten away, although that was certainly worth a chuckle. But what made me grin was the freshly mounted poster on the toppled column that lay crushed below the Gestapo car. It was a picture of Hitler in a Napoléonic pose, with the caption spelled out in big red letters: *Suivez le Führer!*

Follow the Führer!

"You've been a long time," Christien said, recognizing our footsteps before either of us spoke. "We have been worried."

He and Gérard were at the kitchen table, seated across from Madame Moulichon. She gave Claude and me a suspicious look as we entered the room, then went back to staring into the cup of lemon tea that sat untouched in front of her.

"We had a couple of problems," I said. "But it's all right, we took care of it."

Claude flopped into a chair, threw his cap on the table, and shook his head. *"Merde!"* was all he could say. Gérard poured us each a glass of wine while Christien explained that Raymond had gone to return the taxi to his uncle.

"And Eva?" I asked.

"She's taken Abrielle to stay with a neighbor. It seemed a better place for her."

I nodded and glanced over at the maid. "What does she have to say for herself?"

"She is too frightened to speak."

"Can't say that I blame her."

I accepted a cigarette from Christien, leaned against the door frame, and sipped the wine, wishing it was whiskey. When I heard the front door open and close, I slipped out to intercept Eva before she could get to the back.

"Well?" I said.

She smiled, put her hands on my shoulders, and kissed me on the cheek. "It was sewn into the lining of her case."

"And? Is it as good as advertised?"

"It's incredible," she said in an excited whisper. "It's a report, Jack—a recent one—laying out Britain's entire air defense system. Every radar installation along the English and Scottish coasts, and everything you'd want to know about them."

I let loose a low whistle. "That's big all right. Where is it?"

"I've hidden it."

"Where?"

She hesitated. "There's no point us both knowing, is there?"

"I'm not sure I follow you."

She smiled and averted her eyes, glancing around the room, though there was nothing to look at. "I just don't see why we should both know where it is, that's all."

She tried to slip by, but I cut her off.

"I'd like to see it, Eva."

"Why?"

"I'd like to have a look, that's all."

"I've told you what it is. Don't you trust me?"

I was taken aback. "It's got nothing to do with trust, Eva. I'd just like to see what I've been risking my life for."

"It's better that you don't know where it is," she said, trying to close the discussion while making another attempt to get around me. I grabbed her by the arm.

"I think I know why you don't want to tell me."

"Let go of me, Jack."

"You think if we get caught, I'd tell them. That's it, isn't it? You're afraid I'd fold."

She yanked her arm free and gave me a dry look.

"I don't know if you would or you wouldn't. And neither do you. This way, we won't have to put it to the test."

I was trying hard not to say something that I would later regret when Claude appeared from the back room.

"*Oh, pardon,*" he said, looking a little embarrassed that he'd stepped into our argument. "But the maid, she cries."

She was bawling her eyes out, in fact. The poor woman had been able to contain her alarm for several hours by maintaining an absolute stony silence, but her fear had finally reached breaking point, and without warning, she'd exploded into a flood of tears. The boys thought that Eva, being a woman, would know what to do.

She sat down, took Madame Moulichon's hand in hers, and said a few gentle words in French. The maid responded with what sounded to me like a series of whimpering sobs, but everyone else exchanged a meaningful look.

"What did she say?" I asked.

"She thinks we're going to kill her," Eva said without flourish. Then she turned back to the maid, looked her in eye, and lied.

"I promise that no one is going to hurt you," she said, in French. "You've had a shock, why don't you lie down for a while? A rest will help you recover, then someone will take you home." Worn down, Madame Moulichon acquiesced.

Christien told Claude to put her in his bedroom—and lock the door. No one said anything once she'd gone, but no one had to. We all understood that the poor woman had been right. We were going to have to kill her.

Madame Moulichon was an innocent bystander, with no idea of the significance of what she was carrying, and she certainly didn't deserve to be murdered in cold blood. But in war, innocence and justice are not the criteria for who will live and who will die.

She had to die because letting her live would be too risky. That simple. It was possible, of course, that if we'd explained the significance of the document she was transporting, patriotism would've outweighed loyalty to her masters, and she would've told the Windsors that the papers had disappeared from the safe. Maybe she would've promised not to run to the gendarmes with a story about the men from Montmartre who'd abducted her, and maybe she would've even smiled at us, and said we were doing the right thing. But that was just too many maybes, and the stakes were just too high. So we had no choice but to get rid of her.

"Gérard will do what is necessary tonight," Christien finally said, breaking the silence.

I needed a real drink, so I headed to the front room to see what I could find at the bar. As I passed through the door into the club, I was feeling on edge, preoccupied with Madame Moulichon, and I never saw what hit me. Whatever it was, it came down like a hammer—a dull, heavy blow at the back of my head, accompanied by a loud *thwack* and a simultaneous explosion of pain.

Then the lights went out.

I came to in a sitting position, hands bound together and tied to the back of a hard wooden chair. My head felt like it had been hit by a runaway train. I opened my eyes, got a blast of light and pain, tried to break through both. The first thing that came into slow focus was Popov, sitting across the room, at the bar, smoking a cigarette. He looked nervous. Like he was waiting for something to happen.

The room had been pretty well turned upside down. Furniture upended, banquettes ripped open, pictures pulled off the walls and smashed onto the floor. I was momentarily blank, then it all came back in a rush the maid ... the abduction ... the duke's papers. They must not have found them, I thought. If they had, I probably wouldn't be waking up at all.

"Jack ...?"

Easing my head around while trying to keep my battered brain from bumping up against my skull, I found Eva seated on my left, just a couple of feet away. Like me, she was secured to a chair, hands tied behind her back. So were Gérard, Christien, and Claude. The five of us formed a small circle, about ten feet across, in an area in front of the stage that had been cleared of tables and chairs.

"...Are you all right, Jack?"

Her voice was distant, muffled, the words lagging behind her lips, like she was disconnected from her body. Concussion, I thought. Like the time I did a swan dive off a stagecoach and landed headfirst on a boulder. I wasn't myself for a couple of days then, but I didn't have the luxury of that kind of time now. I tried to refocus and must've given Eva a pretty odd look, because she frowned and looked at me sideways, as though she was trying to figure out if I was still in there.

"Jack ...?"

"Yeah ..." I groaned. "I ... I'm okay." Not really, though, because just saying the words sent a knifelike pain shooting down the back of my neck, across my shoulders, and along the length of my spine. It helped bring me back to reality, but I must've cried out because Popov swiveled his head around and gave me a sour look.

"Mr. Jack Teller," he hissed. "So you are awoken."

Slipping off the bar stool, he crossed the room and planted himself a couple of feet in front of me. He stood there watching me for a moment, blowing smoke into the air without saying anything. Just seeing him again made my stomach churn.

"It's better if you have stayed in Hollywood," he finally said, poking his cigarette at my chest. "Better for all of us."

"How about I apologize and we can all be friends again?" Popov, unappreciative of my humor, tossed his cigarette aside, pulled a 9mm Glock out of his jacket pocket, and pointed it at my head.

"You think you are really quite clever, but in fact you are the opposite." He took a step closer, pressed the barrel up against my forehead, which got my full attention. "You have fucked up everything when you take her off this boat."

"That's right, Jack ..." Eva chose an opportune moment to jump in. "Roman would've been the toast of Berlin if you hadn't interfered. Isn't that right, Roman?"

It took him a moment to take his eyes off me, but when he finally looked over at Eva, he lowered the handgun.

"I thought that you were smarter," he said.

"I'm smarter now," she said. "You see, Jack, Roman has British intelligence fooled, as well. They think he's on their side, just as I did. He was sending me off to London to become an agent for them when you showed up and ruined it all."

"You don't know anything," Popov moaned, but Eva kept talking.

"Had I arrived in England," she continued, "I would've been given training and a new identity, then put in the field—back in Germany, or even here, in France. Roman would've been my control agent, so I would've been feeding everything through him, thinking he was forwarding it on to London. But, of course, he wouldn't have been doing that at all. He would've been passing it straight to his friends in Berlin, who would replace it with whatever misinformation they wanted London to have. So you see why Roman is so upset with you, Jack. You ruined quite a good plan by taking me off that boat."

"Silly me," I said.

Popov dismissed the subject with a wave of his hand, and shoved the gun back into his pocket. "You are both fools," he mumbled as he made his way back to the bar.

The door to the back rooms opened and Engel stepped into the room, escorting Madame Moulichon.

"Nichts," he said, which I took to mean that, though he'd found the maid, he hadn't located the missing papers after tossing the rest of the building. Popov nodded, suggested that he put the lady in the car and bring the other one back with him. I couldn't think who he meant by the other one, but it wasn't long to find out.

Raymond was alive, but just barely. Beaten senseless, he couldn't stand up on his own, let alone walk, and his face and torso were so covered in blood that he looked like he'd been turned inside out. Engel dragged him across the room and let him fall, facedown, onto the floor in the center of the circle. He lay there, limbs flailing back and forth like a crushed insect—maybe a last-ditch, pitiful attempt to escape, or maybe just indiscriminate muscle spasms, the result of random electronic impulses firing along his shattered nervous system.

"This is a tragedy," Popov said, shaking his head as he looked down on the poor soul, a snarl of distaste fixed onto his lips. "And it has not been necessary. He told us, in the end, what we wanted to know. Here we are to prove it."

"*Du vergeuden Zeit,*" Engel snarled. "You're wasting time." Popov gave him a look and continued.

"We have brought him here so that you will see what will happen if you try to—"

"He is a hero ..." Christien said quietly, his voice filled with emotion. Popov sighed, put on a vexed expression.

"You are fortunate to be blind in this instance," he said. "Because if you can see your friend, you would know—"

"I know that he is a hero!" Christien shot back defiantly. He leaned forward in his chair and called out.

"*ÉCOUTE, RAYMOND?! TU ES UN HÉROS! UN HÉROS DE LA FRANCE!*"

Claude and Gérard quickly joined in, calling out a chorus of praise to their struggling comrade:

"*RAYMOND! TU ES UN HÉROS! ...UN HÉROS DE LA FRANCE!*"

The battered drummer slowly turned his head up toward the sound and—I can't be sure about this, but I thought I saw a flicker of a smile form across his bloodied face at the very last moment, just before Engel stepped forward and fired a single bullet into the back of his head. Someone gasped, then there was stunned silence. Even Popov looked shocked.

I watched Engel. There was no sign of emotion on his face, no suggestion that firing a bullet into a man's brain had any effect on him whatsoever. It was an execution, carried out with cold, military indifference, and it seemed to give him neither pleasure nor pain, and certainly no pause. I wondered if being able to kill like that was something he was born with, or if it was repetition that had inured him to the act.

He studied Raymond's corpse for a brief moment, then swung around, raised the pistol again, and fired a shot into Christien's forehead. The chair fell backward onto the floor, and just like that, Christien was dead, too.

"Another fallen hero of France," Popov moaned. "I hope there will be no need for more."

Unlike Engel, who betrayed no emotion, the violence was making the Slav visibly edgy. He stepped around Raymond's mangled body to continue his interrogation.

"A document has been stolen," he announced, walking the circumference of the chairs as he spoke. "This must be returned. If one of you chooses to speak now, he—or she—will save all of you. This will be the only opportunity to speak without consequences."

Popov didn't expect any takers, so he didn't wait for any volunteers. He stopped behind Eva's chair, crouched down, and whispered in her ear.

"What can I offer you? The lives of your friends? I can give you that."

He got nothing but stony silence.

"I'm sorry, then," he said, sounding almost genuine. "Truly, I am sorry, Eva. I wish it could be—"

"Get on with it," she said sharply.

Popov sighed and moved away. He seemed to have genuine regret for what was to come, but he knew Eva, so he knew that she couldn't be frightened or threatened into submission. She was too strong to be manipulated, but there are very few people who can stand up to the kind of torture that Raymond had been subjected to.

Popov nodded to Engel, and as the German moved toward Eva, my heart sank into the pit of my stomach. Engel took hold of the back rung of her chair and dragged it into the center of the circle. I could see that she was frightened—who wouldn't be?—but she clenched her jaw and stared the Angel of Darkness square in the face. A trace of a smile appeared on his scarred lips, and I understood that, unlike the others, he didn't see Eva as a faceless victim. With her, it would be personal.

He put on a pair of black gloves, then removed a short leather truncheon from his pocket—the same instrument, no doubt, that had made a cripple out of Raymond, and bruised the base of my skull. I wanted to explode out of my chair, take the bastard by the throat, and choke the life out of him . . .

Stay cool, I told myself . . . It's over if you don't stay cool . . .

"So I guess it's true what they say about Nazis," I said as loudly and clearly as I could muster, waiting for his eyes to pivot around on me before I continued.

"Everyone knows that they're pigs, of course," I said, my voice sounding surprisingly breezy. "But I didn't believe until now that they're cowards, too."

"Jack . . ." Eva moaned, but I kept my eyes locked on Engel.

His expression of utter incredulity would've been funny if I didn't know that behind it he was pondering the best way to take me apart, piece by bloody piece. He didn't budge, didn't blink, I don't think he even breathed. He just stood there, studying me, like a sadistic schoolboy might study a fly before relieving it of its wings.

"It's obvious from the way you smell that you're *ein Schwein*,"

I said, closing the deal. "And now we all see that you're *ein Feigling*, because you're obviously too frightened to untie me and fight like a man."

He struck first at my solar plexus, driving the truncheon deep into my abdomen, just below the rib cage. A visceral blow like that doesn't just "knock the air out you," like most people think. It initiates an acute and sudden trauma to a cluster of nerves that lies behind the stomach, resulting in a muscle spasm that makes it physically impossible to draw a breath.

I doubled over, gasping for air, and was on the verge of blacking out when I was treated to a crushing blow to my kidneys, sending white-hot pain rushing into every corner of my torso. Stuck between a desperate search for oxygen and the paralyzing agony of a bruised organ, my brain seized up and I must've gone into some sort of psycho-traumatic shock.

My head went a little funny.

The next thing I knew I was lying on the floor, still tied to the chair, staring at a pair of leather boots. But when I looked up, it wasn't Walter Engel—*der Engel der Schwärzung*—who was standing over me. It was Mickey Rooney. I don't mean to say that my rattled mind got momentarily confused because Engel looked a bit like the young star. I mean that, as far as I was concerned, I was in the midst of a knock-down, drag-out fight to the death with little Mickey Rooney.

Unusual role for him, I thought. He even has a knife in his hand. I panicked because I couldn't remember what the hell my next move was supposed to be. Was I supposed to win, or was my character supposed to die in this scene? I couldn't figure it out for the life of me. Shit, we'd probably have to do another take and I'd have to listen to the director moan all through lunch. He might even fire me. The actors can screw up till the cows come home, but the stunt guys don't get a second shot.

The knife looks particularly real, I thought, even at close range. Rooney held it like a pro, too. Not like most actors, who look like they're getting ready to butter a roll. I braced for the kill, but was surprised when, instead of plunging the retractable blade into my chest, the actor brought the knife around the back of the chair and cut my bindings free. That's odd, I thought.

Then Rooney fed me a line:

"Maybe you can show me now how you fight like a man." He smiled wickedly, and the German accent wasn't bad, either. Maybe he's playing a bad guy, after all, I thought.

"Get up, Jack! For God's sake, get up and fight!"

Eva's voice snapped me back to reality, along with the sight of Engel's boot heading for my teeth. I did a quick roll out of the chair, got a rush of air as his foot swept by, and ended up facedown on the floor, staring Louis Armstrong in the face.

The big black-and-white photograph had been dropped onto the floor and stomped on by the same boot that had just tried to stomp on my head. And there, lying on top of Satchmo's wild-eyed, horn-blowing face, was just what the doctor ordered—a long piece of thick, razorlike glass that came to a beautifully sharp, flesh-piercing point.

Grabbing the blunt end with both hands, I rolled back the way I came and buried the shard into the first thing I came across, which happened to be Engel's thigh muscle. He hit the floor screaming, spitting out German curses. He instinctively reached for the wound, but just drove the glass farther into the muscle before it broke off, leaving a large piece embedded in his leg.

A shot of adrenaline brought me to my feet. Grabbing the nearest thing available, I lifted my discarded chair high over my head and brought it down toward Engel's head. He saw it coming and was able to get his Luger halfway out of its holster before I caught him across the neck and shoulders.

He fell backward and the gun went spinning across the floor. I got there first, took the pistol in both hands, and spun around, ready to empty it into Engel—

"STOP!"

I pivoted, saw that Popov had the Glock buried in Eva's ear.

"PUT IT DOWN!" he said. "PUT DOWN THE GUN!"

"KILL THEM! JACK!" Eva cried out. "KILL THEM BOTH!"

"I PROMISE YOU THAT I WILL SHOOT A BULLET INTO HER HEAD!" Popov screamed, his voice charged with emotion.

My mind raced. I might get one of them, maybe I'd even kill them both, if I got lucky, but not before Popov pulled the trigger. I had no doubt that he would. He'd pull the trigger as I shot Engel, then it would be a race to see if Popov or I survived. It wouldn't matter, though, not to me, because she'd be gone, and there would be no changing that.

Popov took a step back and planted himself, ready to absorb the gun's kick.

"DECIDE!" he yelled. "NOW!"

I tossed the gun onto the floor.

"Jack . . ." Eva moaned. "Oh, Jack . . . They're going to kill me anyway . . . They're going to kill us all . . ."

Popov exhaled and lowered his gun. He mumbled something to himself which I didn't understand, then looked up at me and nodded.

"Okay," he said. "Now we must see if she feels the same about you." He gave the nod to the Angel, who struggled to his feet, scooped up the Luger, and took aim at my head. I looked to Eva and she looked to me.

"Well, Eva?" Popov said. "Do you love him as much as he loves you?"

I tried to smile at her, to let her know that it was okay, I didn't mind, but I doubt it looked like a smile. Tears spilled onto her cheeks and ran down her face.

"Just say it," Popov persisted. "Say that you love him."

She inhaled sharply and seemed to stop breathing.

"Do you love him, Eva?"

"Yes . . ." she whispered, barely audible. "Yes, I love him!"

"Then you cannot let him die for the sake of a few papers. Do for him what he did for you. You must save the man you love."

She turned her eyes toward me. I wanted to tell her that I loved her, too, and that whatever they did with us, it didn't matter, because we'd had each other, and I was happy with that, I didn't need more.

But I didn't get a chance to say anything. A shot rang out and I fell to the floor.

I cried out in pain and grabbed my leg. The bullet had ripped a hole through my right thigh, in the same spot I'd stabbed Engel with the shard of glass. Payback, I guess—but it was just his appetizer.

He picked up the chair that I'd attacked him with and brought it crashing down across a table, smashing it to pieces. Then he selected a long fragment of wood, with a sharp, splintered end, and limped forward, toward me. He stood there for a moment, expressionless, before he carefully placed the pointed end of the wood an inch over the bullet hole he'd just put in my leg. He moved suddenly, driving it hard into the wound with all his might, then twisting it back and forth sharply. My entire being screamed out in unspeakable agony.

"SCHWEIN!" Eva shrieked from across the room. "HE'S RIGHT! YOU ARE A PIG AND A COWARD!" Engel pulled back, threw the wood aside, and turned toward her tearstained face. He smiled.

"I know that I will break you," he said matter-of-factly "Of this I can be sure. Because you are weak. Your emotions make you so. It has been already shown."

Eva breathed in deeply and cast him a steely glare.

"You are the devil on earth," she said, her voice shaking with emotion. "And there is nothing—*nothing in this world*—that can make me help you again!"

There was a moment of stunned silence, then we became aware of a voice. It cut through the night, like a knife through my heart—outside, on the street, distant at first, but approaching quickly, the high-pitched voice of a little girl singing a carefree song to herself as she made her way home from a visit with the neighbor . . .

> *"Sur le pont d'Avignon,*
> *On y danse, on y danse . . .*
> *Sur le pont d'Avignon,*
> *L'on y danse tout en rond . . ."*

"RUN, ABRIELLE! RUN!"

Eva cried out from the bottom of her soul, but it was too late. Engel grabbed the child as she came through the door. She screamed and tried to pull away, but the Angel of Darkness had her in his grip. She punched and squirmed as he hauled her across the room, until she saw Raymond and her uncle lying lifeless on the floor. Then she became quiet, and perfectly still, her eyes fixed on the horror that lay before her.

"Abrielle!" Eva called sharply. "Don't look at that! Look at me!" The girl looked up, and snapped out of her trance. She tried to run to Eva, but Engel held her back.

"Laissez-moi!"

Abrielle bit hard into the German's forearm, escaped across the room, and threw her arms around Eva's neck. Unable to reciprocate, Eva did her best to comfort the girl with soft words whispered in her ear.

"No . . ." Eva pleaded as Engel came toward them. "She's a child . . . *She's just a child . . . !"*

"You see." Engel smiled as he stood over them. "You show your weakness."

Abrielle clung to Eva with everything she had, but Engel grabbed her by the hair and brutally yanked her away. I tried to get up, but a scalding pain shot up my spinal cord, sending me back to the floor, writhing in pain and cursing the bastard as he shoved the child onto her knees, just a few feet in front of Eva.

"Roman, please!" Eva begged. *"Stop him! You can't allow this!"*

Even Popov had gone a little pale with the turn of events. He gave Eva a sick look and spoke in a shaky voice.

"Tell me now," he said. "Before it's too late . . ."

Abrielle shuddered as she felt the pistol against the back of her head.

"I will count," Engel said calmly. "To five."

Abrielle sobbed and tried to call out, but her voice failed her. She couldn't even manage a whisper.

"EINS . . ." Engel began, letting it hang in the air.

"Eva!" I called to her, but she was fixed on the horror of the scene and didn't hear me.

"ZWEI . . ."

"EVA!" I yelled, and her head whipped around to me. Her eyes were scarlet, overflowing with tears, her face distorted with terror.

"Tell them, Eva! Tell them where it is!"

She shook her head, choked on the air as she tried to draw a breath.

"DREI . . ."

"Listen to me, Eva!" I was trying desperately to stay calm. "We can't let this happen . . . Look at her, Eva, look at Abrielle . . ."

The little girl couldn't breathe and her body was shaking uncontrollably.

"VIER . . . !"

"FOR GOD'S SAKE, EVA, GIVE THEM THE GODDAMNED DOCUMENT!"

Eva shut her eyes and turned away from me, sobbing silently to herself. It was a shocking moment for me, one that shook me to my core, and one that became etched into my mind forever.

I'd accepted that I would die that night, and I was as ready as you can ever be for that. Eva and I had made our silent pact, and at least we would die together, in a good cause and in love. You can't really ask for too much more than that. But Abrielle . . . To turn away from her . . . From that trust that was in her eyes when she looked to us . . . How could that be right? I couldn't conceive that saving England— or the whole goddamned planet, for that matter—could be worth the brutal betrayal of that child's faith.

"FÜNF . . . !"

My heart stopped beating as Engel squeezed the trigger.

The sound of the shot was gut-wrenching. I flinched, and then my entire being froze.

Had I really seen what I thought I'd seen?

Popov had moved quickly across the room and now he stood, his right arm extended, locked at the elbow, a little pistol gripped tightly in his fist. Engel had had only a fraction of a second to register his shock—the time it took the bullet to travel from the chamber, along the length of the Glock's barrel, and across six inches of space—before the slug punctured his eye and exploded into his brain. I wondered if he'd felt the hot metal pass through his head, or if his mind had shut down too quickly to register its own destruction. Whatever the case, the Angel of Darkness was crying blood, and he was soon dead on his feet. His body swayed, his legs buckled, and he dropped to his knees, balancing there for a few long seconds before he fell, face-first, onto the floor.

Abrielle raced into my arms. I held her tightly, tried to stop her shaking, but I must have been trembling as hard as she was. I turned my head to look for Eva and saw that Popov was cutting her out of her bindings.

"What the hell just happened?" I said.

"You have made a big fuckup of everything—this is what happened." He moved over to cut Claude free, too, then Gérard. "You play with things that you don't understand."

"I'm missing something."

"You have missed everything."

Claude knelt down and gently took the girl from me, carrying her away, sobbing, toward the back room. Eva made a tentative gesture toward her as they passed, but Abrielle recoiled. The hurt on Eva's face broke my heart all over again.

Our eyes met. She came over to me, fell to her knees, and reached out to touch the pool of blood that had spread across my leg.

"You've been wounded," she said.

Eva helped me into to the back bedroom, where she dressed my injury in silence. I guess there was nothing to say, not that we wanted to say, anyway. When she'd finished wrapping my bandage, Popov appeared at the door.

"I must now have this document," he said.

Eva gave him a blank look, and I probably did, too. He nodded slowly, sighed, and pulled up a chair. I guess he realized that the time for secrecy had passed.

"There is a group in London," he began. "A highly secret intelligence service, formed only a month ago, by Churchill himself. It is known as the Twenty Committee, so called because it is represented by the symbol XX—the number twenty in Roman numerals, but it can also be read as a double cross. This is the purpose of this group, and the reason for its existence. To double-cross the enemy. I am the first field agent. Eva was to be the second."

Eva studied Popov's face. "Why should I believe you?" she said, her voice betraying her emptiness.

He shrugged. "Think about the facts. You were sent to me by Geoffrey Stevens, in Paris. He told you that I am part of a special branch of intelligence that has just been created, which he did not know much about. He knew only my code name, which is Bicycle . . ."

"Why didn't Stropford know about you?" I asked.

"Stropford picks up scraps that have fallen from the table," Popov smirked. "I have a seat at the table. My work is too important to be shared with others, and I say this not to impress you. It is a fact. Now, please—it is very important that I have this document."

Eva looked to me, and I nodded.

"I hid it in the piano," she said.

It was tucked up under the frame at the high end of the plate, between the soundboard and the strings. Maybe the Gestapo would've found it, maybe not. Eva handed the thin folder to Popov.

"All this was about that?" I said.

"Yes," he said. "A small package, of enormous value."

"Mind if I have a look?"

Popov shrugged his shoulders. "Why not?"

I opened to the top page, which was a map detailing the location of all the radar facilities along the south and east coasts of England. Brixham, Weymouth, Shanklin, Eastbourne, Hastings, Margate— each one marked with a coded number that could be referenced on the following pages. I flipped to a random page, which gave detailed information about the Hastings placement, in East Sussex. It provided the exact latitude and longitude of the facility, along with operational details, telephone and telegraph links to the network, and security information. It even listed the home telephone number of the station manager.

I was no expert, but I'd read enough about the new radar technology to know that without it, Britain would be blind and defenseless. German bombers—thousands of them—would be virtually unchallenged as they rained their Blitzkreig down on the ports, airfields, factories, and cities of England. RAF fighters would be destroyed on the ground in a matter of days, leaving the Channel open to the invasion force. The Wehrmacht, advancing behind four panzer divisions, would cut through the British forces, still reeling from Dunkirk, like a hot blade through English butter.

Of course, it would probably never come to that. Once the radar stations were gone, even Churchill would have to see the futility of fighting on. And if he didn't, he'd be shown the door and a new prime minister—one who could see the Nazi writing on the wall—would be given the key to Downing Street. That was the scenario that His Former Royal Highness, Edward VIII, dreamed about, anyway. The duke was no troublesome peacemaker who naively hoped to save his country from ruin by suing for peace with Germany. He was an out-and-out traitor.

"Impressive," I said, handing the folder back to Popov.

"Will you destroy it?" Eva asked.

"Destroy it?" Popov looked incredulous.

"Yes. Burn it . . ."

"No . . ." Popov shook his head and smiled mischievously. "I will pass it to the Gestapo . . . just as I always intended."

I noticed that he'd placed his pistol on the piano, and edged toward it. "So what you just told us about the Twenty Committee . . ."

"Is absolutely true," he said, picking up the pistol.

"Then—?"

"It's not real."

"What?"

"This document." Popov displayed the folder. "It was created by the Twenty Committee, with the full intention that Hitler would receive it from the Duke of Windsor."

"The duke is part of this?"

"No, no, he is certainly not. The duke and duchess believe they will provide Germany with accurate information."

I don't know if I looked confused, but I sure felt it. Fortunately, Popov was ready to tell all.

"You see, the British government has suspected for some time that the duke and his wife have been acting in a treasonous fashion. Since the ninth of November in 1939, to be precise."

"What happened then?" Eva asked.

"Do you remember Charles Bedeaux?"

"Yes, of course."

I recalled that he was the American businessman who had been Eva's contact in Paris. He'd introduced her to Geoffrey Stevens, who later sent her to Lisbon to find Popov.

"On the ninth of last November, he was seen entering the German Chancellery in Berlin. Once inside, he was escorted to a room where he met two high-ranking officials of the Reich. One was Hermann Göring, the head of the Luftwaffe. The other was Adolf Hitler. The purpose of their meeting was for Bedeaux to provide Hitler and Göring with the entire defensive positions of the French and British forces. As a result of what they heard from him, the German invasion of France was postponed so that a new plan could be devised, one that took account of this invaluable intelligence."

"What's that have to do with the Duke of Windsor?" I asked.

"Three days before that meeting, on six November, in Paris, the duke and duchess dined with Charles Bedeaux and his wife in their suite at the Ritz. At the conclusion of the meal, the men excused themselves to a private room where they spoke for nearly two hours. At the end of the discussion, the duke gave Bedeaux a letter."

"The contents of the letter could not be confirmed, but the following morning, Bedeaux departed by train, traveling first to Brussels, and then to Cologne, where he stayed the night. He finally arrived in Berlin on the evening before he met with Hitler."

"Are you saying that the Duke of Windsor was responsible for the fall of France?" I said.

"The circumstances certainly suggest it. The duke's position as liaison officer between the British and French forces put him in a unique position to access sensitive information. And it is suspicious that the Wehrmacht seemed to know the weakest point in the French defenses . . . But, of course, there was not enough evidence to make an accusation of treason against the former King of England."

"So you gave him some, to see what he would do with it."

"Yes, that's true. There is no doubt that the duke is a traitor now. But this was not the primary reason for the operation. In fact, the duke's treachery must remain an absolute secret. It is essential that the Germans do not know that he is suspected."

The penny finally dropped.

"Because the Luftwaffe will be bombing radar facilities that don't exist," I said.

"They do exist," Popov said. "But they are no more than empty buildings, built specifically to be the target of German bombs. The actual stations are very well hidden."

I had to smile. "So the Duke of Windsor's treason handed France, Holland, and Belgium to Hitler on a silver platter, but it may be responsible for saving England."

"Clever, yes?" Popov couldn't help smiling, too. "It was my idea."

37

Eva and I never said good-bye. She was gone the next morning, leaving me with just a couple of lines on a scrap of paper:

> *Think of me on our train to Paris, Jack.*
> *I wish we'd never had to jump off . . .*
> *Eva*

She stayed in France, of course, becoming an invaluable, and later, much-renowned asset to British intelligence, their primary link to the Resistance in Paris. Her exploits have been well documented in many books and articles, some of which I've read, most of which I've chosen not to.

Eva was hanged at Ravensbrück on March 30, 1945, a month before the camp was liberated. I don't know what her last days were like, but I'm absolutely positive that they never made her talk.

I've never known anyone like Eva. She was, and always will be, unique. A beautiful, sensual woman, with a soft spirit and a will of iron, she had decided that there was nothing in the world that could make her surrender to the forces of evil that she had once been a part of. I think, if there is such a thing, she must have found redemption for her sins.

With time, I came to better understand what she'd done. It wasn't long after that night in Paris that I, as an army lieutenant, was sending kids to their deaths, justifying it by that tried-and-true apology of war, that each one of the lives we sacrifice will save dozens, maybe hundreds, of others. I also came to learn that a piece of your own soul goes off with each one of those young faces that doesn't come back.

That's what they mean by the horror of war.

Along with her note, I found a new passport, a letter of transit, and a second-class train ticket back to Lisbon, courtesy of Roman Popov, aka Bicycle. I spent a lot of time thinking about the rat from Belgrade, who turned out to be not such a rat after all. He was no John Wayne, either, of course, and that, I figured, was the point. Just because the bad guys wear hats that are blacker than black, that doesn't mean that the good guys are wearing pure white. I don't know what Popov's motives were for doing what he did, but I'm not sure it matters. He came out of the war a very wealthy man, but few did more to consign the Nazis to history than he. Popov was what he was—a rat and a hero, who wore a decidedly gray hat.

Abrielle married a doctor, had three children, seven grandchildren, and, recently, two great-grandchildren. Her husband died in 1987, and she's since lived a quiet, contented life in Montmartre, with who knows how many cats. I always let her know where I am in the world, and I get a hand-painted Christmas card every year.

Gérard became leader of the Resistance movement in Paris. He was killed in 1944 when he and his party were surprised by a German patrol as they attempted to sabotage a rail line. Claude served honorably in the Resistance, too. After the war ended, he got a motorized milk wagon, found a lovely wife, and fathered eight kids. One Sunday in the spring of 1957, when I was passing through Paris, the three of us—Claude, Abrielle, and myself—went to visit the Père Lachaise cemetery, where there is a memorial to the fallen heroes of the Resistance. The first two names carved into the stone monument where we laid our flowers were *Raymond Fournier* and *Christien Delacroix*.

In Lisbon, I took a room in a small hotel in the Alfama, preferring not to make an appearance back at the Palacio—not that I could afford it, anyway, having left the remains of Lili's envelope with Abrielle. I did head out to Estoril one afternoon and found Harry Thompson at his favorite watering hole. He seemed happy to see me, and pretended to pump me for information, while I pretended to give him some. We had a few drinks and a few laughs, then we wished each other luck and went our separate ways. I liked Harry. I don't know what became of him, but I felt kind of sad as we parted. He was the kind of guy who'd die alone and be quickly forgotten.

I made my way back to Hollywood, getting passage on the steamer *Excalibur*, which, coincidentally, was carrying the duke and duchess to their new posting as governor and first lady of the Bahamas. I had to stay locked in my cabin for four days to avoid seeing them or Madame Moulichon, who Popov had sent back to Lisbon with the phony documents. I assumed that Espírito Santo arranged to get the papers to Berlin, and over the next three months, I enjoyed reading the story of the RAF's unlikely victory over the Luftwaffe in the Battle of Britain.

I drifted around Los Angeles for a while, picking up a bit of stunt work here and there, drinking too much, and losing at cards. One of the guys I played with was Julius Epstein, the screenwriter. They used to call him Julie. I didn't know him too well, but he ended up driving me home one night when I couldn't manage it myself. We stopped for coffee at some out-of-the-way diner in the San Fernando Valley, and for some reason I told him the whole story of Lili and Eva and me, and what happened in Lisbon and Paris. I don't know why I decided to tell him. I guess I just needed to tell someone.

I'm not sure if he believed me, but I remember him saying that it might make a pretty good movie. With a few changes, of course.

Acknowledgments

I'd like to thank Henry Ferris, at William Morrow, for his continuing faith, his abilities as an editor, and for being such a pleasure to work with. There are many others at Morrow who have worked hard and contributed their talents, among them Eryn Wade and Lynn Grady.

My agent, Bill Contardi of Brandt and Hochman, is always a reliable counselor, and takes care of business with an ease and directness that is much appreciated.

Others who have made valuable contributions to the book along the way are Francie Gabbay, Ian Howe, Susan Schulman, Susan Gabbay, Harry Von Feilitzsch, and as always, my wife, Julia, who continues to tolerate a husband with a very odd job.

11/16/11